To my Aunt Raven and Uncle Albert

HERE HE COMES. My very own Prince Fucking Charming, Cal Scott. He walks in, and his eyes quickly skim the packed suitcase in my hand and briefly rest on my face. He lets out an exasperated sigh, tosses his keys on the table, and then takes off his coat. His eyes fall on the empty bottle of wine I finished today. A smirk spreads across his face before he passes me, heading into the living room.

April 26th, 2011

I expected his lack of response, but it hurts all the same. I'm pretty sure he regards me more as his personal high-class escort than his wife.

I clutch my suitcase, full of the very few things that are mine. He can keep the cars, the money, and the penthouse—the things he believes should comfort me in my loneliness. All the material things in the world can't make up for the growing disconnect between us. The four-carat yellow diamond on my finger is a beautiful but painful reminder of the vows he broke.

I look over at him now, slouched on the couch with a self-assured cocky grin plastered on his face, the same one he wore the day I met him. I walk into the living room. He's watching a basketball game on his obnoxiously big television screen like he hasn't a care in the world.

He glances back at me, still not speaking, and my anger boils over. If I were a man, I would kick his ass. I pull the calendar from my bag, marked with the very few days he's been home, and force it into his lap.

"Don't start this shit, Lauren. I texted you," he says with obvious exasperation.

My questions come rapid-fire as I walk in front of the television, waving my suitcase in his direction and trying my best to obstruct his view.

"You texted me? That makes it okay? Do you see my bags at the door and the one I'm holding? Do you not get it? I'm leaving, Cal. Fuck you and your texts!"

He shifts his position on the couch and gestures to the empty wine bottle I forgot to discard. "I'm not talking to you while you're drunk," he says dismissively.

"Yes you are!" I insist, moving closer to him.

"Weren't you leaving?" he asks sarcastically. His face is stern, while his eyes smile.

He's not taking me seriously, so I lean down and growl in his face. "You are such an asshole!" He kisses me—right on the lips—and laughs. He fucking laughs! I try to slap him, but he's quick and my fingertips barely graze his face.

"I fucking hate you!" I roar and storm away from him. I start to take off my engagement ring. I want to throw it at him, but then I realize I like my ring. It's fucking gorgeous. So I throw the stereo remote at his head instead before I march to the door.

He's off the couch, coming after me, but I keep walking. He grabs my arm, turns me to face him, and takes my suitcase.

"I'm done. Leave me alone!" I yell, struggling to break free from his iron grasp. Suddenly, I'm picked up and swung over his shoulder.

"Let me go! Stop it!" I cry, but he doesn't listen. I'm failing miserably in my attempts to escape.

"No more bottles of wine for you, Mrs. Scott," he utters, unfazed by my protests.

"Let me go!" I scream again, punching him in the back as he carries me up the stairs and into our bedroom, where he drops me unceremoniously on the bed.

"Sleep this off," he says simply.

Who the hell does he think he is? I rush towards the door, but he quickly slips out, shutting the door behind him. I get to the door a split second later and yank on it. It's locked. The bastard has locked me in.

"So, you're kidnapping me now? You're adding that to your résumé along with shitty, emotionless husband? You can't keep me here! I'm leaving you! I'm tired of this! You're never home! I didn't sign up to be the only person in this marriage!"

My outburst is futile. I can hear the play-by-play of the Bulls game echoing up the stairs, and I'm certain he's turned up the volume on his stupid-ass giant TV in order to drown me out. I sit on the floor and cry until I can't cry anymore, until I am too tired to do anything but sleep.

I ADJUST MY eyes as I wake. My head is pounding. The bottle of wine I consumed is coming back to haunt me. I realize I'm no longer on the floor, but in our bed with the covers over me.

The moonlight shines through the window, rather than the sun my conscious brain last saw. I've been out of it for a while. I place my feet on the plush carpet, leaving my bed and heading out onto the terrace to enjoy the fresh evening breeze. Looking over Chicago's glittering downtown, I think about how many nights I have spent out here alone, staring at the skyline and wondering where my husband is. I feel sick.

I move back inside where the bedroom door is now unlocked. I open it, only to find that all the lights in the penthouse are off and it's silent. He's gone again, which doesn't surprise me. Being inside alone feels suffocating. I walk back out onto the terrace.

The loneliest time of my life didn't begin until I married the one person I would have given my life for. His touch awakened every nerve in my body, his words and promises hypnotized me, and in his arms, I felt safer than I'd ever felt anywhere else. For so long, I couldn't *breathe* without him.

Nothing is certain now. The bond between us, once so real—so tangible, I believed in it with every ounce of my being—is now in tatters. Whatever we had has been lost, our home void of warmth and love and filled with anger instead. We are participants in a war of words that continues to be recycled over and over again. Any hope I had for us now lives in the past, and that is really fucking depressing.

I laugh at my naiveté and wipe a few tears from my cheek. Dammit. I promised I wouldn't cry over him anymore, but what's another promise broken to myself? I try to not care so much, but I'm not fooling anybody.

I know I still do.

The front door opens. I walk back inside and into the hall and look over the banister to see that he has a dozen pink roses in his arms. I watch him place them on the table before I go back into our room, saying nothing.

Returning to the terrace, I survey the city. After a few minutes, the bedroom door opens and I sense him walking up behind me, his scent giving him away before he's even near me. He's wearing my favorite cologne. As smoothly as ever, his strong arms wrap around my waist.

I hate the fact that I still get chills when he touches me. I wish I would cringe instead. I hate it even more that he knows the effect he has on me. His lips find the back of my neck, making his way to the crook of it, while his hands caress my stomach, lingering lower before finding the button on my pants. He begins to undo them. I hate him so much sometimes. I hate even more that no matter how mad I am, somehow, some way, my body always betrays me and forgives him.

Taking my hand, he turns me around to face him. He knows exactly how his beautiful gray eyes affect me, and he uses it to his advantage.

I know he feels me giving in. He knows I'm faltering because he smiles at me with that subtle, self-assured grin of his before he leans down, places his lips on mine, and parts them. When I don't pull away, he slides his tongue in my mouth, playing with mine, daring me to resist.

I don't.

A soft moan escapes my lips. *What the hell am I doing?* I was supposed to be leaving him tonight. His grip tightens on my waist. He knows he has me, and damn it, I know it too. I hate that he knows it first. I hate even more that he knows me so well.

I pull away and look up at him, frustrated by how he can read me like the back of his hand.

"I hate you sometimes," I say bitterly, but even with my tone, the moment he looks at me, he knows I don't mean it. Those freakin' eyes of his have hypnotized me out of my better judgment—and my clothes—since I've known him. They tend to see right through me.

"I know," he says before pulling me into one of his intoxicating kisses that make me feel like I'm floating.

He lifts me up and carries me inside to our bed. This is what he does, after all. He's the master of manipulation, the king of allure. He knows me inside and out—and probably better than I know myself. That I allowed that to happen at all was my first mistake. My second was falling in love with him. But how could I resist someone who's so irresistible? How could I run away from something that had already caught me? That's what happened to me. I was caught before I even knew I was being hunted, and by the time I realized it, it was far too late.

He has me addicted, and that's how he wants it. How the hell did I let this happen?

April 15th, 2008

SOMETIMES DAYS AT work can be fun and easy. Other days it can suck, and today is a day that sucks.

"So, that'll be two vodka tonics, a Long Island Iced Tea, and four beers?" I ask, trying to hear over the pulsating music that comes with the territory of waitressing at one of the hottest nightspots in Chicago. The Vault: where the music is always loud, the drinks aren't watered down, and you're guaranteed to catch a glimpse of the hottest celebrity in town. Still, after six months, I haven't adjusted to it. Initially, waitressing was going be a part time thing, only for a couple of weeks. Slowly, weeks turned into a couple of months and here I am at six months and counting.

Not that I'm complaining. The tips are great, and I get paid pretty well. I'm now used to what I call "after-hours" people. They're your classmates, coworkers, and relatives—but in their sluttiest clothing, three times more makeup, and drunker than you've ever seen. Most girls would kill for this job. I know for a fact the waiting list for getting an interview is about a mile long.

Still, I can't help feeling tired of it. It's better than working at a fast food restaurant, but the atmosphere is intoxicating. I've seen so many girls swept away by it in my short time here. I'm thankful I haven't fallen prey.

"Can you have one of the beers poured in a glass, with extra ice?" the girl at the table I'm serving asks weakly.

"No problem." I give her a reassuring smile.

"I swear to God, you are such a little priss sometimes," her *friend* announces loudly for everyone to hear. *Obnoxious bitch.* My customer's skin flushes a bright pink and I feel sorry for her; if I weren't working, I'd be her. God knows I've had enough obnoxious friends in my lifetime.

"Are you guys hiring?" the guy sitting with them asks. A question I get five times a night.

"I know we're looking for another bartender. My manager's name is Ryan. Call tomorrow afternoon. His assistant takes calls then and can set up an interview if you have experience."

"Cool! Thanks," he says, his excitement apparent.

"You must love working here. Good music, hot guys, and you get to dress up every night. Very cute shoes, by the way," O.B. adds.

"It's okay." I shrug and walk away.

Truth of the matter is, the cute shoes kill my feet every night. Dressing up was fun until they implemented the butt-crawling shorts that became mandatory. But it pays well and college tuition isn't cheap. I squeeze through the crowd and head to the bar area. My friend Steven, the bartender, is standing with my ex, Michael—Mr. Worst Mistake of My Life. I slide my drink slip over and count down the minutes to when my feet will get to rest.

"It's really packed in here tonight, isn't it?" Michael yells to me over the music. Our relationship didn't exactly end on *friendly* terms. In fact, this is the first time I'm even contemplating responding to him since our breakup two months ago. The best I can do is remain civil with him, but it's so hard.

"When isn't it packed in here?" I reply abruptly. Well, I said I'd be civil; I didn't say polite. His smile drops. It's not like he needs me to be nice to him. He has enough women being nice to him. In fact, the reason we broke up was because I caught him in the storage room, being too *nice* to some girl.

"Hey, Lauren. You look like you could use a break." My friend Angie comes to the rescue as she hands her drink slip to Steven.

"A break? More like a vacation." I chuckle, taking the tray full of drinks. My customer 'Extra Ice' is the only one sitting at the table now. Her expression looks less than jovial. I smile, hoping to lift her spirits a bit.

"Here are your drinks," I say, setting them down.

"Thank you," she replies, taking the glass of ice. She pours her beer over it, glancing up at me. "I'm probably the first person you've seen do this." She laughs then sighs.

"It seems all my friends have abandoned me for the dance floor," she explains, probably afraid of offending me. "What a great birthday this turned out to be," she mumbles before taking a sip of her beer.

"Happy birthday!" I say, probably a little bit too enthusiastically. "This one's on the house," I offer.

"Thank you." She lifts her glass and goes back to getting acquainted with her drink.

I know the feeling of being in a place you'd rather not be. Anyway, it's sometimes better not to think about it. I head back over to the bar. My watch informs me I have two hours left, which might as well be an eternity. It's strange how I can be so bored in such an exciting atmosphere. Maybe it has to do with the fact that I'm always in this atmosphere. Out the corner of my eye, I see Michael flirting with a petite redhead. He's always flirting with a petite something. I was the petite brunette. I can't believe I still care who he's flirting with; maybe care is the wrong word—irritated. I'm irritated at the fact he's flirting with other women.

"Hey, L." Angie pinches my side and slides another drink slip to Steven, who passes it to Michael since he's standing there being worthless.

"Don't take a second look," she whispers in my ear. I realize I must have been staring.

"Hey, Mikey, why don't you stop chatting and actually do some work since you're here?"

He shoots her a sarcastic smile and saunters over to us. "Nice to see you, too," he replies, looking over her slip but passing it back to Steven.

"Hey, Lauren, look what I have for you!" Trish, another waitress, shouts, holding up a Long Island Iced Tea and showcasing it to me.

"What's that?" I ask curiously.

"Compliments of a gentleman from VIP." She grins, handing the glass to me. I set it down. I make it a habit not to accept drinks from guys while working.

"Ooh, VIP. Now you have to take it," Steven teases me with a wink.

"Isn't it a bad policy to accept drinks from customers?" Michael butts in. We all stare at him in disbelief; he's been known to accept a lot more than drinks from customers.

"Well, you know, Ryan expects us to be extra nice to VIP customers. Plus it is your favorite, Lauren," urges Angela.

"The guy is a cutie, too," Trish adds.

Michael glares hard in my direction, but it totally has the opposite effect on me than he probably wants. Staring straight back at him, I moisten my lips, put them on the straw, and suck up a good, long sip.

I turn back to Trish.

"Tell him thank you, and that it's my favorite." The disappointment on Michael's face makes me giddy.

"Oh, he knows. I told him. It's his birthday too," she adds before disappearing into the crowd.

"L, you should go tell him happy birthday," Angela urges me with a nudge.

"I'm not doing that," I say indignantly.

"Oh, come on. Why not? A little flirting would do you some good." She laughs.

"It's desperate and unprofessional. I sent him my thanks for the drink. That's all I'm doing," I declare, making my way from the bar.

I would rather work than hear her urging me to talk to some guy like she does every night.

I GLANCE AT my watch. It's 1:30 A.M., and my bed is calling. I hope my roommate Hillary isn't home. If she is already home at this time of night, she usually has a companion. The amount of money I have invested into earplugs is crazy, thanks to all the noise they make. I've already put my coat on to leave when see my manager, Ryan. He's heading my way, and it's too late to go in the other direction—well, without being completely obvious.

"Lauren, I'm so glad I caught you." He's beaming and his tone seems, dare I say, nice. He's hardly ever nice, and I place a bet with myself he's going to ask me to stay another hour.

"Hi, Ryan," I reply warily, beginning to change into my flat shoes.

"Oh, you're leaving," he says with a pout resembling that of a two-year-old, only not as cute.

"Yes, I'm off now," I remind him, praying he won't ask me to stay, or worse, tell me to stay.

"Would you mind doing me a tiny favor?" he asks, walking over to me. I knew it was coming, I still haven't learned to leave faster. What am I supposed to do, tell my boss no? My body screams hell yes! My mind directs me to smile weakly.

"Sure," I give in with a sigh.

"A very good customer of mine wants to meet you. He's been eye-humping you all night," he explains while helping me take my coat off.

"What?" I snap before even getting a chance to censor my tongue. He is my boss, and, as always, a bit of an A-hole, but who the hell does he think he is?

"Just say hello and nothing else. He's a reporter for *The Tribune*. He can bring a lot of exposure to the club," he says urgently.

"I don't know." I do know. I don't want to do it!

"It's just a quick drink. It is his birthday, after all, and the VIP room is filled with people. Just a drink."

"If you're too tired, I'll switch your shift. Maybe you'd rather have Monday night instead of this *tiring* Saturday shift," he suggests slyly. That's low. Monday is the absolute worst night to have in the club. It's slow, fewer tips, and I have a class Tuesday mornings.

"Okay. I'll do it," I say, finally giving in. I hang my coat back up and start to follow him out, but he stops me at the door before I can even cross the threshold.

"How about I give you time to put on your other shoes and let your hair back down?" He winks. I bite my lip in frustration.

Fuck you, Ryan.

I go back to my locker to get my heels.

"I'll meet you upstairs in a few minutes." He smiles, but before leaving he pops his head back in the doorway. "A little lip gloss wouldn't hurt either," he quips before disappearing.

Jerk-off.

I slip out of my gym shoes and let my ponytail back down. I purposefully don't put on any lip gloss. *Just a quick drink then bed*, I tell myself and try not feel like such a pushover.

THE VIP ROOM is buzzing with people but empty compared to the other floors. With a three-bottle purchase for a table, it makes sense though. Dan, the VIP security guard, is standing at the entrance. He's pretty intimidating to anyone wanting to start trouble. At almost six foot four and at least 290 pounds—his death grip headlock has brought many to their knees—he's a good guy to have on your side. He's busy flirting with two girls who are trying to talk their way in for free, but he gives me a quick nod of acknowledgment.

I take a deep breath and remind myself I need my job. Having a drink with a guy for my boss isn't that bad. Wait, that even sounds wrong. Being pimped out is not a part of my job description. I hope this guy isn't a complete asshole, drunk or sober. Even if he isn't, I hate the dating scene. I've had two serious boyfriends: Daniel, my high school sweetheart, and Michael, who as it turned out wasn't that serious about me after all.

I've been on a handful of dates with guys since I moved here from Michigan, many of which turned out to be complete disasters. I've grown to hate the whole situation. First the obligatory awkward conversations, and ultimately my date's disappointment when I don't put out after the first date. The guys I run into are nothing like the princes in the stories my aunt read to me when I was a little girl. My adult theory: The Prince Charming myth is the other curse God created to punish Eve and every other woman for biting that stupid apple. Looking around the room, I spot Ryan sitting in the corner talking to a short blonde woman accompanied by a man in blue dress shirt and black slacks.

Ryan sees me and waves me over. As I get closer to the guy, I have to agree that Trish was right—he's cute, in an Abercrombie and Fitch sort of way. He has dirty blonde hair and green eyes, even a coy smile, but that still does doesn't mean I like being coerced into talking to him. When I reach the table, Mr. Abercrombie and Ryan stand up while the woman just smiles in my direction.

"Lauren, I would like you to meet Jason Daniels. He's doing a story for The Tribune's entertainment column. And this is his partner, Marie."

"Nice to meet you." Jason shakes my hand, a huge grin on his face. "Very nice to meet you," he repeats again, almost nervously.

"How about I have Diana make you one of my favorite drinks, Marie?" Ryan asks, gesturing towards the VIP area of the bar. I keep myself from rolling my eyes. I guess he wants Jason and me to have alone time, because Ryan can easily have Diana at our table in less than a minute with just a gesture.

"I would love that." She links her arm with his and leaves Jason and me alone. He seems to be tongue-tied at the moment; awkward conversation avoided, maybe?

"Would you like to sit down?" he finally says. Crap, no such luck— he's not mute. I smile graciously as I sit in the plush leather booth.

"Did you like the drink I sent you?" he smiles.

"Yes, it's my favorite." I look down, trying to avoid the awkward silence filling the air. "Even though I'm the one that should be buying you the drink. I hear it's your birthday," I say with forced friendliness.

"Yeah. The big two-four." He laughs.

"How does it feel?"

"Not too different from twenty-three." He laughs and sips his drink. "Oh, would you like something, another Long Island—?" he starts, but something has caught his attention across the room. Maybe it's his girlfriend. This is probably just wishful thinking on my part, but with my luck, who knows.

"Would you excuse me for a minute?" he says, leaving me to sit alone. I wonder if this fulfills the requirement of a drink as far as Ryan's concerned. I wonder who he was looking for—I guess the blonde who was with him, maybe they're more than just friends? Drumming my finger on the table, I wait for my new friend to come back.

Ryan arrives a few minutes later, and I'm still at the table alone. I see he's misplaced the blonde as well.

"Where did Jason go?"

I wasn't aware that I was supposed to be babysitting him.

"Umm, I don't know. He told me he'd be right back in a minute. Look, Ryan, I have an exam I have to study for this weekend and I really need to get some sleep," I explain, getting up to leave.

"Wait! Please, just five more minutes. I'll go find him," he begs, holding my arm.

"Fine," I relent. "I'll be out on the terrace while you look for him."

"Okay. Back in five minutes," he promises before hurrying off, and I sneak away to the terrace of the club. It's my favorite place in Chicago. It makes me feel free when the wind blows just the right way and the lights of the city sparkle in the night. It reminds me why I'm not in my old comfort zone in Michigan. This may be my lucky day since there are only two couples making out in the corner. Usually there are so many it's embarrassing. I stroll to the other side so they can have their privacy. You can see all of Chicago from right here. I could stand here for hours just looking out over the city.

I glance at my watch and notice it's been around five minutes. I decide to head back to VIP before Ryan has a panic attack. Right as I'm making my way back into the club, Michael heads towards me.

"This must be my lucky day," I mumble sarcastically to myself, but loud enough that he can hear me.

"Hey, can I talk to you for a minute?" he asks as I walk past him.

"Actually, I'm meeting someone." I smirk at him before continuing on my way.

"What? Who? I mean, you just got off." He stumbles over his words. I guess I surprised him. I just smile, adding a shrug, but he calls after me, "Well, when you're not busy, I need to talk to you." I don't even look back.

What Michael doesn't understand is I don't care what he needs. He lost that privilege when I caught him banging some girl in the storage room of the club. He didn't even have the decency to screw her in his car like a respectful douche bag would do.

I'm seeing red as I make my way down to the VIP room. I'm in total disbelief at Michael's audacity and sudden resurgence of trying to weasel his way back into my life that I don't even notice the person in front of me that I crash into. A second later I feel cool liquid spread down my blouse. Best day ever!

"I'm soooo sorry," I say, embarrassed. This is completely my fault and I'm even more furious that Michael caused me to do it.

"It's okay," a deep voice replies, and it sends a shiver up my spine.

"I'm sure your shirt costs a lot more than this drink," he says again, and I'm afraid to look up. I can hear my heartbeat pounding in my ears. When I work up the courage to finally see whose voice is causing my heart to try to escape my chest, I find a tall, ebony-haired stranger looking down at me.

And God, he has the most beautiful pair of gray eyes and an amazing smile that's housed by the most perfect lips in the history of mankind. I mentally remind myself not to swallow my tongue and breathe. Is he real? Or have I been knocked unconscious and am being fanned with a cover of GQ magazine? This encounter will probably turn out to just be a figment of my imagination.

The more I look—no, stare, I'm actually staring now—he has to be an illusion. I search for a flaw, taking in every inch of him, from his chiseled features to his chocolate-brown hair falling right over his eyebrows, strong broad shoulders hidden beneath a dark gray blazer and black fitted shirt. No flaw found. He's unsettlingly beautiful.

"I-I'm sorry. I can be so clumsy at times," I choke out, internally cheering as my mind begins taking control again.

"Let me get you something for that," he responds, disappearing into the crowd. I panic. What if he doesn't come back? What if he *does* come back? That scares me even more. But a minute later he's here again with a cloth in hand, and I'm still not prepared to think like a civilized person instead of a cave woman.

"Thank you," I reply sheepishly, taking the cloth from his hand. He's smiling at me like he knows a secret I'm not in on.

"I'm really sorry about your drink. I can get you another one," I offer, staring up at him. He has to be at least six foot two. I subconsciously take a few steps back, so I don't have to look up at him like a little girl.

"You're good," he assures me coolly. No, *he's* good, apparently, since no matter how hard I try I can't bring my eyes to leave his face.

"I work here. It'll be no problem," I reply. His gaze is intense, almost intimate, but his smile is so charming, or rather, welcoming—like he's luring me. For a moment, time slows down. All of the noise around us has disappeared, and it's just the music and my breathing.

I wonder if he hears it.

He steps closer to me and I notice in those perfect gray eyes, the iris is surrounded by a subtle green tint. But, beautiful as they are, they're upstaged when he lets the right corner of his bottom lip free that he's been holding captive between his stark white teeth. His tongue sweeps across those delectable lips, adding the perfect amount of moisture, and right then a wave of heat flushes through my entire body. I cringe to myself for referring to a body part as delectable, a stranger's at that, but there is absolutely no other way to describe them.

"I know." His words jolt me back to reality and I lean forward a bit, the return of the noise making it more difficult to hear him. A second later he leans down towards me, his face near my ear, and my breath hitches.

"Your shorts gave you away," he says into it, and just as quickly he's back in his own space.

"These godforsaken shorts." I'm so embarrassed and begin pulling them down. He nods his head, a grin now on his face as his eyes travel down my body.

"No, thank God for those shorts." He's biting his lip again and I feel myself turning all shades of pink. " . . . and I was actually coming to get a closer view of the woman I haven't been able to take my eyes off of since she walked in," he explains, looking directly into my eyes with a smile that could melt the Arctic. With that, I almost swallow my tongue. What am I supposed to say to something like that?

"She's Lauren," I can't help but whisper. Wait, that wasn't right. *Wake up, genius!* "I mean, I'm Lauren." I laugh, hoping the music covers my ridiculous answer and that I won't drop dead of embarrassment right here. Thankfully, my brain cells are released from my hormones' grip and direct me to extend my hand.

He smiles almost as if he's amused. I guess I'd be amused too if I could reduce a college-educated woman to a bumbling idiot just by licking my lips.

"I'm Cal," he replies.

I OPEN MY eyes and turn over to see Cal still asleep. I remember when I would watch him sleep; he seems like such a different person when he's asleep. When he's awake he's confident, cool, and in control of every situation. I think this is the only time he doesn't have a wall up—when he's not plotting and planning and his guard is down—the one he always has up, even with me.

I touch a lock of his hair and move it back into place. He starts to wake up, so I turn away and settle back on my pillow. He

April 27th, 2011

knows I'm awake, but he won't say anything to acknowledge it.

He runs his fingers through my hair before tracing a soft line down my neck and momentarily resting them on the small of my back. He begins to trace his signature there, causing me to roll my eyes and get goose bumps simultaneously. This is his way of saying good morning, a tease. I feel him get out of bed, his footsteps growing faint as he enters our bathroom and the door shuts. I roll onto my back, entangling myself in our sheets.

A sigh escapes my mouth as my thoughts drift to last night; tingles shoot through my body at the memory, and I try to shake the thought. He can make me feel wanted and be so in tune with me, *physically*, but his mind can still be miles away in an emotional desert. It didn't used be like this with him. I can't pinpoint when it changed, but somewhere along the line he started to grow resentful towards me, or maybe towards our marriage. I'm not sure which, or if there's even a difference. We used to talk about it—or at least *I* tried to talk and he blew it off, telling me I was paranoid and overreacting. Now I don't talk—I throw fits.

I didn't used to be angry and vindictive all the time, but now it's my defense mechanism with him. It's about the only way to maintain my sanity. He has a barrier up that he won't let me see behind. I only see what he wants me to see. I've known him for three years, and he's still like a puzzle that I'm trying to solve. Sometimes I just get mad and want to throw the pieces at the wall and give up.

Unfortunately, I always come back, letting the mystery of the final project pull me in. It seems that's what we've resorted to—emotional mind games. We both play them. He's forced me to play, and all I want is for it to be over and for us to be how we were before we were married. If it were up to me, I'd wake up every morning and tell him how much I love him.

Now, I just keep my feelings to myself until I have an emotional overload, like yesterday, aided by a bottle of wine—a bad habit I've developed after being left alone for days at a time.

His story is that he's working. I do believe him—mostly—and for a while, I was content to share him with his job—or at least what he says is his job. I've never been privy to the specific details other than that he works in a special division of Crestfield Corporation, a company that has its hand in nearly everything, from real estate to commercial retail and highly questionable financial investments.

Conveniently for Cal, he's in a position that's so confidential he can't even tell his own wife where the hell he is half the time. When I complain, he says I knew this when I met him. And I did, but it was exciting getting surprise visits from my boyfriend when we didn't live together. The picture isn't so rosy when you're home alone most of the time and it seems as if your husband is just dropping by rather than living with you.

I look towards the window, where the sun is shining in. He must have opened the blinds. Two conclusions quickly come to mind: he's either trying to wake me up, or he's just trying to annoy the shit out of me. Whichever it is, I'm not happy about it.

I grab the remote that controls the blinds and close them again. I hate how the weather almost never matches my moods. Right now I would prefer it to be raining and dark out, that way I could linger in my depression, but as always, things never go as I plan.

I hear him come back into the room and I look over as he opens the closet. His typical getup, a gray button-up and black slacks, will be, I'm sure, paired with one of his long black coats. He probably spends more money on clothes than I do. Out of the corner of my eye, I watch him leave the room, so I turn my attention back to the ceiling. Suddenly, I feel the sunlight on my back. He's opened the damn blinds again. I was right. He's trying to bug the shit out of me.

"What the hell is your problem?"

"It's time to get up." He glances up at me now while rifling through his drawer across the room.

"It's morning. I'd like to sleep," I growl before burying my head beneath the covers.

"Morning?" he asks, sarcasm dripping from his voice. "It's one o'clock." He laughs.

One?

I roll over and maneuver myself to see the clock on his dresser. Damn. He's right.

"I'm sorry I tired you out. I won't keep you up so late tonight," he says, smugness lacing his voice. He turns his attention to his cell phone. I roll my eyes at him and start to get up, making sure the sheet covers my entire body. He notices.

"You have something I haven't seen before now?" he asks deviously. I don't dignify him with an answer. I head to my closet, which he is now blocking.

"Excuse me," I say sharply. He just smiles down at me. When he doesn't move, I push past him, but he holds on to the sheet, so my choices are to either keep walking, bare as an egg, or to stay put and covered. I tug on it, but he won't let go. In a battle of strength, he'll win every time, so I do the only thing I can do to save my dignity. I throw my hands up and twirl around in the birthday suit God gave me.

"Happy now?" I ask sarcastically.

"Well, you are wearing my favorite outfit on you," he says with an amused grin. He points his phone at me, and the flash goes off on the camera.

"Real mature, Cal!" I chastise him before going into my walk-in closet and slamming the door. I look around, see my robe hanging on a hook, and put it on. I go to my dresser and look for something to wear today; I need to get out of this house.

I SINK DEEPER into the warm bath water, grab the remote beside me, and turn on the stereo, hoping to calm my senses. Twisting my hair into a braid and pinning it in place, I realize I should have done this before it became wet. I look at my nails and think it's time for a new manicure. Then I settle in and close my eyes, trying to relax.

I don't really need a manicure. It isn't a necessity; it's just another example of how spoiled I've become since marrying Cal. The fact that it's so high on my priority list is just one of the bad traits I've picked up since being with him, along with a long list of very bad words I use now that never used to escape my mouth. He brings out the worst in me sometimes, but when he wants to, he can bring out the best. Most times, that's only when it's to his benefit. I look up and notice he's leaning in the doorway.

Damn him, sneaking up on me. I swear he has feet like a cat.

He's dressed in one of his many chest-hugging gray t-shirts and a pair of dark denim jeans. The only thing standing out from his outfit is the black Rolex on his wrist. He always does that. At first glance, you'd guess his clothing came off the rack from any local mall and then—surprise! He's wearing an $11,000 watch or a $500 pair of sunglasses, and you'll know otherwise.

I note that it's not the same clothing he picked out earlier. I'm surprised; he's usually very decisive when he chooses things. He's never been one to second-guess himself. Since I've known him, he's always been very particular and exactly sure of what he wants. So I'm curious as to why he's changed clothes. I grab my sponge and dip it in the water before I run it up my leg. I know he's there. He knows I know he's there, but I have no reason to address him.

He walks toward the sink and I can't help but think how good his hair looks since he's grown it out—that fresh-out-of-bed-look.

He takes off his watch, making me wonder why. He then opens up the stereo control above our sink and presses the "scan" button, changing the radio station I had it on. I roll my eyes. I'm not going to do this with him. My first instinct is to change it back, but I came in here to relax, and I won't let him interrupt my attempted moment of peace.

"How do you listen to this crap?" he asks, shaking his head in disgust. He finally finds a station he's happy with and closes the stereo control back up. I open my mouth to insult his choice, but I like the song.

I have to admit, I've stolen his iPod more than a couple of times. His musical choices have exposed me to songs I'd probably never have discovered had I not known him. He's not into pop at all; his favorite genres range from Alternative to R&B, with Classic Rock dominating.

I'm so lost in the song that I don't realize he's now beside me, squatting near the side of the tub so we're close to eye level. I try to play off my surprise as he smiles at me knowingly. The shirt he's wearing highlights those gray eyes of his.

It would be a lot easier if he had a beer belly, bad breath, or an ugly scar. I look away from him, continuing to busy myself with my soap sponge. I see him out of the corner of my eye, but I won't give him my full attention. Unfortunately, he knows he has it, and he'll make sure I know he knows.

He grabs the remote and turns down the radio. I still don't look his way. Out of the corner of my eye, I see a smile play on his lips; he walks behind the tub and starts to caress the back of my neck. I bite my upper lip to keep from moaning, it feels so good. I curse him silently for knowing each and every sensitive spot on my body. With one touch, my hormones usually drown out my anger, stubbornness, and better judgment. I feel his hands start to slide down my shoulders as he massages them. I try to maintain my aloofness, continuing to wash myself. I don't know if it's helping or making this situation worse. I know he either wants something, or is going to tell me something that's going to really piss me off.

"What do you want, Cal?" My question comes out as a whisper, which is not what I intended. He doesn't say anything, but I feel his lips on my shoulders, making their way up my neck.

"Isn't it obvious?" he whispers in my ear before his tongue makes its way inside it. This time I can't help but let a small gasp escape. I try to wiggle my way out of his grasp. I don't want to let him have the satisfaction of doing this to me, but one of his arms crosses beneath my breasts, holding me in place while his other hand makes its way past my belly button, slowly trailing downward.

"Cal, leave me . . . S—s—" I'm unable to finish my incoherent sentence as one of his fingers slips inside of me, finding a place only he's been able to discover. I freeze as his fingers start to work their magic on the two most sensitive places on my body. I draw my legs up, my previous defensiveness disappearing as I close my eyes and lean back, giving him complete control to finish his intended task.

"What were you saying?" His voice is low and husky. I want to scratch his eyes out, but I settle for digging my fingers deep into his shoulder as I feel myself going over the edge. It has little effect on him as his rhythm speeds up. I start to fidget, unable to control my panting, and I feel it coming on. As bad as I want it, I wish it wouldn't.

"You started that little show out there," he continues in between sucking the back of my neck.

"But I just wanted you to know . . ." I hear his voice, and I want to slap his patronizing ass, but a moment later everything in me rises and releases, and I involuntarily let his name slip past my lips. Moments later, my body is coming down in ripples, and for that instant, I just enjoy bliss.

"I'm the finale." He snickers, and it wakes me out of my moment of ecstasy. I push him away from me, irritated at the satisfied grin on his face. "What, no thank-you?" he asks condescendingly.

I make my way out of the tub, dripping wet in more ways than one. As I grab my robe off the counter, I see what's lying there next to it and get a wicked idea.

"Lauren, don't do it." His eyes widen, reading my thoughts, and before he can reach me, I grab his watch and throw it into the water.

"Fuck!" he yells out and races towards the water. But it's too late.

"That was really fucking evil, Lauren!" He holds up his watch helplessly. I try to keep myself from laughing.

"Why the hell did you do that?" he shouts. His brow furrows and his skin turns a shade of red.

I shake the thought of how good he looks. "Because you're a

condescending asshole, that's why!" My voice matches the volume of his. He thinks he can do and say whatever he wants with no consequences. He shakes his head incredulously and then leaves the room, slamming the door behind him.

I smile to myself, but there's a twinge of guilt somewhere inside me. He's being such a baby—but the guilt is still there.

I let out a much-needed breath and let the tub water out. I quickly dry myself off and slip on my underwear and robe. I walk to the mirror, letting my hair down.

Cal buys expensive things, but he isn't frivolous. He takes great care of everything he owns. From his most expensive car to his least expensive shirt, he treats all of them the same. I hate feeling guilty or sorry. I know he doesn't most of the time. Yet, maybe I did go overboard today.

I grab my sweater to put it on, but give in to my conscience. If I'm going to apologize and get him to accept it, the fewer clothes I have on, the better. I peek in the bedroom and see that he's on the phone; he's changing into the gray button-up and black slacks from earlier. I see his travel bag and cringe; I really want to burn that thing. Even though I'm upset with him, there's still a sinking feeling in my stomach that he's leaving.

"What time is he going to be there?" I hear him ask.

"Around seven thirty. That's two hours, your time," I hear a voice boom through the speaker.

"I'll call you when I'm there," Cal answers. He sits down on the bed and begins putting on his shoes. I sit beside him quietly, trying to sense how mad he is at me.

"The watch was waterproof, wasn't it?" I tell him dryly, trying to cover up my sincerity.

"Would it matter to you if it wasn't?" he asks, surveying my outfit—or lack thereof. I love how he asks me a question and disregards mine.

"Maybe . . . maybe I overreacted a little," I admit, watching him change out of his gym shoes to his black loafers. I pout that he's ignoring me. I stand up and walk in front of him. He doesn't bother to look up at me.

"And that makes this time any different because?" he asks,

unenthused.

"How long are you going to be gone?" I ask, pushing myself between his thighs, purposefully ignoring his previous comment.

"You're going to miss me?" he asks, but it's a statement more than a question. He loosens the tie on my robe. I don't answer but look him in his eyes, knowing mine will give away my answer. He slides the robe down my shoulders and pulls it off me.

"The next time you try to get out of apologizing." His voice is low and deep in a way that causes my heart to beat faster. His eyes look from my body into my eyes.

"*This,*" he says, unhooking my bra. " . . . isn't needed," he continues.

"Who said I was apologizing?" I retort before he pulls me onto him.

His lips crash against mine. I don't fight his tongue for dominance but allow him to have his way, freely exploring my mouth. I wrap my legs tightly around his waist as he frees me from my robe completely and drops it onto the floor. I unbutton his shirt, looking into his eyes. Sometimes, I swear he can read my mind.

Hopefully he can see in my eyes what I can't bring myself to say to him. At the very least I know the longer he makes love to me, the longer it will be before he leaves, and I try to take solace in it.

HERE I AM again for the second time today, with nothing but a cool sheet covering my body. The space Cal previously rested in is cool. He's getting dressed after his shower, and I know in the next hour I'll be alone again. This is how it usually goes. Physically he has no boundaries with me, and none of my needs go unmet, but anything beyond that is a no-man's land that I can't seem to escape. He goes from attentive, responsive, and connected to withdrawn, distant, and aloof; and I wonder *why me?*

Any nameless woman could fulfill this need of his. He won't let me be there for him in any other way except sexually. It's starting to get harder to see the difference between being his wife and a favored high-class escort.

"I'll be back tomorrow . . . or more likely Thursday," he states quietly. I glance at him and turn in the opposite direction. I can't believe how upset I still get; this is routine, after all. I fight back my tears. He doesn't deserve them. He sits down beside me.

"What's wrong?" he asks, sincerity intermingled with sarcasm. I sigh.

"I don't know, Cal. What *is* wrong?" I ask him sarcastically.

"What's the matter? It's not like you're going to miss me." He's kissing my shoulders with the same lips that once could make me forgive him for anything. "But I'll miss you. Just a little." He adds the last part playfully. I watch him put his coat on and grab his overnight bag. I could practically narrate this scene from memory.

"Come walk me to the door," he says, heading out of the bedroom. I start to pull the sheet around my body.

"Leave the sheet. Please." He smiles with a twinkle in his eye that I've missed. I feel myself start to blush, but I comply. I walk through our bedroom door as he holds it open, and I playfully roll my eyes at him. A moment later I feel his hand slap my backside.

"Cal!" I yell at him, massaging the tingling on my backside. I should have seen that one coming.

When we reach the front door, I cross my arms, starting to feel cold, standing with no clothes on.

"Thursday at the latest." I grimace.

"I'll see what I can do," he vaguely promises.

"Well, I guess I'll see you," I say, irritated with his lack of an answer.

"Stop pouting; it's way too sexy when I'm leaving," he says before stealing a quick kiss from me. I quickly close the door behind him. There's only one other apartment on the floor and that's been vacant, but I wouldn't want to flash any potential tenants.

I lean my head against the door. I swear our relationship is so back and forth that it's like we're playing tennis, except he makes all the rules. When it's bad, it's really bad, but when it's good, it's so good. I hate it and love it at the same time. But that's how Cal is.

Sometimes, even if briefly, he's funny, fun, and open like he used to be. Other times, he can be a total bitch, which is not fun for anyone but him. When I first met him, I thought he was mysterious. Now I try to remember if he was this moody when I met him, and I was just blinded by his good looks and carefree attitude.

"SOMEONE'S GETTING ALL dressed up," my roommate Hillary teases as I put my hair in a French braid.

"Well, he says we're going to do something fun, so I'm dressing casually." I defend myself, referring to my sweater and blue jeans. Of course she thinks I should be wearing a skirt that barely covers my ass and a tight blouse—what she wears on her dates.

Hillary and I are like night and day. She's a statuesque blonde. Well, when she's wearing

April 30th, 2008

her natural color. I was blonde once in an experiment that went terribly wrong. Normally though, I'm brunette and only reach five foot five with the aid of four-inch heels. I'm content to spend my nights off work wrapped up in a good book or watching a movie. Hillary, on the other hand, loves to drag me down to my job at the club to go party all night.

I can't blame her. We both grew up in small towns in Michigan, but our childhoods couldn't have been more different. Hillary's father is a well-known preacher and kept her and her sister on a pretty tight leash. She says her mother didn't do much to loosen it.

My parents died in a car crash when I was three, so I don't have the luxury of complaining about an overbearing dad or sheepish mom. My aunt Raven raised me, and her parenting style was the perfect mix of discipline and freedom, which isn't bad for a woman who never wanted kids.

I guess being the girl with a dad who wouldn't even let her go to school dances means she's just making up for lost time and enjoying the freedom she missed out on. Somewhere within me I admire her free spirit. She never lets anything bring her down, and she does what she wants regardless of what other people say or think about her. She's dyed her long curly hair multiple colors more times than I can count and is the only person I've ever met that wears purple and green contacts over her gorgeous baby blues. I sometimes wonder if she is bipolar on a constant high.

"Maybe when he says fun, he means *fun*." She snickers, wiggling her eyebrows. I look back at her and can't help but laugh.

"First off, I don't even know this guy. So there's not going to be any of that kind of *fun*," I assure her.

"Well, of course not *that* kind of fun. Tight pants Lauren Brooks isn't revealing *Victoria's Secret* to just anyone." she laughs and flops onto my bed.

"You're five seconds away from being locked out of my room," I tell her playfully while putting on my gym shoes.

"It's not like anything *fun* goes on in here anyway," she says mockingly with a wink.

I pout at her and she laughs.

"Aw, girly. You know I love you. Besides, I want to hear all about the guy who was able to talk you into a date with him after just one drink," she says, flipping through a magazine on my bed.

"It wasn't a drink. In fact, he doesn't drink, which I think is a plus. It was just a conversation, and we have a lot in common. I thought it would be fun," I say, turning around to face her.

I ask God to forgive me for lying. We didn't have a long conversation; he had clients waiting for him and asked me out before he disappeared into the night, so to speak. I don't know if I have anything in common with him. I just know he's one of the sexiest men that I have ever seen and he literally had me at a loss for words.

I don't know why I'm reluctant to tell Hillary. Well, more like embarrassed. I hope my cheeks aren't burning at the thoughts I'm having about him—thoughts I shouldn't be having before I've even gone out with him. He sent me a text about the date. I was hoping for a phone call, but I'm pretty sure verbal communication is going to die out soon anyway.

"A lot in common, huh?" she says sarcastically, as if she knows my secret.

"Yes, a lot in common," I repeat, maintaining my innocence.

She's about to say something else, but the doorbell rings, interrupting her. She jumps from the bed and bolts to the door, yelling, "I'll get it!"

I go to grab my jacket and bag, glancing at myself once more in the mirror. I walk out and see Cal standing in the doorway, looking quite different from the last time I saw him. His blazer and slacks have been replaced with a t-shirt, leather jacket, and dark jeans. But those gray eyes and mesmerizing smile are still right there.

Hillary is standing there with her mouth hanging open. I assume she's having the same reaction I did when I first saw him. I then immediately realize she's wearing a cleavage-revealing cut-off sweater, and leggings that are hugging her curves a little too tightly. I now wonder why I let my over sexed, half-naked, cute roommate and her double Ds greet him. I'm immediately self-conscious about how conservative I look in comparison to Hillary.

"Hey, gorgeous. You ready?" he says, flashing a devilish grin. He walks over to me and, with one arm, lifts me right off my feet into a hug without even looking in Hillary's direction.

"Hi," I say breathlessly as he puts me down. I'm so caught off guard I almost stumble into Hillary.

I notice she has a look of shock on her face all her own. I don't think she's ever had a man look totally past her the way Cal just did. And I don't know if I should be turned on at his confidence, or insulted that he assumes he could invade my personal space like that.

I'm definitely going to have to explain the boundaries of Lauren Brooks later on, if that's his first date hug. Even though whatever cologne he's wearing has hypnotized my senses; he smells so good it should be illegal.

"Can I talk to you for a minute?" Hillary says, pulling me by the arm without waiting for a response. I smile back at Cal helplessly and he winks at me—butterflies invade my stomach at the gesture before Hillary and I escape away to my room.

"She'll be right back. You can sit down," she informs him. As we get in the room, she shuts the door and starts talking a mile a minute.

"Did you see how he just ignored me? How fucking rude is that?"

Hillary asks me sharply. I have to keep myself from laughing out loud at how serious she is.

"I'm sure he would have spoken to you if you didn't drag us out of the room in 0.2 seconds." I try to appease her even though I'm extremely amused.

"And what was with that hug? Didn't you guys just meet? Who the hell does he think he is?" She says, resting her hand on her hip. For the first time ever I think my roomie/friend is a little jealous. I have *never* seen her jealous before. I also think how ironic it is that she's saying all this when I know for a fact she's hooked up with guys the first night she's met them. One of whom she met just the week before.

"But other than that, he's fucking hot. Like hot as hell," she relents with a contemplative smirk, returning to the friend I know.

"Isn't he?" I sigh, relieved it isn't just me reverting to a fifteen-year-old hormonal girl. Hillary looks at me, surprised. I'm usually not into a guy just based on looks. I couldn't date anyone who I'd consider hideous, but I've learned that a relationship can't stand on attraction and the last two 'hot guys' I was with barely stood at all.

My first boyfriend, Daniel, had brown eyes, matching hair, and the most adorable dimples. I had known him since we were kids. My aunt always said he had the face of an angel and the mind of a demon. If only I'd known how right she was. When Daniel and I first started dating, we were both virgins and promised we'd be each other's first, and I thought we'd beat the odds until *after* I actually slept with him. Two days afterward *and* on my eighteenth birthday he revealed not only had he *not* been a virgin when we had sex, but he wanted me to have a threesome with the other girl he'd been screwing while waiting for me.

Then there was Michael. Of course that ended with me catching him screwing a girl where we both worked. So in all honesty I should be running in the other direction from Cal. But there's something else to him that makes me nervous and excited at the same time. It's not the way he looks. Aside from that, he exudes this sexual magnetism that I can't even describe—that I've never felt before and I'm kind of afraid of.

"Wow," Hillary says, interrupting me from my thoughts.

"What?" I ask curiously.

"You're blushing!" Hillary exclaims excitedly.

"No, I'm not," I deny quickly.

"Lauren Brooks, if I didn't know any better, I'd think you were in lust with him!" she says, her excitement growing.

"Shut up, Hillary," I whisper loudly, hoping Cal doesn't hear us.

"Yeah you are. I may not know about love, but I know aaaallllll about lust and it's all over you." She giggles, thumping me in the chest with her finger accusingly.

"You reek of it! Lust at first sight." She bursts into laughter.

"Shh!" I say again, pressing my index finger to my lips as hard as I can. She's never going to shut up about this. "Okay. Maybe I am just a little," I admit, and I start to have doubts.

"You know what? I'm not going to go!" I proclaim. I don't know what I'm thinking. I can't even think straight around this man. Why would I go anywhere with him alone? I don't need a repeat of Michael mixed in with Daniel. Who knows what dumb decision I'll make?

"What? Why? Are you crazy?" she yells at me.

I look at her with a perplexed expression on my face. A moment ago she was just bad-mouthing him, but now since she thinks I want to sleep with him, she's all for it.

"But you just said earlier—" I exclaim, confused.

"You're my friend and I love you, but you can be a little naïve when it comes to men. You've fucked what, two guys? Both of which you were in relationships with. And, sweetie, that guy out there does not look like a relationship kind of guy," she explains, taking a seat on my bed.

"Okay, so, again, why do you think it's crazy that I don't go out with him?" I say, confused.

"Because you're in lust with him, Lauren!" she exclaims, as if it should be obvious. I rub my temples, becoming extremely frustrated with this situation.

"Look, go out. Have fun. Fuck his brains out, but be prepared to only hear from him when he wants . . ."

I raise my hand up to cut her off. I can't hear any more of this. She's giving me a headache.

But she continues, "Lauren, it's not a bad thing to just hook up.

Especially after all the boring *let's make vows to one another* sex you've had. Trust me, it will be liberating! And how long has it been since you've gotten any? Have you ever even had a walk of shame before?" she asks like I'm seriously going to answer her.

"Not having this discussion with you right now," I say, heading to open the door when she stops me.

"Look, every guy isn't going to be 'the one.' Some guys are just meant to be good screws. That is why God put them on the planet! You're a senior and haven't even had the freshman experience," she says with a way-too-serious face.

"And this Cal guy is like the perfect candidate," she continues.

I don't even know where to start in on how wrong this conversation is.

"How do you know he's even good in bed?" I ask her sarcastically.

"Did you see how big his hands and feet are?" she says as if stating the obvious.

"Okay, we're going to go out there, and, Hillary—don't stare at his feet anymore, please!" I say before opening the door.

I walk back into the living room to see Cal sitting on the couch on his phone.

"We'll have to take care of this later," he says sternly into it and hangs up.

"Girlfriend?" I say jokingly.

He looks up at me. "Jealous?" he asks, a smile playing on his face.

"You have a strange sense of humor," I tell him. He winks at me before opening the door and allowing me to walk out ahead of him.

"You two have fun," Hillary sings out as we leave.

"Have a good one," Cal says, giving Hillary a little smile that I'm sure just made her day.

"So, where are we headed today?" I ask him curiously as we walk outside.

"You'll see when we get there," he replies, leading me over to a beautiful black motorcycle. I stop to admire the piece of sexy metal on wheels. It almost distracts me from the fact he hasn't told me where we're going.

"This is yours?" I ask, surprised. I don't know that much about bikes, but I do know that anything that reads Lamborghini on it doesn't come cheap.

"Lauren Brooks, meet Mrs. Scott." He smiles proudly, patting her affectionately. Guys and their toys . . .

"Well. Mr. Scott. I tend to feel a tad bit more comfortable when I know where I'm going with a stranger. Even one as tall and handsome as you," I tell him honestly.

He turns around and looks over at me, amused.

"You think I'm trouble, don't you, Lauren?" he asks, stepping closer to me and leaving only inches between us. The same rush of heat I felt last time returns and runs through my body, and I have to swallow my nerves. I try to think of a way to say it without offending him. But, yes, I do think he's trouble. I'm just not sure exactly what kind of trouble yet.

"Are you?" I smile up at him playfully even though I'm nervous as hell. He cocks his head slightly to the right and pauses a moment, as if he's thinking about his answer.

"Only as much as you want me to be." A wicked grin rests on his face, and for some unexplained reason it excites me. Then his smile softens. "But I guarantee you're safe with me," he says, and he seems genuine.

"So, I can assume you're not a serial killer, ax murderer, or crazy psycho?" I laugh now, only a tiny bit apprehensive.

"Only if I can assume you aren't," he retorts, getting on the bike.

I scratch my head. I guess it's now or never. I'm already downstairs with him and he is on a bike, not driving a big scary van . . . and he's incredibly attractive.

"You know how to get on?" he asks, noticing I'm just staring at him on the bike.

"Yeah . . . well, I think so. I've never ridden a bike, well, motorcycle before," I tell him skeptically.

"Well, I'll be glad to help you with your first time," he says as I get on. I can't help but feel excited, and we haven't even pulled off yet.

"So what now?" I ask as if I'm getting a lesson.

"Don't stick out your feet and hold on tight." He hands me a helmet and I look at the ugly, bulky object. I imagine myself looking like the human fly with it on. *Screw it, you only live once.* I shake my head, refusing it. He smiles with an arched brow as if he's surprised by my response but puts on his sunglasses and takes the helmet back.

"Hold on to what?" I don't see any railing or handles.

"To me," he answers. I see his smile widen in the mirror. *Duh, Lauren!* I laugh at myself, and I hesitantly put my hands on both sides of his waist and try to brace my legs on both sides of the bike.

"Ready?" he asks.

"Yeah," I reply. I hear the bike start and my heart starts to pound. He pulls out of the parking lot with ease, and our speed is pretty slow. This isn't too bad.

"This isn't that bad. I was a little scared," I admit.

"Just wait." A few moments later, he turns onto the freeway and we speed off. I feel like I'm on a roller coaster. The space that was between us is now gone. I've involuntarily scooted as close to him as I can, my arms as tight as they can go around his waist. After a few minutes of be- ing scared to pieces, I feel like I'm flying.

"This is great!" I yell, laughing.

He nods his head. "It's the closest thing to flying while you're on the ground!" I look at the sunset. It's absolutely beautiful. I can't believe I haven't done this before. I'm on a bike, going at least seventy miles per hour with a man I don't know much about. What I do know is that I hav- en't been this at ease with anyone in a *very* long time.

"I CAN'T BELIEVE you got me on the back of a motorcycle and bun- gee jumping in the same day," I say with a laugh, taking a fry and dipping it into some ketchup.

He just smiles and bites into his hamburger.

I try to look at him without staring. I expected a totally different type of man. I mean, the expensive suit, the VIP section of the club, seeming- ly manicured hands and styled hair—it didn't exactly scream motorcycle riding and bungee jumping.

"You're different than I expected," I confess.

He looks up at me with an arched brow and a smile playing on his lips. "You mean between me back at the club and now?"

"Yes." I smile.

"Is that a bad thing?" he asks, those incredible eyes flirting with me.

"No! It's just—you surprised me. I mean, when I first saw you at the club, I didn't expect you to be the outdoorsy, leather-jacket-and-jeans-wearing type, I guess." He doesn't say anything but flashes that million-dollar smile of his.

"So what other amazing things do you do?" I ask and run my hand through my tangled hair, free from its earlier braid. I wonder if he can tell how nervous I am. He opens his mouth to say something and then stops.

"What?" I notice his slight hesitation.

"Never mind. You've already given me this bad rep in your head. So I'll keep my thoughts to myself," he says, feigning hurt feelings.

"Now my curiosity is quite piqued, sir. I'm sure it won't change my view of you in any way. Tell me," I demand playfully.

He arches his brow and leans in, and I follow his lead, as if he's about to tell me a secret.

"I'd rather show you, but I think you're the type of girl that would require a few more dates before that happens."

I feel my mouth fall open. Is he referring to what I think he's referring to? He's watching me, waiting for my reaction. I decide not to push it any further, at least not directly.

"Hillary was a little irritated that you didn't speak to her earlier." I change the subject, wanting to know his thoughts. "She's not used to a guy ignoring her the way you did."

"I'm sure she's not." He chuckles, and I arch my brow questioningly.

"But I'm not like most guys. It takes more than big tits and a face full of makeup to get my attention," he adds. I'm a little taken aback by his frankness. He notices.

"I just mean there's nothing original about that. I see it every day. She's hot, but I've seen her type."

"And what exactly is her type?" I ask, irritation evident in my voice. Hillary and I see things through different eyes and we disagree a lot, but she's still my friend, and I won't let him speak badly about her, no matter how incredibly sexy he is.

He sighs, noticing my defensiveness. He clasps his hands together.

"Can I be one hundred percent with you right now?" he asks, and I nod apprehensively.

"Her *type* is usually empty, demanding, feeding on everyone else around them to boost their ego, jumping from one guy to the other," he continues to explain. "So absorbed in her own sense of self-worth that she doesn't realize that any man who can stand her is doing it just long enough to get laid."

I'm caught off guard by his answer. I won't confirm or deny what he's saying, and decide to steer the conversation in a different direction.

"So, are you saying you're not interested in sex?" I ask, surprising myself.

He folds his arms and flashes an amused grin. He leans in and, like a magnet, I do the same.

"Oh no. I'm *very* interested in sex." His voice is low and sensual, and for a moment I think he's going to kiss me. I'm disappointed when he leans back in his seat.

"That doesn't mean I'd screw any girl that batted her fake eyelashes at me. So, what about you?" he asks, focusing those piercing gray eyes on me.

I smile to hide my nervousness. Most guys I know fail to look me in the eye, which I hate, but it's like his eyes can see right through me, and I don't know which is worse. His candor is refreshing but unexpected. I don't know how to answer his question; he's been so honest, it would be hypocritical if I didn't return the favor.

"Well, it's been a—a while since the last time," I stutter nervously.

"I actually meant 'what do you like to do,' but I'm sorry to hear that." He smiles teasingly.

I think I'm going to die of embarrassment.

"Oh, God," I whimper, covering my face.

Then I feel his hands on mine and he brings them down. I look at him, surprised, his touch giving me butterflies.

"Don't ever hide those gorgeous eyes from me again," he tells me, and I'm even more embarrassed, but this time it feels much better.

"Well, I'm pretty boring, actually." I laugh, slightly disappointed when he lets go of my hands.

"I'm sure that's not the case." He rests his arms behind his head.

"I like to paint, draw, sculpt . . ." I tell him.

"Oh, an artist?" He grins.

"Yeah, kind of." I smile.

"So, is that something you want a profession in?" he asks. Somehow, it actually seems like he's interested, and not just for the sake of conversation.

"Well, sculpting and painting are more of a hobby, but drawing is what I love. If I could wake up every day and do it for a living, it'd be great. Unfortunately, there isn't a demand for artists, so I don't know how far I can go with it professionally." I sigh.

"Are you any good?" he asks.

I'm a little caught off guard by that.

"Well, I hope I am. It'd be kind of heartbreaking if I sucked at something I love so much," I remark with a chuckle.

"So am I going to see some of this work of yours?"

"I don't know. I'm sort of private about it," I say apprehensively.

"If you want to stun the world, you have to show it first," he says casually, and for the second time I have nothing to say.

"And you can practice on me," he offers.

"Maybe." I smirk. "So, are you from Chicago?"

"I've lived here most of my life," he answers. "What about you?"

"No, I go to school here at Chicago University. I was born in Michigan; Saginaw, to be exact," I tell him.

"Beautiful, smart, and Saginaw—I've been there before," he says.

"Really? I've never known anyone from Chicago who willingly went there," I say, surprised.

"I used to know some people who lived near there," he says, his mouth turning downward. "You didn't like it?"

"No! I love it. It's my home, where I grew up. There's just not much opportunity there. Well, you've been there. You probably understand."

He nods.

"It's weird how you don't appreciate something until it's gone," I continue. "When I was younger, I always dreamed about coming to Chicago and never looking back. But now that I'm here, I can't wait until I'm able to go back for a visit."

"So you're a small-town girl?" he jokes.

"I guess you can say that." I laugh. "Is that a bad thing?"

"Not at all," he replies convincingly.

I glance down as my phone vibrates. I look at the caller ID and see that it's Hillary. Why didn't I turn it off and why isn't she texting me? I roll my eyes.

"I better get that," I say with a sigh. Pressing the answer key, I say, "Hello?"

"Hi! How's it going so far?" she asks, excited and loud. I know he can hear her through the phone.

I look at him and he smiles.

"Excuse me a minute." I laugh as I stand up and walk to another part of the restaurant. "Everything is fine," I tell her.

"So what did you do? Where'd you go? Have you kissed him? Tell me everything!" she demands.

"This couldn't have waited until I got home?" I laugh.

"Well, yeah. It's one o'clock, and being that I'm the best person in the world, I wanted to act motherly and make sure you're okay, of course." More like nosey.

"Thank you, Mom. Wait, did you say *one?*" I ask in disbelief.

"Yeah! This is the longest you've ever been out, other than when you have to work! That's why I thought I'd check on you. Oh, and FYI—your boss man has called here three times. He wants you to call him ASAP or something like that."

What does he want?

"Okay, thanks, Hill. I'm going to hang up on you in about three seconds. But I'll talk to you when I get home," I inform her jokingly.

"Wait! Before you do that, you have to tell me if you're going to sleep with him," she says giddily. I roll my eyes and remain silent.

"Come on, Lauren! I'm bored as hell! Please, give me some kind of amusement. Give me *something*. I'm going to be here all alone tonight." I'm thankful to hear that. Now I know I can get a good night's sleep.

"Hillary, I haven't even kissed him yet," I say, almost disappointed.

"Well, the night—or morning—is still young," she sings.

"We'll see. I've got to go. Talk to you later, Hill."

"Yes, because you will tell me everything, or I'm jumping on your bed with you in it," she jokes. At least, I think she's joking.

"Okay, Hillary," I say before I hang up.

I walk back over to the table.

"Everything okay?" he asks.

"Yeah. Hillary checking up on me." I laugh.

He looks at his watch and frowns. "Yeah, we better get out of here." He stands up, puts on his jacket, and pulls out his wallet.

"You know, I can pay for this. You've already paid for everything else," I say, getting my purse.

"I asked you on the date. That's the point." He laughs.

"But—" I protest.

"When you ask me out on a date, you can pay." He winks at me as he puts a fifty on the table. I know our food didn't cost that much.

He looks up and sees my surprise.

"Don't worry. I have a pretty decent job." He throws me a smile before he leads the way to the front door.

I quickly pull on my jacket and follow him.

"I never asked—what do you do?" I say as I head through the open door he's holding for me. He ignores my question, distracting me with the thrill of the bike ride.

I OPEN MY eyes, feeling the bike's engine turn off. The lull of the engine and smooth ride almost put me to sleep. I look over to see that we're in front of my apartment building. I let go of him and get off the bike. I have an urge to stretch. We've been on this bike for over an hour.

"I have to tell you I've fallen in love with this machine," I say, only half-joking.

He looks at it and grins. "She has that way about her," he jokes as he dismounts and gives the gas tank an affectionate pat. He walks me to the door.

"This is one of the most interesting days I've had in a while. I really had fun," I tell him.

"You're not as boring as you've made yourself out to be," he kids.

"This is just me on a good day," I say, giving a mock warning.

As much as I've enjoyed myself, this moment has been drifting through my thoughts all day. There have been a few moments throughout our date when I thought he was going to—and then, nothing. I know for a fact he's not afraid or nervous about doing it. After all, he lifted me off the floor into a passionate hug when he greeted me. But he's done nothing but surprise me the entire night. Maybe he won't kiss me at all. I'm being ridiculous. I usually don't want to be kissed on dates, and now that I do, it's not going to happen.

"Well, thank you for everything," I say as I make my way toward the entrance to my building. I want to get inside before he sees how disappointed I am.

"I've been wanting—" he starts, but my phone rings, cutting him off. "May I?" he asks, gesturing toward the phone. I look at it, unsurely. Before I can answer, he takes the phone from my hand and answers it. I'm a little perturbed that he's answered my phone without waiting for my response—until I realize it's Michael calling.

Cal interrupts the confused voice on the other end. "No. This is Cal. Lauren's going to have to call you back at a decent hour. Don't you think it's a little late at night to be calling a respectable woman?" he scolds playfully, hanging up the phone and flashing me an innocent smile.

I can't help but laugh. I then wonder why Michael would be calling at two A.M. He's probably drunk and trying to apologize again, hoping I'll cave in and ask him over. Not going to happen.

I look at Cal, who shrugs innocently. He hands me my phone back and I remember how he did that, without my permission, and I frown at him.

"You're not mad, are you?" he asks, seemingly surprised.

I did think it was funny, but he shouldn't have just assumed it was okay. What if I did want Michael to come over? Not that I *ever* would, but still.

"No. But it could have been important. And you asked but didn't wait for my answer," I say, my voice strong, and for the first time all night, I'm not nervous. He laughs as if he's shocked, I'm a little insulted.

"Goodnight, Cal," I say, turning to open the door, and he grabs my hand.

"It's just that—I don't usually have to ask for things. So, I'm not used to waiting for the answer," he says in a joking tone, but his expression is serious.

"That's probably something you should work on, then," I say sarcastically, glad to have my nerve make an appearance for the first time since I met him.

"Well, can I kiss you?" he says, stepping closer to me, his eyes flirting with mine. It causes me to swallow my breath. He smells so good, but no. I'm going to ignore how good he looks and smells. Cal needs a lesson that he can't get everything he wants or do everything he feels like. Now, I'm going to explain the boundaries of Lauren Brooks.

"Cal, I like you, but you should th—" Before I can finish, he pulls me toward him as he did earlier, but this time, he presses his lips against mine.

I wrap my arms around his neck to keep my balance. I don't know how to react, but my body starts to respond as he sucks on my bottom lip. Before long my mouth opens, allowing his tongue into play, and he begins coaxing out my own. I feel lightheaded, tingles running up my spine, as his fingers trace circles on my lower back.

I can feel him smiling as one of his hands runs through my hair and cups the back of my head, while his other hand makes its way underneath the back of my sweater. His skin on mine sends sensations through my body that I'm not ready to experience. His fingers linger, tracing the same spots as he was earlier, but now there's no material as a barrier to the warmth of his skin, countering the cool wind. It sends heat flushing through my body. I feel hot, anxious, and . . . unsatisfied. If our kiss gets any deeper, I'm going to drift away. But I want more.

I wrap my arms tighter around his neck, my body demanding to be closer to him, almost acting on its own. In response, his hands move to both sides of my waist, gripping me tighter as he backs me into the door—or maybe the wall. I can't say for sure. But now I'm pressed between him and something. I can feel his heart starting to beat faster, or maybe it's my own. We're so close I can't tell the difference. I run my hands up his chest, the cool leather of his jacket smooth against my hands. I've never wanted to feel bare skin so badly in my life, and I realize I'm thinking crazy things—like, if only I had a dress on this would be a lot easier, and if only he drove his car, how fast we could have been in there. I wonder how hard Hillary is sleeping and if she'd hear us if I brought him up. I realize I'm close to doing something extremely stupid, and with every ounce of willpower in my body, I prepare myself to break our kiss. But before I do, *he* pulls away. I immediately miss the warmth of his lips.

"Lauren," he whispers in my ear, setting me back on the ground. I'm in a haze. He can't expect me to have a conversation with him right now. I need a minute to compose myself. *Ugh, Lauren, let's start thinking again, shall we? Way to show him your boundaries.*

I look up at him and he licks his lips, his hands palms-down on both sides of me. He leans down and rests his head on mine.

"I'm going to go, because if I stay here another minute, *I am* going to be trouble for you," he says, his tone dangerously low. But his smile is so innocent it should belong to a Boy Scout. I nod, unable to force any words out of my tight throat.

"Good night, gorgeous," he says and kisses the skin beneath my earlobe, causing my heart to flutter. In a flash, he's walking toward his bike, but stops midway and turns back toward me.

"Oh, and I'm going to work on the asking thing. I promise," he says, walking backwards. A smile spreads across my face. He gets on his bike, pauses, and leans on the handlebars.

"Are you going in, Ms. Brooks?" he asks, a hint of sarcasm in his voice and a glint in his eye that's daring. My body is screaming, *Hell no, I'm going with you* and as if he can read my mind, he says, "Or are you coming with me?" and I contemplate. I'm actually contemplating! But my mind wins out over my body's insistence, almost as if recovering from a knockout punch. "No, you said yourself it's a little late for a woman of my *respectability* to be out," I tease him and he laughs, relenting.

I take out my keys and open the door. "Good night," is all I manage to say, and before I shut it I look back at him. He gives me a wave, a tickled grin on his face. I close the door, hoping I'm not wearing a big goofy grin.

My phone starts to ring again, and my heart beats rapidly, thinking of Cal. My heart sinks when I see that it's only Michael. He's probably steaming right about now over what Cal did, but so am I, for an entirely different reason of course, and in a *very* different way.

As I let myself into my apartment, I hear the roar of the motorcycle's engine and I run to the window. I catch a glimpse of Cal turning the corner, and for the rest of the night I dream about what would have happened if I'd ridden away on it with him.

May 5th, 2011

"**A**RE YOU FREAKIN' kidding me, Cal?" I make sure the disbelief in my voice is apparent to him on the other end of the line. But coming from Cal, I should expect this.

"Calm down, babe," he says steadily.

"Don't fucking call me babe, Cal! You said you were coming home Monday. And it's Thursday!" I yell, pacing the room.

"I know. Things came up," he explains. He sounds distracted, which sets me off even further.

"Things came up, huh? What the hell has surfaced from out of nowhere that has kept you there almost a week?" I scream into the phone.

"You know what? I'm going to talk to you when you calm down." He hangs up on me.

Again.

I growl and throw the phone on the bed in frustration. As usual, our conversation ends with me ready to punch a face that's conveniently not here.

He hasn't called at all, just sent a text that asked if I was behaving—whatever the hell that means—and telling me he'd be home today. I don't know where he is or who he's with, and when we do talk, he never grasps the severity of the situation and thinks hanging up is going to stop me. Oh, he's wrong! I'm so not done. I snatch the phone back up, hit redial, and wait for him to answer.

"Yeah," I hear him say shortly.

"Cal, you are such a selfish asshole!" There's no response, and I glance at the call screen on my phone and see that it's ended. I direct a kick into the side of bed and throw my pillow across the room. He almost never argues with me! I can't seem to get a human response from him. He ignores me, laughs at me, or, when he *is* home, picks me up and takes me into another part of the house, which pisses me off even more. How do you argue with someone who won't say anything? But considering that in order to argue, you have to communicate, it's no surprise that he won't do that with me, either. He's a brick wall, and I'm tired of trying to break through.

I never thought this would happen to us. I knew he could be closed off, but I never thought it would go this far. Sometimes, I want to go back to that first minute I saw him and scream to myself, "Run the other way!"

The phone in my hand rings again. It's him. I push the answer button, but I don't say anything.

"You done?"

I bite my tongue in a stubborn effort to not call him every foul name I can think of. "Cal, where are you?" I say as calmly as I can.

"I'll be home tomorrow," he says, ignoring my question. I hear music blaring in the background, and it almost sounds like . . .

"Are you at a club?" My voice almost squeaks on that last word because I can't believe what I'm hearing.

"Around two," he continues, deliberately ignoring me.

"Cal, are you at a fucking club?" At this point, being calm and civil is out of the question. He's at a damn club, God knows where, when he told me he'd be home today. I take a deep breath. I'm so mad my hands are shaking, but I demand my tone to be calm.

"I'm so sick of your shit, Cal. I don't give a shit when you get home, because I won't be here." And I extend the same courtesy to him as he's shown me. I hang up. I won't keep doing this. I am not his doormat. He can't do anything he wants and then come home whenever he's done without any repercussions. This is it. I won't play these games with him anymore.

I'm a good—well, I *was* a good wife. I don't know if he understands, but I do know he doesn't appreciate how much I love him. Of all the men for me to fall for, why did it have to be him—a man who's incapable of showing his love for anyone, *especially* his wife?

Before we were married, I knew he loved me. He made me feel as if I was the most important person in his world. Thinking back, maybe I was so in love with him that I didn't even notice the person he's in love with is himself. He *says* he loves me, but his actions show me he doesn't give a flying fuck.

The house phone rings, breaking into my thoughts. I walk over to the wall and pull the line out. I'm done talking to him, or rather, I'm done with him talking at me. I walk into my closet to find my suitcase. Opening drawers, I start pulling random things out and throwing them in. I ignore the dressers filled with nothing but lingerie, the things I wear only for him.

I watch what I eat and work out every day so my body is still attractive to him. But he doesn't care. It's not like he's around often enough to see it. I pick out a few more shirts and pants and stuff them into the suitcase as well. I walk back into my room and put on my leather boots, glancing at myself as I walk past the mirror. I'm wearing a black cashmere sweater and leggings; I spent two hours curling my hair. I look nice. Stupid me, actually believing he'd be home when he said he would, waiting for him.

My cell phone starts to ring again. On impulse, I walk out onto the balcony and drop it off the side with satisfaction. That'll stop it from ringing.

Feeling much better, I go back into my room and try to zip my suitcase, but it's too full. Of course, folding everything neatly would solve that problem, but I'm in no mood to mess with that crap. I stomp on the lid with my boot until everything is finally squashed enough to get it zipped up.

I grab the leather jacket that he bought me while on our honeymoon and throw it across the room. The thought of wearing it sickens me. In the closet, I find another one that I bought myself. I grab my suitcase. It's a big one, stuffed full and heavy as hell. Thank God it rolls, or I'd have serious trouble. I drag it out into the hall to the top of the stairs. I turn it on its side and give it a good shove. It stops halfway, so I kick it the rest of the way down.

At the bottom, I grab the handle and roll it to the door. I look around at what I once thought was a beautiful penthouse, with its huge picture windows, boutique furniture, and state-of-the-art electronics. In my mind, though, all I can see now are barred windows and a cold bed— the prison where I remained silent. Well, that's a lie. I have caused a lot of hell, but nothing unwarranted. I can feel tears forming in my eyes, and I try to fight them back. I really shouldn't cry; he's not worth it.

Losing the battle, I reach up to wipe away the tears and catch sight of the spectacular ring on my finger. It means nothing. I pull it off and slam it down on the console table next to the door, precisely where he sets his keys when he walks in. At least he won't be able to miss that.

Taking a deep breath, I open the door and head to the elevator, pulling my bag behind me. There's really no need to lock the door. Security here is better than in a Vegas casino, so the chances of the apartment being robbed are slim. Not to mention we're over ten stories up. I press the button and step back to wait, fidgeting with my hair.

I don't even know where I'm going. I mean, the logical place would be my aunt Raven's, but I'm not sure that's where I want to go. Instead of showering me with hugs and kisses, she'll probably shower me with questions and opinions. Questions like, 'What's going on?' and comments like, "You really should talk to him." I'm not in the mood for that kind of shit right now. Still, I have no plan at this point. I'll have to figure something out to tell her. I need to think about what I want and what I'm going to do. I've been with Cal so long that I can't remember what it's like being without him. I've wrapped myself up in him, something no woman should do with any man.

The elevator has arrived. I drag my suitcase in and hit the garage floor button. I hate the way my stomach feels as it's going down; it reminds me of the butterflies Cal used to give me when we first met. Finally, it stops and the door opens to the parking garage. Cal hates for me to come down here alone, but I always remind him there are cameras everywhere and Jeff, the security guard I've just waved at, watches everything like a hawk.

I head down to our parking spaces and over to the white Audi Cal bought me for my birthday. I remember getting up that morning, being blindfolded and led downstairs. There, I found a jewelry box and opened it to find a beautiful emerald necklace inside. I was so enamored with the necklace that I didn't notice the car key—though, I did wonder why he brought me to the parking garage to give it to me.

That was one of our good days, just a memory now. There's no sense in fantasizing about those, dwelling on the past when I live in the present, even if the present is falling short. It's only been six months since I became Mrs. Scott, and now I think the name is temporary.

How long do I hold on to those memories when they're fading further and further away? I pop the trunk on my car to heave my suitcase in and slam it closed. I take a deep breath as I get into the car and shut the door. I sit for a moment, leaning back and gripping the steering wheel. Suddenly, the enormity of what I'm doing washes over me and I lean forward to rest my head on the steering wheel.

"What am I going to do now?" I say softly to myself.

May 3rd, 2008

"I CAN'T BELIEVE you really considered screwing him." Angela chuckles as she wipes down the bar. We've been doing inventory on all the alcohol, our regular routine before the club opens. Angela is the one who pulled a few strings to get me my job here. Her mother and my aunt Raven used to go to college together and, thankfully, stayed in touch, so when I moved here to the big city I wasn't just a nameless face with no one to call a friend. Angela got me this job and introduced me to Hillary, who needed a roommate to help her cover the rent.

"I know. I feel like I'm Hillary," I joke, pulling the case of Patrón Tequila.

"Nah, Hillary would have fucked him right on the front door." Angela chuckles.

"That's what she told me I should have done. She said it would have 'liberated me,'" I say, using air quotes.

Angela laughs and sighs. "Well, I say you only live once. But you shouldn't do anything you'll regret either," she says, her tone going from playful to serious over the span of the sentence. "So, when are you going to see him again?" she asks giddily.

"I don't know. I'm waiting for him to call. He hasn't yet," I admit grudgingly.

"After a kiss like that, he's going to call. You need to think about what's going to be your excuse to not screw him if he picks you up in a car." She nudges me in the side and we laugh before her attention turns to the door.

"Look who's entered the building," she says sardonically. I look over to see Michael strolling in. How ironic, one of my biggest regrets walking right towards me.

"You know, for someone who doesn't work here anymore, you spend an awful lot of time here. Shouldn't you be out arresting criminals?" she mocks, snapping him playfully with her rag. He's working a part-time security job now.

"And good afternoon to you too, Angie." He smirks, walking past her.

"Well, it was. Then you got here," Angela sings before heading to the back, twisting her cold black hair in a faux bun and leaving us alone.

"Lauren, we need to talk," he says, the playfulness in his voice turning serious.

I arch my eyebrow at him. "No, Michael. We don't," I say shortly as I walk past him. I can feel him following close behind me.

"Please," he insists, grabbing my hand.

"Michael, we haven't been on speaking terms for at least two months. What's the big deal now?" I ask, snatching my hand back.

He doesn't say anything for a moment, but then blurts out, "I miss you. I want us to at least still be friends. Like you and Steven are. You guys stopped going out and you're still friends!"

This time, both of my eyebrows go up.

"Seriously? Steven and I went out a few times. We weren't in a relationship and he didn't feel it necessary to screw some other girl while I was upstairs working," I say more bitterly than I intended.

"Lauren, I don't know what I was thinking that night. If you would just listen . . ."

"You're talking a lot. But you're not saying anything worth listening to," I interrupt him.

"I messed up. I'm sorry. I'm so sorry!" His eyes are pleading. For a moment, I think he may be sincere. Then I think back to the girl he had pressed up against the wall in the stock room—her skirt hiked up, his pants down—and how he lied, saying nothing happened . . . and I remember he's just a liar.

"Apology accepted. Happy?" I flash a fake grin at him and try to walk away, but he grabs my arm. I look back at him; my eyes are daggers. "Don't touch me," I warn him, my tone laced with ice.

He ignores me. "If you would just give me a chance to talk to you," he pleads.

I snatch my arm away from him. "What, Michael? What do you want to talk to me about?" I yell and throw my hands up.

"What I did that night. I've regretted it every day since then. If I could change it I would, but I can't. I keep trying to remember what I was thinking and what the hell my problem was, but I can't count it toward anything but drunken stupidity. Never in a million years have I ever wanted to hurt you like that. I just—" He stops mid-sentence, and I follow his look to the door to see Angela walk in.

"Lauren, someone's here to see you." She smirks, not forgetting to roll her eyes at Michael.

"Michael, I've already told you. I'm over what you did, we're not to-gether anymore, and it no longer concerns me. I don't care what you did, what you are doing, or what you are about to do. I've moved on. I just want you to leave me alone," I tell him before walking away.

I have to take a deep breath once I get out of the room. He will never know how hard that was for me. Michael and I had a complex re-lationship from the start. I had just broken up—well, kind of agreed to be friends—with Steven, and one night, after a little too much drinking, he kissed me, and we kind of fell into a relationship from there. In the end, I think we probably should have chalked it up to drunken attraction instead of deciding to be together. But, you know what they say about hindsight . . .

The man sitting at the bar is Jason, the newspaper guy.

"Hey, Lauren." He stands as I approach him.

"Hi, Jason," I say hesitantly. After all, the last time we spoke, he did ditch me.

"I just wanted to say how sorry I am about the other night," he starts off.

"It's fine." I smile at him. In fact, if he hadn't ditched me, I never would have gotten up for some fresh air, which means I wouldn't have bumped into Cal.

"I just . . . I thought I saw someone that . . . Never mind. It was no excuse, and I wanted to apologize," he says.

"Well, apology accepted." I laugh slightly. I'm accepting a lot of apologies today, it seems.

Michael walks up to us, looking a little angry. *What the hell does he want now?*

"Remember me?" he asks Jason in a sarcastic tone. Jason looks at him with a perplexed expression.

"No, have we met b—?" His question is cut off by Michael's fist in his face, knocking him to the floor.

"Michael! What the hell!" I scream. I immediately jump out of the way as Jason stands up and rams into Michael.

"Steven, Dan! Do something!" I call. Hearing the commotion, Angela rushes our way.

"Dan! Dan, get out here!" she screams. Soon Dan runs out to break them up, followed by Steven.

"Let go! Let go, guys!" Dan growls as he tries to pull the two of them apart. Steven grabs Jason and succeeds in separating them right as Ryan walks in.

"What the hell is going on here?" he yells angrily, his usually subdued British accent flaring. Everyone looks at him, none of us knowing what to say.

"I don't know! This—this lunatic just attacked me!" Jason yells.

"What the hell happened, Michael?" Steven asks.

"He hung up on me when I called Lauren!" Michael yells.

Oh my God, I can't believe this. I cover my face in embarrassment.

"I have never spoken to this guy!" Jason yells. "I hang up on a lot of people, but you don't see them coming up to me and punching me in the face! For the record though, I've never spoken to you before!" Jason yells.

"Jason, I am so sooooo sorry for this," I say, walking around the bar to get him a cold towel for his eye.

"Jason? Your name isn't Cal?" Michael says as stupidity starts to take over his expression.

"No," he says sharply.

I hand Jason the towel. "No, Michael, this isn't the guy; but even if it were—oh, God! I can't even believe you!"

"What is this, *Melrose Place*?" Ryan yells. "I haven't even opened and I'm already breaking up fights. From now, on no one who is not currently employed here is allowed in before opening unless I personally approve it!" Ryan frowns at all of us.

"I-I'm sorry," Michael murmurs.

"Michael, get the hell out!" Ryan yells.

"I'm sorry, Ryan, and I'm sorry to you too, Jason." Michael glances at them briefly before scooting quickly out the door, escorted by Steven and Dan.

"Jason, I am sorry about this, mate," Ryan says, dusting Jason's suit off.

"It wasn't your fault," Jason utters, rubbing his eye, which is already purple.

"I'll be back," Ryan says angrily and walks out, cursing Michael under his breath.

"I'm really sorry again; he can be a douche sometimes," I tell him sincerely.

"Don't apologize. You aren't the one who punched me in the eye," he says.

"I know. But still . . ." I feel bad about the entire situation.

"So is it always this hard to ask you on a date?" He laughs slightly.

"Y-you're asking me on a date?" I chuckle.

"Yeah, I was about to when that guy—who I take it is your ex-boy-friend?—attacked me."

I stuff my hands in the back pocket of my jeans. This has been a busy week; two *sober* guys ask me out in the same week.

"I, well . . ." I'm thinking hard about it. This could be fun. Another date wouldn't hurt. I mean, this guy did just get punched in the face for me. I can't turn him down after that. And Cal hasn't called, so . . .

"I would love to," I tell him.

"Well, maybe this day won't turn out so bad after all." He smiles broadly.

"I can't Friday night, but how about Thursday?" I ask.

"My eye should be down by then. Hopefully." He laughs.

"That's great. I'm sure it will," I agree. Well, I'm sure the swelling will be down, at least. Whether his normal color will be back, I doubt it, based on the way it looks now. I'm still shocked Michael hit him. He's studying to be a police officer; you'd think he would know better.

"Great!" he says with enthusiasm.

IT'S 11:00 P.M. I can't sleep. That is what working the night shift will do to you on your days off. I had planned on catching up on my sleep, but I'm utterly restless. Switching on the lamp beside my bed, I pull out the sketchpad I keep under my bed and start to draw. The phone rings suddenly, startling me.

"Hello?" I answer hesitantly.

"Hey, gorgeous."

The voice is a familiar one and it immediately awakens the butterflies in my stomach. "I guess that would be me," I say, a grin spreading across my face.

"I'm not calling too late, am I?"

"No, it's fine. I'm a bit of a night owl myself," I tell him.

"Note this: me working on the asking thing." He chuckles. I think back to his earlier promise and grin.

"Look at you, sir. I am so very proud of you," I tell him playfully.

"Well, you'll have to show me how much," he flirts back. I bite my lip at the thought. "I was going to text you. I didn't know if you'd be at the club or not."

"No, today's my night off. But yesterday I was. I restocked the bar, had to help clean the stock room . . . watched an innocent man get punched in the face over the stunt you pulled with my cell phone the other night." I chuckle.

"Really? This is a first, me causing a fight I didn't get to be in. Well, maybe next time." He laughs. "And you said I was trouble. It seems trouble follows you, Ms. Brooks," he says playfully.

"Ha-ha," I say dryly.

"Listen," he goes on, "if you're not too busy breaking up fights around Chicago, I wanted to ask if you were going to the AIC opening Saturday?"

It takes me a few seconds to register he's talking about the Chicago Museum's 80th Anniversary charity ball. I wish I were, but unfortunately, it's an exclusive, invitation-only event. It's the only thing my classmates have been talking about the past month. They're furious that Crestfield Industries, one of the largest companies founded in Chicago, weaseled their way into sponsoring the event and privatized the entire affair.

"I wish. It's invitation-only," I tell him. Too bad I'm not rich or famous, since those were the people on the invite list.

"Well, I guess you're going to have to come with me." He sighs.

"Wait. Are you telling me you have an invitation?" I ask, my voice rising with excitement. I hear him laughing now. "How did you get that? You're not screwing with me, are you, Cal?" I ask him cautiously. I don't want to sound like an art geek, but it would be an absolute dream come true to attend.

"We're on the phone, you know—what would be the fun in that?" His voice deepens with insinuation, making my skin tingle.

"I would love to go!"

"I'll have you picked up at eight," he says.

Have me picked up? Is he not coming? "You aren't picking me up?" I ask curiously.

"Well, I'm in New York, and I won't be getting back until that night, so I'll have a limo pick you up and then it'll swing by the airport to get me. Is that okay?" he says. Of course it's okay. I'm going to the Chicago Museum's anniversary ball!

"Yes, it's perfect," I tell him. "I can't wait!" I really should tone down my enthusiasm just a few notches.

"Look, I've got to go. But I've been thinking about you, Lauren . . ." He quietly trails off. I grip the phone a little tighter, feeling my heart rate speed up. I didn't expect to hear that from him.

"I-I've been thinking about you too, Cal," I say sincerely.

"Good," he says. I can hear the smile in his voice, and one spreads across my face as well.

After I hang up the phone, I twirl around like a seven-year-old on Christmas. I rush to my closet and start to rummage around, hoping there's something there. I don't even know if I'm going to be able to get off work. I'll have to trade shifts or something.

I sigh, disappointed with the contents of my wardrobe. Jeans, jeans, and more jeans, along with a few dresses I used to be able to wear to work. Nope, nothing seems worthy of the occasion. I come to the conclusion that I'll have to buy something. I have a Visa card for emergencies with a couple hundred dollars I've never used. Cal has been thinking about me! I want to make sure my dress leaves a lasting impression.

I wonder if he's he been thinking about me as much as I've been thinking about him. I rush to the door, ready to tell Hillary all the details. Then I remember her telling me to keep it simple and fun with him, and the thought stops me in my tracks.

What if Hillary is right? He said he was thinking about me. He didn't say in what way. I ignore the sinking feeling in my stomach. Well, right now it doesn't matter; it's just a date, to one of my favorite places on earth, and on the arm of an incredibly handsome man. And here I am trying to find something wrong with it. I'm not going to let anyone ruin this for me, not even myself.

"SAGINAW, MICHIGAN." I can't help but feel a little nostalgic as I read the sign welcoming me back to my hometown. It's as if I'm watching a home movie, picking up random memories as I drive.

May 5th, 2011

It's been a while. The last time I was here was right after Cal and I got married. I sigh while driving past the endless rows of cornfields. In fifteen minutes, I'll be on my aunt's doorstep, lying about why I'm there and putting up with her well-meaning bullshit. Well, maybe ten if I rush it, but speeding through Saginaw in an Audi isn't the best idea.

When I come to a stop sign, I rifle around in my purse for my cell phone before I remember I dropped it out the window. My stomach's growling. I've only eaten a bagel all day, and that was four long hours ago. I see a gas station a few blocks down and decide to stop for a bite. I turn off my car and lock the door. Even though there's really no need to lock it, living in Chicago has changed my habits. Walking in, my eyes gravitate to my favorite strawberry shortcake roll-up. I walk to the counter and wait for the clerk to come to the front. She approaches the counter with a warm smile, reminding me of the friendliness of Saginaw.

"Good afternoon. Is this all you'll be having?" she asks.

"Yes, that's all." I smile and hand her a dollar. She puts it in the register and hands me back a quarter.

"Have a nice day," she replies.

"You too," I tell her, leaving the store while opening the wrapper of the cake. I break off a piece and pop it in my mouth before stuffing the rest in my purse and getting into the car. As I drive off, my thoughts drift to Cal. I wonder what he's doing right now. He's probably pissed, or maybe he isn't. Maybe he doesn't care that I left. I'm usually clueless as to how he feels.

I hate the fact that I'm thinking about him at all, or even considering his feelings. I shouldn't, but how do you stop loving someone in an instant? It's almost ludicrous how many times I've tried to do that. It never works because the feelings just pop right back to the surface moments after my anger has subsided. It would be so much easier if he weren't so complicated. Cal is the most complex person I've ever met. He always has this air of mysteriousness to him, which is beyond frustrating after all these years, but that's what attracted me to him. When I moved to Chicago, it was a totally different world from Saginaw. In my hometown, almost everyone knew each other, or at least of each other. I had grown up with most of the guys I went to high school with, so there was never the excitement of meeting a new person, or having to learn about someone from scratch.

When I transferred to my school in Chicago sophomore year, it was like the men there could smell fresh meat. I was asked out by so many different types of guys, especially when I started working at the club. There were some with tattoos and piercings, others who wore expensive suits and glasses, black, white, tall, short, it was so much to take in.

Thankfully I had Angela and Hillary to guide me through the dating scene, which got old really quick. I started to miss the familiarity of Saginaw. I ended up only kind of dating Steven, who is now a really good friend, and Michael, who turned out to be the exact guy I should have been avoiding—good-looking, closeted douche bag. Other than him being attractive, I think it was the familiarity of working around him that caused me to convince myself there was something there that wasn't. There was always something missing, and whatever *it* was, Cal had more than enough of. He always has had this way of exuding this sexy confidence without appearing conceited, a way of making mundane things seem exciting and new, so Cal has been my gift and my curse. Curse more often than gift, I suppose. When we first met, I couldn't have known I was only scratching the surface of the mystery of Cal, an enigma in himself. Unfortunately, one I still haven't solved.

I always pictured him being the man I wanted him to be, yet now I wonder, is it fair he's not my expectation of the husband that I thought he'd be? I assumed after marriage he'd open up, let me know the secrets that were hidden behind his smile; that I'd understand why, when we're alone, his presence is peaceful, but when I look into his eyes I see something completely different. I thought I would get answers to all of these questions when we married. I was wrong.

I arrive at my aunt's house and memories instantly start to flood in. I remember Raven walking out onto the porch, successfully ruining the goodnight kiss at the end of my very first date. She cleared her throat and stared at me until all I could do was kiss him on the cheek and say, "Good night."

I laugh now, but in that moment I was angry and embarrassed. She was both sweet and sour. She had to play mom and dad to me growing up, a woman who never wanted kids but did a better job than she could have imagined. She always made sure to let me know how much my parents loved me and how proud they'd be of me.

Raven never married, so I've never felt comfortable asking for advice about my own marriage. I often wonder what advice my mother would give about Cal and me. My dad would probably wring his neck for the stress he gives me. I turn off the car and grab my purse, stepping out and heading towards the porch. I leave the suitcase because I really don't feel like getting the third degree at the moment. I'll find a way to slip it in later on during a conversation. I'm sure I'll get an opening. "Lauren, I found the most wonderful sweater," she'll tell me, and then I'll say, "Oh really, because I have a ton of sweaters in the car, since I'm leaving my husband." Yep, it'll be really simple, really quick. I ring the doorbell and check my appearance in the reflection of the window, making sure I look presentable. Raven always stresses that if the day is bad, you have to dress better to hide it.

I ring the doorbell again, this time adding a knock. I still have a spare set of keys, but I don't want to intrude. It doesn't seem like she's home. I take a seat on the top step of the porch. She's probably gone shopping, hopefully not for clothes because that could take hours. I'm really regretting that little fit of rage that sent my phone over the balcony railing this morning. I look at my watch, realizing it's only one o'clock. Raven could be out all day.

I decide to go ahead and let myself in rather than wait on the front porch like a FedEx package. I find the spare set of keys at the bottom of my purse and open the door. As I step inside, the radio is on, and I can't help but smile. Ever since I can remember, 91.3 has always been Raven's favorite radio station and it plays a constant soundtrack in the house. I lock the door behind me and set my purse on the table. This place still brings me comfort—a real home rather than just a place of residency, which is how I feel when I'm alone at the penthouse. I walk upstairs and find the doorway to my old bedroom. Another smile spreads across my face as I walk into the room, still the same way I left it. I sit on the bed and breathe deep as I face the window and let the sunshine wash over me through the curtains. On my dresser sit awards, ribbons, and medals aligned in the same place they were when I was in high school.

There is one new addition, though. My eyes glide over to my wedding photo with Cal, and I feel a sense of jealousy towards my past self. The couple in the picture no longer exists; they are light years from where Cal and I are now. I pick it up and turn it downward. If only I could see into the future. A door shuts downstairs; Raven must be home. I give myself a little pep talk: *I can do this; just don't let anything slip.* I take a deep breath and walk out of the room. From the top of the stairs, I can see Raven setting down her bags. I knew she'd been shopping. She looks up at me, a huge grin spreading over her face.

"Lauren! I thought that was your car!" she squeals, dropping it all on the floor.

"Hi, Raven," I say cheerfully, running down the stairs. She meets me at the bottom and wraps me into a big hug.

"It's so good to see you! I've missed you so much!" she says, squeezing me tightly.

"I've missed you too," I tell her honestly, letting her scent take me back to my childhood, when any problem I had could be solved with a piece of chocolate cake, albeit from the store, since Raven couldn't bake a piece of bread if her life depended on it. She steps back, scrutinizing my appearance.

"You look beautiful. I love the sweater," she says, gliding her hand across my shoulder. Raven, fashionably inclined as always, and I often wonder what would have happened if she had grown up in a big city. I'm sure she wouldn't have ended up a librarian. "So what brings you here? How long are you staying? And where is that handsome nephew of mine?"

Okay, Lauren, let's start thinking. Think, think, say something, keep smiling. Unfortunately, all I'm doing is smiling because I can't think of a word to say. I really need to start planning ahead.

She frowns at me and brushes her scarlet bangs out of her face.

"Uh huh. How about you help me take these in the kitchen and tell me all about it?" she says, grabbing two bags herself and leaving the room. I pick up three bags and follow behind. I need to think of something; I'm definitely not ready to tell her that I've left my husband. I walk into the brightly lit kitchen and set the groceries on the table. Being here reminds me how gloomy Chicago is sometimes. Even though she doesn't cook, she makes sure to have all her favorite snacks and plenty of fruits and vegetables in the refrigerator. She starts to unpack bags and put groceries away, but I can tell her full attention is on me.

"So, how is everything?" she asks casually.

"Everything is good." I nod, pulling a carton of milk from the bag.

"You didn't call me this week."

"I know. I um, I wanted to surprise you." I say, hoping that doesn't sound like a lie.

"You did! When I saw that Audi parked in the driveway, I couldn't believe my eyes! So, again, how long do I have you guys?" she asks as if she's a hotel desk clerk.

"Oh, well, I was thinking I'd stay a week or two," I tell her, busying myself by taking out a bottle of juice and avoiding her eyes.

"You are?" she asks, surprised.

"Yeah, well, if that's okay with you," I say hesitantly.

"Of course it is, honey. I love your company and you know that you're always welcome here. It's just . . . two weeks is quite a long time. Is Cal here?" she inquires.

Here's my chance. Just tell her. Just say it!

"N-no, um, that's actually why I'm here," I say meekly. She stops going through the bag and gives me her full attention; her look is intimidating.

"What's wrong?" she says, raising her voice slightly.

"Oh, nothing's wrong. It's just that Cal's gone on another business trip, and the penthouse gets lonely at night. I thought, I haven't seen you in a while." I laugh slightly. *God, why didn't I just tell her?* I missed the perfect opportunity. Now this whole time I'm going to be on pins and needles and have to remember my own lies.

"Oh." She looks at me skeptically, the look quickly replaced by a smile. "Well, I'm really glad you're here," she says, giving me another hug. "How about I finish up here, you go to your room and get settled, and I'll order us some lunch?"

"That'd be great." I get up from the table. "You sure you don't want any help?" I ask again.

"No, I'm fine. Go get settled," she insists.

I walk out of the kitchen and head for my car. I hate lying to my aunt, or lying in general, but if I told her why I was really here . . . I open up the trunk and heave my big suitcase out, setting it on the ground with a plop. As I roll it up the walkway towards the house, I notice Raven standing at the door with a huge smile plastered on her face and the phone close to her ear.

Please tell me she's not talking to who I think she's talking to.

"Lauren, honey, Cal's on the phone!" she calls. My heart stops for a minute. She loves that man so much, I swear, if he weren't my husband and he were just a little bit older, I know she'd be on him like a Chanel bag in the clearance section, if there is such a thing.

"I'm kind of in the middle of something," I call to her as sweetly as I can, squashing my annoyance and anger as I head back over to the car, trying to look busy shuffling through my bags.

"Lauren Brooks! Get over here right this minute. You can bring your bags in later," she says in a calm but forceful tone. I feel my shoulders drop as I slowly walk up to the porch, a small pout on my face. I remember I'm supposed to pretend I'm happy. I take the phone from her.

"I'm going to take this in the house."

"Sure," she tells me. I walk into the dining room and close the door behind me. I take a huge breath and bring the phone to my ear.

"I knew you were going to be at Raven's," he says before I even let him know I'm there. *How wonderful of you*, I think to myself and roll my eyes.

"You're not talking to me?" he asks. I sigh in disbelief. He still thinks I'm "not talking to him." I've left him, and he's shrugging it off as a temper tantrum. Obviously, he doesn't get it.

"Two calls. It must be my lucky day," I mumble sarcastically, pacing the room.

"I know. I was wrong," he says.

"You really mean that? Or are you just saying what you think I want to hear?"

"I mean what I say." He sounds offended.

"Cal, I'm tired of doing this with you," I sigh.

"Well, what do you want me to say?" he asks defensively.

What do I want him to say? What the fuck do I want him to say? I want him to say he's sorry for everything, sorry that he's played with my emotions, sorry that he's such an ass, that he leaves me alone at home for days without a single phone call, sorry that he's made me into a person I don't even recognize, that he's eroded my self-confidence, sorry that he exists in my life!

I don't hear anything except silence on the other end. Oops, I must have said all that out loud.

I'VE BEEN SITTING here in my old bedroom in silence for twenty minutes, waiting for him to call me back. I shouldn't be waiting for him. I *should* be happy that he's not attempting to call me back. I brush my fingers through my hair and sigh. I hear a soft knock on the door.

"Honey, is everything okay?" Raven asks, quietly walking into the room.

"Yeah, everything's fine," I say to her, forcing another smile.

She opens her mouth as if she's about to say something, but then she changes the subject. "I completely forgot I told Mrs. Ingram that I'd have lunch with her today, before I knew you were coming. Would you like to join us? She'd love to see you."

"No, it's okay. I think I'm just going to stay here and think some things through. Tell her I said hi."

"Ok, if you need anything just call my cell," she tells me, as if I'm a twelve-year-old again.

"I'll be fine," I assure her.

"I'll see you later, honey," she says, shutting the door. I suddenly feel exhausted. I start stripping the big quilt and colorful sheets off the bed, replacing them with some sheets I brought from home. After I'm done, I look around the room, taking a deep breath. This place will take some getting used to again. I crawl into the bed, hugging the pillow as if it's a stuffed animal.

"I WENT TO University Of Illinois for two years before I transferred to Indiana State, where I played football. Believe it or not, I originally majored in criminology. It's funny how I jumped from criminology to journalism because they're so different from each other. Initially, I only took it in high school because of this girl I had a crush on. Then I changed it because criminology was getting too complicated. I thought it was the best thing I ever did in my life. So when I graduated, I moved back to Chicago. My dad helped me get a job at *The Tribune,* where my boss assigned me the Entertainment section. Who the hell reads that? But anyway, the point is . . ." Jason can't shut up.

I continue to nod and smile, pretending to be interested in what he's saying. He's been going on like this for twenty minutes; he hasn't asked a single question about me except what I wanted to order. He then told me the dish he's having is better and I should order that. I glance at my watch for the third time. I've never been this bored in my life. I don't know if he's nervous and he's just rambling on to cover it up, or if he's really that self-absorbed. He seemed so different back at the club. Looks can sure be deceiving.

I take a sip of my water. The ice has melted. Looking around, I admire how elegant the restaurant is. The piano is playing softly in the background. I could really enjoy this atmosphere—if Jason would just be quiet for a minute.

"I remember my first piece for Journalism 101. It was on a Dean sleeping with a student. I had a lot of fun with that, even though it only received a C. My professor always told me I could do better, and on my last paper I finally had an A," he continues.

"So what about you?" he finally asks.

I almost choke on my water; the opportunity to talk is unexpected—I thought he'd at least give me a rundown of every article he'd ever written before he asked *me* a question.

"Well, I attend Chicago University. I'm majoring in English and minoring in art history," I tell him.

"The art world is a hard world to break into," he tells me, as if I don't know.

"That's why I'm majoring in English," I tell him, a little annoyed.

"So what kind of work do you do?" he asks.

"What do you mean?"

"I know you're an Art History Major, but do you do any artwork?" he asks absentmindedly while signaling the waiter.

I just told him art history was my minor, but whatever. Close enough.

"Well, some painting and sculpting, but my passion is drawing," I tell him.

"Yes, can you get our check?" he asks the approaching waiter, who nods and walks away. He turns back to me. "I'm sorry . . . you were saying?"

I shake my head. "It's not important." It's not like he was paying any attention anyway.

"Have you heard about the museum's anniversary gala?" he asks. Has he already forgotten the art history thing?

"Yes. I have," I tell him, trying not to sound sarcastic.

"You would probably have a wonderful time there. It's too bad you can't get tickets. *The Tribune* only received three. I was lucky enough to get one of the press passes, since it will be the entertainment event of the season," he boasts.

Should I tell him I'm going or should I not? Hmm.

"I'll be sure to have a full report on it for you." He grins. I decide not to tell him. I will keep smiling, and maybe he'll get the hint. My phone begins to vibrate in my purse. I take it out and see it's Hillary. *Oh, I love you Hillary!*

"Excuse me for a minute," I tell him, walking to the front entrance. "I've never been so happy to hear from you," I say gratefully.

"I take it your date sucks?" she asks excitedly.

"Other than the food, yes. I'll be home in an hour. Jason is probably the most self-absorbed person I've ever met. The whole conversation tonight was all about him. I probably got three sentences in," I tell her.

"Aw, you poor thing!" she states. "Well, you can't strike gold twice."

I smile, thinking about my date with Cal, which makes this seem like an appointment with a dentist.

"So, does he have anything else planned after dinner?" she asks.

"I don't know, but I can't take any more of this."

"Remember the guy I met at the party you didn't want to go to last week, Jinere, or Johnae—I'll never be able to say it right. Anyway, something foreign, and he's ridiculously hot. I'm making him dinner and I may be his dessert . . ." she warns with a hint of excitement in her voice.

"Have fun, Hillary," I say. At least one of us will be having a good time tonight.

"Want me to wait up for you?"

"No, I'll be fine."

"Okay, night, hun," she says, and I hang up the phone. I look at my watch; it's only 9:12. This night is going way too slow. I walk back into the restaurant and see that Jason isn't at the table. I suppose he's gone to the restroom. Thank goodness. It'll be quiet for a few minutes.

"Excuse me, miss?" asks a small voice from behind me. I turn around to see the hostess who seated us when we arrived.

"The gentlemen who was with you had an important call and had to leave, but he's called you a cab," she informs me.

He's ditched me? He's ditched *me*. After an hour and a half of listening to him talk about his boring job and attendance history in class, he leaves me? I sigh and notice that the hostess is waiting for my response.

"Thank you," I say, smiling to hide my annoyance.

She nods and walks away. I take my jacket from the back of my chair and put it on. Who would have thought at the beginning of this evening I would end up sitting in the lounge alone, waiting for a taxi to take me home because my date ditched me?

I STARE AT the blank canvas in front of me and see . . . a blank canvas. I have no inspiration. I see nothing. I move the easel back to the wall and grab my sketchbook off my desk. I have to flip all the way to the back to find an empty page.

I start to make a light mark with a pencil in the middle of the paper. All of my drawings start off this way, and then I go with what I feel. Painting is not that easy; you have to have your colors mapped out, your setting, and you can't paint stray marks and wait until they turn into something.

That's why I love to draw; it's therapeutic. My thoughts drift to the anniversary of the museum tomorrow. I feel butterflies starting to play in my stomach. Since it's the anniversary, I know they're going to have all types of new collections flown in just for the night, even though they will probably already have new pieces I haven't seen. It's been forever since the last time I was there. I've always enjoyed being there alone, in my own world. Tomorrow will be the first time I'll actually go with another person outside of school. I've always kept art as a private reward for myself. I wonder if Cal is into art. He didn't seem too excited about the event, but most people wouldn't be. He does get credit for actually suggesting a date based on my interests, aside from the fact that he had tickets to an event that would be difficult for an average person to get.

I put down my sketchbook and go to the closet to pull out the dress I'm planning on wearing tomorrow. Angela was kind enough to let me borrow it, since this is probably the only time I'll ever need something to wear for an occasion like this. I admire it again, along with the six-inch black heels that Hillary contributed. They'll murder my feet, but they match perfectly, and it will all be worth it.

Any artist in Chicago would die to be there, and I get to dress up for something other than work. Oh, and Cal isn't too bad of a perk either.

I laugh at myself and hang the dress back up in the closet. Cal . . . I really don't know what to think about him. I thought I had him all figured out the first time I met him, that he was either a suave businessman or some rich playboy. I couldn't have been more wrong. He's neither of those, but even though I can say what he isn't, I still don't know what he is. I know less about him now than when we first met, which is intriguing and scary. He's invited me to this party because he could guess how much I'd love to go, so I know he's got at least that chapter of my autobiography, yet here I barely have a snippet of his birth certificate.

The only thing I really know about him is that he's mysterious, outspoken, and incredibly sexy. I still can't believe I wanted so much more after that kiss. Usually I never even let a guy approach my lips, pulling the old kiss on the cheek or awkward hug move. Letting a guy slip his tongue in my mouth is something that's sacrilege in the "Code of Lauren Brooks," but I've broken a few codes already when it comes to Cal. By now I'd usually know his age, what he does for a living, how many siblings he has, and what his first pet was, but it occurs to me that I didn't even ask him a single question about any of those things. Well, his smile and eyes kept distracting me. They draw you in and make you stay there . . .

May 5th, 2011

I WIPE THE steam off the mirror and crack the bathroom door open to let some air in. One shower and the room is up to 105 degrees. I wrap myself in the plush bath towel and slip into the flip-flops I've left by the tub. I yawn a little, even though I shouldn't be tired at all. I woke up at ten P.M. I couldn't believe I had slept the day away. But I guess sleep is the best thing to relieve stress, and I had tons of relieving to do.

I know I shouldn't feel like this, but I can't help wondering why Cal hasn't called me back yet. I check the phone for messages, even though I know he probably won't leave one, especially on Raven's voice mail. I flick a piece of wet hair off my face. I should blow-dry, but I'm way too irritated to do that right now. On the way down the hall back to my room, I notice Raven has gone to bed, so I back up to turn off the light that's illuminating the tiny hall. As I walk into my bedroom, a slight breeze blows in through an open window, so I walk over to close it. A hand touches my lower back.

I shriek, spinning around and backing up at the same time. Cal is standing in front of me. He grasps my arm to keep me from falling over. *What the hell is he doing here?* My impulse is to wrap my arms around him, but then I remember I'm pissed at him, so I retreat to the other side of the room.

"What are you doing here?" I ask, shocked, still out of breath, and a tiny bit happy he's here. This was the last thing I would have expected. He hadn't even called me back.

"Oh, come on. No 'hello' or 'nice to see you here, honey'?" he teases. The moonlight reflects off of his chiseled face, and he brushes past me to sit on my bed. I inhale his scent. It lures me to him. It's the cologne I bought for him last month, and it makes me want to . . . *Dammit, snap out of it, Lauren!*

"Maybe, if I was in the mood to say it. But I'm not." I mean to be short, but I'm not sure it has the effect I was going for since he's caught me off guard. He looks up at me, and his eyes drift down from my face, reminding me I'm naked under the towel. I cross my arms around myself tightly to show that I'm determined to keep it on. He smirks at me and picks up a plastic pig that I won at a carnival in high school. I snatch it out of his hand.

"Careful! You wouldn't want that towel to fall off," he whispers, and he starts to work his hand up my leg. I step away quickly and tell myself to ignore the chills that shoot up my spine.

"What are you doing here?" I ask again sternly.

"You're here, so I take it I should be here too." He seems genuine, but who knows with him.

"Really? Because forty-eight hours ago, it wasn't at all important for you to be where I was," I tell him bitterly. He stands up and walks toward me.

"I'm sorry," he says, looking me straight in the eye. I quickly look away; I hate when he does this. I swear he can see straight through me and read my thoughts.

"That's what you say."

He rests his hands on my waist. "That's what I mean," he says, taking a step closer and leaning into me.

I shake my head and step away from him. "Well, how am I supposed to know?" I say quietly to myself as if I'm trying to wake up from a bad dream. "I'm tired of not knowing, Cal!" I say louder.

"Have I ever said anything to you and not meant it?" he reiterates. Cal has done some pretty mean shit to me. He'll ignore me, avoid the questions I ask, or leave me without a warning, but he's not a liar. I'm trying to think, but I get distracted as he starts to run his fingers through my damp hair, massaging my scalp. How am I supposed to think while he's doing that? I need to think. His lips softly glide across my neck, and he pulls me against his chest. I'm trying to figure out how to respond to this. I'm mad, and I have the right to be. Whatever I want to do, I need to do it fast, before he gets me all the way over to the bed. *Say something!*

Say it now!

"W-we can't," I tell him breathlessly as the towel drops to the floor. It's too late. He lowers me down to the bed. His weight covers me, as do his lips. I need to talk with him, not sleep with him. This always happens when he touches me: first the shivers up my spine, the heat between my thighs, and then I get light-headed and forget my thoughts. He's casting some kind of spell over me. What else could this be?

"C-Cal, stop," I say, so softly that I can barely hear myself as his fingers trail down my body.

"Do you want me to?" He's beginning to nibble on my ear.

"I don't know what I want anymore," I say honestly, trying to catch my breath. I turn my head to the window. It's still open, and a soft breeze is blowing in.

"This isn't what you want?" he says huskily before deepening his kiss. It takes all my strength, but I break it and gently hold his chin in my hands. He looks at me, surprised and somewhat curious.

I stare into the eyes that I usually try to avoid. I look into them for answers to see what he is thinking, what he is feeling. The light from the moon beams down on us through my window. I can't read them. I can't see what's behind them; they are a smoke-covered glass. I can't see anything more than he wants me to.

"I don't *know* anymore, Cal," I whisper, trying to hold the hot tears in my eyes, and I let go of his face. The wide grin on it softens. He sweeps a piece of stray hair off my forehead and looks into my eyes for what seems like an eternity, but in reality it's only a minute.

In an instant, he lifts his body off of me and out of the bed. I maneuver myself to one side and rest my head so I can see what he's doing. It's cold, so I slip underneath the covers. Resting my head on my hands, I watch him grab his jacket and get something out of it. I sigh and turn my body, so I'm not facing him anymore.

A few minutes later, he's in bed beside me, his bare skin against mine. Kisses cover my shoulders, and he pulls me toward him. This time, I avoid eye contact. I don't know what to think or what to feel; I don't want to get lost in him. I don't want to keep falling for him, caving in to whatever manipulation this is.

"Lauren," he beckons quietly. He takes my hand, bringing it to his face and caressing it. I still don't answer him. Hot tears sting my cheek. He hasn't seen my tears flow like this in a long time; my facade of anger and vindictiveness is usually perfect for camouflaging them. Tonight, I'm too exhausted for any of it. He wipes them from my face and gently kisses my cheek.

"I'm so tired. I can't. I can't keep doing this; it-it's destroying me," I whimper. My voice is choked up, and I look away from him.

He cups my chin, making me look up at him. "Lauren. I'm here," he says earnestly.

I look away from him. "But how am I . . ." I can't finish; my voice caves in.

"I'm *here*, gorgeous," he says. His voice is unrecognizable and almost pleading. I can't look away from him after that. His gray eyes are showing that faint hint of green. He squeezes my hand, which is tiny in comparison to his. He brings his other hand into view and shows me what it was he was looking for in his jacket a minute ago. Slowly and deliberately, he slides the wedding band down my ring finger, restoring it to its rightful place. I begin to cry harder because tonight I'm so confused. I wrap my arms around his neck and he holds me close.

I have a lot of confusion about his love for me, but what I have never been confused about is my love for him. I love Cal. That's it. There's been nothing I've been able to do to stop loving him yet. No matter how angry or how frustrated I get. He knows the exact moment, to do the exact thing to make me fall in love with him all over again.

I close my eyes, feeling at peace in this instant. For this moment, I've gone back in time to when I used to lie in his arms, when he made me feel like it was just the two of us in the world and nothing stood between us.

While I have this moment—this peace—I'll sleep and worry about the rest tomorrow. I finally feel myself drifting to sleep, wrapped in Cal's arms. And at least for this night, the couple in the picture that I turned down earlier doesn't feel so far away.

WHY DO I stay? It's a simple question, really. Why don't I just leave? I have no children with him. We're married, but divorce is so easy and common these days. Why do I care so much?

These questions run through my mind as I stare at the ceiling. The same ceiling I used to look up at every night when I was a little girl. The teenaged dreamer is now a woman. I glance at the ring on my finger and it commands my attention, not because of the gorgeous princess-cut yellow diamond, but what it once stood for.

It's supposed to be a symbol of our love, trust, and commitment to one another. When I made those vows, I knew without a doubt that we both had those things.

I love him, but my trust in him has waned. I sometimes doubt his commitment to me, our commitment to make our marriage work. I've taken off this band easily because the things it stands for, I don't believe in anymore. Still, time after time I allow it back on.

Why is it that when Cal isn't with me, I miss him so much it's worse than physical pain? Why is it when I see his eyes, sometimes I swear I see a side of him he won't allow me to fully know?

His eyes—I think I fell in love with his eyes. They reveal so little and so much. Sometimes I look into them and they're vacant, cold, and void. Yet there are moments when there is something kind and warm behind them.

His mystique used to excite me, drawing me in, too intriguing to let go. Now, the fact that my husband is still a mystery to me is frustrating, and it makes me realize his mysteries are just secrets that he won't trust me with. I grow more resentful of that every day.

I've allowed myself to stay because there are times like last night when I'm madly, deeply in love with him all over again. Other times, I feel like I barely know him at all. I'm afraid I've wrapped myself up in him for so long that it would be hard to stand on my own. The realization of that is sickening, and a part of me blames him for that. I know I let this happen. I've allowed this icy exterior to take over and change who I am. It started out as a way to deal with him, to keep from feeling sad, lonely, and insufficient. It started out as a temporary defense mechanism, but now it is a cornerstone of the woman I've become.

It's morning. I've been lying here for a while, not able to sleep, still trying to figure things out. I feel Cal wake up, and the mattress shifts as he sits up. I roll over to look at him. He glances at me, yawns, and begins grabbing his clothing scattered about on the floor.

"Morning," I say, quietly resting my head on my arm. He puts on his boxers and shirt, but he doesn't answer. His brow is furrowed and he's moving like he's in a hurry for something. He walks to my old closet, shuffling through it impatiently. I sit completely still, trying to figure out what he's doing in there.

"What are you doing?" I ask, trying to maintain my composure. I don't want to do this with him today. I'm trying to not be a bitch, but he's really pushing it. He finds my suitcase and pulls it out.

"Get dressed; we're leaving," he says.

"What? No, I'm not going anywhere."

"Look, I don't have time for this shit. Get up and put your clothes on."

"So that's it? After everything last night, you wake up with a fucking stick up your ass, throwing out demands. Maybe you don't get it, but I didn't come here for an overnight trip."

"You know what, Lauren? I'm tired of this bullshit. I may have really fucked up a business deal for Dex to come after you and hold your fucking hand. I want to go home and at least sleep in my own bed!" he snarls.

I throw my pillow at him. Jumping out of bed, I grab my robe from the floor and put it on.

"Here we go." He laughs angrily.

"Why did you come after me? Why did you bring me this?" I thrust my hand in his face, showcasing our ring.

"Yeah, I brought it to you. You're my wife. Why the hell do you keep taking it off?"

I'm taken aback by his question and it causes me to pause.

"Because I miss you, but I'm starting to feel like this is just something to pacify me!"

"But I'm here! That's what I don't get! How do you miss me?"

I take a deep breath. I know he's not the only one to blame in this and decide to take on some of it. "I miss us," I correct, lowering my tone. "What we used to have. How we used to be. What's happened to us?" I walk toward him, my eyes pleading, and his brow softens, but he turns away from me.

"What are you saying?" His tone becomes defensive.

"I-I'm not, I'm not going back to Chicago with you," I say sternly, but my head is down; I can't look at him as I say it.

I love him, yes. I'm in love with him, no question about it, but it's a problem when I'm questioning whether I love him more than myself, and if he loves me at all.

"You're not coming home?" he asks as if he didn't hear me.

"As of now, Cal, we don't have a home. I don't think of where we live as a home," I say angrily.

"Great, now we don't have a home. I guess the penthouse I've worked my ass off to pay for is what, pretend?" he says sarcastically.

"You know what I mean, Cal!" I growl at him, and he laughs, shaking his head defensively.

"No, I don't know what you mean. I came here. I spent the night with you. I don't want to be in fucking Saginaw the next few days I have off. Why are you making this into something it's not?"

"Because! I don't want you to think this is just a temper tantrum. I'm serious, Cal. If I go back, I'll be saying what you're doing—what we're both doing—is okay. I'll be saying it is okay for you to leave me for weeks at a time. It's okay for me to miss you so much that it's painful. That I'm fine with not knowing what you're feeling or thinking ninety percent of the time. I question whether you love me every day." My voice is starting to crack.

His hardened expression softens and he walks toward me. "Why? Why do you do that?" He holds the back of his head in both hands and sighs, exasperated. "You know I love you!" He gestures toward me angrily and starts to pace the room. "If you only knew what it took for me to be here with you!" he says aloud, but it seems as if he's saying it to himself.

"Of course, you're tearing yourself away from work. How difficult it is to be with your wife—because we're desperate for the money, of course. I need the Louboutins, and you need those Rolexes and foreign cars!" I shout back through my tears, sitting on the bed. "I-I feel like you've grown resentful towards me. You used to be—well, I thought you were happy. You were fun, you made me laugh and feel sexy and wanted." I smile, remembering happier times.

"Now, I feel like you're distant. I know you're slipping away from me. The only time I feel connected to you is when we're having sex. And recently it's just been that. You don't make love to me anymore . . . Maybe marriage turned you into this. I never imagined it being like this for us," I say, using all my strength to finish.

I close my eyes and let out a much-needed breath, which feels like I've been holding it in forever. The silence in the room after all of the noise seems odd.

He's been sitting on my desk chair, arms folded across his chest, with a range of emotions passing across his face. None of them have looked remotely sorry or understanding.

"I've never wanted anything more than our marriage, Lauren. You're the one thing that belongs to me. The only pure thing I have is us. I used to have a different reason for being. It came from a dark place. My motivation changed when I fell in love with you. You're my strength and my weakness. *You're* the reason I fight to be here."

I open my eyes and remember that those were his exact words in his wedding vows to me. I can't believe he remembers them. I don't even remember mine to that extent. My heart warms, thinking of that day on the beach in Rio where we were joined together, where I became Mrs. Scott. I *was* the happiest woman in the world.

"I meant that then, and nothing has changed since that day." His voice is low and wavers just a tad. I start to approach him slowly and touch his shoulder gently. He seems to be deep in thought.

"I want you to stay with me, here." I look towards him, my eyes pleading for him to give me the answer I want—no, that I need to hear.

"I'm not moving to Saginaw!" he says adamantly, arms still crossed as he stares out the window.

"I didn't say that," I tell him.

"Do you mean like a week, or a couple of days?" he questions.

He's pondering. That's a good sign.

"However long it takes," I tell him, trying to keep my voice steady. He exhales and runs his hands over his face.

"What about my job? I'm just supposed to . . ."

I rest my head on his shoulder. "Oh, come on. You're Mr. Big Bad Cal. Just tell them you'll be back whenever." I smirk at him.

I touch his face and turn it toward me so I can look into his eyes, and he can see in mine.

"If you love me, you'll do this," I whisper to him. "I know you say you do. I just need to feel it," I plead. If he says no, I don't know what I'm going to do.

He's thinking, which is always a good sign. I stop looking at him and rest my head back on his chest. "This isn't really an option, is it?" He sighs.

"Not really," I say honestly. If he leaves, I'm done. I can't do this with him anymore. I'll learn to forget about him, as hard as it may be. I can't keep feeling like this. If he stays . . .

"LAUREN BROOKS IS wearing one of the newest dresses from the House of Angela. This stylish ebony gem is perfect for the hot date, business affair, or even a sophisticated gala. The top of the dress with sequined fabric gives this vintage silhouette a modern twist, while still keeping the garment classic. Her dress features a flocked sequined sweetheart neckline, a deep V back with invisible zippered closure, and flattering split to get any red-blooded man's juices flowing," Hillary announces in her Joan Rivers voice. Angela and I die of laughter.

May 10th, 2008

Hillary taps me warningly. "Stop, you're going to wrinkle," she scolds me, still in her faux, fashion-extraordinaire persona. "Do a spin for us, darling," she says.

"Work it, girl," Angela howls, supporting the foolishness. I begrudgingly oblige, rolling my eyes at their whistles and catcalls.

"Lauren Brooks, you look so fucking hot right now!" Hillary exclaims, returning to her normal self.

"I'm going to the anniversary of an art museum. Hot isn't exactly what I was going for," I joke as I keep my focus on the mirror. I must say, the dress is exquisite. Angela came over to work her magic on my hair, giving me deep romantic curls. And after much scolding, I was able to tone Hillary's dramatic smoky eye down to a comfortable highlight.

"She means you look absolutely fabulous," laughs Angela.

I look back and see Hillary going through my purse.

"Hillary, what are you doing?" I ask.

"Making sure you have all the essentials," she says in a matter-of-fact tone.

"Makeup, gum, wallet, keys . . . Lauren, do you not know you're forgetting something muy importante?" she asks. Angela and I look back at her with a curious expression on our faces.

"Where are the condoms?" she demands.

"Oh . . . I don't have any condoms," I say plainly.

"Exactly!" she states.

I roll my eyes at her. "It's not like I'm going to need them," I reason with her.

"Oh, come on, I've seen the man. You'll need them." She winks. I playfully snatch my bag from her.

" . . . and you remember what almost happened last time," says Angela in a sing-song voice as she flops on my bed.

I ignore them both, trying unsuccessfully to make this little black dress a few inches longer.

"Hey, stop that." Hillary swats my hand.

"So what does he do? Is he in school?" asks Angela.

"She doesn't know." Hillary laughs mockingly.

"You don't know? What the hell is that supposed to mean?" asks Angela, confused. I open my mouth to defend myself, but Hillary jumps in.

"That's what lust will do to you . . ." teases Hillary. Angela starts to laugh.

The phone rings, and my heart skips a beat. Angela's closest, so she picks it up. "Hello? She'll be right down." She gives me a wide grin.

"The limo is heeeeere," she sings. I take a deep breath and glance at myself in the mirror once more.

"You look fine!" they yell in unison. I grab my purse and we all head out the door. Once we get downstairs, there is a beautiful black Town Car with the driver waiting by the door.

"Damn!" says Angela, taking in its appearance.

"Which one of you lovely ladies is Lauren Brooks?" the driver asks in a friendly tone.

"She is." They both point to me.

"Good evening, Miss Brooks. I'm Byron, and I'll be your driver for tonight."

I give them both a hug and head over to the car.

"Have a good time," calls Angela.

"Too good of a time," yells Hillary with a wink as I step into the Town Car. I wave back at them before Byron shuts the door. I look around at the plush leather interior that surrounds me. There's a TV with a remote and a champagne bottle on ice, nestled in its own station.

"Wow!" is the only thing I can say. I hear the phone ringing next to me. I look around, as if there's someone else in here with me. I reluctantly pick it up.

"Hello?" I say hesitantly.

"Hey, gorgeous. I can't wait to see you tonight. Has everything gone okay so far?"

I release a slow breath, relieved it's him and not someone calling for him. That would have been embarrassing. "Yes, everything is fine . . ." I drift off, still wowed by my surroundings.

"If you need anything, just tell Byron. He'll take care of it."

I want to ask him if this is rented or his, but that would be rude, wouldn't it? "I will, but I really don't think I'll need anything; it all seems to be right here . . ." I say, still astonished.

He laughs a little. "Well, I'll see you in about an hour."

"I look forward to it." I smile and hang up. I let the wide grin I've been keeping hidden spread across my face. This should be fun. I sing along to my favorite song.

I think I feel the car stop, even though it's a little hard to tell since the ride has been so smooth. Butterflies start to play in my stomach. The phone rings again, so I pick it up.

"Miss Brooks, we've reached Mr. Scott," Byron tells me.

"Thank you, Byron," I say and hang up. I step out and the cold air whips around me, causing my dress and shawl to flow in the wind. I look up to see a huge plane—or jet?—fifty feet away from me. I mean, what was I expecting, really? Not this. Cal steps off with a phone in hand. I survey his appearance as he gets closer. He has on a black suit with a silver button-up underneath it, no tie. What really shocks me is that he's wearing glasses, something I've not seen before, and it's extremely sexy. When he nears me, he hangs up the phone.

"You look . . ." he says with a dazzling smile on his face, his eyes trailing from my five-inch heels upward. "You've got to do a spin for me," he says, licking those lips that I'm really starting to crave.

"Actually, hold that thought," he says, biting his lip, and he begins to circle around me, his gaze predatory. Once he's fully made his way behind me, his arms cross over my stomach and he kisses me softly on my neck. My whole body tingles.

"I'm glad you could make it," he whispers in my ear, and I hope to regain my composure before he sees my face. Luckily, he takes my hand, and in an instant he's leading me in the opposite direction of the Town Car. I'm confused but try to keep up with him in these five-inch stilettos while mentally scolding my hormones to control themselves.

"Where are we going?" I finally manage to speak.

"I thought we'd arrive in something a little more personal for the night." He smiles back at me. He pulls a pair of keys out of his pocket, and when we stop at a car parked right next to the hangar, my jaw drops on the floor. In front of me sits a magnificent all-black Aston Martin.

"This-this can't be yours," I say in disbelief. I've never been one to fawn over cars and make a big deal about expensive things, but this is an Aston Martin, for crying out loud. I remember what a big deal Steven and Angela made at the car show they dragged me to, and here I am about to get in one.

"It's not mine. It's a company perk," he explains, opening the door for me with a playful glint in his eye.

I CAN'T HELP but appreciate the car's warmth contrasting with the cold wind outside and, of course, the pure luxury that I'm smack in the middle of. The Aston reminds me of a plane, it's so futuristic; I feel like I stepped out of this year and fell into another decade. Cal is watching me, amused.

"You must be an extremely valuable asset to your company." I chuckle, still in awe.

"I'm a hard worker. At *all* things," he says, and I wonder if that's an innuendo, or if my brain is just in the gutter. *Stop it, brain!*

"What is it that you do again?" I say "again," but he never told me the first time. Now that I'm riding in *this* car, I'm a lot more curious than I was.

"I work for Crestfield Corporation," he replies, turning on the radio. Okay. Not quite what I asked, but I'll take a where instead of a what.

"How old are you?" I ask, trying to figure out if he's a lot older than he looks. He must be in an invaluable position to receive a perk like this.

"Two decades and some change," he retorts playfully.

"Why do you wear glasses?" I ask curiously. He seems like a guy who would wear contacts if he had the choice.

"To make people think I'm smart." He grins slyly and takes them off. They're sexy on him, but I'm glad when he removes them so I can see those mesmerizing eyes of his. "You're excited about the opening?" he asks, changing the subject.

"Very excited, actually. I still can't believe I'm going."

"Well, at least one of us is," he groans.

"You're not interested in art, I take it?"

"Someone once told me everything is art, so I wouldn't have to go to a museum to see it."

I frown a little; it would have been nice to go with someone who shared my interest in art, but I'm too thrilled to be brought down.

"So, I decided I should at least have something beautiful to look at," he says, throwing me a flirtatious grin. So far, the night is starting extremely well. I can't wait to see what other surprises Cal may have in store for me.

May 9th, 2011

I LOVE THE spring breeze in Saginaw. I close my eyes as the cool breeze passes, leaving tingles from the temperature change. I look at my watch and see that it's 3:00 A.M. We've been in Saginaw for four days. Four days that have passed like moments.

He's stayed—a small gesture, but one that means so much. It's been a long time since we've been like this, just with one another, no pretenses or agendas; having him the entire day and not dreading the phone call he'll get that will pull him away.

I've been able to let the ice melt and Cal has shown me a side of him I haven't seen in a long time. I know we have a long way to go, but his being here is a step in the right direction. Still, there are moments when he seems lost in his own thoughts, where he'll go off to be alone, leaving Raven and me to ourselves.

Those are the times my heart reaches out to him; I feel like he's struggling with something he won't share with me. I don't bother him about it, though I hope he'll eventually learn to lean on me the way I have on him.

I've been sitting here on the balcony since 1:00 A.M. I really should try to get some sleep. I walk back into the room where Cal is sprawled out on the bed. I can't help but smile; he always looks like a little boy when he sleeps, so innocent and peaceful. I tiptoe to the other side of the bed, slip out of my robe, and climb in.

I settle under the covers and lay my head on his chest. It's been months since I've done this, and I tentatively put my arm around him. I've missed this so much. When things started going wrong, I hated my desire to be near him. I resented my longing for the touch of someone who didn't seem to need mine, so I pulled back.

I turn toward him now and watch his breathing pattern; it's never deep, but subtle—almost as if he isn't breathing at all. He's always quiet, he never snores, and most of the time his expression is calm. But then there are the moments his breathing is faster, as if he has a million things going on in his head at once. I try to enjoy this moment and not think about anything else, but he's so unpredictable it wouldn't surprise me if he jumped up all of a sudden and said he was going back to Chicago.

He must have heard my last thought. He's up now, observing me, possibly attempting to read my mind. I would say he's given me his attention, but it's more like he has mine.

"You think too much," he whispers, massaging the small of my back.

I sigh. "So do you." I put my hand on his. He smiles for a minute and gets out of bed. I watch him as he grabs the bag he brought with him and disappears into the bathroom. I hear the water start to run. The walls are so thin here. I shift in the bed, trying to get comfortable. It's no use; I'm utterly restless. I know I can't sleep now. Once I'm up, it's so hard for me to get tired again.

The crickets are singing. It's been a while since I've heard them. When you live in a high-rise, you miss out on the luxury of hearing their lulling, albeit sometimes annoying, song.

I get out of bed and turn on the radio that's sitting on the dresser. The smooth sounds pour out of the speakers, the only thing Raven listens to. I've learned to appreciate it more than I did in my younger years, when I found it beyond boring. But now the music hypnotizes my mind into forgetting the stresses that burden most of my thoughts.

My eyes drift to the alarm clock sitting comfortably between three books and an old photo of me in high school. The light green numbers tell me it's 3:20. I really need to be asleep. I cover my mouth, trying to hide the yawn that sneaks out. I'm not tired. Well, my mind isn't, but my body disagrees.

I flop back on the bed and lie across it, resting my face on the mattress, absorbing the remnants of Cal's warmth that remains on the bed. I close my eyes, hoping the music will work as a lullaby to put me to sleep. I start to hum along with the song, catching on to it after a minute. I feel the light shining in from the hall, but it soon disappears. I recognize his scent and open my eyes. I love his cologne, but the truth is he doesn't need any. His own scent is intoxicating.

"I'm hungry," he says, standing at the foot of the bed.

"You want to go get something?" I ask, getting out of the bed and searching for something within my reach to throw on, even though we'll be driving a while to find something open around here. I grab his black button-up on the floor and put it on. It, of course, engulfs me.

"Come make me something," he says, leaving the room.

"You must really be hungry if you're going to eat what I cook." I snicker, and we both head down the stairs and into the kitchen. He turns on the light and sits down at the table. I look at him curiously.

"Are you going to stand there and look at me all day? My stomach's kind of growling," he says teasingly while rubbing his stomach, and then he rests his head in one of his hands. I playfully roll my eyes at him.

"Excuse me." I touch my chest indignantly and make my way to the cabinets. I pull out a loaf of bread and open the fridge and retrieve a packet of ham.

"Nuh uh," he says. I look back at him with my brow arched.

"Cook me something," he dares, his eyes smiling.

"You really want me to cook?" I ask in disbelief. He folds his arms with an amused grin on his face. In the entire time I've known Cal, he's never asked me to cook *anything*. I told him I was a terrible cook when we met, and so far, he's taken my word for it; but I can plate a meal like nobody's business.

"Only if you promise you'll eat whatever I cook," I dare him, folding my arms.

"Deal."

I assume the "thinking position," with my chin in my hand, trying to come up with something that is at least edible. It's morning; eggs are easy. I've seen them cooked before a thousand times.

"Get ready for the best eggs of your life, Mr. Scott," I brag as I start to unload the fridge, grabbing cheese and eggs.

"Just promise me it won't be my last meal." He laughs. I shoot him a warning glare and prep my cooking area. He walks over to the counter and leans against it, the better to watch me, I guess.

"You want a cooking lesson?" I joke while washing my hands.

"More like making sure you don't burn Raven's house down," he says.

I jokingly nudge his chest. "So, first you crack the eggs," I begin to explain, demonstrating the process. The egg falls neatly into the bowl, but . . . oh crap.

"I don't think the shells are supposed to be in there." He muffles his laugh with a hand over his mouth.

"It adds to the texture," I say sarcastically. He shakes his head and grabs a fork and attempts to get them out.

"You'll eat those shells and like it, remember?" I say, referencing his earlier promise. He sighs. *Not feeling so smart now, huh, buddy?* I sprinkle the salt and pepper into the bowl and then reach for the butter to add.

He grabs my wrist. "Okay. I think the butter goes in the pan, and not the actual eggs." He laughs.

"Well, in my eggs it does," I say, swatting him away. He suddenly puts his hands on both my shoulders and moves me out the way.

"I think I'll take it from here." He snickers, and I pout.

"But I thought you wanted me to cook," I whine.

"I thought I did too," he mutters, and I playfully hit at him. Begrudgingly, I walk back to the table and watch him make his way around the kitchen. I have to admit he seems to be much more acquainted with it than I am.

"Since when did you become a master chef of the kitchen?" I question him as he whips the eggs like a pro.

"You don't have to be a five-star chef to make eggs." He winks.

I'm really starting to regret not honing my cooking skills during all the times Cal has been gone. In what seems like no time at all, the eggs are cooked, and he sets before me a plate of the most mouthwatering eggs I've ever seen. He scoops a spoonful and lifts it to my mouth. Oh, sweet Jesus, it's delicious.

"Okay, you win. I'll work on the cooking thing," I say as we both dig in.

After a few moments, I decide to take advantage of his good mood to tell him something. "So, I've been thinking of going back to school to get my master's," I tell him in between bites.

"Why would you want to do that?" he asks, unimpressed.

"Well, I haven't really done anything with my undergrad. It's been something I've been thinking about." He's quiet. "Your thoughts, sir?"

"You know how I feel about that sort of thing," he says, finishing his food.

"A master's isn't like a bachelor's, Cal. It holds more weight and prestige."

"It's a crap piece of paper you have to drop thousands of dollars on and waste years of your life over, to work in a miserable job that you're going to end up hating." He gets up to take his plate to the sink.

"It's not only about that. It's to prove to myself I can still do something on my own. I can achieve something outside of . . ." I trail off at his disapproving look.

"Look, I think it's good that you want to do something to challenge yourself. I think with me working like I have, something to occupy your time is good, but why a Master's in English? Do you want to teach now? You despise the corporate world. What are you going do with it?"

I push my plate away, annoyed. This really isn't going like I wanted it to.

"I think you should open a gallery," he says, taking a seat back at the table.

My eyes widen in surprise. "Really?" I ask in disbelief.

He folds his arms. "Yeah, why not? Your stuff is just as good as the shit Dex has on his walls," he says.

I bite my tongue, deciding to take the compliment for what it's worth. Then I dare to give the idea a serious thought. "Well, it wouldn't just be my work. I'd need to get more prestigious artists. It would be a lot of work, and the money . . ."

"I guess you'd have to sacrifice some of those shoes, and I can do without a few Rolexes," he quips, throwing my earlier words back at me.

I jump up and go over to him, settling myself in his lap. "You really think I can do it?" I ask, looking him in the eye.

"Well, I sure as hell didn't marry you for your cooking skills," he retorts playfully, and I laugh.

It's these moments when I know the reason I'm here, and why I fight so hard against the wall he puts up.

"There's so much to do. I—oh my God, I'm so excited, babe! I don't even know what to do first," I say excitedly.

"I can think of one thing I want to do right now, in multiple ways." His eyes are mischievous, and they're locked onto mine, as his hands creep under my shirt. I hop off his lap and start to back away from him, a smile playing on my lips.

He stands up to follow me, walking slowly until I've stopped, trapped between him and the kitchen counter. He places his hands on both sides of me.

"No," I say half-heartedly before he lifts me up onto the counter, squeezing himself between my thighs, and begins kissing my neck.

"No, Cal, not here," I plead before his lips take mine. It takes all my strength to pull away.

"What if Raven wakes up?"

He groans, and before I know it, his hands are on the bare skin of my bottom and I'm being lifted off the counter and carried into the pantry. He closes the door behind him.

"But—Raven!" I protest as he lifts the loose silk shirt I have on up to my belly button, his fingers caressing me.

"You'd better be quiet, then," he whispers in my ear before his tongue makes its way there. A moment later he's inside me, and I'm helpless. I hold on tightly to his neck, wrapping my legs around his waist and trying to muffle my moans by burying my head into his shoulder. He pins me against the back wall, taking my arms from around his neck and capturing my wrists over my head. As my body opens up for him, he exploits it, pushing deeper into me. I bite my lip, trying to prevent a moan from slipping from my mouth. His mouth sucks the skin above my collarbone and I give in, unable to keep quiet any longer. I'm lost in the moment. My body is in heaven as he moves rhythmically inside me, and I feel the climax building, but in the distance, I hear footsteps. That's not good!

"Cal . . . dooo . . . y-you h-h-hear that?" My sentence sounds incoherent, even to me.

"Shut up," he says, his grip on my wrists tighter than before. I wrap my legs around him tighter and start to move with him. This needs to happen faster.

Oh God, please don't let Raven be in the kitchen.

"Oh fuck, Lauren," he groans and releases my wrists, and I'm thankful I can bury my head back into his shoulder.

"Right th—" And I'm cut off when the door opens, the light from the kitchen illuminating what I can only assume is the last—and most traumatic—thing Raven's ever expected to see in her pantry.

"Oh my God! I'm so sorry, honey!" Raven screeches. I don't see her face, but Cal looks as if he's seen a ghost. The door quickly shuts and Cal sets me down. Seconds later he bursts into laughter. I punch him multiple times.

"I told you we shouldn't have been in here!" I scold him angrily as he pulls his boxers up.

"I'm sorry, babe, but you shouldn't have been wearing that around me!" he defends himself, gesturing at his shirt that I claimed as my own.

"And, it's morning," he adds, trying to maintain a straight face. I don't find this funny at all! How am I ever going to look at Raven again? I'm only thankful I couldn't see her face when she caught us.

"I'll tell her it's my fault!" he says, swallowing a laugh.

"Of course it's your fault! God no, you don't talk to her. That'll make this even more weird." I fold my arms, upset at this entire situation.

He pulls me into a forced hug. "Don't worry, babe. I'm sure Raven has had a little pantry action before." He chuckles, and I push him away.

"Ewww." I shudder and hit him again.

"What? Raven's hot!"

May 10th, 2008

"SO, YOU'RE TELLING me this painting doesn't awaken the inner creativity of your soul?" I say condescendingly, nudging his arm. This will be the fifth painting he hasn't liked. He smiles at me and sighs a little.

"Not really," he says with a smirk.

"Seriously? How can this not captivate you?" I ask, looking back at him. A whimsical expression is on his face. He walks beside me and puts his hand on his chin, mimicking deep thought.

"It's a train running through a wall—genius!" he says sarcastically. If that damn smile of his weren't so hypnotizing I'd find his blasé attitude irritating, but instead I'm quite intrigued by it.

"Okay, maybe modern isn't exactly your thing," I relent. I look around the museum. It has been a while since I've been here and they've added so much for the event. I get an idea. Taking his hand, I pull him behind me, walking quickly until I finally spot the painting I'm looking for. Triumph! I glance back at him to see his eyes aren't on the back of my head but on a lower region. I'll just pretend I didn't notice that.

I stop in front of it, and he looks at me expectantly.

"Okay, what about this one?" I ask him curiously. I watch him as he steps closer and examines the painting.

"*A Sunday at La Grande Jatte*," he reads.

"So, do you like this one?" I ask him.

He shrugs. "It's okay," he says dryly.

"Okay?" I laugh in disbelief. "Georges Seurat was mastering the form of pointillism before it was even thought of, really. These all just started out as dots and look. . . ." I trail off, feeling his body heat behind me. I stop mid-sentence. I feel his breath against my neck as he brushes my hair aside with one hand. His other hand finds my waist and his fingers start to slowly slide down, reaching my hip.

"Like I said before . . ." His fingers trail down my neck as his lips graze my ear. "I think there are much more interesting things to look at," he whispers.

Lauren, get a grip. Just calm down. I can't help how my body just reacted to that and he barely touched me, but it was in all the right places. *STOP!* I fold my arms across my chest, just to make sure he doesn't see exactly how obviously my body reacted.

"Don't you think?" he retorts playfully, walking away backwards with a sexy smirk. God help me. We've only been here an hour and I'm having thoughts about him that really should be more like fourth or fifth date thoughts. I take a deep breath, trying to regain my composure before joining him in front of a huge black-and-white photograph of the ocean.

"This, I like," he says, gazing into it. I look at it. I've never really been into photography, but I have to agree, this is beautiful.

"I can see why," I state, becoming mesmerized by it.

"It's real. No embellishments or sensors. It is what it is," he says quietly. "So, what type of drawings do you do?" He breaks the spell and turns his attention back to me.

"What type of work do you do?"

"A lot." He smirks at me.

"So do I." I grin. If he doesn't want to tell me anything, I won't tell him anything either.

"I'll show you my favorite painting." I lead him to the last place I remembered it was. Luckily, it's still there, so I don't look like an idiot.

"Degas is my absolute favorite painter. The way he captures light and color is just amazing."

"*The Dance Lessons*," he reads off the information card below. "I saw this in Washington last year."

"I think they made a trade for another painting. Wait, you were in a museum?" I smirk at him.

"Something like that," he hints. He loves to talk in codes.

"Hmmm, a hint . . . Do you work in a museum? You're an art collector? Or you're a notorious thief, and you're scoping out your next grab,"

I guess, joking with him.

"You really want to know what I do?" he asks with a sly grin. Suddenly, he gets serious, stepping closer and holding my gaze. I stop my eyes from drifting to his lips. He leans down slowly and whispers, "I work for the mob."

I sigh and gently push him away, seeing the wide smile on his face. "Fine, fine, I'll stop asking," I assure him. "It is legal, right?" I ask unsurely.

He casually shrugs with a slight smirk. "Maybe, maybe not," he says, even more cryptically. I roll my eyes at him. Suddenly, his jacket pocket begins to buzz and he pulls out his phone.

"This will only be a minute," he promises and I nod, excusing him. I hear him say, "Hello?" as he walks a little ways down the hall.

A voice at my side interrupts my enjoyment of the view that is walking away from me.

"Hi, I'm Darrell Comings, a photographer from *The Journal*. Do you mind if I take a picture of you looking at this painting?" he asks, already prepping his camera. I don't even know where this guy came from.

"Um . . . sure," I say, but when I look back down the hall, Cal is nowhere to be seen. I could have sworn he was just there.

The cameraman ushers me in front of a painting. "Just look up at the painting naturally," he orders. I look up at the painting, seeing it for the first time.

"Is that good?"

"Perfect, stay still." I hear the quiet click of the camera, followed by, "You're done.

Thank you." He says, and he and his companion walk away.

I look through the crowd, trying to spot Cal. Walking out to the main hall of the museum, I observe the crowd of people, all impeccably dressed, servers carrying trays of expensive champagne, navigating between them all. The comforting quiet of the other section is replaced with a low hum of chattering, clicking heels, and soft piano music playing overhead.

I make my way through the crowd, trying to spot my handsome, six-foot-something companion, and I feel someone lightly grab my arm. I let out a sigh of relief until I see that's it's Jason.

"Lauren, I thought it was you," he says happily.

"Hi," I say, trying to match his enthusiasm. God, I don't want to get stuck talking to him all night. I continue to glance around, hoping to spot Cal somewhere.

"What are you doing here?" he asks, oblivious to my anxiousness.

"I . . . I was invited."

"Really?" he asks, stepping forward, a little too close for my liking. I step back, trying to reclaim my comfort zone, but he continues to move in on me.

"I'm really sorry about dinner. My boss called," he explains. *Too busy to call and see if I made it home safely, hmm?*

"It's fine. I understand." God, why am I so nice all the time?

"Yeah, well. I know this was the second time. I really just want to apologize. It won't happen again," he assures me. I know it won't happen again because we'll never be on a date again. We both stand around awkwardly, and I start to scan the crowd for Cal.

"Would you like some champagne or something?" he asks.

"No, I'm fine." I say weakly. "Your eye looks better," I tell him. It's still a bit swollen, but the makeup over it is doing its best job to hide it.

"Oh yeah. It feels a little better," he says, running his hand across it. He smiles at me. "Y-you look beautiful," he says as his eyes drift from my legs upward. I wrap my arms around myself out of irritation. I feel like he can see through my clothes, and it's creepy.

"Thank you. I like your suit," I reply mechanically.

"Thanks, I just bought it," he says, tracing the rim of it proudly. "Umm, are you doing anything after this?" he asks, moving closer to me again.

"Actually . . ." I say, starting to excuse myself from another date of boring torture, when I feel a strong arm wrap around my waist, and Cal is back at my side, looking down at me with an arched brow and a sexy smirk.

"I lost you for a minute," he says.

"It was more like I lost you," I retort, thankful for his return. For a moment I forget Jason is even standing here. I glance over to see him looking annoyed, but more confused.

"Jason, this is Cal. Cal, Jason," I introduce them. I should feel awkward about this, but I'm more amused than anything.

Jason sticks out his hand, and Cal takes it. For a moment, a look of anger crosses Jason's face.

"The infamous Cal." He laughs tightly and runs his hand across the bruise over his eye. I then remember that Cal is the reason he has the bruise. I glance at Cal and see his expression is still calm—and a little smug, if I'm reading it right.

"Lauren, I thought you would keep our midnight escapades a secret," he says, pulling me closer. I look over at Jason, who is turning red from either anger or embarrassment; I'm not sure which. I feel a little sorry for him, but I'm unwilling to pull away from my comfortable position in Cal's arms.

"Well, I better get going. I have a lot to write for the paper," he bumbles, already starting to walk away.

"It was nice seeing you." I give him a slight wave.

"Oh, Jason, you may want to get that looked at," Cal says, gesturing to the cut above his eye. Jason presses his lips together tightly and walks away in a huff. I let out a much-needed sigh of relief.

"So let me know if I'm wrong, but you seem to have lot of options here?" He laughs, amused.

"Are you implying something, sir?" I say, hoping my sarcasm covers my embarrassment.

"Oh no. It's just, I thought I was on a playing field all my own," he says, crossing his arms, a smug grin on his face.

"You don't seem to be the type that's easily intimidated," I retort, playing along.

"Oh, I'm not." He laughs haughtily. "I guess I'm going to have to do something to make myself more memorable," he says, leaving me behind with a seductive smile that I can't help but follow.

May 9th, 2011

I'VE BEEN TIPTOEING around the house for the past few hours, admittedly trying to avoid Raven. I haven't faced her since the most embarrassing moment of my life happened. I suspect she left quite soon after she found Cal and me in the pantry. We've run the poor woman out of her own house. How terrible is that?

I've been trying to think where I can go to use a Wi-Fi connection in Saginaw. My mind has been all over the place, coming up with ideas and dreams about opening my gallery. I don't know why I never thought of it myself. I smile, thinking about the epiphany Cal had this morning. He can be distant, aloof, and distracted most of the time, but however far his mind is, it doesn't change the fact that he knows me—what makes me happy. And at this point, he should know what makes me sad, too—what can hurt me deep down to the core.

I head downstairs to see that Cal has fallen asleep on the couch watching SportsCenter. I snuggle in beside him. I inhale his scent; after all these years, I still can't believe how good he smells all the time. He adjusts his position to let me climb up beside him. I reach for the remote resting on his chest, but he grabs it.

"You're sleeping," I whine.

"But I'm still listening to it," he retorts, his eyes still closed.

"You're so selfish," I pout, snuggling closer and enjoying his warmth.

"No, you were just too chicken to come downstairs first."

"How did that go . . . with Raven?"

"It went fine. I apologized and told her it was my fault."

"How did she take it?"

"She said she was young once and for you not to worry about it. I told you she's gotten pantry action before." He snickers.

I swat him playfully. "Have you talked to Dexter yet?"

"No, he's in Ireland. Why?"

"Well, you said coming back here could have messed up a business deal for him. I wanted to make sure everything was okay between you two."

"Yeah, it's something I was working on—on my own. I wasn't going to tell Dex until it was secured. It's not a big deal."

"Well, what was it you were . . ." I trail off as his phone starts to ring. I can see the caller ID from here. It's him.

"Speak of the devil." He laughs before picking it up.

"Dex! How's the whiskey over there?" he asks, a wide smile on his face. I hear Dexter's voice on the other end, but it's not loud and joking like he usually is with Cal. After a few moments, Cal's smile fades into something more serious.

"Cal, what's wrong?" I ask, noticing his demeanor change. His face shows something I've never seen before.

"Yeah, I'm still here," he says, almost absentmindedly. His face is drawn into a look of concern, but his eyes are almost glazed over. He slowly sits up, forcing me to sit up as well. "When did they get that information? How bad is it? . . . Yeah, she's here. We're in Saginaw at her aunt's."

He stands up and walks to the other side of the room. I stand up too, following behind him. He puts the phone down to his side.

"I need a minute, okay?" he says. His voice is unsteady, and it makes my heart beat faster. I've never seen him this way before.

"Babe, what's wrong?" Instinct is screaming at me not to leave him alone.

"I need a minute." His voice is cold and stern. Against my better judgment, I nod and step back to let him walk out the front door. I watch him from the window, pacing back and forth as he continues to talk on the phone. I've never seen him distraught before—angry, yes, but not this. I'd give anything to hear what is being said. I'm getting a sinking feeling in my stomach—the same one I get when I see the familiar bag he takes on his overnight trips, except this is worse.

Raven's car pulls up. I watch as she passes Cal on her way into the house. He acknowledges her but continues pacing and talking. I meet her at the door.

"Honey, is everything okay with Cal? He seems upset," she asks, closing the door. "Are you okay?" she asks, touching my shoulder.

"I-I don't know. He got a phone call from Dexter, and, whatever he's saying, it-it's not good," I explain, folding my arms around myself.

We both stand there, watching him through the window. "Is it something going on back home?" she asks.

"I don't know. It could be, but I think it's something more than that. Did he look angry to you?"

"No, more like worried or alarmed," she says, confirming my fears. In three years, I've never seen him afraid or alarmed about anything.

"Cal doesn't get like that over work," I say aloud, but more to myself. Cal is good at what he does, and I would say he's dedicated, but it doesn't affect him like this. There has only been one other time I've seen him emotional about work and, well, that was right before things started to change between Cal and me. Still, this is different. He finally puts the phone down and runs his hands through his hair in frustration. I head towards the door, and Raven gently grasps my arm.

"Honey, maybe you should give him a minute," she says. I watch him kick the dust as if it's someone's head.

"I can't," I say apologetically. Maybe he does need a moment, but I can't help it. I have to know what's going on, and if he's okay. I quickly run out the door and down the stairs.

"Cal, what's wrong? What happened?"

He glances at me briefly and turns his attention back to the ground.

"What's wrong? Talk to me," I plead. I move closer to him and hold his face in my hands. For a second, he's vulnerable, and the gray eyes that engulf me are the seldom-appearing faint green. He opens his mouth, beginning to speak, and I imagine he's about to tell me what's wrong. He's finally going to let me in on whatever it is that's bothering him. The thing that keeps slipping between him and me, pulling us apart, is about to be revealed. And then, just as quickly as the moment came, it passes—it's gone. His expression turns cold, and he takes my hand off of his face and walks away from me, heading swiftly towards the house.

"Cal, talk to me!" I yell, following close behind him as he enters the house.

"What did Dexter say? Is this about the deal?" I follow him up the stairs and into my room. He grabs his wallet and keys.

"You're leaving? What's happened?" He walks out of the room without saying a word, quickly heading back down the stairs.

"Where are you going? Can you say something?" I grab his arm, and he snatches it away from me and walks out the front door. Following behind him out of the house, I swallow my anger. I know something's wrong. He hits the alarm on his Porsche and walks to the driver's side. I open the passenger door, get in, and buckle my seat belt.

"What are you doing?" he asks bluntly.

"I'm coming with you," I tell him.

"No, you're not," he says shortly.

"Yes, I am. Something is wrong, and you won't tell me what. I won't let you leave here like this." I fold my arms across my chest and look forward, avoiding his heated glare. I cross my feet over each other, feeling a little ridiculous I don't even have on any shoes, but if I leave this car, he's pulling off without me.

"Lauren, get out of the car," he says, his voice rising.

"No, I'm going with you," I say adamantly.

"Lauren, get out of the fucking car! I don't have time for this!" he yells.

"No!" I shout back at him. In an instant he's out of the car, walking over to my side. He opens the door, and I stare him down.

"Don't make me pull you out of the car," he says quietly, and I ignore his intense glare. In a second he's reaching over me, undoing my seat belt. I push him away and he wraps his arms around my waist, lifting me out of the seat.

"I'm not getting out!" I grab the steering wheel, holding on for dear life, but he somehow manages to loosen my grip. I've hit the horn somehow in the process. So much for not attracting any attention.

"Stop it, Cal!" I scream at him as he carries me towards the house. I struggle to get out of his arms. One of Raven's neighbors has stepped out of their house and is watching us. Cal must have noticed also, and he puts me down. I start to head back to the car, and he steps in my way.

"Lauren, fuck! Go in the house. You're not coming with me!"

"Why? Why can't I go with you?" I scream at him and he covers his face in frustration.

"You just can't, okay! You're wasting my time making me do this with you!" he shouts. "Just . . . just go in the house," he continues angrily, and I burst into tears. He shakes his head defiantly. "Please!" he says, his tone still loud but softer.

"What is going on!" Raven shouts frantically from the porch, obviously having heard the commotion we've caused. The last thing I wanted to do is embarrass her with all our drama here on the front lawn.

"Fine, just go," I say, swallowing my remaining tears and gesturing towards the car.

"I'll be back," is his only reply as he heads back to the car. It is a few seconds before I notice Raven is beside me. She says something, but I don't really know what. My attention is on the black Porsche zooming out of her driveway, taking with it all of the progress that's been made over the past few days, and I realize our time here was just a bandage on an open wound that's not even close to healing.

"HERE WE ARE," he says as we step towards one of only two doors on the entire floor. He opens it, standing aside to allow me to enter first.

It seemed like a good idea in the car to come up to his apartment alone, but now I'm second-guessing myself. After leaving the museum, he mentioned how beautiful the skyline is from his place. I said I'd never seen the Chicago skyline before from anywhere other than the club and then he said he had a great view of it.

May 10th, 2008

I look up to see he's still waiting for me to go in. I bite my lip. Maybe this wasn't such a good idea. I don't know what he may think this implies. Maybe I should just say I'm feeling sick and go home. I look up again and see an amused grin on his face. I smile back at him, ignoring his humorous demeanor at my indecisiveness, and walk past him.

"Thank you," I say quietly as I enter the apartment . . . or more like penthouse. The butterflies in my stomach have tripled. The click of my heels on the chocolate-colored hardwood floors echoes throughout the house. I let out a small gasp as I take in the tall vaulted ceilings that reveal a second floor being introduced by a long, wraparound staircase.

The next thing that catches my attention is the open-concept kitchen with all stainless steel appliances, separated from the living area by an island, which I can bet is granite. There isn't much furniture, just a white chaise and a matching long sectional that stretches for miles in front of what has to be a at least a seventy-inch television; there's also a circular glass table separating the two. But what stops me in my tracks, making me wonder what took me so long to notice them, are the beautiful floor-to-ceiling windows that surround the entire left side of the apartment, revealing a breathtaking view of Chicago.

"This—this is amazing," I quietly say. I feel Cal touch my shoulders, and my nerves cause me to jump out of my skin.

"Can I take your coat?" He asks, gesturing towards it.

God, Lauren! CALM DOWN!

"You shouldn't sneak up on people like that," I joke, allowing him to remove my small jacket, if the thin material I'm wearing can even be classified as such.

"I'll remember that," he says whimsically, taking what would better be described as my shawl and disappearing into another part of the house. I rub my arms, suddenly feeling vulnerable with just this thin piece of clingy material on me. I run my hands through my now fallen curls as I walk over to the large island and take a seat on one of the tall white chair-like barstools. I slip off my stilettos, hoping my throbbing feet won't develop any blisters. I look up as Cal reappears, heading over to the stereo.

"This is really beautiful," I tell him, taking in the scenery around me once again.

"Thanks." Music begins to fill the house, a song that is haunting and hypnotizing at once.

"I love this song," I tell him, taking in the slow, sensual rhythms.

"It's one of my favorites," he replies, removing a glass pitcher from the gigantic stainless steel refrigerator. He pours ice water into two glasses.

"It's interesting." Actually, the word that comes to mind but that I won't use out loud is sexy. I've heard songs about sex, vulgar ones, but I've never thought of a song not about sex being almost erotic.

"I think it's sexy, but maybe that's just me," he says casually. His smile is wicked, and as he hands me one of the glasses I smile too, feeling my ears heat up.

"That's the word," I agree, taking a sip of water; it seems as if the temperature has gone up at least ten degrees. I start to look around the apartment to distract myself.

"Are you here a lot?" I ask absentmindedly. Most of the guys I know don't do a lot of cleaning. Even when they have a girl over, if they can sweep all the trash off the table, they consider it a job well done. But this house is spotless. Not one thing seems to be out of place, and every surface shines, dust-free.

"What do you consider a lot?" he asks seriously. I raise my eyebrow curiously.

"Um, I don't know. I guess I'm always home when I'm not at work or school." I giggle. Did I just giggle? I also start to realize how unbelievably boring my life is.

"Have you ever been out of the country before?" he asks.

"The farthest I've been is Florida for my cousin's wedding." I laugh, watching him come from behind the island. I quickly slip my shoes back on.

"That should change," he says, taking a seat on the barstool next to me. My skin starts to tingle at our close proximity now that we're alone. I take another sip of water. "I've never met a woman like you before, Lauren," he says, his intense gaze on me once again. His eyebrow arches as if he's trying to figure me out.

"What do you mean by that?" I ask, gulping my water down.

"It's just that you're one of the most beautiful women I've ever seen, and you don't exploit it. I haven't seen that around here," he says, taking my hand and leading me into the middle of the floor. I don't really know what to say to that.

"I'll tell you a secret," he says as he wraps his arm behind my waist and takes my hand. *Please don't be married or a serial killer.*

"The day I met you wasn't the first time I'd seen you," he says, placing my arms on his shoulders with a sly grin. I chuckle nervously. "I'd noticed you the first time I was at The Vault. You were the only waitress who seemed like you didn't belong there."

"Is that a compliment?" I ask him, laughing.

"It's a compliment," he says, a small grin resting on his face.

I take my arms off his shoulders and wrap them hesitantly around his neck.

"You're pretty good at this," I say, a little amazed. He's the first guy I've danced with who hasn't stepped on my feet in the first ten seconds.

He spins me around expertly. "I don't know what you're talking about," he says innocently.

"Sure you don't." He pulls me back into his chest and resumes the dance. His hand starts to caress the small of my back, sending chills up my spine; his touch, along with this music, is almost intoxicating. I close my eyes and lay my head on his chest. As we sway back and forth to the music, he's leading me in every way.

"I've never felt like this before," I say softly, not recognizing the tone of my voice

"Is that a good thing?" he asks. I can't even get my words out. I just nod. "I can make you feel like this every night."

"You think so?" I laugh lightly, feeling as if I'm floating on air. He suddenly stops dancing, and I look up to find him gazing at me intently.

"I'm positive."

"But would you?" I ask. I'm not sure why I said that. I'm feeling a bit lightheaded, even though I've only had one glass of champagne this evening, not wanting to make him feel uncomfortable at the benefit since he doesn't drink. Yep, I'm feeling a little out of it, but not at all in a bad way.

"If you asked," he says. The sarcastic tone is back, breaking the moment for now.

I laugh quietly. "So, is this what you say to all the girls?"

He spins me around again and pulls my back against his chest, wrapping his arms around my waist and swaying with the guitar rhythm in the song. "Who says I have to say anything," he says quietly. His lips are dangerously close to my ear.

"I'm sure you don't," I say, trying to appear indifferent. "So that makes me different?"

"You are. From the first time I saw you, I knew you were different."

"How?" I'm curious.

"Well, you didn't throw yourself at me once you saw the Aston Martin." He laughs.

"Well, I have an incredible amount of self-control," I reply sarcastically, "and high personal standards." I've found myself using sarcasm as a defense mechanism with him. Truth is I can't blame any girl who did throw herself at him. He definitely has that effect, even without the car. I feel a soft chuckle rumbling in his chest, but he doesn't say anything.

"So, tell me, what happens next?" I close my eyes and concentrate on his hands as they lift to rest on my shoulders then slowly slide down my arms, sending tingles through my body. I twist my head to look back at him.

He's smiling slyly. "That's up to you."

"Is it?" I say, closing my eyes again, and I feel his breath on my neck, causing me to bite my lip to keep from letting him know the effect it's having on me. "If I didn't know any better, I'd say you were trying to seduce me," I purr as his hand slowly creeps across my stomach.

"Tell me. How am I doing?" His voice is husky and is barely above a whisper. My little inner voice is going crazy, screaming at me. This is where I should tell him good night and that I had a nice time and it's time to go, but I'm having trouble doing that.

A crash of thunder snaps me out of the trance I'm falling into. I disentangle myself from his embrace and walk towards the window, watching the raindrops paint the city. He comes to stand beside me. I don't look at him, but I know he's watching me.

"I didn't mean to make you uncomfortable," he says quietly.

"You're not. It's . . . it's just—this is all . . . I'm not used to this," I admit, stumbling over my speech.

"I don't want you to do anything you don't want to do tonight. As hard as it is." He lets out a long sigh and laughs.

"I'll keep my hands to myself the rest of the night." He smiles innocently, crossing his arms over his chest and deliberately tucking his hands under his muscular arms. The thing is, I don't want him to keep his hands to himself. I want them all over me and it's terrifying. I've never wanted someone so bad in my life, and it's overwhelming.

"Do you do this? I mean seriously, is this just a routine for you?" I ask him, my heart in my throat. I'm afraid to hear the answer.

He looks at me, surprised. "Well, I'm not going to lie and tell you I'm a saint. I'm far from it. I love women and I've never had to work too hard to get one," he says bluntly. I cross my arms as well. I think somewhere inside of me I'm jealous, imagining all of the women who have stood in this same spot, who have walked through his door and been in his bed.

"But you're the first woman I've been with that I can honestly say if you left here tonight without letting me see what's under your dress, I would still call you," he says with a slight chuckle, and I'm appalled. What a douche-bag thing to say!

"It's time for me to go home," I say, irritated. Definitely time for me to go. I turn to walk away, but he grabs my hand.

"Wait! That came out wrong. I'm sorry. I'm not used to having to explain myself to anyone," he says. He runs his fingers through his dark locks and chuckles nervously.

"I like you! I love *being* with women. But I usually don't *like* being with them, if that makes sense," he tries to explain, and he seems a little confused. It's the first un-cool moment he's had, and for the first time tonight I notice flecks of green glimmering in his gray eyes; they twinkle at me.

"You seem like the type of guy that doesn't think beyond the night. I'm not like that," I tell him.

He steps towards me and the familiar heat rushes between us.

"Well, I see you past tonight," he says, cupping the side of my face. I lean into his hand and close my eyes. I don't know what to do. My mind is telling me to leave at this point, to leave right now. My body is begging me to stay and let him do whatever he wants to it. My heart is lonely; I've been alone for so long. Even with Michael, something was missing, and I know this pull he has over me has to be lust, but there's something else. If it was just lust, I wouldn't be so afraid, right?

I turn away from him, back towards the window, trying to collect my thoughts—my wants versus my fears.

"What do you want from me?" Who am I kidding? I know exactly what he wants.

"I want you to tell me what you want," he whispers, and a second later his lips have found the secret spot on my neck that sends a thrill over me.

"What if I don't know what I want?" My voice goes up an entire octave.

He turns me around so we're facing each other now. He leans down, pulling me into a breathless kiss. I have to wrap my arms around him tighter to keep from losing my balance. I softly whimper as his tongue begins to explore my mouth, and he begins to slowly unzip my dress, almost as if he's waiting for me to stop him. When I don't, he slides his hand beneath the thin material; the heat of his hand seems foreign but amazing.

As I open my eyes, the room is spinning, but my focus is on him. Each movement in rhythm, every kiss, every touch—he shouldn't be able to make me feel like this; it's almost like he can read my mind.

"I want to be the one to show you things you've never seen," he whispers in my ear as he unhooks my bra. "Make you feel things you've never felt," his voice pours into my ear as his hand slides up my thigh.

"Just let me," he says, picking me up. The strap of my dress slides down my shoulder.

"And what do I have to do?" I whimper out, completely under his spell. He lifts me higher so I'm looking into his eyes, and brings his mouth to my ear.

"Say yes."

There are so many reasons I should say no: I barely know him, we've only been out twice.

"Yes," I say, breathless.

THE TIME IT takes for Cal and me to reach his bedroom on the second floor of his apartment passes within seconds; he's carried me as if I were a feather. Once we enter the room, he pulls me into a slow, deep kiss that leaves me hungry for more. After his lips leave mine, we catch our breath. With the few seconds apart, my mind begins to race.

"Wait, um. Do you have any . . . any protection?" I ask, immediately feeling the awkwardness of the question as soon as it leaves my lips. Still, this is the first time I've ever been in a situation where I haven't been in a committed relationship with a man I'm about to share my body with. I hadn't quite planned for things to go this far tonight, and Hillary's earlier premonition mocks me.

I open my eyes as I feel his arms loosen their grip around my waist.

Damn, those gray eyes are spellbinding. He sets me down, and my toes are revel in the softest plush carpet I've ever walked on. I shift my focus out to the rest of his face, searching his expression to see if there is any hint of anger. I've heard horror stories of men who refuse to use condoms. Thankfully, he flashes me a wide grin, takes my hand, and leads me toward the bed. He sits and busies himself, rummaging through a drawer built into the headboard. I try to calm my nerves and hormones by distracting myself and surveying my surroundings.

His room is large with walls that are a stone-gray color. A large fireplace sits high on the wall adjacent to his California King bed that seems to stretch for miles, decked in blue and gray linen. My eyes quickly scan the room for personal effects, but there are none. No photographs, trinkets, or clothing scattered about. I do notice an unopened king-sized Snickers bar on the mantle above the fireplace, which starts painting shadows across the walls. A woman's voice pours from the surround sound system in the bedroom.

I feel his hand slide across my stomach, and it reels me back into the moment at play, causing every nerve in my body to awaken. The gold foil wrapper is sitting beside him on the bed, waiting for me. I take a deep breath and move to sit beside him, but his hand on my wrist stops me.

"Here," he says, gesturing to the space in front of him in a deep, authoritative voice. My body begins to tingle all over, and I move to where he's told me to. He shifts forward to the edge of the bed and gently pulls me closer toward him; his face is now only inches from my stomach and his lips caress the space above my navel gently as the muscles in my stomach and lower flex in response. His fingers slowly trail up the back of my thighs as I look into his eyes—dark gray now, lust replacing the light green specks that dawned in them earlier.

"I want you to know that you're in control," he says, sensuously licking the lips that I badly want to cover mine. He moves his hands up my thighs, sweeping across my backside to my waist. He bites his lip but suddenly leans back on the bed, resting his weight on his elbows. His eyes are locked with mine, and I feel like he's teasing me. I'm confused, but then I remember his earlier words. He's waiting on me. I feel myself flush all over and let out a small breath. I turn around so that my back is toward him.

"Take off your clothes." My voice is low and unrecognizable, but I can't help feeling some satisfaction at the confidence that courses through me. I feel him behind me and hear him removing his clothes. A few seconds later, I hear the wrapper opening. My heart is beating a mile a minute.

"Now, take off mine," I say, the nervous pit in my stomach transforming into an excitement I've never felt—a rush that's foreign, a craving I don't recognize. I feel him behind me. His hands move the hair falling down my back to one side of my shoulder; he licks each shoulder blade, sending tingles up my spine. He slowly unzips my dress and pulls it down my shoulders. I can feel his arousal pressing against me. His tongue caresses the back of my neck. One of his hands explores my body, while the other removes my bra. I'm free.

Usually, this would be the point where I feel awkward, nervous, and self-conscious about the first time my body is revealed, but this is different. I reach my arm up to hold on to his neck, my knees literally weak, but a slow excitement has been building since I told him to take off his clothes. His touches and dragging kisses on my body are becoming torturous.

His fingers find their way between my thighs, pushing the thin, now moist, lacy material aside, and slip inside of me. I gasp, involuntarily throwing my head back. I push his hand away and swiftly turn around to face him.

"I didn't say you could do that," I whisper, a teasing grin on my face that disappears as soon as I see his perfectly sculpted bare body. I don't have long to admire it before he picks me up, capturing my mouth. His tongue dominates mine into submission, and it's not until I'm on the bed, with my body captured beneath his, that he releases it.

I catch my breath and he smiles down at me wickedly. He brings his mouth to my ear and I slide my hand up his back.

"Do you know what you want *now*?" he asks before his lips start trailing down my breast, enrapturing one of my nipples. I try to focus on what he's saying. He stops and I look at him pleadingly.

"Tell me what you want," he demands again, facing me, his eyes hypnotizing. My body's yearning for him, craving him, almost on the brink of begging him to enter.

"Everything," I admit almost desperately, never having spoken a more honest thing in my life.

He smiles at me, seemingly satisfied. "That's what you're going to get," he promises, granting my wish.

"LAUREN, SWEETIE." RAVEN'S voice wakes me up. I open my eyes and see the sky is dark, but lit with stars. I've fallen asleep on the patio couch waiting for Cal to come back.

"What time is it?" My body is stiff. I sit up to work out the kinks in my back. "Is Cal back?" I grimace, trying my best to keep the urgency out of my voice. I feel anxious; butterflies are lining my stomach again.

May 9th, 2011

"I'm sure he'll be back soon, and that everything is fine." Raven unsuccessfully tries to sound confident. I can't even hide my disappointment. I'm too tired to try to play the role of a happy and content wife. It isn't even worth it after the show Cal and I put on for her neighbors.

"Can you think of why he wouldn't tell you what happened?" she asks, and I roll my eyes. If only I could think of a reason other than he doesn't want to.

"Lauren, do you mind if I ask you a personal question?" she asks, taking a seat beside me. *Okay, here it comes.*

"You're going to ask it anyway, aren't you?" I reply sardonically, and make room for her to sit beside me.

"I don't mean to pry, but honey, something doesn't seem right with you both," she says softly.

Her tone is eerie and sensitive, the tone people use when approaching an unpleasant subject.

"What makes you think that?" I say sarcastically, and I immediately regret my snide remark as she looks down at her feet, defeated.

"I'm sorry, Raven." I sigh and look into the distance. I'm angry and frustrated, but it has nothing to do with her. She's done nothing but show concern for me, and I have no right to patronize her like that.

"Sweetheart, it's okay," she says, squeezing my hand supportively, and I feel tears in my eyes. God, I hate this. I hate that she can still read my face, and that she can bring whatever emotions I'm suppressing to the surface.

"Honey, don't cry," she says before wrapping her arms around me into a long, warm embrace. I can feel myself breaking down. I hug her back, tears flowing down my cheeks.

"It'll be okay, sweetheart," she says, stroking my back.

"I-I don't think it will," I reveal to her.

"I knew something was wrong when I first saw you. I was hoping it wasn't this." She pulls a Kleenex out of her jacket pocket and hands it to me, taking a seat beside me as I wipe the tears from my face.

"Is it another woman?" she asks almost nervously.

"I don't know what he does; he's gone so much," I admit. "Honestly though, I may be in denial, but I don't think it's another woman or women. Then again, Cal would never let me find out; he's too smart for that," I say undecidedly. I think back to the night where we had a huge fight about my theories on why he's gone so much, when I first became tired of his frequent disappearances and how that ended and led to the pattern we have now.

"Well. What is it? He doesn't hurt you, does he?" Raven asks worriedly.

"NO!" I say quickly. "That's not it at all. Cal has never hit me, pushed me—he even hates to argue. He always just leaves. That's the problem."

"Well, honey, sometimes it's best to leave, especially if he has a bad temper. A long walk . . ."

I knew she wouldn't understand. She'd probably think I was silly or over-emotional if I told her how I really felt. "I don't mean it like that. It's more than that. Cal, he's . . ." I exhale. I can't even say this out loud to anyone without sounding like an oversensitive idiot.

"Lauren, you can tell me anything," Raven says reassuringly.

I go to stand at the railing on the other side of the porch. If I tell her this, I can't look at her.

"When we first met, it was like . . . it was like I was dreaming. He was this handsome, mysterious, rugged, and intelligent man. All that I could ask for. I'd never felt as attracted to anyone as I was to him. My hormones took control and left my brain behind." I look back awkward-ly at Raven, who has a small smile on her face.

"Go on," she says, clasping her hands.

"It was like I wasn't living in the real world. It was just us. In the real world, I wouldn't just go with a guy I barely knew without asking any questions. But with Cal, I basically knew nothing about him, and I didn't care. Because though I didn't know facts, I thought—well, I *felt* like we were connected. I told him things that I'd never told anyone." I pause, reflecting on the many nights in bed with Cal when I'd revealed all my soul, wrapped in his arms, his eyes on me as if I were the only person in the world.

"God, his eyes . . . Those eyes were what I fell in love with. They're what make me forgive him a thousand times over." I wipe the leftover tears on my face. "How can our marriage work if he doesn't trust me? Today just proves it, and it's not just today. He rarely tells me how he feels. He leaves when he's angry. And then he comes back and thinks everything can be fixed with a good fuck!" My jaw drops as I realize what I've just said out loud. I look at Raven, feeling embarrassed, but I see that she's not. She's listening attentively.

"I-I just don't know how to get through to him. I don't know how to make him open up. He won't let me in. I used to try so hard, and then I got sick of being turned away or shut down. Today was just a reminder of that. If he doesn't trust me, can you imagine the secrets he has? If he gets to pick and choose what I get to know and not know, I'm more of a child than a wife." I take a much-needed breath.

"Well, from what you've told me, his job is confidential in nature. That would explain . . ."

"It's not the job!" I interrupt her, shaking my head defiantly. "It's something else. I can feel it. Whatever happened today . . ." I trail off as I catch sight of the black Porsche pulling up to the driveway.

Raven walks over to me, puts both hands on my shoulders, and looks me straight in the eye.

"What's in the dark, will always come to light," she says, giving me a reassuring smile before pulling me into another hug. She then with-draws into the house, and I turn my attention to Cal getting out the car.

His face is expressionless, and he glances up at me as he slowly climbs the stairs.

"I don't—" I begin, but he holds a hand up, stopping me mid-sentence.

"I'm not doing this with you tonight. If you want to fight, stay out here and argue with yourself," he says disdainfully. I look at him standing there, expressionless. Like I'm the one who likes to fight and argue all the time. Like I didn't sit on this porch for hours since he left, worried about him, waiting on him to come back safely.

I think of how he has the nerve to stroll up as if he didn't fly out of here like a bat out of hell after kicking me out of his car. I want to throw a fit and yell at him and not stop until he tells me what's going on. A part of me wonders if everything earlier was an act, an excuse to get away. Maybe the answer is obvious: he's a cheating bastard.

. . . Yet, when I think of him earlier, how his eyes pleaded with me, how he was distraught and vulnerable, and that one moment when I saw the panic and worry I'd never seen before, I know he's genuinely struggling with something. I fight every urge inside of me to smack him across the face. Instead, I hug him. I hold him close for a long time. Tomorrow I will need answers. I'll demand them. I can't go on with him like this. Tonight, though, I know he needs me, even if he doesn't say it.

BEFORE TODAY I'D never been asleep and afraid to wake up, open my eyes, and realize that what happened was just a dream. Too perfect, it had to be surreal. So wonderful it couldn't have existed. That's how I feel today. I can feel the warm sunlight beaming down on my face and I'm afraid to open my eyes. I'm afraid when I do I'm going to be back in my own bed and my night with Cal will turn out to have just been a dream. Fate's cruel, artificial trick, a hoax being played on me because it was unlike any-

May 11th, 2008

thing I've ever experienced. I wish I could relive the entire day. My own personal fairy tale—being whisked away in a carriage, then swept off my feet in a dance—and, well, the next part is not so much like the endings I've read about, more amazing than I ever thought it could be.

I turn over on my back and wrap myself in the softest sheets I've ever felt and smile, knowing these definitely aren't mine. I could sleep in this bed forever . . . this bed, that I didn't get much sleep in last night. Where things were done to me that all next week I'll be blushing over whenever I think about them. All by a man who I know little of, but one who's made me feel as if he's known me forever, like he's spent an eternity with my body, knowing the exact way to do each thing as if he wrote the instructions for my body's creation. He looked into my eyes and made me feel things I never felt in any of my past relationships. I feel guilty somewhere inside because I don't know him and he doesn't know me but was able to get me to share a part of myself I've been afraid to let anyone else see. The first time I've lost myself in a moment of passion that caused me to drop every reservation I've ever had, to let go of any inhibition I've experienced.

Michael always complained that I held back when we had sex, and I know I did. Something in me wouldn't allow myself to fully let go, but last night was different. That feeling I never allowed to come over me with another person washed over me completely, any hesitation gone in the wind from the moment I agreed to let Cal give me *everything*. I run my hands through my hair and massage my scalp. I barely know him, but I feel like I've given him a little piece of my soul. His eyes hypnotized me into wanting him to experience every part of me, and my heart is starting to beat faster as I fully realize this.

I look over and see that I'm wrapped in this sea of sheets *alone*. The lull I'm in is starting to wear off, and my thoughts start to race at the idea of . . . what happens next?

This is the first time I've ever been faced with waking up in the bed of a guy with whom I'm not in a relationship! Here I am, having all these strange thoughts, and he can easily be counting down the minutes until I'm gone. What if I have to do my first walk of shame? After the most amazing night of my life, I'm going to have to walk out of this building onto the busiest street in Chicago in last night's wrinkled clothes and wonder if I'm ever going to see him again. *Ugh. Stupid!*

Dammit! If this is one of the liberating experiences Hillary says I need to have, I'm going to kill her, because I don't feel liberated at all. I'm horrified! What if he's just left or is hiding somewhere, waiting for me to leave? But no guy would leave a strange girl in his house alone. Oh, gosh, I'm just a strange girl to him!

I start to scan the room, looking for my clothes, feeling a near-panic attack starting. I get out of bed and tiptoe around it, expecting to find my dress and underwear scattered on the floor, but there's nothing. Where the hell are my clothes! Okay, calm down, calm down. There has to be a reasonable explanation for this, and why am I tiptoeing?

"Breathe. Just breathe," I tell myself aloud, taking a deep breath.

"Please do. If you pass out, I don't know CPR."

His voice causes the hairs on my neck to stand up. I turn to see him leaning in the doorway, arms folded across his bare chest, pajama pants resting a little below his hips, and on his face that same amused grin from the day I met him. A grin spreads across my own. I let out a sigh of relief until I realize the only thing I'm wearing is a smile. I quickly grab the sheet from the bed and wrap it around myself.

"Um, I—good morning," I finally manage to say.

"Good morning." I can hear him holding in a laugh and he bites both of his lips, seemingly to keep from doing so.

"You're laughing at me." I chuckle at how ridiculous I must look, depending on how long he might have been standing there.

"A little bit," he admits, walking toward me. With each step, I grow more nervous but in the best way possible. His hair is tousled, but almost perfectly so. His skin looks amazing in the sunlight and his eyes are showcasing their green hue. I remind myself I'm twenty-one, not fourteen, and command my big-girl voice to make an appearance.

"Well, you did hide my clothes," I retort as he sits down on the bed in front of me.

"As good as you look without them . . ." he says as he gives my entire body a once-over. "I didn't hide them. I sent them to the laundry." He rests his weight on his elbows, his eyes staring up at me playfully. That's a relief. If he wanted me gone super fast, I reason, he wouldn't have done that. I breathe a little easier.

"Thank you," I say, my eyes resting on my feet.

"You're shy?" He chuckles and stands up from the bed.

Is it that obvious? Ugh, stop acting like a spaz.

"A little," I admit, laughing at myself. I want to tell him it's only around him but decide not to. He steps closer to me. My heart beats faster with each step.

"Not what you expected?" I say, wishing, at this moment, that I'd had more experience with this kind of thing.

He looks down at me and his smile softens.

"I'm just surprised." His chest now touches mine, and I instinctively step backward. "After everything you let me do to you last night . . ." he adds, again closing the distance between us. He bites his bottom lip and beams down at me, and I know I'm turning every imaginable shade of red.

"I think you like making me nervous," I say, my back now against the wall and his arms on both sides of me.

"No. I just like getting you all worked up," he says and leans down, bringing his lips only an inch away from mine. His breath smells like mint and his skin like vanilla, and I realize mine doesn't.

I slip from underneath his arms and he's caught off guard. "Can I use your shower?" I ask, smiling at his surprise.

"Is that an invitation?" he asks, walking past me, going into what I assume is his bathroom. He gestures toward it, and I follow. Once I'm in the doorway, a wicked grin appears on his face. I feel my stomach drop at the gesture. But whether he knows it or not, I'm too sore to even contemplate what he's hinting at.

"Privacy?" He laughs, and I nod my head gratefully. He steps back, but not before his hand slides down my back and he squeezes my butt.

"Too bad." He sighs before slipping out, and I playfully roll my eyes at him, demanding my body to behave.

When he's gone, my mouth almost drops. The bathroom is huge, almost bigger than my bedroom. It's stone gray and navy blue, matching the hues of Cal's bedroom. There's a deep stone tub in the center, and adjacent to that a shower with two heads and a clear glass surround. There are his-and-hers sinks, with faucets that flow down like a fountain. This place just gets better and better.

There are body towels and face towels neatly stacked on a bench. There's a little cup on the sink next to what I assume is mouthwash, but the bottle matches the bathroom decor. I open it and smell the cap to make sure it's the mint I noticed earlier. As I contemplate whether to shut the door or not, I peek out into the bedroom and see that Cal's nowhere in sight.

I swish the wash around in my mouth. It's minty with a mix of something else I can't put my finger on, but it's mild, unlike the burning kind my aunt used to buy. When I'm done I make my way into the shower. When I turn it on, I'm startled when the showerhead behind me sprinkles down my back. Once I figure out the settings, the shower is absolute heaven. I'm a little excited about smelling like Cal throughout the day, after using his body wash and shampoo. They both have the exact right hint of vanilla for him to smell good but retain his masculinity.

After I dry off, I wrap the towel around my body and head into the bedroom, which is still empty. I look on the bed, hoping he might have left me a shirt of his to put on, but there's nothing.

I head down the stairs and hear a television on. Cal's at the fridge, a container of orange juice in hand. Wearing an amused smirk, he does a quick glance over me.

"Pulp or no pulp?" he asks, shutting the fridge.

"No pulp." I chuckle as I sit down on the side of the island that's closest to me.

"Good choice," he says, pouring me a cup and setting it in front of me. Before grabbing it, I secure my towel to make sure it will stay. I notice him laughing and he shakes his head disapprovingly.

"What?" I ask curiously.

"Nothing," he says, amused, the fridge hiding him.

"How was your shower?" he asks, at last fully appearing with a bowl. When he sets it down, I see it contains cut-up fruit, all kinds.

"It was wonderful. I definitely have shower envy," I admit, popping a piece of cantaloupe in my mouth.

He takes a grape, does the same, and sits across from me. I grab another piece of fruit and make sure my towel is still in place. He leans over on the island and tilts his head slightly to the right.

"You should take the towel off," he says, his eyes beaming at me.

I bite my tongue instead of the fruit. *Ugh!*

"*What?*" I laugh in disbelief at what he just said.

"What's so funny?" he asks, a wry grin on his face.

"It's just how casual you said that and how serious you sounded," I joke.

"I am serious," he says, resting his chin in his hand. His eyes set on mine, causing me to shift in my seat.

"I'm sorry. I'm not going to sit in your kitchen completely naked." I laugh off my nervousness. He can't be serious. He stands up and walks around the counter. He's heading towards me, and with each step, my heart pounds faster. I swallow as he rounds the corner of the island, turning in my direction, and I suddenly feel like I'm prey and he's the hunter. But the doorbell rings, the spell is broken, and he lets out a breath. He makes a beeline to the door, pointing at me as he walks away.

"Saved by the bell, gorgeous," he says, a residual smile resting on his face.

A moment later, he's back with two containers. He hands me one before making his way to the other side of the island.

"You were still asleep when I ordered, so I got pancakes and bacon, because who wouldn't like that?" he jokes.

The aroma when I open the container is tantalizing, and I have to stop myself from grabbing a piece and stuffing it in my mouth. I glance up at him as he stuffs a strip of bacon in his.

I watch him as we eat, trying not to stare at him as I fill my empty stomach. I keep trying to figure out this enigma sitting in front of me. He's young, but this house is decorated with the taste of someone older. He's straightforward, but sometimes it seems like he wants to say something but doesn't. He's seductive but has a boyish charm to him—well, that disappears when his eyes squint a little and lust clouds them. He's blunt but seemingly mysterious about simple things. He seems to want me to be more assertive but is turned on by my reticence with him.

"What's going on in that head of yours, Ms. Brooks?" he asks, his eyes squinting at me as he finishes off his piece of toast.

"You want me to be honest?" I ask bluntly.

"Always," he says, just as bluntly.

"I—I guess I'm trying to figure you out. *This* out," I admit.

He stretches his arms over his head, and for a moment I'm distracted by his muscular physique.

"This?" he asks curiously.

"This whole awkward, day-after-the-night-with-a-guy-I-don't-really-know-how-to-act-around," I ramble.

"The only thing awkward is you trying to eat and keep that towel up," he says playfully.

I frown at his playfulness, then decide to lay it all out on the table.

"You're the first guy I've ever done this with. And I know it sounds cliché saying I'm not that type of girl, but it's true, and I'm not sure what the etiquette is for 'this.' I don't know what to make of you. I kind of thought you'd be hiding somewhere this morning, waiting for me to leave or something." After I let out my spiel, I take a deep breath and glance at him nervously, not knowing what he's going to do next.

"So you think I'm an asshole?" He laughs boisterously and plants his elbow on the counter. I'm caught off guard by that.

"No, I—I didn't say that." I'm a little embarrassed I didn't really consider he'd take that as an insult.

"You pretty much do, if you think I'd sleep with you and then hide from you in my own house. That would make me an asshole *and* a coward." He counts on his fingers with a grin.

"Okay, I'm sorry. But I'm just trying to figure you out," I admit, feeling more than embarrassed.

"It's okay, I'm sure this won't be the last time you think I'm an asshole," he says, tossing out his now empty container. I feel my eyebrow rise.

"Well, unless you just planned on screwing me and never calling again," he adds with an almost knowing smile.

This time, it's my turn to finish up the rest of my orange juice.

"It's not only that. I just . . ." I let out a deep sigh. "I like you, and I'd feel a little better about myself if I knew more about you," I tell him honestly. He's leaning back on the island.

"Okay," he shrugs his shoulder. "What do you want to know?"

"For starters, how old are you? Um, how do you like your eggs? What's your middle name, your favorite color, and what do you do for a living?" I say, rattling off questions to which I usually know the answers before I drop my panties for a guy.

"Twenty-six, scrambled hard, I don't have one, black, and I am a liaison between Public Relations and Research and Development at Crestfield Corporation." He rattles off the answers just as quickly.

"Now it's my turn. Are you always this neurotic after sex?" He laughs and my eyes widen.

"I'm not neurotic. I just—I usually know these things before I have sex with someone," I retort.

"How many guys have you had sex with?" he asks, way too simply for such a personal question.

"Why?" I ask, feeling my defenses rise.

"It seems like you don't have sex that often, that's all."

"Excuse me?"

"You're a little uptight about all of this." He chuckles, unaffected by the anger in my tone.

"You're kind of being a jerk right now," I say sharply, and he grins.

"I answered all of your questions and you haven't answered any of mine," he counters. "I don't feel like you're allowing me to really know *you*," he adds sarcastically, and I roll my eyes and take a deep breath.

"I've been with three men and I just had sex last night, for your info." I say the last part equally sarcastically.

He leans over the island, his eyes narrowing in on mine. In an instant his smile has gone from playful and aloof to dangerously sexy.

"How was it?" he asks. His tone has deepened and he's looking me directly in the eye.

My frustration with him starts to dissipate. "Amazing," I breathe out, looking him right back in the eye. After an intense stare-off, his smile widens.

"Well, do you feel okay to like me now?" he asks in an almost condescending tone. His wide grin softens. I bite my lip, internally arguing with myself, even though that boat has sailed and the deed's been done.

"I'm not going to lie. I can be an asshole. I can probably be worse than that, but I don't talk out of my ass. I like you and I meant everything I said last night. So don't spend the rest of the day wondering if I'm genuine or not. I'm a lot of things, but a liar isn't one of them." He says all of this casually, but with it I feel as if a weight has been lifted off my chest. I bite my thumb, letting everything Cal's just said sink in.

"Still think I'm a jerk?"

I nod. "Maybe just little bit of a jerk," I reveal. With that amused grin again, he stands and makes his way over to me. I let out a much-needed breath and turn towards him on my barstool.

He parts my legs, causing the towel to rise a bit over my thighs. He stands in between them.

"Good, because I am. And I still think you're a little bit neurotic," he says, bringing his lips to mine and his hands to the knot in my towel. I push his chest away playfully. He looks into my eyes, still grinning.

"You didn't ask," I scold him teasingly.

"I want to take your towel off," he whispers in my ear.

I bite my lip and look up at him playfully.

"No." I shake my head, amused. He looks up at the ceiling, feigning frustration, then moves his face near my ear, kissing the skin beneath my earlobe, then makes his way to my neck, kissing it so softly the sensation causes my eyes to involuntarily close.

"Please," he says again, as his fingers trail between my thighs and one slips inside me while his thumb starts to play around the only other area that's much more sensitive. I can't help the moan that escapes my mouth. I lean away from him a bit and slowly unravel the knot, letting the towel fall from around me. He licks his lips.

"You better get used to this," he says, wrapping his arms around my bare back.

"Get used to what?" I ask, wrapping my legs around his waist. I guess I'll just have to be a little sorer.

"Being in my house naked. I kind of like it."

I wrap my arms around his neck and pull him in for a kiss.

I kind of like it, too.

May 10th, 2011

I'M AWAKE. IT'S early, and I haven't slept much at all. What happened last night consumes my thoughts, along with Cal's constant tossing and turning in the full-size bed that was once comfortable to me as a teenager, but now feels cramped for a woman and her six-foot husband. Even if he'd been still, I doubt I could have slept. A million thoughts have been running through my mind. I keep going over all of the things I've accepted, all of the times I've forgiven, that I've caved despite my better judgment. I glance at him and he seems to finally be still, resting. I double-check to make sure he's sound asleep and ease out of the bed as quietly as I can. Grabbing his phone off the dresser, I tiptoe out of the room and pull the door shut behind me.

Throughout our entire marriage, I have never invaded Cal's privacy, not once. But there is a first time for everything and this is completely warranted. I need answers, and I need them now—if I have to snoop for them, so be it. I hit the power button, and of course, it's password-protected. I tiptoe past Raven's bedroom and down the stairs to find the cordless house phone and dial Cal's number. When it rings, I answer it and put it on speaker so that I can get into his contact list.

I only want Dexter's wife's phone number. Granted, if I hadn't thrown my own phone off the balcony before I left home, I wouldn't have to do this, but that's beside the point. I'm tempted to go through the call history. After a short debate, I give in, and when I search through it, I see it's been cleared. I roll my eyes at that. He wouldn't need to delete his call history unless he had something to hide. But I knew that already, didn't' I? I grab a pen off the end table, and write Helen's number down on a piece of paper.

Resting Cal's phone on my lap, I sit back on Raven's plush lounger and dial Helen's number on the house phone. I hope she'll answer an unknown number. I know it's a long shot; it's only 6:30 A.M.

"Hello?" she answers, and I thank God for my luck.

"Helen. Hi, it's Lauren. Is this a good time?" I say quietly, not wanting either Raven or Cal to hear me.

"Lauren? How are you? And where are you calling from? I almost didn't answer. Is everything okay?"

"Um, that's actually why I was calling you." I take a glance at the hallway to make sure no one is there.

"Has Dexter mentioned anything to you about him and Cal having a falling out?"

"No, I don't think so. You know how they are, though. Why do you ask?"

"It's just that Dexter called Cal yesterday and told him something that really upset him. I thought it might have been business related. Or if not, maybe you have some idea what happened."

"Dex hasn't said anything to me, but he doesn't usually keep me up to date on his business affairs." She laughs.

"And if it wasn't business related?" I ask.

"Dex is in Ireland right now. I can have him give you a call . . ."

"I'm asking *you*, Helen," I interrupt her, hoping the urgency in my voice is apparent. "Is there anything that you can tell me, anything I should know?" I ask pleadingly. Helen and I have never been the best of friends. Yet we still share a bond, even if unspoken. We both are in love with men who seem to only trust their secrets with each other. However, I believe Helen chooses to stay in the dark, while I'm forced to. I've never talked to her about my relationship with Cal. I've never dragged her into our personal affairs or thrown myself into theirs, but today, I'm hoping she hears my plea and, by some miracle, offers me something to go on. I think I've shocked her, since there is a long pause on the line.

"I'm sorry, Lauren. Dex hasn't told me anything."

I roll my eyes. "Of course he wouldn't." I don't believe that at all.

"Lauren, I'm sorry, but . . ." Cal's phone suddenly vibrates in my lap, making me jump. It's an unknown number.

"I've got to go, Helen. Thanks anyway," I say before hanging up the phone. I stare at it and contemplate whether to answer it or not. I've already snooped for numbers, might as well go all the way now. I pick up the phone and bring it to my ear. I don't say anything, hoping that the person on the other line will say something first. Seconds pass, but the person on the other end remains silent.

"Hello?" I finally say out of frustration. The person on the other end of the line doesn't say anything. "Is anyone there?"

"I'm sorry. I have the wrong number," a voice says and abruptly hangs up. A woman's voice, older than me, maybe around Raven's age. It doesn't sit right with me. I call the number back from Raven's phone.

"Thank you for calling Madison General Hospital. Your call may be recorded for quality review. A representative will be with you shortly," the recording tells me. I hang the phone up. Well, that couldn't be less helpful. Maybe it was just a wrong number.

I head back upstairs to my room. He's awake and sitting at the foot of the bed when I walk in. I take a deep breath, preparing myself for what's to come next. Biting the bullet, I hold the phone out to him.

His expression is blank. "So, you're going through my phone now?"

"I wanted Helen's number," I reply, trying to remain calm. I wait for him to take the phone back, and when he doesn't, I sit down beside him.

"And why would you be calling Helen?" he asks sharply.

"Well, I thought she could tell me what happened yesterday, seeing as you don't feel the need to," I snap back at him.

His jaw clenches. "If I don't want to tell you, you should respect my decision," he says, rubbing his temples.

"And if I tell you that I need to know, you should respect that request and tell me," I retort.

He runs his hands through his hair, takes the phone from my hand, and turns his attention from me to it.

"I want to know what made you so upset yesterday and where you went," I say, trying to keep the edge from my voice.

"Helen couldn't fill you in on that, huh?" he says sarcastically.

"Now!"

"Here we fucking go," he says irately, slamming his phone on the bed.

"Is it just me, or does it seem that every time we take one step forward, you run two steps back?" I can feel my frustration level rising as I speak.

He stands up and turns, towering over me. "Because every time we're okay, you find something, anything, to start arguing with me about!" he yells.

"Cal, you left here visibly upset yesterday. You didn't tell me what was wrong. I tried to be there for you, and you kicked me out of the fucking car! Why would you think everything is okay after that?" I ask. He's far from stupid, but this is the dumbest shit I have ever heard come out of his mouth.

"Well, you seemed fine last night!" he says sarcastically.

"I wasn't fine! I knew that whatever you were going through, you were still dealing with. I knew that you needed my comfort, and that what I needed could wait. I compromised, that's what a marriage is about. Now it's your turn!" I shoot back.

He ignores me, grabbing his shirt from the bed and putting it on.

"I know that whatever it was, it wasn't about work. I want to know what it is," I say, walking behind him. He's ignoring me, pulling his shoes out from under the bed and putting them on. I see where this is going, so I quickly grab his keys from the dresser. He laughs in frustration.

"How do you think that makes me feel, as your wife? That you cut me off completely whenever you feel like it? That whatever happened, you won't even tell me; what am I supposed to think?"

"You're never satisfied. Every single day it's something. When I'm not here, I'm a jerk who doesn't spend time with you, but when I am here it's not for long enough, and when I'm here long enough, I'm not telling you every fucking detail on my mind?" he snarls as he finishes tying his shoes.

"That's not what this is, and you know it! What is going on?" I shout, feeling my throat starting to burn. "I should have done this a long time ago. I trust you with my life, Cal, and I've gotten nothing in return. I've tried waiting and waiting, trying to earn your trust. I fight with you to try to break down this emotional wall between us and nothing has worked, so tonight is the last night I'm going to wonder where you are, who you're with, or whatever it is . . ."

"You want it all out? Okay, let me tell you, Lauren," he yells sharply, interrupting me. "When I first met you, this was how I was. This is how I am, and I'm going to be like this tomorrow. You knew this when you met me! You accepted it then. I never promised you anything different. You're the one turning shit around. I've never lied to you! I tell you what you need to know. I'm not cheating on you. There is no other woman, and that's all you need to know!"

"You think I'm going to accept that?"

"Why not? Why do you focus on shit that isn't important? What's important is I am here! At the end of the day, all other bullshit aside, I'm here with you!" he yells.

"Because I'm your wife, Cal! I'm not a fucking pet," I shout back at him in disbelief. His hard frown softens, and he runs his hand through his hair. I wait for him to say something else, but he doesn't. I guess he really doesn't have to; what else can he say? He's told me exactly how he feels, and I can't deal with the fact that the man I've been so in love with, that I've compromised myself for, doesn't love me enough to trust me.

"Get out, Cal," I whisper.

"What?" he asks, as if he didn't hear me.

"Get the hell out," I growl.

"You're kidding." He lets out a light laugh. That sends me over the edge.

"Get out now! I can't even look at you anymore!" I yell so loud that I surprise myself.

"Lauren, what the fuck is your problem?" he shouts back.

"Cal, I swear to God, if you don't leave right now—"

He looks at me as if I'm speaking a different language, and I hear a knock at the door.

"Is everything okay in there?" Raven asks urgently on the other side of the door.

"Is it, Lauren?" His tone sounds dangerously like an ultimatum, but today is the wrong day for him to go there with me.

"It will be when you leave," I say, looking him straight in the eye.

"Lauren, Cal, open the door, please!" Her knocks turn into pounds.

I step back as Cal walks toward me, stopping only inches away.

"I don't know what's going on with you, but you need to fix it because next time you tell me to leave, I'm not coming back," he whispers coldly in my ear.

"If it's that simple for you, maybe you shouldn't." I hold the keys out and drop them. He's quick, though, neatly snagging them out of the air before they hit the ground. He licks his lips and smiles, then grabs his jacket and opens the door. Raven walks in, glancing back and forth between both of us. Cal stares back at me with a smirk on his face. I can't look at either one of them. I wrap my arms around myself and stare out the window.

"See you, Raven," I hear him say quietly.

"Goodbye, Cal," I hear her say, and she walks toward me slowly.

"Lauren?" she says quietly.

"Raven, I don't want to talk right now," I say in the most polite tone I can muster.

"Lauren, you can—" she tries to urge before I cut her off.

"Not now," I plead with her, heading to the bed.

"O-okay, sweetie. When you're ready to talk, you know where I am."

I nod, watching through the window as the Porsche pulls away.

October 2nd, 2008

I PLAY WITH my fingertips as I feel the elevator take off. It's a nervous habit, and I haven't been this nervous since I was in high school.

"Don't be nervous," Cal says, wrapping his arms around me.

"That's easy for you to say. Here I am about to meet two of the most important people in your life, and oh—by the way—they own most of everything in Chicago," I whine, resting my head on his chest. It's been almost six months since my whirlwind romance with Cal began, and he's still a mystery to me. I think this is a pretty big step in unraveling that mystery.

"Just pretend they couldn't buy and sell your soul if they wanted," he jokes.

"Oh, that makes me feel much more comfortable."

"Don't worry; they'll love you. Just be yourself." Cal nibbles on my ear, making me forget about my problem for a microsecond. I pull away from him as the doors of the elevator open.

"Come on." He takes my hand, leading the way out. I inhale deeply and follow him. Then my jaw drops as I see the huge hall that stretches before us.

"See? It's just like a museum." He winks, leading me down the empty corridor. In amazement, my eyes follow the paintings that line the walls. Each one is framed in what I assume is gold. I mean, why skimp on the frame when you can afford the masterpiece? I'm pulled out of my trance as I hear Mozart's Symphony #40, coming from the grand piano in the middle of the room, being played as easily as if it were a game of cards. Large, ornate double doors are partly open on the left, and we walk into an impressive parlor.

"Trying to show off again, Dex?" Cal interrupts the musician, announcing our arrival.

"You actually showed up on time? What's the occasion?" the man says, getting up from the piano. His eyes skim past Cal and land on me.

"Miss Brooks, I presume." He smiles knowingly. I swallow my nerves. He's a smaller man—maybe five nine—but taller than me, with almond-shaped brown eyes and dark hair; but for some reason, his presence intimidates me.

"Yes, I'm Lauren," I say awkwardly. I have no idea what's appropriate, so I just hold out my hand.

"I'm Dexter Crestfield," he replies, taking my hand, and to my surprise he brings it to his lips for a kiss. I can't help my giggle.

"Nice to meet you," I finally get out. Dexter Crestfield Jr., the man whose father is the richest man in the Midwest. I just read an article in the paper about him for a class, for God's sake.

"Your home is beautiful. As if you don't know that," I say like an idiot and step closer to Cal.

"I'll give my decorator your compliments." He walks over to the bar area and pulls down a couple of rocks glasses. "Would you like something to drink?"

"No, thank you." I feel like I need to let my nerves settle before I try to hold something breakable in my hands.

"Where's Helen?" Cal asks, taking off his jacket and tossing it onto a chair beside him as if he's at home. He gestures for me to sit next to him on the massive sectional sofa.

"She's around somewhere," Dexter replies, pouring what I assume is scotch into a glass.

"So, Lauren, Cal tells me you're an artist," Dexter says, taking a seat next to us.

"I wouldn't say that. I'm an art student," I say modestly.

"She's an artist; I've seen her work." Cal gets back up, walks over to an oddly placed pool table, and begins racking the balls.

"I'd always wanted to be an artist until I found out I lacked the patience," Dexter says. I see him look over, irritated at the noise Cal is making. "So, in one word, how would you describe Cal?" Dexter asks suddenly.

I'm a little caught off guard. "Umm. Cal is unique." *Unique? Where did that come from?*

"I've never been called unique before," Cal laughs, resting on the pool table.

"I think that's the most honest *flattering* description I've heard about him." Dexter laughs. "I like you already." His expression softens for the first time since I've met him. My nerves start to subside. Dexter seems pretty cool. I should have known Cal wouldn't hang out with people with sticks in their asses, even if he is his boss.

"Too bad; she's mine." Cal walks back over behind me on the couch and leans over to wrap his arms around me. His lips touch my neck, and I feel my cheeks heat up.

"Yes, you'll have to settle for me." A beautiful tall brunette woman comes in with a bag that distinctively says Harry Winston, and she tosses it to Dexter as if it were from Wal-Mart.

"How much is this going to cost me?" He looks up at the woman curiously.

"Nothing you can't afford," she retorts, then casually sits across his lap and pecks him on the lips. Her attention turns to Cal and me for the first time.

"You're on time," she tells Cal sarcastically.

"I'm not late that much," he defends himself.

"No, you just never show up when you say you will," she retorts with a smirk.

She turns her attention to me. "You must be Lauren," she says. Her eyes survey me as women usually do. She leaves Dexter's lap and offers her hand.

"I'm Helen, Dexter's wife," she explains as we shake hands.

"Very nice to meet you," I reply.

"So, has Cal been behaving himself?" she asks, giving Cal a faux warning look.

"I'm always on my best behavior."

"Of course you are."

"So, what's the plan for the evening?" Dexter breaks into the exchange.

"Well, I made a reservation for Luc to come and serve dinner at eight," Helen says with a toss of her hair. "Which is perfect since you and Cal should be back by then."

I see Cal shoot her a warning look.

"You're leaving?" I ask him tightly. He has said nothing about leaving me here alone. Helen seems nice and all, but the whole reason I did this was to finally meet the people closest to him. I didn't want to just be dumped on his best friend's wife. I look behind me to see him standing there with his hands in his pockets. The tension in the room goes up a notch.

"Helen, how about you come show me what else you bought, because I know this isn't all of it," Dexter says, excusing him and Helen. When they've disappeared from the room, I stand up to face Cal. He walks toward me, but I look away from him. This was not part of *my* plan for the evening. He wraps his arms tightly around my waist, pulling me against him

"I won't be gone that long," he promises, caressing my back, which always distracts me from what he's saying. "It'll give you and Helen some time to get to know each other," he says, slipping his hand under my blouse. I step away from him. I'm can feel my temperature rising, and by that sly grin on his face, I see that he can too. He puts his fingers through a belt loop on my pants and pulls me back toward him, our chests colliding.

"I'll make it up to you," he whispers before covering my mouth with his, biting my lower lip gently. I feel his hands slide down my back, his warmth sending sensations through my body that are completely uncalled for at this moment. I wrap my arms around his neck when he deepens the kiss. He always does this. I can be completely focused on what he's saying or what I'm saying, and then he goes and kisses me like this and everything just seems unimportant. He pulls away with a satisfied grin resting on this face.

"You're good?" he says quietly, knowing I'm okay. I nod and lick my lips.

"Dex says he'll meet you downstairs." Helen's voice interrupts us and I remember we're in someone else's house. Helen is walking back into the room. An amused look spreads over Cal's face at my reaction and he lets me go. I glance at Helen in total embarrassment, but she just smiles as she flops on the couch and crosses her legs.

"I'll see you later, okay?" he says and steals a kiss from my neck.

"Stay out of trouble," Helen says in a motherly tone as he grabs his jacket.

"Don't I always?" He winks at us both before leaving the room. I fold my arms around myself. Here I am in a strange house with a woman I don't know at all. What's there to be nervous about? I expect awkwardness to fill the room, but before it does, she begins to speak.

"You'll get used to that," she says, lighting a cigarette.

I look at her curiously. "Used to what?" I ask, hoping she's not a chain smoker. I have to deal with enough of them at work.

"Oh, sweetie." She laughs and walks toward me. I hold my breath from the smoke. "We have a lot to talk about." She smiles deviously before linking arms with me. "Let's go on the terrace," she says, leading the way. I can already see this night is going to be interesting.

WHEN WE REACH the terrace, my jaw drops to the floor. I thought Cal's view from the penthouse was amazing.

"Beautiful, isn't it?" she says, making herself comfortable at a beautifully set table to the right of us. "I was the same way when I first saw it."

There's all-white furniture on the terrace, which stretches for miles, and candles are alight, drowning out the smell of her cigarette before we reach the door.

"Of course it wasn't like this," she says, waving her hand at the impeccable outdoor furniture and luscious greenery that lines the balcony wall, "but I saw the potential."

"You did this?" I ask in shock as I sit down in a seat next to her. It's in a completely different tone from the Gothic rooms that I walked through.

"Well, the design and such. I told the decorator exactly what I wanted and she did it," she says, putting out her cigarette.

"This is so beautiful," I admit, still taking in my surroundings.

"Thank you. I wish Dexter would let me have my way with the rest of the house, but he says a man's house is his kingdom, or something to that effect," she explains with another toss of her hair. This seems to be her signature move, and she uses it to very good effect.

"So, give me the story of you and Cal. I know the watered down version Dex passed on to me. Men are so vague about things like that." She rests her chin in her palm as if she's ready to hear a good tale.

I exhale. I don't really like getting into details, either. I never feel comfortable talking to people about things like that. "Well, we met at the place I work. I ran into him, literally, and he spilled a drink on me," I tell her, remembering the night that shaped the past few months of my life.

"And how long have you been seeing each other?"

"About five months." Actually, it's been five months and fourteen days, but who's counting?

"And now I'm here to get approval from you guys, I suppose," I laugh, feeling a bit more comfortable with her.

"Oh no, Lauren, don't worry about us. Cal does what he wants. He's here to show you off," she states in a matter-of-fact tone. "In fact, just between you and me?" She leans in as if she's giving away a top secret. "You're the first girl he's brought to meet us, or at least me." She winks at me. I can't help but smile, but for some reason, knowing that makes me feel nervous all over again.

"So, there must be something to you other than being stunning." Helen giggles. I blush at the compliment. "Dex and Cal have a thing for beautiful women, and beautiful women have a thing for them." She sighs, shifting in her seat. I swallow my nerves, but she notices my expression. "Don't worry; it takes more than a pretty face to sway them. They aren't idiots like the average male." She chuckles.

"How long have you known Cal?" I ask, still feeling a little uneasy.

"Let's see, I think this year, about six years. Yeah, that's about right."

"So Dexter and Cal are really close?"

"Like brothers. It's good for them, especially since Dex is an only child, and Cal doesn't really have anyone." I can't help but feeling sad at the last part of what she says. I knew Cal was adopted, but I never really thought about him not having anyone. I know his parents have always been a sore subject. After my parents' death, I felt alone, but really I always had a great relationship with Raven. I just assumed he and his adopted parents were cordial, if not close.

"How did you and Dexter meet?" I ask, changing the subject. She smiles softly.

"He was at a benefit for Chicago General, where I used to work. I didn't know who the hell he was, but he walks up to me and says, 'I'll donate a million dollars tonight if you go out with me.' Now here I am, disgusted by this audacious man, who, I assume, is a liar. So I told him, 'If you donate a million dollars, I'll run around this hotel naked,' so he laughs and walks away. I didn't think anything else of it. Ten minutes later, the superintendent of the hospital announces that Dexter Crestfield Jr. has just donated ten million dollars to the hospital, and when I see him walk up there, my heart just stops." She starts to laugh and I join in with her.

"It gets better. After his speech—during which, by the way, he held eye contact with me the entire time—he walks right up to me, leans over, and whispers, 'I'd prefer my house,' and leaves me his number," she finishes with a grin on her face.

"Wow," I say, shocked. "That's a great story."

"Yeah, he's such a snide son of a bitch. But I like that about him, and he's sweet when he wants to be."

"Well, you know what I mean. Cal is a cocky bastard himself."

I've never thought of him as cocky, more so confident. He doesn't care what anyone says or thinks about him because he knows that they all either want to be him or sleep with him, depending on their preferences. He does what he wants, when he wants. It's just routine.

"Enough about us. What about you. Kids, marriage?" she asks, lighting up another cigarette.

"With Cal?" I ask, confused.

"Well, yes, or period," she says, taking a drag.

"I, well, we haven't known each other that long." I stutter a little over the answer. She's really getting to the point, isn't she?

"Well, are you the type of girl who dreams about getting married or wants to put it off as long as possible?"

"I see myself married with a family one day. I'd love to travel abroad then come back and do something that really makes a difference, but I don't know. Marriage at least is pretty far away." I laugh.

"You never know." She chuckles. I look at the sunset. "What I mean is that I was the same way. When I met Dex, I planned to just have fun with him and ended up falling in love. Two years later, he asked me to marry him, and no one says no to a Crestfield." She laughs, putting her cigarette out. She then pulls out a pack of gum.

"For some reason, I don't think Cal is the marrying type." I laugh.

Helen walks to the ledge and sits on it. "Trust me, the worst thing you could do with Cal is assume." She turns her attention away from me to the sky. I wonder what she means, but I don't question her any further. I almost feel like I'd be going into territory Cal wouldn't want me to. The sunset settling on the horizon is amazing.

"Would you like a piece?" she says, offering up the pack of Winterfresh.

"Thanks." I guess you have to keep gum when you smoke. I look up and see Helen staring at me. I look away quickly.

"Lauren, I'm going to share something with you." My stomach drops at her sudden change of tone. "I don't know how you feel about Cal. From what I can tell, you really like him. From what Dexter tells me, he really cares about you. I've known Cal for so long, he's like a brother to me. I'm going to tell you this, something I wish someone had told me so I didn't have to learn it the hard way. Dexter is a very complicated person, and so is Cal. There are going to be times when you won't know what his problem is, but for there to be any hope for you two to have a meaningful relationship, you need to have full acceptance of this. You're going to have to accept him for who he is—all of him—even the part that you may never know . . ." She breaks her serious expression, and the whimsical grin from earlier returns.

"Who knows, maybe Cal isn't like Dexter. Maybe he'll be a lot more open with you than Dex is with me. It doesn't bother me at all. Frankly, the less I know the better, but some people can't handle that." Her gaze is intense and makes me uncomfortable. Suddenly, I feel as if I'm on trial. I clear my throat. "It is getting chilly out here; I'm going to go inside." She stands up.

"I think I'm going to stay out here little while longer," I tell her.

"Okay, I'm going downstairs. Luc should have arrived by now. I'm going to see how he's doing. The kitchen is on the first floor, far left. You'll see it as soon as you get there," she explains. I nod.

"Well, that's where I'll be. If you want a jacket, we have some in the closet in the room we went through to get here; just grab one."

"I'm fine. I just want to soak this all in, if you don't mind."

"I understand completely. Come down when you get ready, or wander wherever you want to go in the house. Make yourself at home—just don't get lost." She laughs before leaving.

THE SUN HAS fully set, and the sky is black with the stars and candles lighting my space. I don't know how long I've been sitting out here. I've been trying to analyze and justify the words Helen so kindly shared with me.

I try to make light of the heavy words hidden behind her whimsical, sarcastic demeanor as she spoke.

They scare me, and I don't know why. I've been with Cal for five months and my feelings have grown stronger every day I'm with him, but I haven't thought about marriage. Sure, I've fantasized about it but not taken it seriously. I know I can't see myself married to a man who has a world full of secrets. I'm just being silly; there's no way I'd marry Cal and feel like I didn't know him. That just wouldn't happen. Besides, Dexter and Cal are two different people, even if what she said is true. Or maybe she's looking for something that isn't there or trying to scare me off. I'm snapped out of my thoughts when I feel a warm hand slip up the back of my shirt. I turn to see Cal smiling at me. He sits beside me and pulls me onto his lap.

"What's wrong?" he asks, searching my eyes.

"Nothing. Why?" His body heat surrounds me, and I realize how cold I am.

"Well, I come out here expecting some kind of welcome, and you sit here in a daze. You didn't even realize I was here. I'm a little insulted." He smirks.

"Just daydreamin. .," I say, resting my head on his shoulder.

"Liar." He laughs, but drops the subject. "How long have you been out here?" he asks, wrapping his jacket over my shoulders.

I smile thankfully. "About half an hour." Well, more like an hour and a half.

"How'd you like Helen?" he asks curiously.

"She's nice," I say before kissing him softly on the lips.

"Nice. Helen isn't nice; she intimidates, manipulates, and frustrates. And that's when she likes you." He laughs, amused.

I roll my eyes playfully. "Then why did you leave me with her?"

"I knew you could handle it." He glides his lips across my neck and then brushes them across my lips. "So, what'd she say about me?" he mumbles. He's such a tease sometimes.

"Other than you're a ruthless playboy who breaks hundreds of girls' hearts? Nothing much," I kid before giving in to his teasing and entangling his lips with mine. I pull away to catch my breath and look into his eyes.

"What?" he asks curiously. Maybe Helen was just manipulating me, like he said earlier. Maybe she's wrong; she has to be.

"Nothing." I smile.

May 11th, 2011

I WONDER IF it's too late to turn things around, if I've accepted the way things are for too long. Is it too late for him to break the hard mold he's created around himself? He says he wants me to accept him for who he is, but how can I do that when I'd be settling for a person I can never fully know? Accepting him this way would turn me into a doormat. I-I can't, can I? I take a deep breath and finish placing the last item into my suitcase and grab my keys from the dresser. I glance in the mirror, assessing my appearance. My face is tired; even after showering and applying a bit of makeup, my eyes are still puffy from crying all night. I don't want to give up on him—on us—but he has to see that I'm serious. Yes, I told him to go, and I wanted him to at that moment, but the root of the problem is that he's so far away from me. Now he is, both literally and figuratively.

I slip on the pair of Chuck Taylors that are older than my marriage, but are more comfortable than the five-inch heeled boots I wore here and more suited to the wide-legged jeans and t-shirt I'm wearing.

I grab my bag and the handle on my suitcase and drag it downstairs and into the kitchen, where Raven is sitting down with a cup of tea in hand. She smiles as I enter, her eyes drifting to the bag on my shoulder.

"Let me get you some tea," she says quickly. I start to protest but realize it's easier to just accept it. "I thought you'd sleep later," she says, pouring me a cup. I set my bag down on the floor and take a seat across from her.

"No. I wanted to get an early start," I tell her, taking the cup as she offers.

"On what?" she asks before taking a seat next to me.

"I'm leaving."

"You're going back home?"

"No," I say after taking a sip of tea. "I'm going to stay with a friend in Chicago for a while—until I decide what I'm going to do," I tell her.

"Lauren, I wish you'd stay here. I don't—"

"I need to get away. Not away from you. I just need a change of scenery," I interrupt. I see she doesn't approve, but she doesn't protest either.

"Are you going to be driving?"

"No. I'm leaving the car here. There won't be anywhere to park. I called a cab to take me to the bus station, and I'll take that the rest of the way."

"I'll drive you," she offers.

"No, it wouldn't make sense for you to drive me all the way to Chicago, then drive all the way back right after."

"It's fine. I don't have much to do today anyway," she says, pouring me some more tea, though my cup is far from empty.

"No, Raven, it's not necessary, and the ride there will give me some time to clear my head," I tell her, desperately not wanting to argue with her.

"Well, at least let me drop you off at the station," she says in a pleading tone.

I sigh, feeling a small smile spread across my face. I give in. "Okay."

"So, who is this friend you're going to be staying with?" she asks curiously.

"Someone I used to work with," I say, running my finger around the rim of the cup.

"This is a woman, right?" she asks nervously.

My eyes widen in surprise. "Of course," I say quickly.

"I was just asking." She smiles, relieved. I can't help but giggle. If Cal found out I was staying with a man, I can't even imagine what he'd do. He's never been the jealous type. He never needed to be. I've only had eyes for him since we've been together. No other guy could stand a chance, and he knew that. But if he even thought it, I'd hate to see what he'd do. I've only seen his temper once in my life, and it was like a lion was let out of the cage. He was furious; I'd never want to make him like that.

"How long are you going to stay with this friend?" she asks, taking the cup from me that I've only taken a sip from.

"I don't know. I just—I need to get away from everything I've gotten used to." I sigh.

Raven continues to busy herself about the kitchen, then turns to face me with her hands on her hips.

"Well, I'd really like for you to stay here and let me help you with whatever it is you're dealing with. But whatever you feel you need to do, know I support you one hundred percent."

I can't help but smile. Sometimes Raven just surprises me. She does the exact opposite of what I think she's going to do. I get up from my seat and hug her tightly, recognizing the scent of her perfume from when I was younger.

"Thank you," I tell her quietly, taking a cleansing breath.

"Everything will be fine, sweetie," she says, rubbing my back.

"I hope so. I-I don't want lose my marriage. It's just starting to be so much. I think taking a step back from all of the issues we're dealing with would be good for both of us."

"This is just a rocky time. Every marriage has them," she tells me, hugging me a little tighter. She stands back and lifts my chin up. "It's the strong ones that make it through them," she says, with a stern smile. I nod, wiping away the tears building in my eyes.

"In fact, this will be good for you, some time to find yourself. Sometimes you forget about yourself when you've been with another person so long." She smiles, putting in place a stray hair. I pictured this conversation going differently. I thought she'd tell me to stop being so sensitive and stick by my husband.

"What?" she asks with a smile.

"It's just, I thought you would take Cal's side on this," I tell her.

"Lauren, I don't really know what's going on between you two to take anyone's side. But you're my niece and I love you. I care about Cal very much, but if he's making you feel like this, I can't stick up for him. You come first. In the end, I'm going to support you, right or wrong. But I don't see you being wrong on this."

I hug her again.

"LAUREN, WE'RE HERE," Raven says, nudging me gently. I open my eyes and see that we're parked in front of the bus station. I stretch lightly. I feel like I've been asleep for hours, and could still sleep several more days.

"Honey, are you okay?" she asks, eyeing me with a worried expression.

"Yeah, just tired," I tell her, gathering my bag off the floor and setting it on my lap.

"I was talking, and before I knew it, you had drifted off to sleep. I hope I wasn't that boring." She smiles, and I return it.

"Not at all; I just didn't get much sleep last night," I assure her.

Her expression shows she's not convinced. "You're sure you don't want me to drive you? It'll be no trouble," she tells me again.

"I'm going to be fine. I'll feel better knowing that you won't be driving back from Chicago alone," I tell her as I get out of the car. I walk around to her side, and she steps out.

"I guess there's no convincing you otherwise," she relents. I laugh at her persistence, and she sighs. "Well, honey, be safe," she says, pulling me into a long hug.

"I will," I promise her.

"I'd feel a lot better if you gave me this *friend's* number." She frowns. I shake my head. I would, but Raven would just call a thousand times to make sure I was okay, not to mention the fact that I don't want Cal to know where I am right now. And as many times as Raven says she wouldn't give it to him or tell him where I am, I know how convincing Cal can be. He is a master in the art of persuasion, and anyone not immune to it gives into him within minutes.

"Do you want me to wait with you until the bus gets here?"

"No, thank you, I'm fine. It should be here soon . . . See? There it is." I point to the bus pulling into the loading area.

"Okay, honey." She smiles weakly and gives me another hug.

"You call me the minute you get to your friend's house, okay?" she warns me.

"I will. The moment I hit the door," I assure her as she hesitantly gets back into her car.

She pauses to look at me one more time, her hand on the keys. "I promise," I tell her. She smiles and blows me a kiss before she finally pulls off. I reposition the strap of the bag on my shoulder and head to the booth to buy a ticket.

"WE'RE HERE," THE tall, gray-haired man tells me. I smile awkwardly.

"How much is it?" I ask him, opening my bag for my wallet.

"Twenty sixty-two," he replies. I hand him a twenty and a five.

"Thank you, ma'am. Have a good one," he says.

"You too," I say, getting out of the cab.

"No problem," he says before pulling off. It's almost eerie how quiet the street is when it is so near downtown Chicago. Usually there's the noise of cars, people, or music playing loudly, the soundtrack of the city. I look at the names listed next to the doorbells and smile when I see Davis. I push it in and wait for a response.

"Who is it?" I hear her voice ask. I smile widely.

"It's Lauren." I giggle.

"LAUREN! I'm coming right down."

I can't help but laugh; her excitement is contagious. A few moments later, the front door swings open and she almost knocks me on the floor with her hug.

"I can't believe you're here. Oh my God!" she shouts in my ear as I try to keep my balance.

"Yeah, I'm here." Somehow, I don't feel like I'm matching her energy.

"I thought you were lying about coming, still. You always say you're coming, and then call with an excuse." She laughs at me, taking my bag.

"Well, not this time." I sigh.

"Come on," she says, leading me up the stairs. I take in the surroundings of the building; it reminds me of my apartment in college. The white walls, wooden floors, and windows letting the sun pour through them.

"These stairs have made me lose at least five pounds." She laughs as we round another flight. But by the time we make it to her apartment, she's huffing and muttering under her breath, "I hate living on the third floor." Putting her hand on the doorknob, she announces, "This is it!" and leads me in, shutting the door behind us.

"It's kind of small, but I love the neighborhood. It's always quiet since there's a hospital up the street, but it's still near the city. They have this quiet zone thing," she tells me. I smile as I look around the small apartment and walk to the window with the sun seeping through, lighting the entire room. I close my eyes as it falls on my face and open them again when I hear her footsteps coming in my direction. "So this is it. Like I said, it's small, and you'd have the couch," she explains.

"The couch is fine," I assure her. She gives me another big smile. That's one reason I love being around Angela—she always has a way of looking at things positively, and there's only been a few times I've ever seen her sad or mad at anything.

"I still can't believe you're here." She laughs, linking arms with me. She leads me to the off-white sofa situated behind a wooden coffee table. "So, how have things been going?" she asks, making herself comfortable. I debate whether to tell her the truth with a fake smile, or just pour out all my problems to her.

"Okay." I sigh, deciding to go with the less time-consuming route. She frowns at me.

"Okay?" she asks sarcastically. I nod and start to play with my fingertips.

She sighs. "Well, I know something's wrong, but I'm not going to pester you, since I have a feeling you're not going to tell me now."

I giggle. She still knows me so well.

Now it's my turn to sigh. "Cal and I aren't the best of friends right now," I say tightly.

Her smile immediately softens. "Do you want to talk about it?"

This is why I love Angie; any other person would just dive into the questions without considering how I felt about it. "Not really. Right now, I'm so tired I just want to sleep," I tell her.

"Of course! Well, I have class in, like, thirty, so you're more than welcome to crash in my bed to get some rest," she offers.

"Oh no, this is fine." I gesture to the couch.

"Are you sure?"

"I just spent the last half hour in a cramped cab; this is a vast improvement." I laugh.

She stands up. "Well, let me go get you some sheets and pillows," she says, disappearing for a moment and coming back with a crisp pink sheet and pillow. She sets them next to me.

"Thanks," I say gratefully. "I see you're still into pink." I giggle.

"Look who's talking." She nudges me playfully, referring to my stint of wearing various shades of pink for at least a year; I needed something to brighten up my then-dull life, and it seemed like a good idea at the time.

"So, my class is over in three hours, and after that I'm going to head to the library for maybe an hour or two. When I come back, you be all rested up so we can do the girl talk thing and order some takeout, okay?" she says, grabbing a brush and quickly running it through her hair.

"That sounds good," I tell her, slipping out of my tennis shoes.

"Lauren, how old are those?" she squeals.

I cover my face in embarrassment. "They're the only flats I have," I admit, and we both break into a fit of laughter.

"Wow. Anyhow, there's some leftover pizza in the fridge, which you're welcome to, though I wouldn't recommend it. Pepsi is all I have to drink—I've become addicted—and if you want to take a shower, turn it on ten minutes before; it takes forever to heat up, believe me," she explains, grabbing her backpack off the table in the kitchen. "The bathroom is back there next to my room. I don't have to show you the kitchen, and yeah—" she gestures quickly.

"I feel so bad about leaving you here alone when you just got here. I feel like I should be showing you around or something," she whines.

"Ang, it's not like I'm a tourist; you don't have to show me around.

And I did kind of call you on short notice. I'll be fine," I reassure her.

"I know. I still feel really bad, but I'll have to do that later." She laughs, grabbing her keys off the table. "If I miss the bus I'm virtually screwed," she says, rushing to the door.

"Like I said, mi casa, su casa," she tells me before she exits, and I hear the lock click on the door.

I look around the cozy little apartment, remembering the days when Hillary and I used to room together. How tiny our apartment was, but how warm it felt. That's exactly what's missing from my own home—warmth and happiness. I search for a phone, hoping she has one, and spot a cordless on the kitchen table. I dial Raven's number.

"Raven, it's me. I've made it safely. I just got here a few minutes ago, and just wanted to let you know. I'm really tired, so I'll call you again tonight. Love you," I say after the beep and hang up. I crawl back onto the sofa and spread the sheet over my head. There aren't any lights on, but the sun is filling the apartment. My eyes are so heavy they feel like bricks. At last, I let them close.

"LAUREN, LAUREN." I open my eyes to see Angie standing over me.

"Hey," I say, starting to wake myself up.

"You've been sleep this entire time?" she asks, turning on a lamp beside us. My eyes adjust to it; the sun has completely set.

"I guess so," I tell her groggily, sitting up on the couch.

"Are you feeling okay?" she asks worriedly.

"Yeah, I've just been really tired," I tell her.

She feels my head. "You're warm. Do you feel sick?"

"No, I feel fine. I just haven't been getting much sleep," I lie. I've been getting tons. It seems as if all I've done is sleep—or cry.

"Are you sure?" she asks skeptically.

"I'm completely fine," I assure her. The last thing I need is another person worrying about me; that's the reason I left Raven's house.

"Okay, well I picked up some Chinese on the way home. I thought you would have been up by now." She giggles, grabbing a remote. The stereo comes on. "We need some life in this house." She laughs, starting to shake her hips to the beat. I laugh at her as she shimmies toward me with the most serious face in the world. "I've seen you shake it at the club. Don't act all shy," she warns me then grabs my hand and leads me to the kitchen.

"What did you get?" I ask, hearing my stomach growl.

"Fried rice, orange chicken, and onion pancakes" she says, passing me a plate and silverware.

"So, how is grad school going?" I ask her as I wash my hands.

"Boring and difficult, but it beats getting a job." She laughs, grabbing an onion pancake and sitting on the counter. I roll my eyes playfully. Angela's parents have agreed to pay for everything she wants or needs as long as she's in school, and she's taken it to the extreme.

"Come on, don't look at me; Cal spoils you rotten." She giggles.

"Well, that's because he's never home," I say dryly, taking a seat at the table.

Her expression softens, and she sits down next to me. "Is he still working for Crestfield Corp?" she asks casually.

I nod.

"Long hours?" she says skeptically.

"Yeah, maybe that's it." I laugh to myself sarcastically.

"You don't think he's cheating on you, do you?"

"He says he isn't, but how many cheating husbands tell their wives that?"

"Do you believe him?"

"Our problems, I believe, are much bigger than a woman, but I can't rule it out." I laugh, pouring myself some fried rice. I take a spoonful, feeling awkwardness fill the room.

"What can be bigger than an affair?" she asks suddenly.

"I wish I knew," I say, pushing my plate away. I've suddenly lost my appetite.

"You know, when you called me, I was sort of surprised, to say the least," she reveals.

"I'm sorry about the lack of information; I just needed to get away,"

"It's okay. I know how it is." She smiles warmly. "I remember how you and Cal were, how in love you guys were. Not to mention how extremely jealous me and Hillary were." She laughs. "I mean, he was incredibly hot." She sighs.

I smile. "He still is," I admit.

"You remember Devon? I'd want to jump his ass whenever I saw him. The problem was that so would every other woman that saw him." She laughs.

"Devon, the basketball player, right?" I ask, as if I didn't know. He was unforgettable, with tanned skin, cold black hair, and a pair of greenish eyes.

"Yep, and every city he played in he had at least three women." She giggles. "You know, I've dated Asian, Black, Hispanic—oh, and Italian—and honey, you know what they all have in common? The inability to understand the concept of being in a monogamous relationship," she explains with a frown, pouring more rice on my plate. "I'm determined to find one though. Up until now I've had the worst taste in men."

I feel sad for my friend. I remember her and Devon and how infatuated she was with him. He was beautiful, but Angela matched him in looks, having caramel-colored skin, exotic eyes, and a face that could pull off short hair. She attracted men of all kinds, just never the right ones.

"Don't we all," I mumble, taking another bite.

"Well, at least we're as not bad as Hillary. That girl could pick the devil himself out in a line-up." She sighs.

"Yeah, the only good guy she had was John, and she dumped him for that terrible jerk, Aaron."

"God, I thought *I* could pick bad ones. She takes the cake though."

My thoughts drift away from Angela's voice. I remember all too clearly the night that I saw how bad a man could be, how truly helpless and lost a woman could be. That same night, I saw a side of Cal I never wanted to see again, but a small part of me was thankful it was there.

April 2nd, 2009

"I'LL NEVER GET tired of this," I say while resting my head on Cal's chest. The roof of his building has one of the best views of Chicago.

"Then get used to it." He smirks, unfazed. I roll my eyes playfully and ignore him to look up at the sky. I've grown quite accustomed to his aloofness over things that I'm quite fascinated with.

"I could stay here forever." I sigh, gazing up at the stars. I glance up at Cal, whose intoxicating gray eyes are allowing faint hues of green to shine. God, when he looks at me like that . . .

"What?" I ask with a smile. He laughs lightly.

"You're no good for me," he says, wrapping his arm tighter around my waist. I look at him with a perplexed expression.

"Why is that?" I ask playfully. He pauses.

"You remind me of something," he says quietly. I arch my eyebrow in question. "It's not another girl." He laughs, feeling my unspoken jealously.

"Then who?" I ask curiously, and his smile softens.

"More of a feeling, anyway," he mumbles, running his hands through my hair.

"Is that so bad?" I ask with a smile.

"I don't know yet," he says before he presses his lips against mine, pulling me into a sensual kiss. It still makes me lightheaded.

"No, you're no good for me," I giggle.

He smiles. "And why is that?" His fingers are trailing down my stomach.

"You distract me," I tell him, ignoring the chills he's giving me.

"From what?" He grins mischievously and continues his path.

"From things I'm supposed to concentrate on, like life, bills, school," I begin to rattle off.

"Well, that's boring," he states plainly, starting to unbutton my shirt.

"You know everyone can't live your life. Stealing away on jets, living in an expensive penthouse, doing whatever you please," I tell him, trying to focus on my words and not the tightness in my stomach.

"Well, they should," he says before his lips find my neck and kiss it hungrily.

"The world would be in chaos," I explain to him as he continues to undress me. Little does he know, I will not be letting him have his way with me on this roof. I mean, I *probably* won't.

"I've lived life the other way. It wasn't too interesting," he mumbles, pursuing my lips with his.

Before I get lost in his kiss, I pull away. "And when was this? In between you jumping out of planes or jumping off buildings?" I purr, wrapping my arms around him.

"Another lifetime." He grins, massaging the back of my thighs. "*This* is how you should live."

"I'm sure everyone would like to live like this, but this is a fantasy. You can't live like this every day."

"I do."

"Well, that's because you're *unique*," I tease him, remembering the word I used when Dexter asked me to describe him. It still seems to fit.

"Normal is boring; it's getting up every day, working a nine-to-five at a job you hate, coming home to the little wife and monsters running around the house, then going to sleep and starting over again. I don't want the highlight of my life to be getting a promotion and still earning less than fifty grand a year." His voice is lighthearted, but there is seriousness in his eyes.

"Life doesn't have to be like that. Marriage doesn't have to be routine, your kids don't have to be screaming monsters." I chuckle.

"Why work all your life with nothing to show for it, only wishing for things that you could never afford? Dreaming about places you'll never get to go? I wouldn't trade this for normality. It's overrated," he mumbles, getting up from the hammock.

"You make it sound like all you care about is money."

"It's not. It's about living life to the fullest. Doing what you want instead of just fantasizing about it. You need money to do that," he says, as if it's simple.

"There's more to life than traveling the world and living by the moment, Cal. Those things are great, but what makes it enjoyable is that you're getting away. If you're doing it all the time, what's the point? What about having a family, settling down?" I ask him.

"You hear what you said? Settle? I never plan to settle for anything," he states.

His words sting me. Getting married and having a family is settling? Is this, now, all there is to him? Doing what he wants and not considering anything else? And where do I fit into this equation? I've been with him a year and I don't really know. My feelings for him are getting stronger every day I spend with him, and all of these feelings are entangled with lust.

It scares me that I'm too afraid to ask these questions because, well, I'm not sure that I even want to know the answers. Cal is unlike anyone I've ever met. I'm important in his life today, but what happens when I'm not? I've seen how quickly he gets bored with things.

It was inevitable that I'd develop feelings for him after all the time we've spent together. He makes me feel like no one else has. A year has passed like moments and when I'm with him, time isn't really a factor. I wrap my arms around myself, feeling the cold now that I'm out of Cal's arms. I let out a much-needed sigh. My phone rings, and I ignore it.

"So, is that what I am to you? A little bit of fun, something you just want to do for a while?" I ask.

He walks over to me and lifts me into his arms. "The reason you scare me is because you're not," he whispers in my ear. I look into his eyes, feeling helpless. This man could easily break my heart. He stole it with a smile, and I don't think I want it back.

"Do you want me to be?" I ask him, taking a cleansing breath. He lifts my chin so I can see him.

"Never." He gives me a boyish grin.

He still gives me butterflies, and his touch has given me tingles since the time we first met.

"I'm still not entirely comfortable around you," I say honestly.

"That's a good thing; when you're comfortable, that's when you get bored."

"Tell me what doesn't bore you?" I ask him sarcastically.

"I can think of a few things," he says with a mischievous grin.

My phone rings again. It's the ring tone I specially assigned to Angela. She wouldn't call me twice in a row unless it was something important. I slink out of his arms to pick up my phone and answer it.

"Hey, Angela. What's up?" I giggle, ignoring Cal's hands roaming down my body.

"Lauren . . . Hillary's here. I . . . I don't know what to do . . . She doesn't want me to call the police." Her voice is shaky and high pitched.

"The police? Hold on, Angie, what happened?" Cal stops bothering me and looks on, concerned.

"She got into a fight with her boyfriend; she's really bad, Lauren. I don't know what to do," she explains.

"He hit her?" I ask in disbelief.

"It's really bad this time." Her voice wavers as if she is about to cry. *Oh God, I can't believe this!*

"This time?" I ask frantically.

"She didn't want me to tell you. She knew you'd want to go to the police. I'm sorry, I didn't know it'd go this far."

I can feel myself shaking. "I'm on my way," I tell her quickly, hanging up the phone. I can feel tears welling in my eyes.

"What's wrong?" Cal looks concerned.

"Hillary's boyfriend beat her up," I tell him quickly.

"Lauren, calm down. I'm coming with you," he says adamantly.

"No, I need to do this alone." *Dammit!* If I hadn't been living in fantasyland with him, I would have known how bad this was. I could have helped her. I haven't been doing much of anything except Cal. I knew this guy was bad news and I ignored it because Hillary gushed about him so much. But if I had been home, I could have seen it; I would have known.

Cal holds my shoulders to steady me. "Lauren, this is not your fault," he says, reading my mind. "I'm coming with you. You're too upset to drive," he says authoritatively as I button my top up, shaking my head in defiance. This is a personal time for her; I'm sure Hillary doesn't want me bringing him along.

"Let me help you," he pleads, grasping my wrist as I try to walk away. I can't push him away if I want him to let me in.

"Okay."

"ANGELA?" I CALL out. After I spot her sitting alone in the waiting area, I rush to her side. When she called me saying they were going to the ER, my heart almost stopped at the idea that Hillary was hurt that badly.

"Hey, Lauren," she says, hugging me tightly.

"Hi Cal," she says in a strained voice.

"Hey," he replies, taking a place beside me. Angela's eyes are red and puffy; her hair is wrapped under a silk scarf.

"Where is she?" I ask urgently.

"They have her in the back. She just got back from radiology. The last nurse I talked to says she has a broken rib," she explains, her voice wavering.

"Oh my God," I say, feeling my eyes start to water.

"It's really bad; this is the worst he's done. Her face is . . ." She breaks down, and I hold her in my arms, crying with her.

"I called her parents. They're on their way," she mumbles.

"It's my fault. I should have done something. She kept telling me not to tell anyone and it was only when he was drunk," she cries into my shoulder.

"This isn't your fault," I try to convince her. She only did what Hillary asked her to, but I wish she had at least told me. However, Angela's word is her bond; she's one of the most trustworthy people I know.

"How could I not know this was going on?" I mumble to myself.

"I'll go get you both something to drink," Cal says, giving us needed privacy.

"When she called me, she sounded so normal. But when I got to your place and saw her I . . . I panicked. I'd never seen anyone look like that in real life, face to face. When you see what this jerk did to her—" She growls angrily.

"Did you call the police?"

"No. She told me not to, but the doctors have tried to ask me questions."

I look at her as if she just lost her mind. I haven't seen Hillary yet, but based on what she just described, I can't believe they didn't call them.

"I know, I know! But she begged me. When the doctors asked me what happened, she didn't even want me to tell them," she explains herself quickly.

"She doesn't want him get away with this, does she?" I can't believe what I'm hearing.

"I honestly don't know. It's like he's brainwashed her. I'm hoping this will be a wakeup call. But she said she didn't want me to call the police or tell the doctors he did it to her," Angela explains, still visibly upset.

"Excuse me." A petite blonde woman approaches us.

"Lauren, this is Dr. Carsons," Angela says, sniffling.

I reach my hand out and she shakes it. "How is she?" I ask anxiously.

"She has a broken rib, facial swelling, various abrasions, and bruises. I've seen a lot worse; thankfully, there's no internal bleeding," the doctor explains. I can't believe this is happening.

"She'll be fine. However, the detective would like to ask you some questions." She gestures to Angela. She looks at me skeptically, and I nod my head for her to go.

"Would you like to see her?" the doctor asks me. I nod quickly and she leads me to her area. Dr. Carsons opens the curtains and my heart stops as soon as I see her. Her face is so swollen and discolored, if it weren't for her long blonde hair with pink tips, I wouldn't recognize her.

"Hey," Hillary says, her tone surprisingly cheerful.

"Oh my God," I mumble to myself.

"It's not that bad, Lauren." She laughs weakly.

I walk over to her slowly and pull up a chair. "You don't think *this* is bad?" I ask in disbelief.

"I mean, it looks worse than it is." She sighs.

"Hillary, why didn't you tell me?" I ask pleadingly.

"I didn't tell anyone, Lauren," she says softly.

"You told Angela," I retort.

"She found out by accident. I didn't plan to tell her. I didn't want to tell anyone. I was embarrassed. I never thought I'd be the girl whose boyfriend beats her up. Like a bad Lifetime movie," she kids. Her words are slow. I can only think how it must be painful for her to speak.

"Hil, this isn't funny," I say seriously.

"Well, what am I supposed to do, Lauren? Cry? Whine about how I was so helpless? I wasn't. I chose to stay with him. It's my fault, no one else's. I just didn't think it would get this bad."

"This isn't your fault, Hillary," I assure her. I pause before speaking again. "How long has this been going on?"

She laughs mechanically.

"About three months after we started going out, we had an argument when he was drunk and he slapped me. I was just so stunned. You know, I'd never been hit before. He apologized, saying he was just really out of it and he was sorry. That he'd never do it again. That's the day all those roses came."

I cringe; I remember saying how sweet it was.

"The next time it happened, he showed up at the house, drunk. You weren't home. He was really out of it and wanted to drive home. I took his keys, and he, well, let's just say that wasn't the best idea." She pauses, and I cover my face in disbelief.

"He really is only bad when he's drunk. He's so sweet when he's not. So I just stayed away when he drank. But today his friend had this party and he was drinking. I thought it'd be okay since there were so many people around. I caught him all over this girl, practically about to make out with her. I was so pissed. I slapped him and threw a cup of beer in his face and I left.

"When I got home, he was waiting for me in front of the door. He was so calm . . ." She chuckles angrily. "I was pissed and told him to leave. He apologized and said how sorry he was and that he just wanted to talk . . . I let him in, like an idiot, and as soon as we were in the apartment, he went crazy on me. He'd never been like that before . . ."

"You should have never let him in," I say, my throat burning and tears starting to fall down my face.

"I know. I know now. Things just went from bad to worse," she says.

"I can't believe I never noticed anything."

"No, Lauren. I was pretty good at hiding that fact and making excuses. Even if you had tried to do something, I wouldn't have let you. Besides, he mostly made sure to never bruise me where people could see. I guess that should have been a sign that this wasn't a first-time thing for him."

"Still." I can't help but scold myself for not having the slightest clue this was going on.

"No still. This is my fault; I kept going back and forgiving him."

"A man should never hit a woman!"

"But some do! I should have never kept seeing him after the first time he hit me. You know what's really stupid? I cheated on Kevin with him because I thought Kevin was a jerk. Karma sure kicked me in the ass, huh?" She smiles weakly.

"I should have at least suspected. I've been so busy running around with Cal . . . I think I'm going to stop seeing him," I say, taking a cleansing breath.

"What? Why!" she screeches. "Not because of this, is it? Because this wasn't your fault at all! I told you nothing would have changed . . ."

"No, not just because of this, Hil. It's been a lot of things. When I'm with him, he makes me forget about the world around me, like the people I care about and what's important to me."

"Lauren, that's not true. If it were, when Angie called you, you would have been like 'screw you. I'm about to bang,'" she exaggerates, and I laugh. I just don't see how she could be in so much pain and still so playful.

"You were about to screw, right? Or just finished or . . ."

"Hil, stop," I scold her playfully.

She sighs. "Seriously, Lauren. I've never seen you so happy before. A guy is supposed to put you on cloud nine and help you forget about your problems. I admit I didn't like Cal at first, at least not for you. I thought he had trouble written all over him. I mean, I would know, right? Since I attract it so magnificently," she says sarcastically.

"But, he's stuck with you. I gave you guys three weeks tops and here you are." She sighs and squeezes my hand.

"He's hot, rich, and makes you smile. You could do a lot worse. A hell of a lot worse." She chuckles.

"We're so different. I feel like we're on two different roads going in opposite directions. And he's so unpredictable. What if he gets bored or . . ." I sigh.

"Lauren, that's what falling in love is about. You take a chance. Sometimes you fall on your ass, or, in my situation, it kicks you in the ass. But rarely do you get something amazing. You can't hold back, or keep your guard up. Don't run from it, or you'll miss something special." She rubs my hand, and I hold it.

"What about when you lose it?" I ask.

"That's the risk you take, but it's worth it," she assures me with a yawn, holding her jaw in pain.

"You're not going to see him again, are you?" I'm not able to read her expression since her face is so swollen.

"No, I've learned my lesson. At first I thought it was just because of the alcohol, but now I realize he just likes to beat the crap out of girls. Oh! The house—it's—he trashed it. The tables are broken, and the lamps. I'll pay you back for everything you bought."

"Don't worry about it. I'm just glad you're okay." I squeeze her hand as Dr. Carsons comes in with the police officer she pointed out earlier.

"Miss Green, Detective Long has some questions for you," the doctor explains. "I'm going to have to ask you to excuse us," she tells me.

"Of course. Hil, I'll be right outside," I tell her with a weak smile.

"No. Go home. They won't let you see me until tomorrow. Unfortunately, my parents will be here soon." She waves slightly before Dr. Carsons closes the door. As soon as I'm outside, the tears I've been holding in since I saw her begin to flow. Cal and Angela quickly approach me.

"I-I can't believe he did that to her," I mumble into his shoulder.

"What did the detective say?" I ask Angela, wiping my face.

"He asked me what happened, and I told him what I knew. But what I say doesn't matter since I wasn't there, and if she doesn't press charges . . ." she says, running her hand across her face.

"Even if she does press charges, what he'll get is too good for him," Cal says tightly.

"His parents will get him out on bail. They're from old money down south. He'll get some high-priced lawyer and it won't even matter," Angela tells us. I feel even more horrible that I don't know anything about this guy other than what he looks like and his first name.

"Let's go back to your place and pick her up some clothes," Angela says softly.

"I'll drive you," Cal says, putting his arms around both of us. Angela smiles appreciatively and pats his hand as we leave the hospital

WHEN I OPEN the door to my apartment, my mouth drops open.

"Oh my God." This is unbelievable. The sofa and matching chair are flipped over onto their sides. Our lamps are pushed over, one broken along with the glass table that usually sits in the center of the room. Glass shards cover the floor.

"I can't believe this," I say, starting to pick up the glass pieces. Angela closes the door behinds us and begins to help clean up.

"He must have been throwing her all over the place," Angela mumbles.

"She has to press charges; there's no way she won't after this," I try to convince myself.

"Do you know where this guy lives?" Cal asks, moving the sofa into its original position.

"No, but I know he's always at the Golden Rod. I've been there a few times with him and Hillary. His parents own it. I'd bet my life he's there now. That's where Hillary met him," Angela says.

"That's the bar on 3rd and Wallace?" Cal asks her.

"Yeah," Angela confirms.

"I don't even know his last name," I mumble to myself. I'm her best friend and I didn't even know her boyfriend's last name.

"Lauren, you can't blame yourself for this; what could you have done—" Angela begins, but she's interrupted by a commotion outside our door.

"Hillary, Hillary!" a loud voice is yelling and punctuating it with loud bangs. "Baby, I'm sorry. You know I wasn't myself. Let me in, we can work this out."

Angela and I stare at each other in disbelief. Is he seriously here right now?

"She's not here, asshole!" Angela yells through the door.

"Go away before I call the police," I yell.

"This is none of your damn business, bitch!" he yells back. "Hillary! I'm sorry. I was drunk," he shouts, still banging on the door.

"She's not here!" I scream, rushing towards the door. Suddenly, Cal steps in and grabs my arm, stopping me in my tracks.

"You and Angela go to your bedroom," he says sternly. His face is like stone and his eyes wide. My heart starts to beat so rapidly that I don't even argue. Angela's eyes lock on mine and we both quickly head to my bedroom.

"I know she's in there. Don't make me kick the fucking door down!"

Angela and I are huddled in the doorway of my bedroom, and we hear the door open. I peek from behind the corner wall to see what's going on. Aaron charges into the apartment when Cal opens the door for him, but stops short when he realizes who just let him in. I take it Aaron is surprised to see Cal. I assess his size. He's a lot bigger than I remember—at least 250 pounds, five eleven, maybe. I shudder at the thought of him hitting Hillary, who weighs 120 pounds at most.

"Who the fuck are you?" Aaron says in a surprised tone.

"It doesn't matter who I am." Cal's face is stoic as he shuts the door and locks it. Aaron looks at him suspiciously for a moment but then continues on his mission.

"Hillary!" Aaron yells, slurring as he walks toward the bedrooms.

He stops when he sees us. "Is she in there?" he says frantically. I stand in the doorway. He reeks of alcohol. No way am I letting him in Hillary's room.

"Hillary," he yells again, rushing towards her door, and I stand my ground in front of it. Cal is right behind him. He moves his arm to push me. "Move, bit—" but before he even finishes his sentence, Cal has grabbed him by the throat and has him pinned to the wall. The sound of his weight hitting the wall causes both Angela and me to gasp. Frantically, Aaron tries to break the grip Cal has on his throat, but it's deadlocked.

Cal's voice seems to come from deep in his throat, and it's calm—scary calm. "You low-life piece of shit. You like to hit girls, huh? Does that make you feel good to throw around someone half your size?"

I glance at Angela, who seems to be in as much shock as I am.

"I should throw you out of that fucking window," Cal growls. He steps back and releases his grip on Aaron's throat, but before Aaron can get his balance, Cal punches him in the face. Aaron stumbles to the ground and tries to quickly regain his balance, but before he can stand, another punch has connected with his back, and he falls to the ground.

The scary calm has dissipated and Cal looks like he's on the verge of exploding. "I should fucking kill you!" he shouts, the veins in his neck visible. His foot connects with Aaron's chest. Aaron falls to the ground, attempting to catch his breath and trying to crawl away at the same time. Cal climbs on top of him and squeezes his hands around his neck again, pressing his knee into his chest.

He jerks his chin up and turns him towards me. "Apologize for calling her a bitch!" Cal yells, applying more weight on top of him. Aaron strains to look at me. "Sorry," he squeaks out.

"Would you have hit her if I weren't here? Does it make you feel good to hit women? Well, how does this feel?" Cal asks venomously. "If you ever come near them again I'll snap your neck like a twig. If Hillary calls you, you better hang up. If you see her in the street, you run the other way. Do you understand?"

Aaron is starting to turn blue.

He's going to kill him! I start to realize Cal has lost control. I run to them and try to pull Cal off of him.

"Cal, he's turning blue," Angela yells.

"Cal, stop," I beg him.

"Do you understand me?" Cal yells.

"Cal, you're going to kill him. Let him go!" I tell him, desperately but unsuccessfully trying to pull him away.

Cal looks up at me, and I see fire behind his eyes.

"He's not worth it. Let him go, please," I plead, tears setting in my eyes. "He's not worth it, babe." Cal is in a rage. I have to get him out of it. If he kills the bastard right here and goes to jail for the rest of his life, I'll never forgive myself.

"He's not, Cal, he's not," Angela chimes in, and he nods his head, removes his knee from Aaron's chest, and lets his neck go. Aaron immediately balls up, gasping in as much air as he can. Cal looks at him like a dirty rat, completely disgusted, and kicks him.

I look at Aaron and think about how badly he hurt my friend. What Cal's done still doesn't seem like enough for how he hurt her on more than one occasion, but I can't let Cal dispense what he deserves. We all watch as Aaron starts to get up. Cal steps up to him one more time and Aaron freezes, his eyes full of fear.

"If I ever find out about you hitting another woman again, if I even think you've hit another woman again, you're dead," Cal warns him.

"Do you understand me?" he roars. Aaron nods frantically. Cal punches him in the stomach and he keels over.

"Open the door," he says, looking at me. I do as he says. The next thing I see is Cal pulling Aaron out into the hall and pushing him down the stairs. We watch Aaron roll down the steps. After a few seconds, he manages to literally crawl out the door. I look at Cal. I can't believe what I've just seen. He looks back at both of us but doesn't say anything. I don't know what to say, and Angela looks completely shocked.

"Go get her things. I'll be in the car," he says simply, catching his breath. And then he's gone. I look at Angela, whose mouth is wide open.

"I don't think he'll be bothering Hillary anytime soon," she says softly.

All I can do is nod in agreement.

"**L**AUREN, YOUR AUNT is on the phone," Angela says, holding the phone out to me. I gesture that I don't want to talk. She gives an apologetic smile.

May 12th, 2011

"Umm, she's not here, Mrs. Scott—I mean Brooks," she bumbles. After a moment she laughs. "She says she knows you're here, and she really needs to talk to you."

I roll my eyes and take the phone. "Hi, Raven," I say, trying to keep the dryness from my voice.

"Hi, sweetie, how are you?" she says anxiously.

I arch my brow; I know she's itching to tell me something. "I'm fine. What's going on?" I ask her, feeling almost as anxious myself.

"Cal is here!" she reveals cheerfully.

I feel my stomach drop and close my eyes, a smile spreading across my face. It's about time; it's been three whole days since I've talked to him.

"Lauren, are you there, sweetheart?"

"Yeah. I'm here," I tell her, remembering I'm on the phone.

"He says it's really important that he talks to you," she says urgently.

He thinks whenever he needs something or wants something, it's important. But when anyone else—

"Did you tell him where I am?"

"No, honey, I don't know where you are exactly."

"Did you tell him who I'm staying with?"

"Honey, will you please talk to him? You are still his wife, even if you're upset with him right now," she urges me.

I roll my eyes again. This is back to the Raven I know. "I'll talk to him," I mumble.

"Cal, here she is," she says happily.

"Lauren," he says dryly. His voice doesn't sound too urgent to me.

"Yes, Cal," I say unenthusiastically, even though I'm really glad to hear his voice.

"Where are you?" he asks nonchalantly.

"Why? Do you actually care now? It has been almost a week, if you haven't noticed," I mumble bitterly.

"Look, I need you to get to the house." He sounds annoyed.

"No." He's not my master; he doesn't get to say "jump" and have me ask how high.

"This is important," he says, his tone softening a bit.

"Important, yeah." I laugh, and he sighs in frustration.

"I'm coming to pick you up," he says, as if it's a command.

"You don't even know where I am."

"Do you want me to play a guessing game?"

"You know what, Cal? Whatever it is, I don't care—"

"Lauren. Can you just meet me at the house? Please," he interrupts.

I run my hand over my head and bite my lip. It could be a trick, him just getting me back where I don't want to be, but there's a hint of urgency to his voice.

"Why?" I ask, knowing I probably won't get an answer.

"I need to tell you in person," he replies quietly.

"Of course, in person," I say softly to myself. "Fine. Fine, Cal." I mumble, ignoring that little voice in my head. I've pretty much blocked it out since I met Cal—why start listening now?

"I'll be home before the evening," he says.

"Yeah, okay." I sigh and hang up the phone. I can't believe I'm even doing this.

"What happened?" Angela asks curiously.

"Cal says he needs to see me," I tell her weakly.

She sits on the couch. "Are you going?" she asks, but from her expression, I can tell she already knows the answer.

"I'm just going to see what he wants. He said it's important," I say, trying to convince myself more than her.

"No judgment here," she replies, grabbing the remote and flipping through the channels on the TV.

I roll my eyes at myself and flop down beside her. "I'm so pathetic," I mumble and rest my head on her shoulder.

"Not pathetic, just in love." She giggles, leaning her head on mine.

"I think being in love makes you really stupid."

"No question about it." She laughs. "You don't think this is just a ploy to get you back home, convince you to stay? Because that's what I think." She chuckles.

"If it is, I'll leave," I say pointedly.

"Aww, come on. Once you see him, it's all over. He starts whispering in your ear how sorry he is. Touching you in all the right places, making you forget why you were even mad in the first place . . ." She eyes me. God, how many times has that happened?

"Have you been stalking me?" I tease her, but I realize how perfectly that describes the end of every argument or fight we've ever had.

"Well, let's get you back to the hubby." She laughs, grabbing her keys from the table. "If you're not staying, you won't have to take anything with you." She sticks her tongue out at me.

I laugh. "You're right." I shrug and grab my purse, following her out the door.

I WONDER WHY people take a chance on falling in love. If I could go back through time, would I change the things I've done? My mind says I would, but the decisions I made concerning Cal were never made logically.

Someone once told me when you're in love, your heart takes over and your brain shuts off. I never understood what that meant when I was younger, but I do now. New love makes you look past a person's flaws, which seem magnified later on. I look down at my wedding ring; even when I take it off, I still feel it there.

I open the door to the penthouse. Everything looks the same, as if I never left.

"Cal," I call out, putting my purse on the console table near the door. I didn't think he'd beat me here; it seems I was right. I turn around and lock the door behind me. I head upstairs to our room, and I can tell it's been cleaned since I left. I sit on my bed and look around, realizing that I have actually missed being here in the comfort of my own home. Who knew? I yawn and lie back, my body relishing the down comforter beneath it. This feels amazing after the cramped stay on Angela's couch.

I OPEN MY eyes and first notice that the sunlight vanished while I slept. I look at the clock on the table and see that it's 8:14. I got here around six. Footsteps are coming down the hall, so I jump up, only to get a head rush, and I have to sit back down on the bed. The door opens and Cal steps in. He looks at me, the expression on his face set in a hard frown.

"You're finally up," he says, turning on the light.

"How long have you been here?" I ask, covering the yawn escaping from my mouth as I try to fully wake myself up.

"About an hour," he says, sitting in a chair across from the bed so we're face to face. I wonder when he brought that in. It wasn't here earlier.

"So, what did you want to talk to me about?" I sigh, secretly scolding myself for wanting his arms around me, for missing him, for being ready to forgive him if he just asked. He pulls his chair closer to me and sits back down. I look at him curiously, and for the first time in forever, his eyes avoid mine. We sit in silence for what seems to be the longest seconds of my life.

"Cal," I say softly, purposefully erasing the contempt that laced my voice earlier. His eyes are scaring me. I've always tried to tell what he was feeling from them, but they're avoiding me. He's looking in my direction, but he's not making eye contact.

"What's wrong?" I whisper, almost afraid to hear the answer.

"I've never lied to you," he says, his voice strong and unwavering. "And I'm not going to start now." He sighs and drops his head down, running both hands through his hair.

My heart rate picks up. "Just say it," I blurt out. My nerves are multiplying by the second.

He picks up my hand and holds it tightly in both of his. "I-I have to leave."

My expression hardens, and I pull my hand away. "You called me back for this?" I stand up, feeling my anger rise. He pulls me back down.

"Look, this is different." His eyes widen and his tone lifts higher.

"Everything is different with you, Cal. If you weren't so different, maybe I wouldn't feel so screwed up right now," I snap, snatching away from him. I can't believe how easily he'd fooled me. God, I was eating out of his hands. He frowns and stands up, walking towards the window. He looks out, seemingly lost in his own thoughts.

"I don't know *if* I'll be back." I search his tone for some hint of sarcasm, but I don't find any.

"What?" I say, hoping I didn't hear him right. He doesn't say anything. I walk in front of him. "Would you mind repeating yourself?" I say sharply.

"I'm going to make sure that you're taken of. I put ninety thousand in your personal account . . ." he starts. My heart is beating rapidly, and his eyes still won't connect with mine.

"What? You don't know if you'll be back?" I ask him frantically, trying to get my words out. He's leaving me money? Things are going so fast in my head that I can't even say what I want.

"Why does it sound like you're saying that you're leaving me?" I ask, my stomach dropping. He doesn't say anything, which makes my heart speed up even more. I have to be jumping to conclusions. I mean, *no*— Cal wouldn't leave me. We argue, we fight, we make up. This isn't right.

"I have to," he says. His eyes finally fall on me, and the look in them scares me. He seems helpless, and I'm suddenly terrified. My throat is starting to burn.

"Is this about me, how I've been acting? Is this some kind of revenge thing?" I say, hearing my voice start to crack.

"This has nothing to do with you," he says, almost in a whisper.

"Exactly, Cal! Look what you're saying—I'm your wife. And your decision to leave has nothing to do with me?"

"I don't have a choice."

"What are you talking about? Cal! Talk to me, please," I say frantically. "Look at me!" I yell. His eyes stare past me. "What is wrong with you? Why are you acting like this?" I plead, feeling tears start to fall down my face. This isn't the man I know; he seems broken.

"Tell me what the hell is going on! Tell me what's going on with you for once!" I beg him.

"I can't!" he yells back, and his expression hardens. "This isn't about me," he says tensely, walking away from me to the other side of the room.

"Then who is it about?" I don't understand. This is not how this is supposed to happen.

He doesn't say anything.

"You won't tell me that either, huh?" I say quietly, unable to stop the stream of tears escaping from my eyes. I wipe them away angrily. "What am I supposed to say, Cal? What?" I yell.

"Am I just supposed to accept you leaving? No explanations except 'I have to.' Not that I've ever gotten one from you. This won't be any different except who knows when you'll come back? If you come back."

"My stock dividends from the company will still be deposited into the account . . ." he continues.

Oh my God, he thinks I care about money, as if that's my main concern right now.

"I don't care about the fucking money! I never cared about any of this—the trips, this house—I never needed this! All I wanted . . ." I'm screaming now. "All I ever wanted was you. Can't you see that?" My words get caught in my throat. "Say something." My voice comes out in a whisper.

"Is there someone else?" I ask, trying to maintain what little composure I have left.

"I told you I've never cheated on you," he insists, almost annoyed.

"Then why? People just don't decide to leave out of nowhere. There has to be a reason. Tell me you're in love with someone else, that this isn't working, that you're in trouble. Just tell me something," I plead with him, begging for some type of explanation.

"There's nothing I can tell you," he says coldly, his eyes not even on me. I look at him, the person I've loved all these years, the man I've loved so much that my body ached. How many nights have I cried myself to sleep, missing him? How many times has my mind told me to walk away, and I stayed?

If it's this easy for him, he doesn't deserve a measure of what I'm feeling right now. He doesn't deserve to know how much I love him. I don't even know how to respond to this. How do you respond when your husband says he's leaving you, and he can't tell you why?

"What am I supposed to do?" I ask him, wanting some kind of response, some kind of answer.

"Helen and Dex will take care of anything you need . . ."

"Helen and Dexter?" I ask in disbelief. "They know about this?" I yell. He looks away for the hundredth time today. "How long have you known that you were leaving me? Have you gotten bored with me, or is this just a spur-of-the-moment thing?"

"It's not like that," he says, walking toward me.

I step away quickly. "Then what? Tell me what it's like. Tell me something. Tell me why," I say, as the burning in my throat mounts.

"I can't believe you're doing this to me!" I scream as loud as I can. My throat feels as if it's on fire. My vision is so blurry I can't even see him clearly. I walk over to the bed and rest my head in my hands. I'm completely drained. Every emotion inside of me is spilling over, and all I can do is cry. He walks toward me, reaching out. I get up to step away, but he pulls me into him. "Why? Why are you doing this to me?" I whimper, feeling too drained to push him away, and I don't want to. I want to hold him and never let him go. I can feel myself completely breaking down.

"I'm sorry," he says, stroking my hair. But instead of being endeared by it, I feel like a helpless puppy about to be put to sleep at the pound.

"No, you aren't," I tell him in a daze. I'm not even in this moment. I can only see past it. And I see nothing.

"Yes, I am," he says softly in my ear. I don't detect a hint of sarcasm or amusement in his voice, which makes me start to cry even more.

I wrap my arms around him tightly and look into his eyes. "Don't make me ask you to stay." I begin to cry harder. I can't even control what I'm saying, what I'm feeling. I feel as if everything is crashing down around me.

"I wish I could," he replies in a whisper.

"Don't! Don't you dare make this seem as if it's out of your control. If you wanted to stay, you would!"

It takes all my strength, but I remove myself from his arms. My vision is so blurred that all I see is a vague image of him. I feel his hands touch both sides of my waist, and his lips meet mine. I don't even respond. I can't. I want to kiss him back, wrap my arms around him, but I'm numb, too numb to react, too helpless to pull away. I can't even register this; I won't believe this is the last time he'll kiss me, the last time he'll touch me. I close my eyes, pretending this is all a bad dream and that I'll wake up any minute. But when his lips leave mine, I know I won't wake up. This isn't a bad dream; I'm living this.

I then feel his lips move to my cheek. "You'll get through this," he says after they leave it. "You'll have to."

I wipe my eyes and look at him quickly before they blur again. "If you're leaving, go!" I say, trying to hold on to the last thread of dignity I have, the one thing that's keeping me from begging him not to leave me. I stand up angrily and face him.

"Leave." I push him. "I hate you! I hate you, you fucking bastard!" I begin to hit his chest furiously, a hysterical, sobbing mess, and he stands there and takes it, not even trying to stop me. He looks drained too, and I hate him for it.

I hate that, even at this moment, I hope he's okay. I hate the fact that his expression is soft, and he seems vulnerable. It's all a trick; he's trying to convey that he doesn't really want to go. How could he do this to me and make me feel sorry for him? Why, in this moment, am I worried about him?

"Just go," I whimper. I make my way to the floor, not wanting to feel anything, not even the comfort of the bed we once shared. My whimpers are probably inaudible to him, but it doesn't matter, because he doesn't care. I can't believe that he cares, not now. I have to believe he doesn't. I won't give away my anger. It's all I can hold on to. The alternative is worse, but I feel it winning out. It's about to take over and I silently pray that he leaves before it does, because I'm on the verge of it. It's growing from the pit of my stomach—desperation. I squeeze my fists together and bury my head underneath my arms. His footsteps approach. He nears me, and a moment later the steps grow distant, farther and farther away with each second. And then the door closes, and I feel like my heart has stopped. I lift my head and see that he's gone. My imitation of a prayer has been granted, and that desperation that was welling in my stomach is now morphing into something else, something even more terrifying—complete and utter sorrow.

I close my eyes and my new prayer is for sleep. I want out of this moment, out of this life I've fallen into—that I'm now trapped in, alone. My only temporary freedom is sleep. I close my eyes, squeezing them shut, and wish more than anything that sleep comes and comes fast. But it doesn't, not in the following minutes or even the following hour. I feel catatonic, staring up at the clock over my bed. When I hear the door open again, my heart rate goes into overdrive, but I close my eyes, almost afraid to see him, wondering if he left something behind—if he forgot his keys, or something important enough to take with him. I keep my eyes closed and try to slow down my breathing when I hear him move around me. I hope he'll get what he needs quickly and leave me to my despair.

His footsteps near me again. I hold my breath, hoping if I hold it long enough he'll disappear. But when his hands move underneath me and he lifts me into his arms, I lose my breath completely. I'm afraid to breathe, and only do so when he finally lays me down on the bed. He lifts my legs, removing each of my shoes, and I don't know what to do. Do I say something? Do I kick him away? A moment later, cool sheets cover me. Then his lips rest gently on my forehead and I feel frozen, knowing he thinks I'm asleep. His footsteps grow distant again, the light clicks off, the door opens, and that welling from earlier is coming up again, full force, and I shoot up from my zombie-like state.

"Can you stay?" I blurt out and immediately regret it. He stops in his tracks, his back toward me—there's silence, and I remember I'm supposed to be asleep. But here I am, punishing him for his last act of decency toward me. "Just—just until I fall asleep," I manage to squeak out without my voice breaking, my old self content that the words have been spoken. The jaded, vindictive woman I've become the last few months cringes at the sound of them.

He doesn't answer, but he walks back over toward the bed. I slowly release the sheets trapped between my fingers. He sits on the edge of the bed, still not facing me, resting his elbows on his thighs, his hands clasped together. I feel the burning sensation in my chest starting, followed by the stinging coming up in my throat. In the next few minutes, I'm not going to be able to stop crying.

I immediately regret asking him to stay. I tell myself he has to be here out of pity, or some fucked-up sense of duty, granting his desperate wife a last request. A wife who doesn't even know where the fuck he's going, and what's causing him to sit so far away from me on our bed, like I'm disgusting? I change my mind. I want him out, but I can't tell him without unleashing what will be an uncontrollable, hideous wail. So I quickly force myself back onto the bed, pull the sheets over my face, and try my best to whimper as quietly as I can.

His weight shifts and I know he's risen. I knew this would be too much for him. Why should he have to sit here and deal with this? He's leaving anyway, and being here now isn't going to make the resolution of this any better. He shouldn't have come back in. He should have left me in my grief, lying on the floor, alone. After all, that's what he's ultimately going to do.

When the cover lifts off me, it's like a splash of water on my face. When he climbs in beside me and pulls me toward him, it's a comfort so conflicting it's almost giving me a headache. My mind tells me to push him away, overriding every other thought. I attempt to do it, placing my hands on his chest, but he pulls me toward him, wrapping his strong arms around me, and I don't put up much more of a fight. He holds me tightly. I can feel his heart beating rapidly, but when I look at him his expression is calm. He stares past me, and I wonder if he's here in this moment with me. I don't know if I want him to be, but I do know what I want. I shift in his arms and he looks down at me. I bring my lips to his, pressing against them, holding my breath as I do. And when he pulls away, my heart drops, and I can't face him. I quickly make a break from the bed, but he grabs my arm. He looks confused and conflicted and it's just making things worse. One thing that Cal has never denied me is his kiss, his touch, his body—they were all mine, and it's breaking my spirit that he's doing this now.

"I—I'm still going to have to leave."

His voice is unyielding but soft, and it causes me to melt, his grip on my wrist gentle but firm enough to not allow me to run away, which was my absolute intention. I wish I could stop *him* from running away so easily. I replay his words in my head, trying to decipher the meaning, and in my clouded, emotional state I realize he's trying to give me a choice. For once, he's not trying to use sex as a bandage or as a means of control or manipulation. But I have to say his timing sucks.

I take a deep breath and command my voice to be steady. "I want to go to sleep." My voice is raspy and somewhat harsh. I clear my throat and wipe away any vulnerability and sincerity. I want him to know that him giving me his body wouldn't be a knife stabbing through me, that this is not about trying to keep him here—but that I need this, now. His guilt about it is not a priority to me now.

"Put me to sleep," I say, sternly commanding my normal voice to return, and he raises his eyebrow, skeptical. I can tell he's surprised. Before he can say anything, I attack his lips, this time without hesitancy, with a swiftness I think has caught him off guard and with a force I'm shocked I'm able to muster, considering the state I'm in.

I climb on top of him, ensnaring his body between my legs, and wrap my arms tightly around his neck, kissing him with an urgency I've never felt before. He pulls away this time, trying to catch his breath. He takes my face in his hands, searching my expression, his eyes finding mine—the tables have turned and he's trying to figure out what it is I want. But I don't have time for that. He's trying to give me my last out, and I don't want out. I want the one thing from him that makes me forget about everything else.

"What are you waiting on?" I ask, breaking the solemnness of this moment. Before a second passes, he takes my lips in his, countering my hectic kisses and frantic need with a passionate patience that my fake bravado isn't ready for, an unhurried desire that causes my stiffness to melt away. His lips hold on to mine like he's trying to pull me into him. His hands slowly start to remove my clothes, but his pacing makes me feel vulnerable, almost innocent. The hard façade I'm trying to create is going to break, but I have to hold on to it. I break our embrace, snatch my shirt over my head, and reach to undo his pants, somehow successful even with my rapid, clumsy movements.

"Lauren!"

I ravish his lips to silence him, throwing all of my body weight on him, which causes us to momentarily fall back on the bed. I realize my pants are still on and I swiftly shimmy out of them. When I try to climb on top of him again, he grabs my waist, stopping my pace. His eyes are downcast and his lips pressed tightly together—he's upset, but right now, I don't care. The confusion on his face is unexpected, but I don't want to know what it's about.

I need to be distracted. My lips find his once more but, again, he's pulling me into that slow, sensual kiss that almost broke me before. I pull away. I rest my eyes on his chest—I can't look at him. I work up my nerve to try again and kiss him hard, biting down on his bottom lip. This time he breaks our kiss, and my eyes can't leave his face fast enough. There's a glimpse of something I have never seen before, and I think I see heart, possibly disappointment, and it stabs through me, but the expression is brief. Soon, his familiar wicked grin covers what was just there. His fingers slide between the lacy material on my hip and the skin there. He pulls it down, and I step out of it. Within a second, I'm on the bed, my arms above my head, trapped beneath his wrist. This is what I want. Lust—not love. Physicality—not intimacy.

He's fucking me figuratively, and I want it literally. I don't want to be made love to—that's over. I can't let him in that place, not with him leaving. I won't. I go to suck his neck, and he moves. His finger glides down my arm, and I try to ignore the tingling that jolts down my back at his touch. It's something I'll have to forget. He grips my hands, holds them together, taking the flimsy thong of mine from earlier and tying it around my wrists. It's tight, but I don't say anything. I don't want tenderness, anyway. I want him inside me. I want to be exhausted, but mostly

I want to forget. I want to forget this moment, that this could be or is goodbye.

When his lips find my neck, they stay there only briefly before his tongue glides down to the crook of it, sucking in the skin midway. His path is slow and tortuous, and I shift to stop his trail. His fingers grasp my hair, forcing me to look at him, and I close my eyes. I won't. I don't want to see into him.

His lips are at my ear. "Open your eyes." His voice is deep and stern, but I ignore him. I can't look at him. I bite my lips and squeeze my eyes shut tighter, and soon his tongue finds its way inside my ear. My body involuntarily arches towards him; it's the place he knows causes me to give him complete control. My eyes open. I pray that the tears welling up don't escape them. I try to focus on the waves of lust going through my body and not on the fact that after all this, he's going to be gone. That is what I want to forget. I want to forget that I don't want him to go. I feel his hardness pressing against me. It's torture, and I'm growing inpatient. I want him inside.

"Now," I demand, but it comes out more as if I'm begging, and I realize I'm helpless. I start to try to free my hands. His lips leave my ear, traveling down my neck, past my breasts, and when they reach my belly button, I freeze as his tongue swirls around it. This isn't what I want. I know now where he's going with this, and it isn't what I wanted.

I try to move my body away from him, but he holds me in place as his lips trail lower and lower. I try to lock my legs together, but he easily holds them open and in place, and his tongue starts to trace the one part of my body I have absolutely no control over. I can't help but cry out.

"Cal. Cal, stop," I pant. My mind is demanding that I do something to stop this, but my body is giving in to each stroke of his tongue, causing my thoughts and emotions to crash against one another, my moans of pleasure battling against my pleas for him to stop. This isn't what I wanted. I cover my face as best I can with my arms as his tongue delves deeper inside me. I try to inch away from him, and he grips my thighs tightly and pulls me to him. He goes more slowly, his pressure increasing, and my protests become shorter and inaudible. As my stomach tightens, he begins going faster, and I can barely catch my breath. I give in completely, and as I feel myself building to a climax, my legs trembling, I think of when we first met—our first kiss. I try to block these things out and focus on the absolute pleasure my body is feeling—no emotion.

But my mind isn't giving in. I see the night he proposed and our wedding day. Then, suddenly, our first fight, the *first* time he left for days without calling. I see him walking out the door and me alone on the floor, and I envision getting a phone call from Dexter telling me he's dead. And at that moment, my body gives in, experiencing a pleasure that momentarily overwhelms these terrible thoughts.

My body recovers and my legs stop trembling as an overwhelming sadness washes over me. I begin to catch my breath and recover from the eerie visions that are weighing on me. Now, more than anything, I want him to hold me. I want that slow, sensual kiss he gave me a taste of earlier, but he just undoes the thong on my wrist, goes into the bathroom, and slams the door. I don't know what to think or how to feel, my thoughts clouded. I rub my wrists that are now free and wonder what happens next. Is he just going to walk out? Is he going to say anything? He's angry and I don't know why *he* has any right to be angry. I put my t-shirt back on and hug my knees to my chest.

When he comes out, he leans in the doorway, his lips held between his teeth, arms folded. "That's what you wanted, right?" he asks in a sardonic tone. He's fully dressed again.

"What are you talking about?" I say, rubbing my temples, not wanting to look at him.

"To get off. That's what you wanted from me. A last good fuck, right?" he snarls, leaving the doorway and grabbing his keys from the nightstand. I can't believe he would say that to me.

"What? That wasn't what I wanted!" Deep down I know it's a lie. I didn't want to feel him—I wanted to feel his body, and he was trying to take me to a place I couldn't go. I wanted him to give me something—to *not* think about him, to get away from all this. I know it's wrong, but he's the one fucking leaving at the end of all this.

"Yeah. You wanted me to fuck you, but you couldn't even look at me." He laughs cuttingly, his hand resting on the back of his head. I open my mouth to respond, but I have no valid comeback.

"What do you want from me, Cal? What? You're the one leaving. What do you want me to do? How do you want me to feel!" I demand, getting angrier by the minute.

"I wanted you to let me in." He sounds so dejected it makes my heart break.

Why is he doing this? Why is he trying to take me to a place I have to leave in order to move on? But I guess the reality is he didn't need to take me to that place. I'm already there, living in it. Since the day I met him, I've been there, and he's the only person I want to be there with me.

I swallow my pride and get off the bed. He's hurt and he can easily spurn me, but I still move toward him. When I reach him, he looks down at me, his hands now stuffed into his jeans. I place both my hands on his chest and force myself to look at him, and I know once I do, the flimsy wall I've tried to create around myself today is going to crumble. And when I look into his eyes, it does.

"You're already in. You always have been and you always will be," I say, unable to imagine how he can't know this already. In the back of my mind, I wonder if this is a trick. Is this what he wanted to hear all along? Is this a card he can play, to know he can leave and waltz back into my life whenever he wants, because he can't *not* know how much I love him, how much I need him, and how much his leaving tears me apart? It feels as if my heart is being ripped out of my body.

"Promise me," he says, and for only the *second* time in my life, I hear his voice sound unsteady and unsure. I nod furiously and stand on tiptoe. I kiss him as he did me earlier—passionately, with controlled patience—and in return, he makes it so deep it's as if he's pulling my soul from my body and is trying to take it with him. His hands slide beneath my shirt, and he removes it. I do the same, tugging at his, and soon our clothes are both off and I'm back on the bed, this time with him fully inside me, connected. He doesn't pin my arms over my head but allows me to dig my fingers deep into his skin as he takes me to places of ecstasy only he has. I take in his scent, his breath, his touch. I try to remember each of his kisses; his every single movement I capture in my mind. I allow him to go as deep inside me as he wants, taking in the pain and the pleasure as one. I hold him tight. I say his name, and my body gives into him over and over again as it always does, even knowing the danger in which I'm putting myself.

I tell him how much I love him and that I'd wait if he'd only ask . . . but he doesn't. He's done what I asked—my earlier demand that he put me to sleep. I can barely keep my eyes open, but now I try to fight the sleep that's coming down on me so heavily, the kind I wished for earlier. I'm exhausted emotionally and physically. I look back at Cal and he's already asleep, and I lie as close to him as I can. My eyes are so heavy, but I don't want them to close.

"Don't give up on me." His words are quiet barely over a whisper, and as quickly as they're said, they're gone. I wonder if I imagined it. I close my eyes and know that soon this night will only be a memory within a nightmare I want to forget. Now it's only a dream. Still, I give him my heart and let him take it with him.

Well, that's not entirely true. I can't give him something he's always had.

I OPEN MY eyes and stretch out my body, noticing there's more space in the bed than usual. I sit up and look around to see that I'm alone.

"Cal?" I call out. He'd better not have left me again. I hate being in his house alone. I especially hate waking up in his bed alone instead of in his arms. Looking out the window, I notice the sun has been replaced by darkness, which is interrupted by the surrounding city lights. I step out of bed and turn on the lamp in order to find my clothes. A piece of paper on the nightstand catches my eye. It's a note from Cal asking me to come to the roof.

April 22nd, 2010

"What are you up to now?" I say to myself, a smile spreading across my face. Quickly, I open one of his drawers and pull out a shirt to throw on instead of dragging around this stupid sheet. A brief glance in the mirror tells me my hair needs some help. My brush is nowhere to be found, so I shake my fingers through it to try to settle it back down. It'll have to do.

I hear music playing as I make my way up the stairs. My eyebrows shoot up when I see the candles lighting the way up the stairs and pink rose petals trailing the steps. When I finally make it up to the top, my mouth drops open. The entire roof is outlined with candles and the ground is littered with rose petals.

"Oh my God." A smile creeps across my face. "Cal, I can't believe you," I scold him playfully. "Where are you?" I stop when he picks me up from behind. "How did you do all this?" I giggle when he puts me down.

"Well, technically, I didn't do it—but it was my idea."

"How did you know I wouldn't wake up?"

"Well, I made sure you were pretty tired earlier, didn't I?" He smiles suggestively, pulling me up against him. I push him away playfully.

"This is beautiful, really. It's my graduation present?" I guess. He's been hinting at having a big surprise for me, and it'd be like him to give it to me a month early so I'd be truly surprised.

"Do you remember the first night I danced with you?" he asks, pulling me back in his arms.

"Yeah, I remember what that led to." I giggle as I wrap my arms around his neck, and we sway to the music.

He looks into my eyes. "I told you I'd give you everything."

"You were trying to get me into bed," I remind him with a sly grin.

"That's beside the point."

"That night, it was exactly your point."

The wide smile on his face softens. "I've been with a lot of women." I arch my brow, a little apprehensive about hearing the rest of this speech—it's not getting off to a good start. But I say nothing and let him continue.

"I looked straight through them, and they never noticed or didn't seem to care. When I first saw you, I couldn't do that; you wouldn't let me. It caught me by surprise. Everything about you caught me by surprise."

His hand slips beneath his shirt that I am wearing and up my back. We stop dancing as his fingers begin to trace their infamous pattern on my skin. His touch gives me chills, causing me to bite my lip. His fingers leave their spot and he takes my hand, gripping one of my own fingers, and he brings it to my back again. He then makes the same pattern he's done so many times. This time I recognize it and my heart flutters. It wasn't just a random pattern or symbol; it was his name.

"I want something more permanent than tracing my name on your back." He steps back, looking into my eyes.

"I'm not getting your name tattooed on me," I joke, wrapping my arms around his neck. He chuckles and shakes his head.

"Well, ink fades anyway." He winks before he licks his lips as he shows me his boyish grin. He reaches into his pocket with one hand. The other one glides down my arm, and he takes my hand in his.

"You know I've never lived by a plan. I've always decided to do what I wanted, and no one else really mattered. Since I met you, that's changed.

I never thought I'd feel for someone the way I do about you."

My heart speeds up and my mouth suddenly becomes dry. I look up at him, tears filling my eyes. He pulls his hand out of his pocket and opens it to reveal a yellow diamond ring. My jaw hits the floor.

"I tried to talk myself out of doing this more times than you'd believe. And that's just today. I know you're graduating next month and moving on to a different phase of your life." He takes the ring and slides it on my finger. The ring is a perfect fit.

"I don't want to be a part of your past. I want to be the only person to touch you in ways that give you chills, to whisper things that make you turn red. I know there are a lot of things that you want to know about me that I haven't been exactly open with you about. But know that I love you; I've been in love with you longer than I've admitted to myself."

My tongue is completely stuck to the roof of my mouth. I can't even open it to say anything.

"You always tell me I need to work on asking for things." He gets down on one knee. His eyes are bright and his expression soft. I'm trembling. He takes my waist and pulls me onto his bended knee.

"I want you to, I mean . . . will you marry me?"

He's in front of me; the ring is on my finger and this still doesn't seem real. I never would have guessed this would happen now. I can't even say anything. *Open your mouth!* I want to say yes. I want to jump into his arms and tell him yes a million times, but something's stopping me. It's not me; it's him. Is he ready? There are so many reasons this might not work. I get off of his bended leg, which easily holds my weight, and stand, and he does the same.

"Are you sure?" I whisper, trying to wipe away the tears that keep falling. He stands up and pulls me closer to him, gently cupping my face with his hands.

"No doubt in my mind," he says adamantly

I rest my head on his chest. *Oh God, help me.* When I look into his eyes, I lose all doubts, but they don't go away quietly.

My mind is telling me one thing, my heart another. I can't help but hear Helen's words echoing in my head. Have we really come that far since then? I lift my head and look into his eyes. In a moment they ease my doubts but increase so many of my fears. I know that he could break my heart in the blink of an eye.

"Yes," I say softly. I can't say no. Why should I? I love him. I've been in love with him longer than I want to believe. If I couldn't touch him, talk to him, feel him, I don't know what I'd do. I could very easily spend the rest of my life with him. Still . . .

"Yes," I say again, mostly to myself. I throw myself into his arms and softly kiss his lips before he deepens it. He lifts me in his arms, and the world spins around me. The little voice in my head is quiet, as tears of joy roll down my cheek.

But all I can think is . . . please don't break my heart.

I WISH I wasn't here. Out of all my worries, my assumptions of what Cal was doing while he was gone, wondering who he was with, what was he doing? The jealousy, loneliness, and fear of my imagination used to choke me like a noose. Now, being here without Cal is worse. So much worse than I could ever have thought, imagined, or prepared myself for. There was no way I could prepare myself for this. I think somewhere deep down I knew that this was coming, but I hoped it was unsubstantiated

June 7th, 2011

fear. I'd always tell myself that I was paranoid, that my nightmares were my subconscious feelings about him always being gone so much. Still I felt it coming stronger and stronger as I looked into his eyes these past weeks, as he held me but I looked in the other direction.

The connection I've forged with him was trying to tell me, and I didn't understand. I couldn't figure it out. Or I didn't want to. Maybe the entire time I was with him was just a countdown until I'd lose him. It's been hard living with Cal, loving him for all that he is and all that he wouldn't let me know about him, but I know it's going to be harder living without him.

The day after he left me was one of the longest, hardest days of my entire life. It seemed as if it would never end. The hours passed like days and there was nothing I could do to make it go faster. I knew when I woke he wouldn't be here, but still I hoped when I opened my eyes he'd be lying beside me.

He wasn't; he was gone.

He didn't take anything with him. The house looks as if he never left.

That's why I had to leave the house too. Every time the phone rang, my heart began to beat faster. I thought of it being him, but then I'd hear a message from Dexter, Helen, or Raven—anyone but him. Everything I looked at triggered a memory that I didn't want to think about. Trying not to think about him led me to only thinking about him more.

After about a week of almost losing it, I went back to Angela's. She welcomed me with open arms again, without asking any questions, even though I'm sure she wanted to. I did my best to hide my feelings; it took all I had to make it look like I was okay, especially when I'd spent an entire week just crying endlessly, not able to control it. The only time I wasn't crying was when I was sleeping, and then I'd just wake up and start crying again.

"Lauren." I lift my head to see Angela standing in front of me with a slightly worried expression. She's been so sweet to me, and I've barely said three sentences to her other than "I'm fine," "don't worry," and "goodnight."

"Yeah," I say, quickly putting on a fake smile, which, I'm sure, isn't convincing.

"Can we talk?" she asks, biting her lip. The talk, I knew it would come eventually; even the most patient person in the world would have to ask me about what I'm doing here sooner or later.

"Sure." I nod, sitting up from the fetal position, my default these past couple of weeks.

"Good." She smiles and then disappears for a moment, while I get up to fold up my sheets. As I finish, she returns with a gallon of ice cream and two spoons. I smile, wishing this was going to be as fun as ice cream and girl talk. She sits down on the couch and pats the seat next to her. I sit beside her and take the spoon she's handing me. I quickly pop a spoonful of ice cream in my mouth to avoid speaking first.

"So, you know I'm not nosy or trying to pry, right?" she asks quietly.

I nod, knowing what's coming next.

"But since you've come back, you've been like a zombie. You don't say much, which is fine. I can understand that you may not feel up to talking about how you're feeling. But whenever I'm home all you do is sleep. You're not just napping, Lauren, you're like in REM when I leave and when I get home." She pauses, giving me a chance to respond. I really don't know what to say to her. She's right.

"You don't have to talk to me, but I'm here to listen," she tells me.

I take a deep breath. "Nothing's wrong," I mumble, taking another spoonful of ice cream. I look at her through the corner of my eye.

"I heard you crying last night," she reveals quietly. "I've heard you crying the past three nights, and I'm worried about you."

I open my mouth to tell her again that she doesn't have to worry, that I'm okay, but suddenly, my stomach starts to churn. I run to the bathroom as fast as I can. Thankfully, the contents in my stomach don't spill out until I'm over the toilet. When I lift my head up, Angela is staring in the doorway silently with her arms crossed. I look away from the skeptical look on her face and grab my toothbrush.

"Can you guess what I'm about to ask?" she says, handing me the toothpaste beside her.

"It's not what you think." I stuff the paste-filled brush in my mouth, taking as long as I can to brush so I won't have to face her.

"And you know this for sure?" she asks, sitting on the edge of her tub. I see she's not going to let up on this. I smile tightly and rinse my mouth.

"I know my body," I tell her simply, and leave the bathroom. There is no way that I can be . . .

She follows me back to the living room. "When is the last time you had your period?"

"Three weeks ago," I say off the top of my head, hoping the questions will stop.

"Was it a full one or . . ." she continues.

I stop and turn around to face her. "It doesn't matter, because I'm not pregnant." I should have gone to a hotel.

"Willing yourself not to be pregnant doesn't work."

"Well, birth control does."

"It isn't a hundred percent."

"Well, it is for me," I say, anger creeping into my voice.

"You're telling me that you never missed using it, or whenever you and Cal had sex, he always wore a condom?" She laughs.

I cover my face with my hands. "I don't want to talk about this, okay?" I whine, covering my face.

"Lauren, you can't ignore this!"

"I'm not ignoring anything, because there's nothing to ignore. So what? I've thrown up once. It could be what I ate. I could have the flu. It doesn't mean I'm pregnant."

"No, but since you've been here, you've done nothing but eat, sleep, and cry. I don't know what happened when I took you home. I haven't asked you anything, but you aren't the person I know. Tell me what's going on," she asks sincerely.

"He left me, Angie! Cal left me. That is why I've been crying," I say, my voice rising. I bite my lip, begging my eyes to stop watering. "I sleep so I won't have to think about him being gone. I miss him, and I want him back. As screwed up as our relationship was, I want him back. I love him." I cover my face again.

Angela wraps her arm around me. "Lauren, why didn't you tell me?"

"I was embarrassed. I don't know what I'm going to do. I didn't want you to feel sorry for me, but I couldn't stay in that house or go back to my aunt's. I didn't want to be alone either. I didn't want to admit that it's happening," I tell her amidst the tears falling from my eyes.

"I'm so sorry, Lauren. I didn't know. It's okay to miss him. There's nothing wrong with that—you've been with him the last three years of your life. I'd be worried if you didn't. I'm sorry. What did he say to you? He didn't tell you why or where he was going?"

"It's not important. He's gone; that's all." I grip my forehead in my hands. "Just gone." I try to compose myself, and I sit down on the couch that has been my bed for the past week. "I don't know, Angie," I say honestly, wiping my face.

"Don't know what?" she asks, carefully sitting beside me.

I run my hands through my hair out of frustration. "The last time I had a full period was two months ago. So I really don't know if, if I'm pregnant. It's possible. What I do know is that this would be the worst time, the absolute worst," I whimper, covering my face. "A baby is not what I need right now. I can't be pregnant." I fold my arms around my stomach.

"Well, let's not jump to conclusions; you may not be. After all, stress would cause your period to stop, and you've been sleeping because you're emotionally drained." She tries to comfort me, but the look on her face is anything but convinced.

"The important thing is that you find out, and then you can figure out what you're going to do about it, okay?" she says, lifting my head. I smile weakly. She goes to the fridge and hands me an iced tea.

"So, I'll run to the store and get a test. You stay here and chill. Don't go to sleep—watch TV, listen to some music, but I'm kicking your ass if you're passed out when I get back," she jokes. I smile.

I'm not pregnant. I'm not.

"IT SAYS TO wait five minutes. It'll be a plus sign if positive, a minus if negative." She smiles, trying to cover up her own nervousness.

"I know, you've told me that twice," I tell her nervously.

"Sorry," she bites her lip anxiously.

"God, why is this taking so long? It seems like it's been twenty. How much time left?" I ask, pacing the kitchen again.

"Three. Only two to go," she says after looking at her watch. "Maybe we should go for a walk. Just sitting here waiting is going to drive you crazy," she suggests.

"No. I need to know that I'm not as soon as possible," I tell her, playing with my fingertips.

There's no way I can be pregnant. Not now. Not now!

"Okay. It's been five." I feel my stomach drop. Suddenly I wish I hadn't taken this test. I want to run out of the house and not look back. If I don't know I'm not, it's better than knowing the other possibility. I can't deal with this right now.

"Lauren, are you okay? You're turning pale," Angela says with a worried look on her face.

"I'm fine," I say, trying to convince myself.

"Are you going to go get it?" she asks. I look at the bathroom door; my heart starts to beat faster.

"I can't. You look," I tell her, sitting down.

"Are you sure?" she asks me again.

I nod.

"Okay."

I close my eyes and hear her footsteps move farther away. When I hear them coming back, I squeeze my eyes tighter. She taps me lightly on the shoulder. I look up, trying to read her expression.

"Good news," she says with a soft smile.

I breathe a deep sigh of relief. "Thank you, God," I say, as if twenty pounds have been lifted off me.

"This is just so much off my mind. You don't know how scared I was. If I was pregnant, I can't even think about what I would do. I don't even know what I'm going to do now. Having a baby, that just would have made things so much more complicated," I say, hugging her. Suddenly, I notice she's not hugging me back. I lean back and see her face is blank.

"Maybe I should have said bad news," she says, covering her forehead. "I'm such an idiot, I'm sorry!"

"What?" I ask, confused, and she hands the test to me. My stomach drops when I see the deep pink plus sign.

"No. NO!" I throw the test on the floor. "I can't have a baby right now! This can't be happening!" I say frantically, my tears returning.

"Lauren, calm down," she pleads.

"Calm down? I can't be pregnant! I don't even know where my husband is. This cannot happen! It has to be wrong," I shout. "I can't be a mom right now. It's wrong, right? Most of the time they're wrong." I try to convince myself. Angela grabs my hands.

"Yes, it could be wrong. These things aren't 100 percent, but you have to prepare yourself for the possibility that it might not be," she urges, which makes me cry harder.

"I can't raise a child alone. I'm not ready for a baby." I shake my head defiantly.

"Lauren, listen to me, okay? You can do this. You don't need Cal. If he comes back, I'll be so happy for you, but if he doesn't, screw him. You're a strong, wonderful, kind, beautiful woman. If he doesn't know that, he doesn't deserve you. He certainly doesn't for making you feel like this, and he won't deserve the wonderful, beautiful baby you might be having. You are not going to do this alone. You'll have me and Hillary and Raven. We'll all be here for you."

I look at her; she seems genuine, but she doesn't understand. I stand up and walk over to the sink and splash water on my face. I stoically walk out of the bathroom and grab my purse, heading for the door.

"Where are you going?" she asks worriedly.

"I need some air. I'm going for a walk," I tell her as I open the door.

She starts to get up. "I'll go with you."

"No, I need some time alone."

"Lauren . . ."

"I'll be fine. I'm fine," I tell her with a dry chuckle as I close the door behind me.

November 7th, 2010

"LAUREN, YOU'RE TAKING forever, babe," Cal complains, standing in the doorway dressed in a square-collar silver button-up paired with a hand-tailored black suit. I slip on my black leather pumps and observe myself in the mirror, making sure the clingy silver dress that's hugging my body hasn't bunched up.

"You look fine." He's left his former resting spot in the doorway and is now behind me, his arms wrapped around my waist, pressing his body against mine. I shimmy out of his arms and grab my flat iron, determined to get the one portion of my hair to cooperate.

"If we're going to be late, let's make it for a better reason." His voice is in my ear and his hand has slid beneath my dress. I whip around and push his hand away playfully.

"No, Cal. Not tonight," I warn him, backing away. I have got to learn to get ready faster, because it seems when I don't and we're heading towards being late, he decides to use it as an excuse to make us even later. He blocks my path, and I'm trapped between my vanity and his chest. He takes the flat iron from me and sets it down.

"We're already late," he says, and in one swift swoop is lifting me onto the vanity.

"But—" My sentence is stopped by his lips covering mine. Only *we* would be late for our own engagement party. I start to give in when I hear our house phone ring. The only person who calls the house phone is the building concierge.

I pull away from his kiss. "It's just going to keep ringing." He groans and turns to grab the phone, answering it as he walks back to me.

"Yeah," he says impatiently as his lips find my neck again. A second later, he stops and gives his full attention to the phone call.

"What's her name?" he asks.

I'm watching him, but he turns, so I don't see his reaction when the person on the other end answers.

"I'll be right there," he says and hangs up the phone.

"What happened?" I ask, maneuvering myself off the vanity and adjusting my dress.

"I think it's a solicitor or something," he says, adjusting his jacket coolly.

"A solicitor?" I follow him as he heads out of our bedroom and downstairs. "At five o'clock on a Saturday?"

My tone is joking, but the expression on my face is revealing the seriousness of the question.

He stops in his tracks and looks at me.

"I'm going to see who it is," he says. "I'll be right back."

"I'll go with you," I inform him.

"No, finish getting ready. This won't take me five minutes," he says, casually resting his hands in his jacket pocket. I stare at him, searching his expression for a hint of nervousness or twinge of guilt. He sighs in exasperation.

I fold my arms across my chest. "Well, you get this strange call that there's some woman downstairs to meet you and you say it's a *solicitor*." Cal never rushes to do anything, and then he gets a call about a woman being downstairs to meet him and I'm just supposed to say, "Okay, honey"?

He seems amused by my reaction. A smile spreads across his face and he reaches out, pulling me to him.

"You're sexy when you're jealous," he says, his arms encircling my waist. I move his hands off me, feeling slightly embarrassed. I've never been jealous over a man before, but I do tend to be with him. Wherever we go, he's like a magnet for female attention. He's never been disrespectful to me or encouraged it, but it gets annoying, really annoying.

"She isn't here to see me; she's here to see you," he retorts, stepping towards me again, and I arch my brow in surprise.

"Me?"

"Yes, you, and if it has anything to do with shopping, I figured I'll save time by having her come back later," he teases. I don't shop that much to have personal shoppers tracking me down. I try to think who would come here to see me.

"Go finish getting ready and you can meet me downstairs," he says, and a moment later he's out the door. I head back to my dressing room, adjust my dress, and run my hand through my hair. I start to grab my flat iron, but there's a nagging feeling in the pit of my stomach—the kind you get when you feel like you've left something behind. I set my flat iron back down and grab my purse and jacket. I rush down the stairs, almost breaking my ankle in these pumps, and head out the door. I push the elevator button multiple times, and it seems like an eternity before it opens.

I push the main floor button and wait for the doors to close. As it starts its mile-long drop, I take a deep breath. I don't know why I'm nervous, but something isn't sitting right with me about this. When the doors open, I try to exit quickly without running. I start to walk past the desk when Lamar, one of the concierges, greets me. I want to be rude and wave and walk past, but I always stop to say hello. In the distance, I see Cal speaking to a woman. Her back is to me, showcasing a mane of long red hair hanging down her back. She seems to be shifting from side to side.

"Lauren, your dress is fab," Lamar says quietly, so the other tenants don't hear him.

"Thank you. Lamar, did you call upstairs for me?" I ask. My attention is on Cal and the woman.

"Yes. Mr. Scott answered and said he'd be down instead," he replies, his attention turning to my shoes.

"Did she say who she was?" I ask, a little impatient that his attention is on my outfit more than the matter at hand.

"She said she was reluctant to do so," he says, arching a brow. Mine matches it in understanding. I reach into my purse and hope that I have some money in it, happy to find a twenty-dollar bill already folded. I bite my lip and rest the money on the counter, covering it with my hand.

"Anything else?" I ask, looking Lamar square in the eye. He looks around before taking it and leans closer across the desk.

"She seemed to be a bit on edge when Mr. Scott appeared instead of you, and they went outside. She didn't look too pleased to see him though."

"What did she look like?" I ask mechanically, unable to keep the words from escaping my mouth, and Lamar's eyes light up as if I asked a question that made his day.

"Well, she doesn't seem like she's from around here," he says with a frown.

"What do you mean?"

"Well, you know how everyone dresses around here? She didn't look homeless or anything, but she seemed out of place. More like she got lost on her way to the suburbs and wandered in." He chuckles.

"How old do you think she is?" I ask curiously.

"She was an older woman. Maybe early fifties," he says, and then he pauses. "But there was something about her that seemed familiar, like I've seen been her before, but maybe not." He shakes his head, dismissing the thought, and turns his attention back to the computer as the manager approaches the desk.

"Is everything okay, Ms. Brooks?" Ms. Riley asks me with a wide smile.

"Yes, everything is fine," I say, leaving the desk and hurrying towards the door. By the time I reach it and step out, the red-headed woman is walking down the street and Cal is walking back towards me.

"What was that about? Who was she?" I ask Cal, buttoning my jacket.

"Nothing," he says, opening the door for me to go back inside. I hesitate a moment, and the woman turns back and looks towards us. She's far in the distance, but her expression is sullen.

"Are you coming?" Cal asks impatiently. In the second I look at him and back at the mysterious red-headed woman, she's disappeared into the sea of people.

"Nothing?" I say pointedly.

"I took care of it; she didn't want anything important," he says. He sits on one of the plush chocolate-brown chairs in the lobby. I assume he's waiting for our car to be brought around.

"Well, what happened? What did she want with me?" I ask, sitting beside him.

"She really wasn't making any sense. She seemed hopped up on something. I told her to leave." He sighs, pulling out his cell phone.

"Well, maybe you should have let me talk to her," I say, nudging him so he can give me his full attention.

"I didn't want some crazy woman to upset you about some non-sense before our dinner tonight," he says simply.

"Why would she upset me? How did she know me and that I'd be here? I don't understand."

"Look. She wasn't making any sense. She probably pulled your name off an article about some event we've been to with Dexter. You have to be careful about just anyone trying to see you. When you're as-sociated with the Crestfields, people see dollar signs and will sell you any sob story thinking you can write them a check. Most people have some type of agenda, and I'm sure she did, but she won't be back. You can't just trust anybody now, okay?" he says, grasping my hand at the last part of his speech.

I nod and try to accept the explanation he gave me. It makes sense, but that nagging feeling doesn't go away and the woman's face doesn't disappear from my thoughts easily.

I WALK INTO the office, and the first thing I see is a woman trying to hold her baby and read a magazine at the same time. She smiles at me, and I try my best to return it before approaching the receptionist's desk.

"Hello. Welcome to Dr. Green's office. How can I help you?" she says with a wide smile.

"I need a pregnancy exam," I say bluntly. The young woman seems caught off guard by my candor.

June 7th, 2011

"We can do that." She smiles, after taking a few seconds to recover. "I'll need your name, and for you to fill out this form, and I can schedule you an appointment," she says, handing me a packet of papers.

"No, you don't understand. I need one now," I tell her quickly.

Her eyebrow rises. "I'm sorry, but you'll have to make an appointment," she informs me nervously.

"This—this is an emergency," I tell her quickly.

"An emergency?" she questions.

I see I'm not going to be able to maintain my composure. I plaster a big smile on my face and lean closer to her. "My husband walked out on me last week, and I have no fucking idea where he is. I took a pregnancy test this morning, and, you guessed it! Positive! So, I need a doctor in there to tell me that the test was wrong, and that I don't have another thing to add to my list of things to worry about. I don't have any cash with me, but I have these credit cards and a checkbook. I'll pay anything." I take out my wallet and put it on the desk.

"I'll sign a piece of paper saying if you happen to kill me during the exam you're not to blame, but I can't go another minute guessing, okay? I can't guess about another thing in my life. I'm not crazy, but every minute that passes, I'm inching closer to it. So if you don't want me to go ballistic in this office and cause more of a scene than I already have, you'll tell the doctor you have a very desperate woman out here in need of his or her assistance!" After that spiel, I take a breath and hope, after the look on the woman's face, she doesn't call the police.

"Um, she can have my appointment. I'll go later." The woman who smiled at me earlier looks at me sympathetically.

"Thank you," I tell her desperately. A door opens, and a nurse comes out, addressing the receptionist. "Who's next?" The receptionist points to me.

IT SEEMS LIKE the doctor has been out of the room forever. I guess the secretary is telling her what a nut I am. I probably shouldn't have come here so soon, but I felt like I couldn't breathe. I need to know what my situation is for sure. When the door opens, I breathe a sigh of relief.

"How are you, Mrs. Scott?" she asks, sitting on a stool across from me.

"Well, I've been better," I mumble.

"When is the last time you had a normal period?" she asks, her eyes still examining the clipboard.

"About two months ago. Well, three weeks ago I had it, but it only lasted for a day."

"You told the nurse that you took an at-home pregnancy test and it was positive?" she asks, scribbling on the chart.

"Yes, but I hear that those can be wrong, right? At-home kits aren't a hundred percent."

"No, at-home kits are not one hundred percent, but they are pretty close. Most are up to ninety-seven percent accurate."

"But there's still a three percent chance that I'm not," I say quickly.

She finally stops writing and her eyes connect with mine. "Mrs. Scott, I am going to be honest with you. You seem like right now you need honesty and not vague reassurances from me," she starts.

"Brooks. I'd prefer if you called me Brooks," I say quietly. I guess I'll have to get used to it.

"Miss Brooks, an at-home pregnancy test or the pregnancy test I would give you measures for a hormone called human chorionic gonadotropin, the pregnancy hormone. An at-home test uses urine to detect the level in your body. I gave you a qualitative hCG blood test, which would measure the exact amount of the hormone in your bloodstream. This test is extremely accurate—it could detect the hormone as soon as a week after ovulation. Pregnancy kit tests are least accurate if you took the test a week after you ovulated, which could possibly have given you false results taking it too early. But from your statements, in my professional opinion, if you haven't had a normal period in six weeks, the test is most likely accurate. From the symptoms you've described such as extreme fatigue, morning sickness, there is a strong possibility . . ." Her voice starts to drown out after a while. I know I'm pregnant because when things are bad, they only get worse.

WHEN I OPEN the door, I see Angela talking on the phone.

"I've got to go," she says quickly and hangs up. I close the door and lean against it.

"Lauren, I was so worried about you. I didn't know where to look. Your aunt keeps calling, and I don't know what to say. You've been gone five hours," she scolds me in a worried tone.

"Eight weeks," I say simply

"What?" her tone softens.

"I'm eight weeks pregnant," I say, feeling completely numb. I slide down the door and cover my face. From of all the tears I've cried, I'm surprised I'm not dehydrated. I think I've literally cried myself out. She doesn't say anything but sits beside me and takes my hand.

"I went to the doctor's office down the street. After I found out, I walked around for hours, just trying to clear my head, but it helped," I say, clearing my throat.

"I can't cry anymore or feel sorry for myself. I'm having a baby, and

I'm going to have to deal with it. There are so many people who have had children in worse situations than me, so I can't just cry about it anymore. But I am so angry because I shouldn't have to do this alone. I can do this by myself, but I shouldn't have to!"

"You're not going to. You'll have me, your aunt . . ."

"He should be here! I need *him*, and he's not going to be. I remember the night this happened. When I was going to leave him, and he carried me upstairs like I was a six-year-old with a temper tantrum and locked me in my room. That same night he came home and brought me a dozen pink roses. I was so angry with him, and I still gave in. I still wanted him. He made love to me the entire night and left the next afternoon." I stand up. "That was the night he did this to me. And just like then, he left!"

Angela gets up and walks toward me. "It may seem bad now, but when you hold that little baby in your arms, and you see its eyes and its smile, all of this shit you're going through now will be worth it."

I hug her. She has been such a good friend to me. Through all of my crazy mood swings and anti-social behavior, she's never complained and always listened without asking.

I'm going to get through this. I'm going to have to be a better woman, for myself and now for this baby that's growing inside of me. Things aren't just about me anymore. I can't cry for Cal another day. My life can't be wrapped around him or his memory. I guess in some way, he's given me a piece of him, and now I have someone else to love.

NEXT WEEK I'LL be standing in a church in front of over five hundred guests, most of whom Cal and I don't really know or care about—even Michael was invited. I don't hate him so much anymore though. A thousand pictures will be taken as we say our vows for the second time. I'll be wearing a nine-thousand-dollar Vera Wang gown with a diamond necklace that costs even more than that. The wedding will be followed by a grand reception. But that's not *my* wedding; well, supposedly it is, but I call it "The Crestfield Affair."

December 7th, 2010

Cal and I have joked about it. Dexter says it will be good for the company's image—whatever that is. Cal wanted to blow it off, but Helen begged me. I never thought she'd beg a day in her life. Besides, what girl wouldn't want two weddings?

But today, on this perfect seventy-degree day on a private beach in Rio, wearing a little white sundress, pearls, and a yellow flower in my hair, with my toes in the beautiful white sand, I commit to spending the rest of my life with the man who swept me off my feet and captured my heart. My tears flow freely as I hold his hand. He's in a white slacks and a matching short-sleeved button-up with a yellow handkerchief in his pocket. He's displaying a boyish grin, but I know the naughtiness that hides behind it. He squeezes my hand as the pastor—whose English is a little less than perfect—gives him the go-ahead to say his vows. He takes a deep breath and Dexter pats him on the shoulder. He lets out a small laugh, but then his expression turns serious.

"Lauren, you know I love you more than anything, more than anyone," he says, his voice steady, and I hear Raven sigh a few feet away from me. I giggle, but the weight of his words cause a warm rush to come over me.

"You've made me a better man," he says a little more softly, and he pauses. I wipe away the tears from my eyes and resist the urge to hug him tightly. He steps closer to me and kisses away the tears on my cheeks. More swooning comes from the women in our audience, which includes Angela, Raven, Hillary, and Helen.

"I've never wanted anything more than our marriage, Lauren. You're the one thing that belongs to me. The only pure thing I have is us. I used to have a different reason for being. It came from a dark place. My motivation changed when I fell in love with you. You're my strength and my weakness. You're the reason I fight to be here," he says, my face now in his hands, and I can't resist the urge to kiss him at that moment. I give in, nearly jumping into his arms. His lips welcome mine and I rest in his embrace.

"I love you so much, Cal," I say quietly when our lips have separated and only he can hear me.

I'm sure the pastor is shooting me a disapproving look for jumping the gun on the kiss, but I don't care. Nothing has been traditional about us before, so why start now? As long as this ends with me being proclaimed Mrs. Lauren Scott, nothing else will matter—not his secrets, not his past. Every negative echo that rested in my brain has melted away; it just doesn't matter. Our love will overcome whatever issues we'll face. I'm sure they will come up—every marriage has them—but when I see his gleaming gray eyes that sometimes reflect warm green shades behind them, I know we'll get through whatever life throws our way. He may not be perfect, but I think I just may have found my super-sexy, leather-jacket-wearing, motorcycle-riding Prince Charming of the twenty-first century.

"HAAAPPPY BIIRTHDAY TOOO you, haapppy birthday too yooou. Happy birthday, dear Caylen. Haappy biirthdayy too youoooo," Hillary sings. The rest of us are doubled up, laughing at her dramatic, horrible, over-the-top singing.

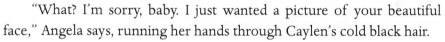

March 7th, 2013

"Screw you all. Caylen liked it, didn't you, honey?" she says, pinching my little girl's cheeks.

"Smile!" Angela says quickly, and a flash almost blinds me. Of course Caylen immediately begins to cry.

"Angie!" Hillary scolds her.

"What? I'm sorry, baby. I just wanted a picture of your beautiful face," Angela says, running her hands through Caylen's cold black hair.

"It's okay, she's sleepy anyway. You old people tired her out," I joke, cradling her in my arms.

"I'm going to put her to bed."

"I'll help you," Helen says suddenly. She's been quiet all night, which is unusual for her.

"Meanwhile, I'm going to steal a piece of this begging-me-to-eat-it cake," Hillary says quickly.

I walk up the stairs, rubbing Caylen's back—the only thing that quiets her down when she's fighting sleep. Helen is quietly following behind me. I open the door to the nursery, which is painted all pink with white furniture. Helen did a beautiful job decorating and supplying everything in the room herself. I still can't believe how different the loft looks since Caylen was born. I look down at my little girl, rubbing her eyes, and my heart melts. It is still amazing to me how much you can love a person who didn't exist in your life for most of it. I hand her to Helen so I can grab a pair of her pajamas.

"She's grown so much," Helen says with a sigh.

"Yeah. She has." I smile, taking off her t-shirt and putting her pajamas on.

"It seems like just yesterday she was in your stomach," she teases.

"Yes, kicking her way out." I giggle. I know why I slept so much in my early months—because I barely got any sleep in the later months of my pregnancy.

"And tomorrow, she'll be a year old. She's so beautiful, Lauren," Helen says, admiring her again.

"Raven's taking her to the zoo tomorrow, so she gets double the birthday fun." I tickle Caylen before I finish putting her clothes on. I'm thankful she's not putting up a fight like she usually does.

"You're going to be a good girl and go to sleep for mommy, right?" I ask, seeing her little mouth open for a yawn. When I put her in her crib she reaches out her arms for me. I lay her back down, placing her blanket over her. I hold her hand until her eyes close.

"It's amazing how much she looks like C—" She stops quickly and folds her hands as if she's a kid who's said a bad word.

"You know, you can say his name around me. I'm not going to shrivel up and die if you do," I joke to lessen the tension in the room.

"I wasn't going to say anything," Helen lies, picking up the stuffed bear Hillary bought Caylen for her birthday.

"Cal. You were going to say she looks just like Cal. You know, the thought has crossed my mind. I'm not blind." Sharpness is creeping into my voice that I didn't intend. Helen looks away uncomfortably.

I take a deep breath. "It's almost been two years. You don't have to walk on eggshells around me. You can say his name. I won't die, or start crying." I understood how weird it was for her to talk about him when it first happened. I remember how angry I was the day after I found out I was pregnant with Caylen. I stormed straight into the mansion demanding to know where Cal was, because if anyone knew, it was Dexter. He proceeded to say how he sympathized with my situation and how he and Helen would be there for me, but he had no idea where Cal was. After three private detectives came up with nothing on Cal, and I was six months pregnant and desperate, I begged Dexter one last time to contact Cal for me. He looked me in my face and told me he didn't know where

Cal was. It was the biggest lie he ever told. I didn't speak to him or Helen again until after Caylen was born.

Helen came to the hospital with dozens of roses, balloons, and teddy bears. She practically outdid everyone who gave me something at my baby shower. I couldn't be mean to her after that. After all, I couldn't blame her for the bond that Dexter and Cal had. I could be dying and Dexter wouldn't tell me where Cal was if he asked him not to.

"I'm sorry, I never realized. Well, actually I did, and I'm sorry. I'm sorry for all that you're going through, Lauren. If I—"

I cut her off. "Helen, you don't have to apologize for anything. You've been wonderful to me and Caylen. I'm not angry with you. I don't resent you. I'm not even upset with Dexter anymore. I've gotten past that. If he hasn't told me where Cal is, it has to be because Cal doesn't want him to. I've accepted that now. I can't blame anyone else for his actions. You tell Dexter that for me. He can come to Caylen's future birthdays or visit her when he wants. He doesn't have to worry about me bombarding him with questions or going psycho on him." I laugh slightly.

Helen smiles. "I'll tell him that. He's been dying to see her. I'm glad you've gotten over him," she says, breathing a sigh of relief.

I look over at her and roll my eyes. "Truthfully, I haven't. I don't know if I ever will, but that doesn't mean I'm going to spend the rest of my life waiting around for him. He gave me the most wonderful gift he ever could have, and I'll always be thankful for that. But I'll never forgive him for not being a part of Caylen's life." I realize I sound more bitter than I intend to. I haven't said his name aloud since Caylen was born, or talked to anyone about him. I guess I can't help but be bitter.

"You have every right to be angry. I knew Cal could be Cal, but I never thought he'd do something like this."

"You aren't the only one," I say quietly before kissing Caylen on the cheek. She's finally drifted off to sleep.

"Night, sweetie," Helen whispers and walks out. Before I follow her out the door, I switch off the main light and turn the night light on.

Downstairs, Raven is taking off her coat and trying to hold three gift boxes at the same time. "I hear I missed the birthday girl."

"Raven, you're here!" I smile widely, giving her a big hug.

"Yes, you wouldn't believe the traffic. I was supposed to be here two hours ago," she says angrily, setting down the gifts.

"Raven, you didn't," I scold her. She's bought Caylen so many things already.

"Of course I did. You didn't really think I was not going to buy my favorite little girl something for her birthday? But since I'm old fashioned, she won't be able to open them until her real birthday," Raven scolds me playfully.

"Well, a Monday isn't the best time for a party. Everyone has work or school."

"Tell me there are plenty of pictures." She smiles, handing me her coat.

I take it from her and hang it in the closet. "Steven recorded everything. I'll get him to send it to your phone."

Her smile fades a bit. Raven hasn't quite taken to Steven as much as I'd like.

"Steven. Oh yes, where is he?" she says, trying to sound cheerful, but I can see the disinterest in her eyes.

"He's setting up Caylen's new bed," I tell her.

"Well, that's nice." She notices Helen, who has taken a seat on the couch. "Hello, Helen, how are you?" Raven asks politely.

"Hello, Ms. Brooks," Helen says, extending her hand. "I'm fine, thank you. Lauren, I think it's time for me to get going."

"Already?" I ask, disappointed.

"Yes, Dexter and I have an engagement that we just can't miss," she groans sarcastically, grabbing her leather jacket.

"Well, let me get you some cake," I say before she stops me.

"No cake. I'm already on a diet, no need to tempt me." She smiles and gives me a warm hug.

"You're in beautiful shape; you don't need a diet," Raven tells her seriously.

Helen smiles graciously at her. "Well, thank you, but there's this certain dress that I'm dying to get into by my birthday, so I'm just going to lose a couple of pounds." Helen winks.

"I'll walk you out," I tell her.

"I'm going to go peek at the little angel. Nice seeing you again, Helen," Raven says before heading up the stairs.

Helen nods, and we both head to the elevator in the lobby. "So, Thursday—girls' day out at the spa—no canceling on me this time!" Helen scolds.

"I won't. I promise." I smile widely as she steps in the elevator.

"I'll call you tomorrow," she says as the doors shut.

I wave before they close, and exhale, shivering and wrapping my arms around myself—they keep the air conditioning on in the hall all year, it seems. She's right to give me a hard time. I've canceled on more than a couple of occasions. I think my excuses are probably getting old.

I turn to walk back into the penthouse. The party is practically over, and my thoughts drift to Caylen, her first birthday, and the fact that her dad's not here.

"You okay?" I look up to see Steven staring at me curiously.

"Yeah, why?"

He walks closer to me, a concerned look on his face. "You looked a little weird."

"I-I'm fine," I say, forcing a smile.

He touches my face gently, and I don't move it. "You sure?" he asks, looking at me skeptically.

I smile softly. "I am now." A movement behind him catches my eye, and I look to see Raven standing at the head of the stairs. I step back from him and fold my arms.

"Lauren, can I speak to you a moment?" she calls.

"Sure," I say quickly.

"Hi, Ms. Brooks." Steven smiles and gives her a small wave. Raven smiles tightly at him but doesn't say anything back. I give Steven a sympathetic look, but he just laughs, heading back to where everyone else is.

I head upstairs and into Caylen's bedroom, where Raven is holding her. "She woke up?"

"She's fine. I have my sweetie," she says, fanning me away. Raven sits down in the rocking chair and cuddles Caylen while brushing her dark locks.

"So, you and Steven have gotten quite close again since I last saw you two together."

I think back to before I was married and before I dated Michael. There was Steven. With his sandy-blond hair and soft blue eyes that are only second to his comical personality, he always knows what to say to make me smile; even after we mutually broke up, we remained good friends, which is something I can't say about Michael and me.

"He's my friend," I tell her quickly.

"Is he still with that nice girl I met who was at your baby shower?"

"No. They broke up a few months ago."

"Well, how convenient," she says airily.

I feel my stomach knot. "Okay. Out with it. What are you asking me?"

"Do you have feelings for him?" she asks casually as she sets Caylen on the floor and hands her a teddy bear to play with.

"What if I do? What if I do have feelings for him?" I ask, annoyed.

Raven continues to focus on Caylen. "Well, if you haven't forgotten, you're still married."

"No, I'm not married, actually," I say sharply.

Her head turns quickly toward me. "You aren't?" she asks, shocked.

"Marriage to me is more than a piece of paper with two names on it."

"So you're going to start a relationship with him again?"

"Look, I didn't say anything about a relationship," I yell, and Caylen starts to cry. Raven hands her to me, and I rock her in my arms.

"Lauren, I think it's time you stop pretending Cal doesn't exist."

My mouth completely drops open at that. That's my Raven, the only person who doesn't shrink away from mentioning him around me, but she's never been this blunt about it.

"Pretend? God, I wish! You think I can just block him out? Well, let me tell you. You don't know how hard it is for me here. Being in this house where everywhere I look, I remember something I'd rather forget. Every time I close my eyes, he's there. Sometimes I swear I can feel his arms around me." I can feel tears building in my eyes, and thankfully, Caylen's finally settled back down. I lay her down in the crib and watch her fall asleep.

"Every time I look at his daughter, I see his eyes, his smile." I run my hands through Caylen's full head of dark curly locks.

"When I look at her, sometimes all I see is him." A single tear rolls down my cheek, and Raven's arms encircle me.

"I'm sorry, honey. I shouldn't have even suggested what I did. I don't know what I was thinking."

"It's okay," I say quickly, wiping my cheek. "This is the first time I've allowed myself to cry over him in a while," I say, almost to myself. One tear isn't that bad compared to . . .

"This thing with Steven?" Raven asks, her expression a lot softer than before.

"I don't know," I say honestly, folding my arms. "He's just been so sweet and kind."

"And here," Raven adds.

"Yes," I admit. "That's the thing," I walk over to the bedroom door and close it. "I don't know if my feelings are genuine, or if loneliness is starting to take its toll," I tell her, picking up one of Caylen's many teddy bears and fiddling with its arms.

"That's understandable," Raven says stoically. I can see that I'm making her uncomfortable.

"I don't want to hurt him, Raven. I just don't know what to do."

"Tell him how you feel. Exactly where you stand—if you feel it's time and this could be something you really want to explore. You need to look into divorcing Cal. He abandoned your marriage . . ."

I cringe at the word. "I don't want to talk about that right now." There's a light knock at the door, saving me from where this conversation is going.

"Come in," I say as loud as I can without waking Caylen.

Angela tiptoes in. "Hey, Ms. Brooks," she whispers, giving Raven a big hug. It makes me happy to see how close they've become through their relationship with me. The past two years would have been horrific without them.

"How are you, sweetheart?" Raven whispers, eyeing the baby, who's turning over in her sleep.

"I'm good. I have to be going; I have to work ridiculously early to-morrow." She laughs.

"Did you get some cake?" I ask.

"Yeah, Steven fixed me a plate. I just wanted to let you know I was leaving, girly," she says before giving me a hug. "See you, princess," she whispers, kissing Caylen on the forehead.

"Thanks for coming, Angie. I know you'll have a long day tomorrow."

"Like I'd have missed this," she says, zipping up her jacket. "Oh, Hillary's knocked out on your couch. I was supposed to give her a ride home, but you know how cranky she is if you wake her." Angela laughs.

"She'll be fine. Steven can take her home or she can sleep here to-night, and I'll take her in the morning," I assure her.

"Come walk me out," Angela gestures. She waves to Raven as we leave the room. "Bye, Ms. Brooks."

"Drive safely, hon."

Angela and I get to the front door, and she stops before opening it. "You okay?"

"Just tired." I smile, letting a yawn escape my mouth. "I didn't think having a party for a one-year-old would be so tiring." I laugh.

"We spent more time setting up the party than having it." She laughs as she opens the door. "I know my way out. You get some rest—you look tired," she says with a frown.

"Gee, thanks." I laugh lightly.

She smiles softly. "You know what I mean."

"I do." I sigh, looking her in the eye. Angela and I have probably grown closer than all of my other friends since she stuck with me during one of the worst times of my life. She doesn't have to guess why or how I'm feeling most of the time. She knows.

"Hey, don't forget your cake!" Steven comes out of the kitchen with a plate wrapped in aluminum foil.

"Thank you. And it looks like you're taking Hillary home." Angela hits him playfully on the chest.

"When was that decided?" Steven raises his eyebrows in mock surprise.

"Well, you're the last one here, so you win." Angela laughs, taking her plate from him.

"Want me to walk you out?" Steven asks her.

"I'm a big girl; I can make it on my own."

"Text me when you get in your car safely," Steven tells her. His big brother instinct is kicking in, and I can't help but smile.

"I will, Dad," she teases. "Bye, kiddies," she says, shutting the door behind her.

I go and lock it. "Now the fun of cleaning begins! Yay!"

"So much fun, I'll do it myself," Steven says with fake enthusiasm.

"No. I can't let you do that," I say, and I start picking up Caylen's toys that are scattered around the floor.

He laughs and starts taking toys out of my hands. "Oh, come on, cleaning to me is all kinds of fun."

"You sure?" He's been doing so much for me lately.

"Absolutely. You go lie down. I'm sure Caylen has tired you out.

I look at his soft smile and feel myself blush.

"Steven," I say nervously and begin to fiddle with my fingertips. "Raven's spending the night, so that basically guarantees me a babysitter tomorrow. I haven't been out in a while, and I was wondering if you'd— if you'd want to have lunch with me?" I feel like I'm fourteen again.

I watch his face as his expression softens, then blooms into a coy smile. "I'd love to."

I begin to giggle.

"Why do I feel like I'm in high school all of a sudden?" he teases.

I laugh. "Want to meet at eleven?"

"Sure."

"Good. Okay, so, in case I'm asleep when you leave, good night." The next thing I do surprises even me. I kiss him on the cheek.

He looks surprised by it, but then his gaze moves behind me and his eyes widen. I turn around to see Raven behind me. Dammit.

"I just came to help clean up," she says, surprised.

"Party time," he teases.

Raven smiles, and I just grin at her. She's actually being nice to him.

"Well, I'll let you two crazy kids get started." I laugh, heading up the stairs. She waves, and they start moving things around. I feel happy. I'm glad Raven's starting to give him more of a chance.

When I reach the second floor of the loft, I peep in Caylen's room to make sure she's still sleeping before heading to mine. When I reach my room, I close the door behind me and walk over to my mirror. I sigh at my appearance. When you have kids, your style sure as hell changes. Glamorous clothes for me now are a clean t-shirt and jeans, and I've traded my flat iron for air-drying, something I *never* used to do.

I grab the baby monitor off my dresser and take it to bed with me. As soon as I lie down, I realize I'm lying on top of Caylen's Speak and Spell Moving it to the other side of the bed, I laugh to myself at how much things have changed in two years. I yawn and feel myself drifting to sleep.

"Hon, I forgot my contact solution. I'm going to run to the drug store and grab a bottle," Raven says, standing in my doorway. "Make sure you lock up."

"Okay, I will," I say with a yawn. Just a few more minutes of rest . . .

I WAKE UP to Caylen's crying. I must have drifted off to sleep. Raven must not be back yet. I get out of bed and head towards Caylen's room, but when I attempt to open my door, I can't. A wave of panic washes over me, and I frantically twist and pull the knob, but it doesn't budge. I can't get out! I can't get to my baby! I turn and snatch my phone up to call Raven.

"Shh, no crying, sweetheart. Daddy doesn't cry, and you're just like daddy." The voice through the monitor sends chills through my body. I hear the crying stop.

"I have something for you," it says again. My heart is racing, but I can't move. I manage to put the monitor closer to my ear.

"I've missed you. No one could keep me from seeing you today." My chest is so tight, I have to remind myself to breathe. A few seconds pass and Raven's voice reaches me faintly from the earpiece of the phone I just dropped. I'm snapped back to reality, this is not a dream.

"It's Cal!" I say in utter disbelief, losing my grip on the phone as I try to pick it up again.

"I've missed your mom, too. I just don't want to complicate things, and I don't want to hurt her anymore," he says. Tears start to pour down my cheeks.

He laughs lightly. "You're lucky you get to see her all the time. This probably wasn't the smartest thing. I wish I could tear myself in half; it'd make things easier for everyone."

A few more seconds pass and I hear Caylen make the sound she makes when she's fascinated by something and studying it intently. "I'm not going to be able to see you for a while, and I don't have much time . . ." His tone changes from regretful to having a sense of urgency.

Suddenly, my body is fully capable of taking action. "Cal!" I shout, trying my best to open the door. I can't get to him.

"Cal, wait!" I shout repeatedly. I don't know how much time passes as I keep trying to open the door, but finally, I hear footsteps approaching. When I stop yelling and pounding on the door, the silence is palpable. I step back from it, my heart seeking freedom from my chest. The knob turns, and I stop breathing, but when the door opens, Raven is the only one standing in front of me.

"Lauren, what's wrong? You hung up on me, the door was still open, you're screaming at the top of your lungs . . ." Raven asks frantically.

"Cal." I race past Raven into Caylen's room. She looks up from her crib and smiles at me. I open her closet and see no one is there. Raven has rushed into the room behind me.

"Lauren, honey, what's wrong? What happened?" She leads me back over to the lounger and sits down, gathering me in her arms.

"He was here. He was here, Raven," I stammer in between sobs.

"Cal was here?" she asks frantically.

"He was here! He was in here with Caylen, talking to her," I whimper, trying to catch my breath.

"You saw him?" Raven asks, confusion evident on her face.

"I-I heard him. On the baby monitor, I heard him talking to her," I sniff.

Her expression changes. "Honey, did you actually see him?" she asks urgently.

"No, Raven, but I heard him. I was locked in my room. He had to have locked the door!" I yell at her.

"Honey, are you sure you weren't dreaming?" she asks, trying to hug me, and I pull away.

"No," I tell her, beginning to cry harder. She looks at me in disbelief. "I wasn't fucking dreaming!" I shout. Her face looks perplexed. I realize how harsh I sound, and wipe my cheeks. "I'm sorry." I begin to cry again. "But I wasn't dreaming. I know I wasn't, Raven!"

"How do you know you weren't, sweetie?" Raven asks in a calm tone, as if speaking any louder will set me off.

"Because I wasn't. I've dreamed before, and this wasn't a dream!" I try to convince her, though my throat is sore.

"Maybe you imagined it."

"I didn't imagine anything. I'm not hallucinating!"

"I didn't say you were," she tells me quickly.

I get up and walk over to the rocking chair I read to Caylen on and sink down into it, my face in my hands. "Why now then, Raven? Why, after almost two years, I've just all of a sudden begun to imagine things?" I plead.

"Well, today is Caylen's birthday; maybe this triggered something. Maybe you feel bad about admitting you have feelings for Steven. I don't know!" Raven tries to reason.

I look at her face; she won't believe me, no matter what I say.

"Lauren, come have a cup of tea. I'm worried about you," she says, heading out of the bedroom. I scowl at her and she sighs, continuing into the hall. I pick Caylen up and take her into my arms. I head back into my room, slamming the door behind me. Sitting down on the bed, I hold her close, thankful she's okay.

"You know mommy's not crazy, right?" I ask her. She stretches and waves her little arms, hitting me in the face. I can't help but laugh.

"Maybe I am crazy. Maybe I imagined it all," I mumble to myself. Then I notice a white gold bracelet on her tiny arm that I've never seen before. It's engraved with the initials D.L.G. in cursive writing.

"Now I know I'm not crazy." I sigh in relief and hug her again.

February 7th, 2011

Today's our two-month anniversary and I'm ecstatic. Cal will be home from New York any minute, and the steamy calls and texts we've been exchanging have me ready to jump him the second he hits the door. But I won't. Tonight is going to be special. I have it all planned. Cal's favorite band is playing at The Vault to a sold-out crowd, but I scored tickets from Ryan. Afterwards, we'll have dinner on the rooftop, made by Luc, Helen's chef, followed by Cal's favorite dessert: me, any way he likes.

When I hear the door open, I rush to it and jump up into his arms, wrapping my legs around his waist.

"Gorgeous." He smiles widely before I attack his lips. He holds me up easily with one arm and sets his bag down with the other.

"I missed you," I purr, kissing his neck.

"You ready to show me?" he says, carrying me over to the couch. He starts to unbutton my sweater, and I lean away from him. His face drops, and I laugh.

"Not until later, babe," I say, climbing off him.

"Later?" he asks, the disappointment in his face like the pout of a five-year-old. He's still following me, but I continue to back away from him.

"Yes. I have it all planned. Just be a little patient," I say with secrecy.

"Just to welcome me home? It's appreciated but not needed. I want it now," he says, catching me and picking me up.

I laugh, but then my face drops a little.

"You don't know what today is?" I ask, a little disappointed—not too much, though. I mean, he is a man.

"It's not your birthday, is it?" he asks.

I frown at him, and he puts me down.

"No, it's silly anyway," I say, trying to sound indifferent. I go and sit on our couch.

He frowns at me. "Babe, please don't expect me to remember all of these stupid little milestones, because if you do you're going to be pissed at me a lot," he says, squatting in front of me so we're at eye level.

"Seriously, Cal," I say in disbelief.

"What?" he asks casually, and I brush past him. He's pretty much told me not to expect anything exciting or memorable from him. I wonder if holidays count? Maybe you don't celebrate an anniversary every month, and it's only been two, but it's been the happiest two months of my life. Stupid me, wanting to celebrate with him. He's definitely making me rethink it.

"You're mad." He sighs, going to pick up his luggage.

"No. Well, yeah, I am. I can give you a pass for forgetting our anniversary, even though it was only two months ago, but if you think I'm going to give you a pass for every holiday because you think it's cliché or arbitrary . . ." I trail off as he pulls out a beautifully wrapped box, all black with a red ribbon tied around it. He sets it on my lap. I look up at him and he's smiling at me knowingly, arms folded.

"You were saying, Mrs. Scott?"

A huge grin spreads across my face, and I roll my eyes at him.

"You're a jerk, you know that?" I say, embarrassed as I untie the red bow.

He sits beside me and kisses my neck as he watches me carefully remove the red ribbon.

"Come on, babe, tear into it!" he urges me impatiently as he tickles my side.

"Okay, okay. It's just so pretty," I squeal, removing the paper, and when I see the golden-tan box that reads "Christian Louboutin," I freeze. He looks at me, and a wider smile spreads across his face.

"You didn't!" I say, and I frantically open the box to see a pair of cherry-red daffodil-crystal-embellished suede pumps—the same pumps I remember fawning over after seeing Jessica Alba wearing them at some awards show I made him watch with me.

"Oh my gosh! Cal," I say, feeling awful for being mad at him.

"Read the card," he says with a smile, pointing to the tiny card lying in between both shoes. I open it and read the words out loud.

"These shoes look like they're straight out of *The Wizard of Oz*, but since sometimes I'm like the tornado that blew you into Oz, I guess you can wear Dorothy's red slippers. And if I'm gone and seem lost, maybe you can do a little click and I'll find my way home."

I look at him and he looks down, a little embarrassed.

"It's corny, isn't it?" he asks with a shy smile.

I nod and climb onto his lap.

"As corny as you being my Prince Charming," I say, cupping his face in my hands and kissing him softly on the lips.

He wraps his arms around my waist, holding me down on his lap.

"Are you going to wear them for me?" he says, a lustful glint in his eye.

"I have the perfect white dress for them," I say, running my hands through his hair.

"No dress. Just them," he says, biting his lip with a playful smile, but I've known him long enough to know how serious he is.

"Later," I promise. "I have to run and pick up your gift," I say, hopping off his lap. I run to the console table and grab my purse.

"No, my gift can be you," he says pleadingly, and I laugh at him.

"It will be. Tonight," I promise again, reaching the door. His expression looks like a sad puppy's.

"Don't look at me like that." I giggle, and he comes towards me. "No. Five feet," I say threateningly, my hand on the doorknob as I laugh. I know if he gets too close, I'll be a goner.

"I hope you've gotten a lot of sleep since I've been gone. Because you're going to be up all night," he says, giving me a faux warning, and my body perks up at the thought.

"Plenty," I say with a wink before slipping out the door.

AS I WALK back into the house, the television is on downstairs, but Cal is nowhere in sight. I grab the remote and turn it off. I start to call Cal's name, but I hear him upstairs.

I make my way up and hear Cal yelling like he's in an argument. The intensity of his voice causes me to pause, not knowing if I should go back downstairs and give him his privacy, or if I should rush into the room. But I don't hear anyone else except for Cal. I make my way up the stairs and pause before I'm right next to the door.

"I'm fucking furious! I can't stop taking it. What the hell am I going to do? You told me you were sure before I did this. This changes everything! I'm not going to stop—I might as well be, Dex! How the fuck am I supposed to explain this? I won't. I can't take her through that shit. Well, figure it out fast." My heart is pounding, and my feet feel frozen on the floor. The only thing that removes them is a thud against the wall. I try to figure out what to do. I don't know what's going on, but I've never heard Cal that angry before when talking to Dexter. I don't know why, but I turn around and go back down the stairs, and when he opens the door, I pretend I'm just making my way up.

Cal comes out, anger radiating from his face. He looks down at me, and it changes to something else. He looks almost remorseful.

"Cal, what's wrong? You look upset," I say, my voice giving away my nerves.

"Um." He exhales and runs his hands over his face, and I see that his hand is red and scratched.

I rush up the stairs to him and hold his wrist in my hand.

"Cal, what did you do!" I ask frantically, leading him into the guest bathroom.

"Don't be mad, but I punched a hole in our wall," he says casually as I run water over his hand.

My head snaps toward him.

"Why did you do that!" I say, grabbing our first-aid kit and pulling out the antibiotic wipes.

"Dex really pissed me off," he says, sitting on the edge of the bathtub while I clean his hand.

I nod and take a deep breath.

"I kind of heard you talking to him," I admit, looking up at him guiltily. His eyes widen just for a moment before his calm demeanor returns. I wait for him to say something, but he doesn't.

"Did it have something to do with me?" I ask, sitting on his lap.

"I'm—I'm going to be gone a little more than I thought I was," he says, his gaze on the floor. I take a deep breath and smile.

"That's okay. I mean, it's not okay, but it's nothing to go punching holes in the wall over," I tease him, running my hands through his hair. If we ever have kids one day, I hope they have his hair. It's thick, shiny, and luscious, like hair from a shampoo commercial.

"I'm a big girl," I add, trying to comfort him, but really my heart has dropped into my stomach.

A shadow of a smile passes over his face but only briefly.

"I'm not feeling too good, babe. Would it be really fucked up if we didn't go out tonight?" he says, searching my expression, and I don't let a hint of my disappointment show.

I give him a wide smile.

"No, babe. If you're not feeling well, it's nothing we can't do another day," I lie with a smile, covering up my disappointment.

"Are you sure? Because we can if you still want to do something. I can just lie down for a few minutes," he says, cupping my chin and looking into my eyes, as if he's searching for my true feelings.

But I won't let him see them. I know whatever happened during that conversation is going to have his mind a thousand miles away anyway.

"No, get some rest. It's your first day back home and you're probably jet-lagged. It's fine," I assure him, kissing him softly on the lips.

"I'm going to make it up to you," he says as I get off his lap and smile.

"And you don't have to sit here with me. You should call your girls and go out," he urges me as he walks into the bedroom and lies across the bed.

"I'm not going to spend our anniversary out with them. As long as I'm with you, that's what's important," I say, crawling next to him.

He wraps one of his arms around me and holds me close to him.

"You know I love you, right?" I'd expect for him to sound playful like his normal self, but his tone is sullen.

"Of course I do," I say, looking back at him curiously.

"No, seriously." He turns my body around toward him, so I'm facing him completely. We're eye to eye. "No matter what. Whatever happens—if anything were to happen—nothing, under any circumstances—" he takes my hand and places it on his chest and holds it there "—will ever take you from here." I try to search for something to say. His words are heavy in the air and he continues. "Even if it doesn't seem like it, always know how much I love you. I've never loved anyone as much as I love you, and even if I screw it up . . ."

I cup his face in my hand.

"Cal, you're scaring me. Is everything okay?" I ask, sitting up and leaning on my elbow.

The seriousness on his face vanishes and is replaced by a playful grin.

"Yeah, just trying to get laid," he kids then pulls me down next to him again.

I smile, but there's still uneasiness crawling all over my body and I can't ignore it.

"You can tell me anything. Nothing would change the way I feel about you. You'll always be my Cal," I say honestly from the pit of my soul, ignoring his playful glare.

"I know. That's why I love you," he says, his boyish grin calming my earlier tremors. As he kisses me, they slowly disappear.

I kiss him back and rest my head on his chest. And even though he said his speech was an attempt to get sex, he doesn't touch me in a way that leads me to believe it. He holds me as if he's just savoring us in this moment, and I lie in his arms and savor it too until we both fall asleep.

WHEN THE KNOCK at the door comes, I try to calm my nerves. I've already cleared Steven with security as one of my guests, so he doesn't have to buzz in to get to my floor.

"Hey." His tone is upbeat and his expression warm—until his eyes drift down to my outfit and he sees that I'm in an over-sized red t-shirt and jeans. Not ex-actly lunch date attire.

"Hi," I say, trying to down-play my apprehension.

May 9th, 2013

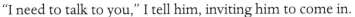

"Are you ready to go?" he asks skeptically.

"I need to talk to you," I tell him, inviting him to come in.

"Okay." He hesitates but follows me in.

I lock the door and take a deep breath.

"Can you sit down for a little bit?" I gesture to the sofa, and he nods, taking a seat. I sit on a chair across from him instead of beside him.

"Is something wrong?" he asks, able to feel the awkwardness of the moment.

"Cal was here last night," I tell him hastily.

His expression goes from concerned to stunned. "Oh," he says. His eyes widen and his mouth falls agape. "Wow. He came back? Is he here?" he says, looking around.

"No, you don't understand." I chuckle. "He's not back. He's . . . I heard him yesterday in Caylen's room." I'm waiting for some sort of re-action, but his expression doesn't change.

"I heard him talking to her, and when I heard him, I sort of freaked out." I stand and begin to pace the room.

"I don't understand," he says, looking as confused as I sound.

"Well, I didn't really *see* him, but I know he was here. He locked me in my room."

He wipes his hand across his face. When I say it out loud, I realize how crazy this sounds. "Are you sure he was here?" he asks, sighing.

"I'd bet my life on it."

He nods. "So I guess that means lunch is off." He laughs dryly.

"I thought I was ready to move on. I really did, but I'm not . . . I-I'm so sorry." I keep my eyes on the floor, too guilty to look at him. He approaches me and places his hands on my shoulders. I look at him but avoid his eyes. I don't know what to say.

"All this time I've been spending with you made me realize how much I've missed you. I started to fall for you again," he confesses, making my pit of embarrassment and guilt deeper.

"Last night when you asked me out, I thought it was a sign. I didn't want to tell you how I've been feeling about you. I didn't want you to think my spending time with you and Caylen was because of some hidden agenda, because it wasn't, and it still isn't. But, my feelings have changed, and I can't just stand by anymore," he continues.

He then looks straight into my eyes. "I know how much he put you through—even when you're smiling, there's sadness in your eyes. Now, you think you might have heard his voice and you're the happiest I've seen you in a year. I can't compete with that."

I try to blink my tears away. What's wrong with me? I have this great guy standing in front of me, and all I can think about is Cal.

"Don't cry," he says, pulling me into a hug.

"You don't hate me?" I whimper against his chest.

"No. I'll get over it. I promise," he says with a light chuckle. I can't help but smile as well.

"I just want you to be happy. You deserve to be happy for Caylen," he says, kissing me on the forehead.

"You're going to make someone really happy one day." I smile, patting his arm as we part.

"Aw, shucks," he jokes. "Well, I better get going then. I'm starving," he says, patting his stomach. "You know, we can still go out if you want . . ."

"I kind of ate before you got here," I admit, a little embarrassed. "I can fix you something, though. Salad or cereal?" I frown as I realize I really need to learn how to cook.

He laughs. "No, I'm probably just going to go grab a burger or something," he says, heading to the door.

I follow him. "Thanks for being so . . ." I start and he puts his hands up.

"We don't want this to get awkward or all emotional." He laughs and I nod.

"I'll see you later," he says, patting me on the arm. I accompany him to the door and watch him walk down the hall to the elevator. I wonder if I'm doing the right thing. I have this wonderful man who wants me, despite my issues, who is nice, funny, and handsome, and I'm throwing it away for—what? I'm not even sure yet. Still, Steven deserves someone who will love him with her whole heart, not a woman who already gave her heart away. I wave as he enters the elevator and the doors slide shut on my innocent, budding romance.

THE DOOR BUZZER sounds, and I look at the camera. Hillary is standing downstairs. Hmm. She didn't say anything about coming over today. I buzz her in and glance at the clock. I still have an hour before Raven and Caylen will be home from the zoo. I get my blanket off the couch and fold it just in time for Hillary to knock on the door. I answer it, and she swoops in, obviously on a mission.

She whirls around suddenly. "You ditched Steven?"

"What?"

"God, Lauren, what's wrong with you?" she exclaims. "Don't you know he has had a thing for you for months now? Then, when you finally wake up and see it, you suddenly ditch him because you *think* you heard Cal?"

"Wait a minute. You've known how Steven's felt all this time, and you haven't told me?"

"I didn't know how you felt, and I didn't want to ruin things between you guys if you didn't feel the same way," she states simply. "And what is this thing about you think you heard Cal? What the hell is with that?"

I try to maintain my composure. I open my mouth to say something, but she cuts me off. "Lauren, he's been gone for a while now; don't you think it's time to get over him? I thought you were over him, for God's sake!"

"Wait a minute, Hillary, you need to calm down. You don't know anything about what's been going on with me, so before you come in here and start chastising anyone, you need to know what's going on." This is why I don't talk to her. This is exactly why I go to Angela before her.

"Okay, fine. Then tell me what's going on," she demands, tapping her foot impatiently on the floor.

"I woke up to Caylen crying on the baby monitor. When I tried to go to her, I realized my door was locked, and then I heard Cal talking to her. I couldn't go to her; I couldn't get out. By the time Raven got back from the drug store and let me out of my room, he was gone."

"And this is the reason you're throwing away your chance with Steven? You didn't even see him, Lauren," she says condescendingly.

Her tone is pissing me off. "I don't *think* I heard anything, I *know* I did. I have proof," I tell her, walking over to the counter and handing her Caylen's bracelet.

"D.L.G. What the hell does that mean?" she asks, looking up from the bracelet as if it's meaningless.

"It stands for Daddy's Little Girl."

"When he was talking to her, I heard him say he had something for her. It was this!"

She sighs, seeming to be unfazed by it, and hands it back to me.

"Don't you get it?" I continue. "I heard Cal talking to her, and then suddenly she's wearing this bracelet from out of nowhere with those initials. You tell me how that's possible," I demand.

"Okay, so what? Let's suspend all disbelief and say it was him. *If* he really was here, what happens now? Are you going to sit around waiting for him to pop up again?"

I open my mouth to say something, but I'm speechless. I don't know what to say.

"If he does come back, then what? You're going to take him back with open arms, wipe the slate clean, forgetting the fact that he was M.I.A. for two years, doing God knows what—or who. That's okay with you? It's fucking fantastic that he left you, *pregnant,* to raise Caylen alone, and he gets the thumbs up to drop in whenever he feels like it?" she asks me mockingly.

Hearing her speak about Cal that way sparks something in me.

"You don't understand. When I heard him talking to her, it was as if something was keeping him from us. That it wasn't his choice." I'm about to make another comment in Cal's defense, but the doorbell rings again and I can see it's Angela on the monitor. I get up and hit the buzzer for her to be let in.

"Okay, let's just imagine, ridiculous as it is, something important caused him to abandon his family and now he's free to come back. What about all the problems you were having before he left? Is everything just going to start over? You're going to pretend like it never happened? Don't tell me you've grown that desperate," Hillary says, staring me in the eye. I look away, feeling my cheeks burn. As much as I hate to admit it, she's right. I've been ignoring everything I shouldn't. I run my hands through my hair and cover my face in frustration.

"Look, L, I'm your friend. Even if we haven't been as close as we used to be. I don't want to see you hurt. I don't want to see you throw away something that could be genuine for a shot in the dark at a world full of heartache *again*," she continues as I bite my lip to keep from really blowing up at her.

Angela's knocking at the door breaks up Hillary's momentum. I answer the door, and she breezes into the penthouse. "Where's the birthday girl?" she sings happily with a gift bag in hand. Her smile fades when she sees the look on my face. "What's going on?" she asks, looking from Hillary to me.

"I heard Cal last night," I tell her.

"She *thinks* she heard Cal last night," Hillary corrects.

"I know I heard him; I showed you the bracelet!" I shout at her.

"Wait. What!" Angela is confused and shocked by the conversation and how Hillary and I are at one another's throats.

I show her the bracelet and brief her on what happened earlier with Cal.

"I think I need to sit down." She exhales, taking a seat next to Hillary.

Angela is looking at me sympathetically, and Hillary is looking at me in disbelief.

"You believe me, don't you, Angie?" I ask her hopefully, focusing my gaze on the more optimistic side of the couch. I need someone to just at least admit there's a possibility that what I'm saying may be true.

"Lauren, I don't know what to say. I really don't." She sighs quietly.

"She wants to say the same thing I have," Hillary snarls.

"Hillary, shut up," Angela snaps at her.

"No, I'm not shutting up! Tell her this is crazy!" Hillary snaps back. She grabs her head and closes her eyes.

"This is driving me crazy! Don't get me wrong, Lauren. I used to like Cal. I thought I was wrong about him, but he turned out to be exactly how I expected him to be," she says, standing up.

"Bottom line is if he loved you, he'd have his ass here. He left you when you needed him most, and not just for a week. It's been almost two years. And you're sitting here crying and pining for him as if he's left for war!" she exclaims.

"I haven't been just sitting here. I have my job, I've been raising Caylen!"

"Yeah, that's a hell of a life. You edit some crap manuscripts because you can do it here alone, shut off from the rest of the world. You were supposed to be an artist and travel the world—what happened!" Her words sting because there's so much truth to them.

"He walked out on you, and you're still here being the faithful little wife, wasting away."

"Hillary, don't!" Angela growls at her, giving her a glare before looking at me sympathetically.

"No one else may tell you this, but I'm not going to lie or ignore what's happening here anymore. That's why I was *so* happy to see you warming up to Steven again, and then I find out this!"

"Cal promised me he wasn't leaving me for anyone else. He just said he had to leave. Cal has done a lot of things, but he never lied," I tell her sharply.

"How do you know that? Because he said he didn't?" Hillary laughs.

My skin is hot and my heart is pounding. "Cal is a lot of things, but he isn't a liar!" I approach her so we're face to face. Angela approaches us quickly, ready to intervene at what she's seeing as an escalating situation.

"No, Lauren! You probably know him as well as I do, which isn't much," she screams, and my anger starts to melt, being replaced by depression. I see the anger leave her face as well.

"Lauren." Her tone is softer than before. "I should have shown you this when I first got it," she says. "I didn't know what to do. I didn't want to hurt you. I figured if you didn't know . . ."

"What are you talking about? What is she talking about, Angie?" I ask her, exasperated, trying to withstand anything Hillary throws at me next about Cal.

"I-I don't know," Angie says, looking as surprised as I am. "You better sit down," she tells me gently.

"What?" I ask her, looking for a brief moment at Angela, who seems genuine.

Hillary sits next to me before she begins, "You remember last month when I went to my aunt's birthday?" she says slowly.

"What does that have to do with this?" I ask anxiously, feeling extremely frustrated as well.

"Let me finish," she says, looking me in the eye. I fold my arms and listen, hoping it's not another load of criticism.

"When I went, my cousin was showing off how her daughter was homecoming queen, and you know, small town, it made the paper . . . and while I was looking through it, I saw this," she says, pulling out a piece of paper. She hands it to me. I read the headline and shrug.

"It's a newspaper from Madison. That's, like, about two counties away from Saginaw . . . What does this have to do with anything?" I ask, my mind reeling with confusion.

"Open it up, the second page. You'll see what I'm talking about."

I roll my eyes and open it, scanning the page. My eyes land on a picture that makes my heart stop. There's a picture of Cal with an older man. I read the caption under it:

Former Madison High alum, Chris Scott, poses with his father, William Scott, after annual pie eating contest.

"Hillary, what the hell is this?" My voice is trembling, my eyes glued to the picture.

"Lauren, what is it?" Angela asks, her voice filled with worry.

"I asked my aunt about him. He played football against her son. He was pretty good. His mom's name is Gwen. They met through some sport fundraisers," Hillary reveals quietly.

"No . . ." I say, slowly shaking my head defiantly.

"No! This isn't him! It can't be!" I yell at her, throwing the paper down. Angela grabs it and I watch her face drop.

"Lauren, pictures don't lie! He's been lying to you this entire time! Now do you understand why I'm so angry and frustrated with you? I'm trying to help you! He's not who he says he is!" Hillary urges, but the anger from her expression has dissipated.

I feel as if I'm going to throw up.

"Tell her, Angie! Is that Cal or not?" Hillary demands, taking the picture and shoving it in front of Angela's eyes.

I very slowly and carefully sit down on the floor.

It can't be him. It wouldn't make sense. Cal wouldn't be in some small-town pie-eating contest. That's not why he left me. He's in danger, or in some type of trouble, not this.

"Lauren, this looks a lot like him," Angela says quietly.

"*Looks*? That *is* him!" Hillary screeches.

Angela sits down in front of me. "Lauren, you said Cal was adopted. Maybe that's his brother, his twin brother . . ." she tries to reason.

"A biological twin brother that he never mentioned with the same last name as his adopted parents? Give me a break; he's a con. He's living a double life," Hillary says with a frustrated groan.

"Hillary, shut up for a minute!" Angela yells. I start to feel dizzy and hot, my vision blurring for a few seconds and clearing.

"I need . . . I need some water," I say, getting up and making my way to the kitchen.

"Lauren, are you okay?" Angela asks, grabbing my shoulder. Her voice . . . their voices . . . are so loud, pounding in my ears, and when I turn around, her face becomes blurry. I feel off balance and fall. Angela grabs me before I completely hit the floor.

"Hillary, get her some water!" she shouts. "Lauren, listen to me. You hear my voice?" She takes the newspaper and begins to fan my face.

"Oh my God, what's wrong with her?"

"I think she's in shock, that's all." I hear their voices, but I can't even tell them apart. I feel as if I'm drunk. I'm trying to wrap my mind around what I've just seen. It looked like him. The article even used his last name . . . but it can't be. It just wouldn't make sense. His name isn't Chris!

"Lauren, say something, sweetie. You're scaring us," Hillary says, her voice full of regret as she puts the cup of water in my hand. When I lift it to my lips and take a drink, they both let out a sigh of relief.

"I'm such a bitch. I shouldn't have told you this way," Hillary scolds herself. "I just couldn't stand watching you care for this jerk."

"You should have told me as soon as you found out," I whisper, setting the glass down. They're both looking at me as if I'm dying. I cover my face.

"Let me see the paper again," I mumble, willing myself not to cry.

Angela looks skeptical but hands it to me. I look at the picture again, his face . . . He's smiling widely, holding a trophy with the older man next to him. He looks so happy, and different. This person has his face and even his last name, but there's something different. I just can't figure it out. If this is him, everything he's told me has been a lie. I've been an idiot sitting around thinking he's in some kind of trouble, but why there? Why in some little county that can't be bigger than my own hometown. I expected Cal to be in New York or L.A. or even some foreign city, not there. And he told me he and his parents were estranged. This doesn't add up. I need answers now!

I stand up and look at them both. They look so worried. I slip on my nearby flip-flops and grab my keys.

"I need one of you to stay here and let Raven know what's going on," I say, going to the closet and grabbing a jacket.

"Where are you going?" Angela asks worriedly.

"To see the one person who can give me some answers," I tell them before heading out the door.

"HI, LAUREN! WHAT are you doing here?" Helen asks, looking surprised as she welcomes me in, though I know security has informed her of my presence. "What's wrong?" she asks, noticing my expression.

"Where's Dexter?" I demand

"He's . . . he's in his office. Lauren, what's wrong?" she asks again, concerned, as I storm down the hall toward Dex's office. I knock hard two times before going in. Dexter looks up from the phone conversation he's having, a mixture of surprise and irritation on his face.

"I'll have to call you back," he mumbles into the phone before hanging up. "Lauren, this is a surprise." He stands and moves around the desk to hug me. "How are you? Helen told me what you said, and I'm really glad that—" He stops short as he watches me struggle to pull the newspaper out of my purse.

"You want to explain this to me!" I slam the newspaper on his desk. He looks at it curiously and then picks it up. A wave of emotions cross his face; I see shock, recognition, and then—yep, there it is!—guilt. After a moment, he glances at me, and for once, it looks like he is speechless.

"What is this?" he begins, placing a fake grin on his face. I can't believe how he can lie to me like this.

"Bullshit!" I yell. He blinks, unfazed. Helen, however, looks as if she's a deer caught in headlights.

"Now I'm going to sit here all day if I have to, but you're going to tell me something, or I swear to God, I'll walk out of this office and disappear off the face of the earth and you and Cal won't be able to find me or Caylen ever again, regardless of how much money you have. So you think carefully before you open your mouth to lie to me," I growl.

"What the hell is Cal doing in Madison?" Helen asks, confused. Dexter doesn't answer. "Answer me!" Helen demands angrily.

"Helen, you have nothing to do with this," he tells her sternly.

"I'm your wife, and not only your wife, but her friend. She deserves to know whatever it is you know!" Helen growls.

"Helen, leave!" he orders sharply.

"No, Dex! This is beyond being loyal to him. You tell her something, or she won't be the only one leaving!" Helen says in a low, vicious tone that makes my skin crawl.

Dexter stares her down as if she's bluffing, but she stands her ground, and a moment later, he walks back to his chair and sits down.

"What do you want to know, Lauren?" Dex asks me calmly.

"Is that Cal?" I ask pleadingly.

He doesn't say anything, but his eyes give it away. I feel my heart start to beat.

"What is he doing? Why is he there?" I wait for an answer, and he doesn't give me one.

"Dex," Helen says curtly.

"Maybe he likes the pie," Dex mumbles.

I can't believe him; he has the nerve to joke about this! "Why does that article say his name is Chris?" I demand, feeling my eyes water in frustration.

"Because that's who it is," Dex says quietly.

I look at Helen, who looks as confused as I am. "You know it's Cal. I know it's him, so why won't you just tell me the damn truth?" I scream desperately.

"It's complicated," he says sharply.

"Then explain!" I yell as my tears start to blur my vision.

"It's not my place to tell you," he says pointedly.

"It's not your place to keep secrets from me. All I want to know is what you know!" I plead with him, but he doesn't even flinch.

"All of this time, all of this time you've known. I went through having Caylen alone, crying night after night, worried about him, sitting around like an idiot, and you knew! You've known the whole time, and you still won't tell me even when I have his damn picture in front of you!" I scream.

"I can't help you, Lauren. I'm sorry," he says in a low tone.

"I thought he left me, for some divine reason to protect me, and it was all a lie. He's been in Madison using some false name. It says he went to high school there, for God's sake. Cal told me he grew up in Chicago!" I scream. I start to feel dizzy again; my emotions are getting to me.

"You don't understand. That's my point!" Dexter states.

"No, I understand completely. I'm done asking you questions that you obviously aren't going to answer. You aren't who I should be talking to anyway." I look over at Helen, who looks as if she's trying to maintain her calm even though her nerves are on edge.

"His address? That's all I want from you. I at least deserve that," I say, exhausted from all this drama.

"I can't give it to you because Cal isn't in Madison," he says adamantly.

"All I want is the address to where he is!" I manage to shout with the anger left in me.

"Dex, tell her!" Helen yells.

"I can't! The person she's going to look for isn't going to be there!" Dexter roars.

"Then I'll find him myself." Madison is about the same size as Saginaw; I can find him in a week's time.

"Lauren, I'm asking you not to go. Give me more time . . ." he says, standing from his seat.

"How dare you?" I spit. "How dare you not tell me anything about where he is, and ask me not to look for him!" I say angrily.

"It's not what you think!" he yells.

"Then tell her!" Helen roars back. For once, I see Helen challenge Dex, going against everything she advised me during one of our first conversations about living with our men's secrets. It's about damn time!

"You don't know what I think! And if you've listened to anything I've said, you'd know that things can't get any worse!" I shout. I then turn my attention to Helen, who looks as if she's ready to march out the door and go search with me.

"Bye," I say before my voice breaks. I wave slightly at her before I leave the office, but she's following right behind me.

"Lauren!" Dexter calls.

I stop in my tracks.

"He never meant for it to be this way. He really did try," he says before disappearing back into his office.

"What the hell does that mean?" I ask, letting out an exhausted and frustrated groan. I've never felt so completely drained.

"Dex speaks in riddles a lot, but you listen to me," Helen says, taking me by my shoulders. "I'm going to find out where he is. He's going to tell me something before the night is over, and when I know, you're the first one I'm calling," she says, opening the door.

"Call my cell. I won't be at home; I'm going to Madison," I tell her, heading to the elevators.

She follows me out. "Now?" she asks, her voiced raised in disbelief.

I hit the button for the elevator to come. "I've been sitting around doing nothing for too long. Now there's no excuse. I know where he is, and I'm not going to wait until he has the chance to go hide somewhere else," I tell her impatiently.

"W-what about Caylen? Where is she? You just can't leave her."

"Caylen is with Raven. She's in the best hands. I'm going to call them on my way. I'm not just doing this for myself. My little girl is not going to grow up without her dad if she doesn't have to. If Cal doesn't owe me anything, he owes her everything!" I say, sharper than I intend to.

Helen looks down, guilty. "Give me a day. Even if Dex doesn't tell me, I'll hire a private investigator. You can't do anything if you don't know where he is," she pleads.

The bell dings and the elevator doors open. I sigh in frustration and walk in. "You think I haven't done that? If it was the other way around and you were in my situation, would you waste another second?"

"I'm not trying to stop you, Lauren, I . . . I just want to help," she says, seemingly offended. Her eyes convey nothing but sincerity, but I always have to guess with her.

I take a deep breath. Helen is a mystery to me sometimes. One minute she's this cool, confident, intimidating woman, and the next she seems warm, genuine, and sincere. When I first met her, Cal warned me about her, but right now, his words aren't holding too much weight with me. I don't have time to figure out what her motives are anymore, and I really don't care if she's on Dexter's side or mine, or if she has her own agenda in this, for that matter, because I have my own.

"If you want to help me, Helen—" I push the button for the elevator to go down "—get me an address," I tell her simply before the doors close. I'm done living in the midst of questions. If I have to knock on every door, drive down every street, I'm not leaving until I find him. And when I do, I'm coming home with my husband or a divorce.

FOUR HOURS. THAT'S how long I drove. I had to stop and ask for directions twice due to my spur-of-the-moment decision to take this trip and my GPS going stupid. My cell phone has been ringing nonstop since I let my friends know about my decision to go to Madison alone. After driving so long, I'm starting to think they were right.

The wiser part of me wishes I would have waited a couple of days to let this sink in, to wait for word from Helen, to at least pack some clothing. I've been pulled over on the side of the road, staring down the "Welcome to Madison" sign for at least thirty minutes. The pissed, angry, and anxious part of me is ready to start randomly knocking on doors. To be honest, that's pretty much the only idea I have. I have absolutely no idea where Cal is, or even if he is still here. I don't know what I'm going to do if I find him. What am I going to say? There are so many things I want to know, that I've never had answers for. The newspaper article just added more questions to the list. Until last night, when I heard him, I've tried to forget about him. I've tried so hard, but the fact that Caylen is his spitting image doesn't help much.

When I first saw her, I cried. There was the happiness of seeing my child's face, and because I knew I'd never be able to forget her father. Every time I'd look at her, he'd be staring back at me, mocking me. And then there's my promise to him . . . but he's definitely broken some of his own.

I lean across the armrest and open my glove compartment, pulling out the worn, stained envelope. I didn't even want it in my house. I open it up and take out my wedding ring. I haven't touched it in so long. The day I found out I was pregnant with Caylen, I took it off and sealed it in an envelope. I couldn't bring myself to throw it away, but I couldn't wear it either.

I think about his picture in the newspaper article again. How his expression seemed foreign, but even in the low-quality picture his eyes drew me in.

I let out a sigh and look at the clock: it's 4:30. Four and a half hours have gone by . . . another sigh. I take a deep breath once more and look at myself in the rear-view mirror. The bags around my eyes can carry groceries. I look like I haven't slept in days.

I pick up my phone and dial Helen's number. I get the same message saying she's not available now and to try back later. I hang up in frustration.

I don't know anything about this town except our school played them in football once or twice. I don't even know if Cal is here.

My phone rings again. This time, it's Angela.

"Hi, Angie." I sigh, watching a car speed by.

"Actually, it's Hillary. I borrowed her cell since you won't answer for me," she says. I roll my eyes, still livid about what happened earlier.

"Well, I didn't answer for a reason," I tell her candidly.

"Lauren, I said I'm sorry. I know I should have told you when I first found out, but I didn't know how," she blurts out quickly.

"Well, you sure figured it out today," I retort sharply.

"You're right. I was the biggest bitch in the world," she says with a laugh. But it's forced and she stops with a sigh.

"I just thought that you starting to see Steven would make things better for you. That you wouldn't stay cooped up in the house with Caylen, and you would start being yourself again," Hillary explains. I admit I have directed my anger at her instead of myself for being so naïve and stupid.

"I'm sorry that things haven't been like they were between us. That Angela and I seem closer, but . . . it's just that Angela saw me at one of the lowest times in my life. So I don't feel so exposed when I talk to her because she's seen me at my worst. I just . . . I don't know when I'll break down, you know? I constantly feel vulnerable, and I hate myself for feeling that way. I'm embarrassed about it." I frown at myself.

"I was mad at you today was because you were telling me the truth. The same thing that little voice in my head keeps telling me, but I stopped listening to that voice the day I met Cal." I let out a small laugh, wiping away the tears that are slipping from my eyes. I hear her laugh on the other end.

"Yep, that's me! The big voice yelling at you that you can't shut up." It feels good to laugh.

"I need that voice sometimes," I assure her.

"Yeah, well, it works for me," she says, giggling, then clears her throat before speaking again.

"I called my aunt, the one I was telling you about who lives in Madison. I was trying to get her to give me Gwen Scott's address." She pauses as if waiting for me to respond. When I don't, she continues.

"She badgered me about why I needed it and we argued. But in the end I just promised my cousin twenty-five bucks for it when I see her." She laughs, but my playful mood is completely gone. The mention of the Scotts makes my heart begin to pound.

"Th-the woman who says she's his mom?"

"Yeah . . . I figured if you were going to start looking somewhere, what better place than his parents' house? Or the people who say they're his parents . . ."

I rub my temples. This is all just so much.

"Lauren, you aren't driving, are you?" she asks suddenly. I guess she's worried that I'll run myself off the road.

"No, I'm actually pulled over in front of the 'Welcome to Madison' sign."

"Are you serious?" She giggles.

"Yeah," I admit, chuckling at myself.

"I didn't really know where to go and knocking on everyone's door sounded kind of dangerous after some thought."

"We shouldn't have let you leave like that. But I don't think you would have let us stop you." She laughs and I join in.

"Probably not."

"Do you have a pen?"

"Yeah . . ." I say, grabbing a pen out of my purse and a receipt from an earlier purchase.

"1206 North Grenton Street," she says, and I scribble it down quickly. I take a deep breath.

"If you have any problems, call me, okay, L?"

"I will."

"Do you want my aunt's address?"

"No. I'll be okay," I assure her, staring at the receipt with the address on it. My hands are shaking.

"Do you think he's going to be there?" she asks meekly.

"Well, I'm about to find out." I sigh.

"Be careful and call me as soon as you get there. Don't do anything that will have you in jail . . ." she says, rambling on.

"I won't, Hil," I say as she continues to talk. "I'm hanging up now. Just tell everyone I'm okay."

I'm pretty sure she's still talking as I hang up the phone and stare at the address on the paper. I pick up my map and see that the directions Hillary gave me are right on. I set the map and address on the passenger seat and rest my head on the steering wheel for a few moments to think.

Cal never told me anything about his parents. All I know is that he was adopted when he was young, and they were estranged.

Nothing is making sense.

He wouldn't leave me to go back home. This can't be his home. He told me he grew up in Chicago. I never even thought about him having close family. He never mentioned anything about them.

At our wedding, the only people who came that were close to him were Dexter and Helen and quite a few of their business associates. This all has to be a lie. There has to be some explanation for this. I can't even imagine what he's going to say when he sees me . . . if he's even at this address. What will this woman say to me when I show up asking about her son? Is this even his mother? All of these questions run through my mind.

I sit up and take a few deep breaths, trying to clear my head, wanting to get away from my jumbled thoughts. Well, there's only one way to find all of this out. I turn the key and start the car.

March 8th, 2011

"HOW DO YOU know he's okay, Dexter? Why is he not answering my calls? I'm about to call the fucking cops!" I say frantically into the phone while pacing the floor. The tone of his voice is pissing me off. He's calm and amused, seemingly unfazed, while I'm losing my mind.

I haven't seen or heard from Cal in four days. No response to my texts or voice mails. I tried to play it cool at first. I didn't want to seem like the bored, crazy wife. Especially since this is just his second trip away since we've been married.

Day One: I didn't call him the entire day—well not for a long time, anyway. Eventually, I did want to make sure he made it to where he was going. I sent him a text, only to get no response. So I called that night. No answer. I call again and the phone goes straight to voice mail.

Day Two: I call again, like any rational person would, but the phone is off and the call goes straight to voice mail.

Day Three: I'm still going straight to voice mail, and I'm just supposed to be fine with this? I don't know where he is or if he's okay. Should I just let it slide? He's not in the fucking Army. I'm sure wherever he is there is an outlet for a charger if his phone died.

Day Four: I'm yelling at Dexter. I know it's not his fault, but since he's not taking this seriously at all, he gets to get yelled at before Cal. According to Dexter, all of this is fucking normal. Nothing to worry about! Well, if nothing is wrong, Cal's definitely going to have something to worry about once he gets home.

"Lauren, I can assure you Cal's fine. This is what he does," Dexter says. "He won't be able to answer your every call. If something was wrong, I'd know, and then you'd be the first to know," he reiterates. Actually, if he knew first, that would make me the second person to know, but I'm not going to argue that point right now.

"I don't expect him to answer every call, but I do expect to hear from him at least once after four days. Why is it that you can reach him and I can't? I do—"

I'm cut off as the downstairs door opens and Cal walks in.

"Never mind," I say and abruptly hang up. Dexter isn't the person who deserves my interrogation or possible anger, depending on the explanation his best friend gives, but I don't care right now. Cal strolls in, dropping his bag from his shoulder to the floor. When he sees me, a wide grin appears on his face. He must not be reading my expression correctly at all, which is somewhere between worried and super pissed.

"Hey, gorgeous!" he says, pulling me toward him. I allow him to briefly kiss my lips, but I pull away shortly after. He seems taken aback by my reaction. Oh, is he about to understand.

I pat him on his chest and touch his face, looking at it from all sides. "Open your mouth," I say with my hands on my hips.

He sticks his tongue out and a second later grabs me and licks my cheek. I push him away, demanding myself not to laugh. I'm still mad, and his little antics aren't going to work today.

"If you want to play doctor, you just have to say it," he says, squeezing my butt. I slap his hand away.

"No. I'm trying to figure out what the hell is wrong with you. It has to be something, since I haven't talked to you in four days," I say shortly, my arms folded across my chest. He looks up at the ceiling like he's bored with my speech.

"Hello!" I say, irritated by his nonchalant demeanor.

"I'm listening," he says, walking away from me.

I follow him. "Do you know how worried I was about you?" I admit, trying to allow the sincerity in my voice to seep through. I trail him into the kitchen. He heads directly to the fridge, his attention seemingly more on what he's about to eat than on listening to me, and I feel my anger rising.

"I told you not to worry when I left," he says, rifling through the fridge. "I'm so fucking hungry." He shuts it, seemingly unsatisfied with the contents.

"Where were you?" I ask pointedly.

"I told you. In Colorado, working." He stuffs a bagel into his mouth before he hops up onto the island.

"Working. Really?" I ask somewhat sarcastically.

"What else would I be doing . . . ?" he states slowly, as if I can't comprehend him.

"Don't patronize me, Cal. This really isn't the time to do it." My patience is wearing thinner as this conversation goes on.

"You're patronizing *me*. This is my third time telling you where I was. I don't know how else you want to hear it," he says sarcastically, getting off the island and going back into the fridge for a soda.

"Why didn't you answer your phone?" I ask.

"I just didn't get around to it," he says impatiently with a casual shrug. A casual shrug!

I bite down on my lip. "That's it? You just didn't get around to it?" I say sharply.

"Yeah," he states simply, his voice just as sharp as mine, and I can't believe he seems irritated with *my* questions. It's almost as if he doesn't understand why I'm asking them. I shake my head in disbelief and walk away from him, swallowing the urge to lash out at him with a verbal assault.

"What's with the third degree on this? This has never been a problem before. Why now?" he asks, following me.

I stop in my tracks and turn around to face him. "Oh, I'm sorry. I don't recall you ever leaving for four days straight and not answering your phone or calling me back," I say.

"I've been gone before, and you didn't freak out the way you are now."

I fold my arms. "This is different," I say.

"Why?" he counters.

"Because this isn't normal! I don't have a problem with you being gone for work, but you don't get to leave and not have any contact with me. I was so worried about you. I didn't know if you were okay, or if you even made your flight. How do you *not* understand how I feel right now? It was four days of utter worry, frustration, and anxiety. Do you think this is how I want to feel whenever you go to work?" I say, trying to take the anger out of my voice. I only want him to hear my concern, but I may not be doing a great job at it since I am furious right now.

He looks away from me briefly, staring at his feet. "Babe, this going to happen sometimes. I thought you got that, that you were okay with it," he says, a hint of disbelief in his voice.

I don't know where he got the idea that I'd ever be okay with him not communicating with me at all on these "trips." The first trip he took since we've been married was a week. He called me when he touched down, and every night while he was there. He sent me texts saying how much he missed me. Before we were married, he called me and kept in contact with me. Now he acts as if no communication is as normal as walking across the street.

"I don't know what gave you the impression that I'd be okay with this," I say in disbelief. He sighs and holds the back of his head.

"I'm going to lie down. I've had a long flight. I missed you. I thought you missed me. But I'm not doing this," he says dryly, walking away from me.

"You missed me?" I ask sarcastically, following him. "Oh, that's nice. I couldn't tell since I didn't hear from you. Not even once," I continue, following him up the stairs. He's quiet as a mouse, not responding to me at all, kind of like when he was gone. Once we reach our room, he sighs as if he's exasperated. *He's* exasperated?

"Hello!" I say, waiting for some type of response, but he still doesn't reply.

He lifts his shirt over his head and removes it, then undoes his pants and takes them off. A second later, he's lying across the bed. "I don't know what the fuck your problem is, but I'm tired and I'm going to sleep." He glances up at me before closing his eyes.

"Seriously, Cal?" I say angrily. He doesn't respond and grabs a pillow, settling it under his head.

"What the hell were you doing for three, four days that you couldn't answer your phone or call me? How the hell do you think I'm supposed to react to this!" I say frantically. This is a fucking joke. It has to be. Still, he doesn't respond and turns his head away from me. I grab a stray pillow beside him and hit him with it as hard as I can. He barely flinches but grabs it and covers his head with it.

"You . . . you know. You're being a real asshole right now. Worse," I say before my voice completely breaks.

I grab my throw blanket off the bed and quickly leave the room before tears escape my eyes. After I make it downstairs, I turn on the television and settle onto the couch, curling up in my blanket. I wonder why on the first night the love of my life is home, we're sleeping in separate rooms. If someone had told me this would happen four days ago, I would have laughed in their face.

A LOUD THUD accompanied by a "fuck" awakens me.

The lights are all off, but the moonlight through the window allows me to see that Cal has tripped over the bag he left downstairs. I'd laugh if I weren't so tired.

I settle my head back onto my pillow and close my eyes. I hear his footsteps coming near me, and my comfortable position is disturbed as couch cushions are removed from behind me. They're soon replaced by Cal's hard chest. He's settling in behind me, one of his arms crosses over my stomach, and he pulls me toward him, nestling his head in my neck. A smile spreads across my face. I can't help it.

"I'm sorry," he whispers. He takes my hand, interlocking his fingers between mine, and kisses them. I squeeze his hand, but I don't say anything.

"I'm an ass for earlier," he says quietly in my ear before kissing me there, and I sigh.

I'm still mad, but that doesn't stop the throbbing he's causing between my thighs. This sucks; my anger doesn't stop me from wanting him. My sadness makes me want him even more.

"A huge ass," I relent with a slight laugh.

I turn over on my back and he leans over me. His lips kiss mine slowly, savoring each of them, and I kiss him back the same way. I cup his face and he pulls me on top of him. I straddle him and lay my head on his chest. He strokes my back, and I feel him trace his signature on me. I can't believe how much I missed that. He leans up, pulling my knees forward until our chests are touching, then reverses our positions so I'm now on my back.

"I just didn't want to argue," he says, trailing off, trying to excuse himself from his earlier behavior.

"I didn't want to argue either." I run my hands through his hair. I missed his kiss, his touch, his scent, everything about him.

"I was going crazy without you," he says, kissing my shoulder and making his way to my neck. "I missed you." His mouth then nears my ear again. "I'm about to show you how much," he adds before his lips trail down my stomach.

I close my eyes and let him have me, my body already revealing how much it missed him. I know we probably should talk about how— or more importantly, *why* our first fight occurred, but we don't. At this moment, I just want peace. We both do, and we get lost in our first married make-up. Still, this only seems like temporary peacetime, our white flags not even raised, just peeking out from behind our bunkers. Deep down, I know this isn't the end of this battle, and I'm content with that. What terrifies me is the little voice in my head saying this isn't what happens at the end of a battle, but it could possibly be the beginning of a war.

March 8th, 2013

"I CAN DO this," I remind myself out loud as I stare at the house in front of me.

I've managed to work up the nerve to get out of the car. Now if only I can manage to walk up to the front door.

I'm standing here, my legs unable to move. I take in my surroundings. It's a stark contrast to the city life I've become accustomed to. The house is beautiful, as if it's right out of a Disney movie; the soft yellow paint and huge front porch remind me of Raven's back in Saginaw, only a lot bigger. I notice the huge barn a few feet away from it; the acres surrounding it are strewn with gated off animals.

I stuff my keys in the deep pockets of my jacket as I get closer to the door. I suddenly start to wonder, what if no one is home. I climb the few stairs of the porch and take a deep breath before I ring the bell. I take a step away from the door and peer through the window; the curtains are slightly open.

From what I can see, the room is spotless with a fireplace in the center. The warm, honey-colored walls give it a welcoming feeling with a tan sofa and chair surrounding a coffee table. I quickly remind myself that I'm peeping into someone's home and move back towards the front of the door.

I ring the doorbell again. I notice myself sort of dancing, trying to calm my nerves and channel my adrenaline. I ring the bell twice in a row and knock frantically; the composure I had managed to muster earlier is starting to dissolve.

"Maybe no one's home," I tell myself and turn to head back down the stairs, but I hear the door open behind me. I stop in my tracks, almost afraid to turn around.

"Can I help you?" *His* voice stops me immediately. I don't even have to turn around to see that it's him. I grab the railing to keep myself from falling over.

"Cal," I say so softly that I'm not sure he can hear me. I turn around and my eyes start to water. I walk toward him slowly, feeling as if I'm going to wake up any second. It's been so long since I've seen him.

When I reach him, he still looks the same, only his eyes are almost all green, gray only intermingled with the dominant green hue. I slowly move my hand to touch his face even though it's shaking uncontrollably.

"It's you." I can't wait another second to be near him and jump into his arms. It's been so long since I've touched him, too long. All of the questions I have don't even seem important right now, just that he's here.

"I've missed you so much." I can't stop myself from crying. I look up at him, waiting for him to say something, but I realize he looks speechless, almost shocked, and I notice his arms aren't around me.

"Chris, who is this?" I look past him to see a tall blonde woman looking at us strangely.

"Chris?" I say, confused. "Chris. His name isn't Chris!" I tell her sharply. My anger starts to replace the initial euphoria of seeing him, as I remember what brought me here in the first place. She frowns at me and then looks at him.

"Who is this?" she asks him irately.

"I-I don't know!" he answers back to the blonde.

"Who am I? Who are you?" I ask defensively. Then I realize what *he* just said. My jaw drops in disbelief.

"What?" I say sharply, turning my attention on him.

"I think you have me confused with someone else," he says, staring at me strangely. My heart drops to join my jaw on the ground.

"She just started crying when she saw me," he explains to the woman behind him. He seems more concerned with her than with me.

"What the hell are you talking about?" I ask, confused and angry.

"She doesn't seem to have you confused!" the woman tells him angrily, eyeing me suspiciously.

"Cal, what the hell are you trying to pull?" My skin heats up; my anger and impatience are about to boil over.

"My name is Chris," he says, stepping away from me. *What is going on?*

"Look, who are you?" the woman asks impatiently.

"I'm his wife; that's who I am!" I say angrily. "Who the hell are you?" I ask sharply.

She frowns at me, but then she breaks into a laugh. "Oh, I see. This is a joke. Good one, Chris, you almost had me for a minute, but you know I can see right through your pranks." She pats him on the chest.

"Does it look like I'm joking?" I tell her frantically, the sting of unshed tears forming behind my eyes. She stops laughing. I look Cal in the face, and he's staring at me as if he has no idea who I am.

"Cal, tell her!" I yell at him, desperately trying not to cry in frustration. This can't be happening!

"My name isn't Cal!" His voice rises in a panic.

"Chris, who is she!" the woman asks him again angrily, the idea of this being a prank now out the window.

"Jenna, I've never seen this woman before in my life!" he tries to tell her pleadingly.

"You asshole!" I scream, pushing him. How can this not be Cal! It's him! It is! It's his voice! His face! I have the same feeling I have when I'm near him . . . almost. And I can feel it so much now since I've been deprived of it for so long . . .

"You don't know who I am now?" I shout angrily as tears stream down my cheeks. "Well, who gave me this!" I ask him sardonically. I pull the ring out of my pocket and throw it at him. The woman scrambles after the ring and inspects it.

"Chris, this is a wedding ring!" she shouts, thrusting it in his face.

"I've never seen that before in my life! I've never seen her in my life!" he yells, pointing at me as if I'm a stranger. He's in a clear state of panic, almost matching my own.

"Chris, don't lie to me!" she screams at him.

"She doesn't even know my name! She's crazy!" he yells back at the woman. She looks at me, trying to determine who the liar in this is. His facial expression softens, and he moves towards her, taking her hand.

"Jenna, I swear to you. I have no idea what she's talking about," he pleads to her more calmly.

I begin to laugh hysterically. I'm about to vomit. I have to be dreaming. This is a nightmare; this can't be happening! "Who the hell is she to you? This is why you left? Is this who you left me for!" I say through my tears, snatching his arm.

"He's my fiancé!" she snarls at me. I begin to laugh again, covering my face as I step back from the couple. I shake my head in disbelief, consciously chuckling. I have to laugh because if I don't I'm going to fucking explode. I feel myself boiling, and finally, I spill over.

"How the hell can he marry you when he's still married to me?" I shout, gripping my head. My chest is so tight and my head is pounding.

"I don't even know you. Who are you? How do you know me?" he asks me angrily.

"All of this time, all of this time you've been lying to me and now . . . Now! You act as if you don't even know who I am!" I begin to cry hysterically.

"You swore to me this wasn't about another woman. You fucking asshole!" I continue, cursing the entire time. This son of a bitch doesn't deserve anything from me. I turn and stomp down the steps towards my car. "I want a divorce!" I shout over my shoulder.

"I never want to see you again! Don't you ever come near me or Caylen again! I'll send your shit through Dexter. I want it all out of my house!" I growl viciously at him.

"How does she know Dexter? How the hell does she know Dexter, Chris?" I hear the woman yell.

"I don't know, Jenna, this has to be a joke!" he says through panicked laughter. Joke? I turn back around and head up the stairs.

"Joke! I'm a joke? You think ruining my life was a fucking joke?" I run back up the stairs and push and hit him with all the energy I can muster, and he tries to restrain me.

"Get your hands off of him!" Jenna screams, attempting to tug me away from Cal.

She has a firm grip on my arm. My anger is in complete control and I push her back violently, one of my hands landing directly on her face, and she loses her balance. She looks surprised, and a second later she rushes back toward me. If she wants a fight, she picked the right day for it! Cal jumps in the middle of us, juggling me on one side and restraining her on the other.

I start to feel hot and my vision becomes blurry. How could I believe him after all of these years? He never loved me. This woman in front of him, who he so desperately wants to believe him . . . He loves her.

A man comes out of the house. He looks bewildered by all the chaos. "What's going on here?"

"This psycho attacked us!" the blonde yells, finally settling down in Cal's arm.

"This has nothing to do with you!" I catch my breath, trying to compose myself at her ridiculous accusation. If anyone is crazy, it's them!

"This was between me and my husband!" I retort.

"What?" the older man asks in confusion.

"Tell her, Dad; she doesn't believe me!" I hear Cal say. The rest of what he says becomes a drone as I'm overcome by dizziness. I've got to get out of here. I can't deal with this anymore. I feel like Jerry Springer is going to walk out onto the porch at any moment. I start to head back to my car, but my legs feel weak and everything begins to spin around me and . . .

I OPEN MY eyes and my vision is blurred at first, but things slowly come into focus. I touch my temples; my head is still pounding as if someone is beating me on the head with a hammer.

I look around and see that I'm in a den. The warm fireplace in front of me is glowing brightly. I look toward the window and see that it's completely dark outside except for the glowing porch lamp. And as I look through the clear glass, I begin to realize that the events from earlier weren't a dream, that I haven't imagined them.

I try to stand up, but my knees feel wobbly, resulting in a quick return to my sitting position. I see my purse sitting on the table in front of me. I wonder how I got in here. I look towards the door and realize

now's my chance to make a break for it, to get out of this horrible situation I've thrown myself into, but I know the answers I need are in
this house. I never thought things would go like this. Never in a million
years did I ever think I would almost fight another woman over the man I
loved, especially one who was claiming to not even know me.

. . . Engaged. How could I have been so stupid? All of his words, his
promises, were lies, every single last one of them, and still what hurts the
most is the way he acted . . . as if he didn't know me. It was like I meant
absolutely nothing to him. And what tears me up inside . . . about the
way he acted . . . he did it so well . . .

Why go through this whole scheme? Why not just divorce me, or be
honest with me and tell me he was in love with someone else? Why did
he come to see Caylen? Why did he feed her all of his lies about missing
me? He has to be a psychopath or a con; Hillary was right. That can't be it
though. If he is, how will I ever explain this to my daughter? How could
he have an entire life with me and have a life here? How is it possible for
him to live two lives? How can he own a penthouse in Chicago and live
on a farm in Madison? The land is vast, but . . . it's just not . . . him. But
then again, I guess I don't know *him*. I'm more confused than I was this
morning, when I knew absolutely nothing.

"You're awake." A soft voice snaps me out of my thoughts. I look up
to see a middle-aged red-haired woman smiling so warmly at me that I
instantly feel as if I know her.

"William. She's up, honey," she calls toward the kitchen. She walks
cautiously toward me and offers me the steaming cup of tea. I look at
her cautiously, wanting to know who she is.

"You need to drink something," she urges me with a smile. I take
the cup and sip it slowly.

William—I now recognize the man from the picture in the paper.
He comes through the door and examines me, warily standing beside the
woman. The man's presence, though non-threatening, is colder than the
woman's, his expression set in a frown, but even with his hard demeanor
his handsomeness shines through. He has to be in his late forties but still
has a full head of light brown hair and sea-blue eyes.

I put the tea down on the table in front of me. I open my mouth to say something, but nothing comes out. The man sighs, almost in frustration, and sits in a big chair across from me. He clasps his hands together and looks at the woman. She stands beside him, resting her hand on his shoulder. They look at me as if they know more than I do, which is very intimidating, since I have no idea who they are.

"You're very beautiful," the woman says in a sullen tone. I shift uncomfortably in my seat, realizing what I must look like, and beautiful is not it. I quickly adjust my shirt and comb my fingers through my hair.

"You don't know who we are." It comes out as a statement more than a question.

I nod my head. She smiles slightly and looks at the man next to her, and he frowns to himself. I watch both of them; they seem to be as uncomfortable as I am. I slide my hands across my lap and sigh.

"I saw your picture in the paper with Cal," I say softly, my eyes falling on the man from earlier.

"When you and Chris won the pie-eating contest, honey." I see her smile softly at her husband. I feel my mouth frown up.

"Why do you keep calling him Chris?" I blurt out. I want some answers, and I feel the exigency of the situation beginning to implode inside of me. When she doesn't answer, more questions fall from my mouth.

"Who are you? What is going on?" The little calmness I have is slowly slipping away.

The couple looks at each other before responding.

"I'm Gwen Scott and this is my husband, William," the woman explains quickly. "We're Chris's parents."

I stand up again. If one more person calls him Chris, I'm going to lose it.

"I want to talk to Cal. I want to talk to him right now!" My voice is rising shakily.

"That's not possible, honey," the woman says calmly.

I start to pace in front of the couch angrily. "Does he not want to see me? The damage has already been done! I just—he owes me an explanation!" I start towards the doorway of the room, determined to find him if I have to search every room in this house myself.

"Lauren, please calm down," Mrs. Scott pleads with me.

I stop walking and turn to look at her standing. "You know my name?" I ask quietly. I can tell her expression is trying to hide some pain as she gives me a pitiful look before looking back at her husband.

He stands up beside her. "We know who you are," her husband says sullenly.

"You're Cal's wife." He sighs, folding his arms. His wife looks at me, almost sympathetically.

"Cal." It feels so good to have someone here say his name. I was starting to feel like I was in the twilight zone.

"So he told you about me? Then why does he act like he doesn't know me? Is it because of that woman out there? I'm sorry, I don't know who . . . he never mentioned you. He . . . he . . ." I feel myself starting to choke up. This is too much. Way too much and I barely know anything.

"He doesn't know who you are," the woman says, walking closer toward me.

"What?" I clutch my purse to my chest and look at her skeptically.

"The person you saw earlier wasn't Cal," her husband tells me.

"I don't understand . . . no, that was Cal. I know it. It has to be," I say, finding myself in need of sitting down once again.

"No. It wasn't," she says, taking a seat beside me. I search her eyes to see if she's joking. Her expression is soft and compassionate. I don't understand. He looked like Cal, he sounded like Cal.

"Are you telling me that . . . is he Cal's brother? He's Cal's twin?" I ask, thinking back to Angela's idea. In fact, it would make sense. That would explain why he didn't know me, why he looked at me as if he'd never seen me before in his life. Cal never mentioned having a twin brother, but then, he didn't mention a lot of things.

Her husband's eyebrows rise on his face. "Yes," Mr. Scott answers rapidly.

Mrs. Scott frowns at him. "William, no. No more lies; she deserves to know the truth," she scolds her husband softly, causing her husband to frown at her now.

"She's not going to understand," he says, walking away from us both.

"We agreed that we'd tell her." His wife stands up, facing him.

"What won't I understand? Is he a twin or isn't he?" I ask sternly.

"We wish it were that simple," Mrs. Scott says, looking pained. I glance back and forth between the two.

"Please, I-I don't know what to think about all of this. I came here hoping for . . . for something different than what I found. I know what I saw, but something within me is hoping it's not what it looks like." I laugh pathetically at myself and the hope I still have that this is just a big misunderstanding. I take a deep breath.

"I've always known Cal was hiding something from me. I didn't know what, or why. All I know is that almost two years ago he walked out on me. That he left me without any explanation at all, but I felt like it wasn't something he did willingly, and now . . . I finally find him today, but he's seemingly in love with this other woman, pretending he has no idea who I am, and it hurts so much. If there is something, anything that you can tell me, even if it's just confirming what I've seen today as the truth. Please . . . please just tell me." I feel tears starting to stream from my eyes. I wipe them away, waiting for an answer. I feel a warm hand on my shoulder and look up to see Gwen with tears in her own eyes as well. "I only want the truth," I choke out.

"Even if he doesn't want to see me again, I just want answers, closure at least," I beg her. Her expression still seems hesitant, and she looks at her husband for agreement. I look away from her and turn my attention to him.

He is now gazing out the window. I stand up and touch his arm. I look into this older man's eyes and see a moment of vulnerability. Then, just like that, it's gone. There's a wall up again. Now I see where Cal gets it. He crosses his arms, letting out a sigh.

"Please," I say softly, barely a whisper.

"The truth is that the person you married doesn't exist," he says, his eyes looking ahead of him more than at me.

I swallow the lump in my throat; I think I expected this.

"So his real name is Chris," I say, hoping my shaky voice will steady. "He's been lying to me all along," I say to myself quietly, wiping away newly shed tears before I wrap my arms around myself for some sort of comfort.

"No, sweetheart, you don't understand," Mrs. Scott says sympathetically, leading me to sit beside her on the sofa.

"Oh, I understand," I say, nodding my head as I close my eyes to try to disallow any more tears from falling.

"I understand he used me . . . He never loved me." My voice betrays me and gives in, releasing a sob.

"Oh, no, sweetheart, you have the wrong idea," she assures me, rubbing my back as if she were my mother. I look at her skeptically, and she takes a deep breath.

"Chris and Cal are . . . They're two different people," she says, taking both my hands. I look at her husband, and he takes a seat in the large chair from earlier with a grunt of apprehension on the discussion of his son.

"I-I don't understand," I stutter, looking back and forth between them. They said he wasn't a twin.

"Chris and Cal share the same body, but the person you met today is Chris, not Cal," Mrs. Scott explains cautiously.

"That's the reason he reacted the way he did. He truly doesn't know who you are," she explains gently, holding my hand, searching my eyes for some kind of reaction to this information.

"Cal is a separate personality from Chris," she tells me again, slowly, as if I don't understand. I take my hands from hers.

"What. What are you talking about?" I ask, my attention going to her husband. "A different personality?" I ask, looking at him, waiting for some form of confirmation.

"I know this may be hard for you to believe, but it's the truth," her husband says sternly.

I shake my head and get up from my seat on the couch.

"We're telling you the truth . . ." his wife says more compassionately. "Chris has what is called Dissociative Identity Disorder."

"Are you trying to tell me that Cal has . . . that he has multiple personalities?" I ask in disbelief. Are they kidding?

"Chris does. Cal is the personality that Chris forged. It isn't the other way around. Cal isn't real," Mr. Scott explains. Yeah, I'm really going to believe this. No. No fucking way.

"You can't possibly expect me to believe this." I laugh angrily. I look to Mrs. Scott, whose expression scares me, because it holds such a look of sincerity.

"I know this may be hard for you to understand, unbelievable maybe," Mrs. Scott says warily, fiddling with her hands in her lap.

"Hard to believe? Well . . . I don't believe it!" I shout angrily, throwing my arms up.

"You—you're both lying for him. You're covering for him!" I reason this is the only possible explanation for this insanity.

"We're telling you the truth. Chris doesn't know who you are. He doesn't know what Cal does," Mrs. Scott tells me with a pleading expression.

I cover my face with my hands. They're all crazy or they're all in on this elaborate joke or lie that Cal has constructed. They can't expect me to believe this. They can't be serious. This cannot be happening! I lower my hands and study their faces; they look absolutely serious. I feel the nervous pit in my stomach starting to grow, and I shake my head frantically.

"You're lying. You have to be!" I exclaim. "You're telling me Cal has some sort of split personality. That Cal is the person I know, but your son, Chris, who I met earlier, conveniently has no idea who I am, and he's the real person," I say in a cynical tone. I laugh at the outrageousness. "So I married a personality, not a person—a persona," I say as I continue to laugh through my tear-blurred eyes.

"Please, calm down," Mrs. Scott pleads with me, coming close to me, but I step away from her. This can't be true. No—it just—NO!

"I want some sort of proof if he has some sort of personality disorder! Doctor's records or statements or something!" I say, my tears being replaced by anger.

"We don't have that right now, but we can get them for you. We'll let you review everything we have," Mrs. Scott says patiently.

"No, I don't want to see anything. Dexter could make this stuff up. I-I don't believe you!" I snap with cruel sarcasm.

"You don't have a choice!" her husband tells me angrily.

"Why should I believe what you're saying?" I say, trying to calm myself, which isn't an easy task right now.

"We have no reason to lie to you!" Mr. Scott yells. "Our son is back home! Chris is back, Cal is gone, and I'm going to do everything in my power to make sure it stays that way!" he tells me coldly.

"William!" Mrs. Scott says, almost appalled. She looks at me nervously, and I can feel my mouth agape.

"I told you she wouldn't believe us," Mr. Scott mumbles to his wife.

"I want to talk to Cal right now," I tell him viciously.

"Please, just let us explain," Mrs. Scott begs, trying to calm the high tension in the room between Mr. Scott and me. "I know this must be overwhelming for you, but if you just give me a chance to explain . . ." she pleads.

After a moment of staring down her husband, I take a seat. In an effort to keep my hands from shaking, I clasp them together tightly.

"Before this started to happen, our son was mild mannered and polite, very hard working and caring." Her warm smile hardens as she continues.

"But around his seventeenth birthday, he began to act differently. It started with little things; he began to act out of character. He didn't want to do chores around the house, which was strange because Chris had always offered his help to us. He knew we didn't have the means to run this farm alone. Then, suddenly, we found ourselves having to ask him for help, even demand it. Soon after that, his teachers notified us that he was missing homework assignments and skipping classes . . . everything that wasn't our son.

"You have to understand that this wasn't like him at all," Mrs. Scott goes on with a sorrowful look on her face. It sounds very familiar to me, the disappearing at random, never showing up when expected, having to beg him for answers . . .

"Chris is extremely bright, and school has always been very important to him. But during this change, his behavior at school became so bad and erratic that we had to have a conference with the principal to keep him from being expelled," she explains.

"They told us that Chris's behavior was atrocious. He had disobeyed teachers, walked out of class when he felt like it, picked fights with other students. Normally, our son didn't even like to argue; he had taken boxing lessons when he was younger but never initiated confrontation, so we couldn't believe what we were hearing." She sighs, taking a cleansing breath and continuing.

"They described him as being a completely different person from the boy they had taught years earlier. We knew he was acting differently at home, but we never guessed it had gone to this extent . . ." She starts to drift off and Mr. Scott comforts her.

"We thought at first it was just a phase," Mrs. Scott continues, "and he was being a normal, rebellious teenager. At home, his behavior wasn't nearly as bad as what his teachers described." She pauses, and a pained expression takes hold of her face.

"When we confronted him about it, he broke down; he told us he didn't know what was going on, and that something was happening to him. He told us he'd get urges to do or say things, and that he had no control over his own actions. He then admitted that he was having blackouts. That he'd wake up in the morning and, in the blink of an eye, hours would pass and he'd have no idea where he'd been or what he'd done. If you can imagine someone telling you that, it's the scariest thing you could ever experience, especially when it's coming from someone you love. If you could have seen the fear in his eyes when he told us about this . . . He was terrified, and so were we.

"We told him we'd have him see a therapist. That we'd find out what was going on with him. That next day, he was gone. We looked everywhere for him, all around town, neighboring counties, but we couldn't find him. Five days later, he came home. He was driving a car that cost more than our farm's annual income, that he didn't remember getting into. And there was over twenty thousand dollars in the trunk of it," Mrs. Scott recalls, shaking her head at the thought of it.

"We had no idea what we were dealing with up until that point," Mr. Scott finally joins in. "Chris had never given us any problems at all, let alone problems as serious as what we were dealing with then. Our son was so afraid of what he was doing when he suffered these losses of time, and so were we. He had us lock him in his room. We turned to the only person that we knew could help us—my stepfather, Dexter Crestfield Sr.," Mr. Scott explains, and I see him clenching his fists at the name.

"He provided Chris with the best psychiatric help money could buy; we hoped it would make Chris better. After three sessions, the doctor called us in to speak with her. She told us Chris was exhibiting a form of Dissociative Identity Disorder, a kind that she'd never seen before. Most cases are caused by a traumatic event that the person can't handle, thus creating an alter who can. But in Chris's case, there was no specific traumatic event that happened. It was as if his personality was always divided; like this alter was growing with him," Mr. Scott says, a look of frustration on his face.

"The doctor told us she'd met Chris's alter during the first session, which was uncommon. She explained that it usually took many sessions to get the alter to come forward, but this one confronted her immediately," he explains and waits for a response from me. I sit quietly, absorbing what I'm hearing and waiting for him to continue.

Mrs. Scott picks up where her husband left off. "You have to understand that we've never faced problems like these. We had a hard time believing what we were hearing, and I know you do too. Even if she was the best in her field, we still had doubts. But seeing is believing; his doctor told us to sit in on a session with her and we'd meet him. We were skeptical the entire time, but she hypnotized Chris, or what she called bringing him to a state of unconsciousness, and she asked for his alter to come out. That was the day we met Cal."

"I was never a firm believer in the mental problem mumbo-jumbo, until I came face to face with it," Mr. Scott says, looking down at his own hands.

"This person looked like our son, sounded like our son, but he was nothing like our son. He was . . . mean, cocky . . . nothing like our son," he recollects.

"He also had a temper," Mr. Scott continues, "and he had no interest in the life that we built for him as Chris, or the life that he had built for himself. He made it clear that he was in no way our son, and that he had no intentions of having anything to do with us. He had big plans for his life, bigger plans than farm life." I look up into Mr. Scott's eyes, and I can almost see hatred there.

I start to feel my stomach knot. This life, these people don't fit Cal at all. But this can't be true. This can't happen. Out of all of the people for this to happen to, why me? Why the person I fall in love with? I close my eyes; even as crazy as this all seems, it sort of makes sense.

"We were afraid he would hurt someone, or do something that would land Chris in jail. We couldn't control him, so we decided to send him to live with my stepfather's son. Dexter Jr.," Mr. Scott says.

"You've met the Crestfields, so you know what that meant," he says, his voice sullen. I can't help but clench my own hands together tightly at the name. The thought of how long Dexter kept me in the dark sends flames of anger through my veins. Mr. Scott notices my discomfort at the mention of Dexter Crestfield and continues, "It's not an association I claim proudly. A name I chose not to take even with its privileges, but it was a good fit for Cal. And we knew with them he'd have everything he wanted and wouldn't have to harm people or steal, endangering our son's life. Of course, Dexter Jr. was one of the people that Cal actually liked. He didn't care for us much. When Chris would regain control, he'd come home, and when Cal took over he'd just leave.

"Two years ago my wife received some news that was life changing for our entire family." Mr. Scott trails off and his wife takes his hand, squeezing it.

"I was diagnosed with stage 3 cancer," she says quietly. "We asked Dexter Jr. to tell Cal. Shortly after that, Chris regained control and came home, and he didn't leave again," she finishes quietly. I try to wrap my mind around everything I've just heard. I think back to two years ago and suddenly, I'm seeing in my mind's eye the last night I spent with Cal, when he left me after getting a phone call from Dexter. It dawns on me that it could have been at that moment. My thoughts are jumbled, but my heart still goes out Cal, knowing what he had to be going through at that moment, and he didn't have anyone to comfort him or help him through what he was dealing with.

"I'm really sorry that happened to you." I try to remain sensitive, but my mind is still reeling from all of this. "This, this can't be true," I whimper to myself, head in my hands as I sit, taking in all of the information I've just heard. What I've just said is to try to convince myself, but what these two people are telling me coincides perfectly with everything that's happened. I feel a hand touch my shoulder, but I pull away, willing myself not to believe what I'm hearing. I don't want to accept this.

"If this is true, if I happen to believe all this, why didn't anyone tell me?" I ask out of frustration at the situation.

"You had to have known about me! Dexter knew about me. I sat in his house. I ate dinner with him . . . He became my friend! And no one told me!" I look them both in the eye.

"We didn't know at first. Cal saw a lot of women," Mr. Scott says dismissively, his words harsh.

"We didn't know Cal was serious about you . . ." He trails off, looking at his feet. His wife stands, wringing her hands together nervously, the tension still high between her husband and me.

"The day Dexter called and told us he was engaged was the first time we were told about you," Mrs. Scott says.

"He said you were a good person . . . that you were good for Cal. He told us that when you were with Cal, he was as close to Chris as he could get. His doctor said that you could probably help him get better, bringing him in touch with a side of himself that he hadn't recognized, with kindness, warmth, and love."

"What about me? You keep saying what everyone thought was best for Cal, for Chris. What about me? Did anyone stop to think what this would do to me? Did anyone for a second stop to look at me as a person and not some form of treatment!" I shout angrily.

"Yes! That made me want to tell you more about him, the real him. I-I came to see you. You didn't know who I was, of course. I asked for you to come down, but Cal did instead, and he stopped me. I asked him not to marry you. I said that he'd hurt you, and he became furious with me. He told me he loved you more than anything and that he'd never hurt you, and that if we told you anything, we'd never see Chris again." She looks down guiltily. And the realization hits me like a ton of bricks. I recognize her now as the red-headed woman who came to see me the night of our engagement party. I feel like I'm going to throw up.

"I begged him to tell you the truth. Told him he couldn't live a lie with you forever," she continues, tears streaming down her cheeks.

"He kept talking about something he was taking that would fix his problem, that would get rid of Chris completely." She says the last part with a sigh. "When I heard that, I was afraid of what he was doing. I hoped he was lying, and my main concern was to make sure he wasn't doing something to hurt himself." She wipes away her tears.

"We wanted to tell you. We knew you deserved the truth, but we couldn't risk losing our son." Tears pour from her eyes like a fountain and I shake the compassion my heart is trying to feel. This isn't about them right now.

They honestly seem like good people. I think back to all the times Cal left, how he never told me anything about his family. I remember Dexter's words, how he told me that if I looked for Cal, I wouldn't find him. I touch my throbbing temples and begin to cry. If this is all true, the person who's my husband, who's the father of my child, isn't real. But no, I can't accept that. Cal is real; at least, he is when he's around.

I lift my head to see Mrs. Scott looking at me with sympathy etched on her face. I don't know what to say. What do I say to this? My mind suddenly drifts to this afternoon's event. I take a deep breath, clearing my throat as best I can, and take the Kleenex Mrs. Scott hands to me.

"So, today, earlier, he's . . . his name is Chris?" I stutter out.

Mrs. Scott nods.

"So I'm . . . nothing at all to him?" I ask, wringing the edge of my t-shirt.

"It's because he doesn't know what Cal does when he takes over," Mr. Scott says in a low, stressed tone.

I stop to think for a second, processing his words. "Wait a minute!" I say, the realization hitting me. "You never told him anything?"

Mrs. Scott looks down in shame.

"We thought it would be best for him not to know. He's already carrying so much that we decided it would be for the best," Mr. Scott explains.

My mouth drops open. "You never . . . ? He doesn't know about Cal? About me? About . . . You let him get engaged to another woman, knowing he was married?" I say sharply, standing up.

"Technically, he's not married to you. You're Cal's wife, not Chris's," he says coldly. His wife immediately whips her head around to look at him.

"I'm Cal's wife?" I shout. "You never bothered to tell me that Cal isn't real, so right now, I'm married to your son!"

"That monster you fell in love with is not my son!" he shouts back.

"Cal is not a monster! He is not this evil person you're making him out to be. He may not be perfect, but he's a good person!" I tell him angrily.

"Cal is the *worst* thing that ever happened to our family!" he growls at me.

"How dare you! You have no right, especially after this, to throw around ethical judgments about anyone. You don't know anything about Cal, and if that's how you feel, you don't deserve to!" I say defensively.

"You don't know anything about him!" he shouts. The words sting me because I don't know what the hell is going on, and if this is true, Cal has ripped our life apart, but I won't let them stand here berating Cal with such hatred. I don't know what to believe at this point, but I won't let anyone talk about Cal that way. He's still my daughter's father, and if his dad treated him like this, I know exactly why he left.

"William, stop!" his wife orders, and he immediately acquiesces.

"Does he even know what he has? That he has this disorder?" My voice starts to shake.

"He knows he's suffered episodes of time loss, but to this extent, no. It's a part of his treatment to slowly tell him about Cal. If we spring it all on him, he could break down and make things worse. He doesn't need this right now. He's finally getting better," Mr. Scott says, his tone calming down.

"Better? You're saying he's getting better? How can he be better when he doesn't know that he has a wife and a child? What do you want me to do? Disappear? Let him have this happy little life with you and his fiancé?" I shout.

"A child?" Mrs. Scott mumbles. Her eyes are wide as she repeats the words.

"You've had almost two years, and you haven't told him anything. You weren't even going to tell me anything . . ."

"We're going to tell Chris. We just need more time. We need his doctor. But you have to understand that you're a part of Cal's life, that Chris has his own. Cal isn't here, and our ultimate goal is to get rid of Cal completely!" he says pointedly, and my heart skips a beat.

"William . . ." Mrs. Scott grabs her husband's arm, her eyes still wide as she tries to get her husband's attention.

"We will tell Chris and Jenna, but we're going to tell them when it's the right time. We hope that you will respect our decision to do it at our discretion," he continues, looking me straight in the eye.

"William!" his wife shrieks frantically.

"Did you hear what she said?" she says, her voice cracking as tears well in her eyes. I wipe away my own tears. "She says they have a child, William."

His frown softens and he arches an eyebrow. They both turn to me. I'm feeling another wave of anger and confusion welling up inside of me.

"You have a baby?" he asks quietly. I don't say anything, frowning at both of them. I grab my purse, take out my phone to show them a picture of Caylen, and hand it to Mrs. Scott. I can't help but notice the shocked expression on her face. I turn to her husband, and his expression matches Mrs. Scott's. From the looks of them, I'd say this is the first time they've heard anything about Caylen.

"D-Dexter never told us you were pregnant. We never knew anything about this," he says, his tone cold but his expression softening.

"According to you, her father's not this Chris person. Her father is the monster that you want to get rid of!" I say harshly.

"What's her name?" Mrs. Scott says, so softly I have to strain to make it out. A smile spreads across her face, and her eyes water as she looks into the picture. "She looks just like him." Her voice breaks, and she covers her mouth.

"You have a daughter with Chris?" he says sullenly. It's funny that now I have a baby with Chris, when a minute ago I was married to Cal.

"Look at her, William. She's beautiful," she says earnestly and tries to show the picture to her husband. He glances at it for a moment then scowls again angrily.

"It's bad enough he took it upon himself to marry this woman, but to have a child. I didn't think even he'd sink that low." He walks back over to the window and hits the window frame.

"William, calm down."

"How could he do this? Why wouldn't Dexter tell us about this?"

"William, we have a grandchild!" she says, trying to focus on the one positive thing in the room.

"That's Cal's daughter! Not Chris's. There's a difference!" he yells at her. Her smile fades, and she scowls at him and takes the picture and puts it close to his face.

"Whose eyes are these? Whose smile is this?" she asks. "It's Chris's. I see my grandchild, William!" she yells at him.

"I can't believe this!" he roars.

"Someone should have told me!" I screech, tired of being ignored. "Secrets aren't okay when you're the one on the other end, are they?" I ask bitterly, and they look down, guilt on their faces.

"No one bothered to tell me that the man I fell in love with, the man I married and have a child with, has a personality disorder? I guess once he came back home, you all were a happy family again, never mind the family he left back in Chicago. It would be too much of an inconvenience to inform me of what was going on! Caylen and I were too much of a liability to your perfect little life!" I shout, feeling my entire body shaking.

"We had no idea that you were having a child. Dexter never told us you were pregnant!" Mrs. Scott tries to explain.

"And if I wasn't? You were just going to let me sulk in the dark, having no clue about him. What's in the past is just forgotten, huh? You may not think of Cal as a real person, but he's real to me, and at the very least I'm real! I'm flesh and bones, and I have feelings. I fell in love with him, a man, not a figment of my imagination or this monster that you claim him to be. When he left me, it hurt more than anything. I cried every night. Every part of me ached. You love your son! I love my husband! Each moment you were happy with him, I was alone, wondering where my husband was! I had no idea if he was hurt, or if he was even alive, but you had the comfort of knowing your son was safe each time he disappeared!" I say, feeling the tears well up from years of being held back inside of me.

"So now that you know that I have a child with Cal, or Chris, or whatever he wants to call himself, what now? Am I just supposed to disappear and take care of her on my own? Leave this Chris person to live his perfect life with his fiancé?" Mr. Scott just looks as if he sees through me.

"W-we—of course not. We're going to tell him; he has a beautiful little girl," she says, looking at the picture. Mr. Scott frowns at her and me.

"I'm going to call Dexter about this," he growls and leaves the room.

"I am so sorry, Lauren" Mrs. Scott says, tears continuing to fall from her eyes. "We had no idea. I know we were wrong for not telling you. But if we knew you had a child, we would have told Chris. I am so sorry." Her voice gives in, and she then takes time to compose herself.

I look at her and almost want to hug her. She seems genuinely sorry, and her presence is so warm. In a different situation, she would have been a wonderful mother-in-law. I put my purse back on my shoulder and take a deep breath. It's been more than a long day. I walk over to her and hold my hand out for my phone.

"Do you . . . do you mind—could you send me one of these?" she asks, reluctantly handing me back my phone. I reach into my purse and pull out the one wallet-size picture I have, which is of both Caylen and me, and write my number on the back of it.

"Her name is Caylen. This is my number." I turn and head towards the door.

She follows me to see me out. "Where . . . where are you staying?" Mrs. Scott asks with a sniff, trying to recover from what just happened as much as I am.

"I don't know yet; it'll be somewhere close," I tell her, opening the door. She looks behind her and looks as if she wants to say something, but doesn't.

"Ritter Inn is a really nice place, not too far away, affordable. Good people work there," she says with a forced smile.

"I'm still not sure if I believe all of what you've told me," I say bluntly. "I mean, no one has been exactly honest with me up until this point." She opens her mouth to say something, but I stop her.

"I know you did what you did to protect your son, because you love him. Just so you understand that I love my daughter, and she's not going to grow up without a father. If it were just me, I'd walk away from this. After all, Cal kept me in the dark just as much as everyone else." I stop, not wanting to shed anymore tears. "But she deserves a father, whether it is Cal, or Chris, or if he decides to call himself Bob. One of them had a part in making her." I try to soften my tone.

"Tell your husband I am not going to disappear. You have three days to tell him whatever you haven't, because when I see him I'm telling him everything. But I think he'd prefer to hear it from you rather than me. I think we'll have enough to talk about without me having to tell him everything you won't," I say frankly. She nods her head, eyes wide. I exit the house and hurry down the front steps.

When I reach my car, I look back and see that she's still watching me. I get in and quickly pull off. So much of what they said could be true . . . but is all of it honest? I'll have to judge for myself. The meaning of honesty seems blurry.

April 1st, 2011

I T'S BEEN THREE days since Cal got back from his last trip. *Working.* It's funny—well, not really. His out of town trips have become more frequent, and not only that, but impromptu. Apparently, they can happen in the middle of the night, with little notice as I've come to learn. I wake in the morning to not find my husband next to me. It isn't too bad. I try to think of it as *exciting*, not knowing if he'll be home or not, kind of like a game. There's nothing *strange* or *disrespectful* about it at all—according to Cal.

I think back three months to our first fight, about his lack of communication. How it was out of character compared to the trips he took before we were married. Well, as it turns out, communicating with me like a normal person . . . *That* was actually out of character for him.

The only thing he's retained from that little verbal spat is to send text messages. Oh, how lucky I am to get those. Usually two words; if I'm lucky, three. 'Made it.' 'Be home soon.' 'Don't be mad.' He probably has them auto-typed. I've decided after this last business trip that I'm done pleading with him to act like a decent human being, to respect me and not cut me off. Now I'm just tired. I'm tired of trying to compromise. I'm done asking. I'm coming close to being done with him and this marriage.

He can say all he wants, that it's his job or whatever the hell he thinks I'm stupid enough to believe, but I'm sick of it. He thinks this is fun for me—being here, waiting around until he decides to show up is not fun. Whenever I see that overnight bag appear, I feel myself slipping into a rage. There is something more than work going on. There has to be.

We haven't been on speaking terms for the past two days. He came home from this last 'business' trip after being gone six days, leaving with less than an hour's notice on the very night he promised to go with me back to Saginaw to visit Raven. I couldn't bring myself to say a word to him since he's been home. He doesn't want to talk about what I want to talk about . . . Things like who the hell he's with when he's gone. I know he probably has a mistress somewhere, maybe one in every freaking state. He laughed when I told him that. It was apparently hilarious, based on his reaction. When I told him his job title should be *"Dexter's Bitch,"* he didn't find that as funny. And now he's not talking to me, either.

The screwed-up part about all of this, though, is that even with me being so mad at him, so furious I just want to hit him, I miss him. I miss him so much that it makes my stomach turn. I miss him, despite us sleeping in the same bed. He hasn't tried to touch me since the first night I pushed him away and told him to keep his hands off me. Still, my body craves his touch. I want to lie on his chest and feel his fingers tracing his name on my back. I'm furious that he makes me feel like this, that he's doing this to us. He thinks I'm overreacting, but I think he is underreacting to the affect this is having on our relationship.

Today, I've been in the gym for the past two hours, beating the track with my sneakers instead of destroying things in my house. I don't know what's happening to me, but I'm becoming someone I don't want to be: a mean, vindictive shrew.

I take deep breaths as I walk into our bedroom and see him shuffling through his drawer, his luggage case near his feet. My stomach tightens and I can feel my pulse beating in my head. He's leaving, and he just got back three days ago.

"I'm going to Seattle tomorrow. In case you give a fuck," he says sardonically. He has to feel my gaze burning into his back.

I turn down the music and snatch the buds out of my ears.

"What?" I say angrily, even though we both know I heard him plain and clear.

"You heard what I said," he says shortly. I laugh angrily.

"Of course you are. Thanks for the heads up on the location but, FYI, I'm starting to not give a fuck," I say venomously. I regret the words as soon as they leave my mouth, but they came out so effortlessly.

He stops shuffling through his drawer, swiftly turning around, and anger radiates from his expression. His eyes climb my body, and for a moment the look he gives me is familiar, something I haven't seen in a few days from him: lust. But I'm too angry to care and it disappears, replaced with his new pissed to shit demeanor. I sit on the bed with force, removing my gym shoes. I'm hot, irritated, and sick of his shit.

"You are, huh?" He laughs in disbelief. I roll my eyes at him and snatch off my other shoe.

"Well, it's the last time I'll tell you where I'm going, since you don't give a fuck," he says angrily.

I open my mouth to respond, but I feel a burning in my throat, and I know that if I say something my voice is going to break and I'll start crying. I won't give him the satisfaction. So instead, I take a deep breath, stand up, look him directly in the eye, and show him my middle finger. I walk towards the bathroom, holding the gesture the entire time until I'm inside and I slam the door as hard as I can.

Once I'm inside, my angry façade quickly starts to break down. I rush to the shower, turn on the water so he can't hear me cry. I strip out of my sweaty shorts and sports bra and make my way into the water, where I let go completely. I'm angry. I'm so angry that I *don't* feel angry. I'm devastated. It hasn't even been three months since he started going back to work, and my marriage is on the brink of falling apart.

I hate the way we've been acting toward one another. That little spiel was the first actual conversation we've had without screaming at each other. Tomorrow he'll be gone again. I'm terrified the cycle will just repeat itself and in a year, I'll be signing divorce papers.

I rest my arms on the wall, cradling my head as the water pours over me and I continue to cry. The hot water isn't washing away the sorrow I feel or numbing the pain my spirit's in. Suddenly, cool air filters into the shower. I turn around and my face automatically sets into a scowl as I see him standing there.

"We need to talk," he says sternly. I hope the droplets of water camouflage my tears. I turn back around, barely glancing at him.

"Go fuck yourself, Cal." I laugh angrily, barely glancing at him. He doesn't want to talk about anything I want to talk to him about, and he's leaving anyway, so any conversation is useless. "Oh, but I'm sure you have plenty of women doing that for you," I add with a bitter chuckle.

A second later he's in the shower, fully clothed.

"What are you doing?" I ask in disbelief. He starts to take off his shirt and undoes his pants, stripping right in the shower. He's lost it. He throws out his wet clothes and closes the shower door. I shake my head in disbelief and shock. I try to move past him as he grabs me. I move to snatch my arm away, but he doesn't let me go. "Let go," I yell, pulling away from him.

"Talk to me!" he demands angrily. Oh, he's angry. No, I'm angry! I'm tired of talking to him. It hasn't helped! I'm wasting my breath. I try to snatch my arm away from him again, but he doesn't let me go.

"No!" I yell, trying to push him out of my path. He moves in front of me each way I try to go.

"I don't want to talk to you!" I say angrily, shoving him away from me, but he forces me toward him. I resort to hitting him hard on the chest, and he grabs me.

"Then just fucking listen!" he demands, pinning me against the shower wall, my arms near my head.

"I'm not fucking anybody else, okay? If I wanted other women, I wouldn't be with you. I know it looks bad! But I swear to God I'm not cheating on you. If you're mad, be mad about me being gone, but I can't deal with you hating me for this imaginary shit going on in your head."

I look up at him. He's breathing hard, his brow furrowed. I want to slap him and kiss him all at once. He's looking directly in my eyes, staring me down and trying to read me, and I look away from him.

"You're all I want." His tone is low as he rests his head on mine. "You're all I've ever wanted." He loosens his grip on my wrists, but still he holds them. He kisses me. I turn away slightly, still trying to process this. He grabs my chin, holding my face toward him, and kisses me more forcefully. When I break away, we both catch our breath.

"I need you," he says. His voice is pleading and he kisses me more urgently, until I start to kiss him back.

His hands move underneath my thighs and he lifts me up effortlessly.

I feel him slide inside of me. I gasp as he enters. My fingers dig into his back as my body adjusts around him. He goes deeper inside me, each movement reminding me of how much my body craves him, each thrust reminding me that he knows its every crevice. My body has given into him, but my heart hasn't; it's bruised and in hiding. While still inside of me, he takes my hand and intertwines his fingers with mine.

"Without you I'm nothing," he whispers in my ear. I try to account the unsteadiness of his voice due to his body recovering from what it's done. But with just those four words, my heart shows itself and gives in to him. I'm still scared, so scared. The heaviness on my chest is gone, and I believe he's not cheating on me, but I realize if he's not, we have a problem—one much bigger than I ever thought. Because if Cal loves me as much as he makes believe he does, whatever is slowly peeling away at our relationship, we may not be able to fix.

Y OU'RE THE REASON I *fight to be here . . .*

I open my eyes, trying to get away from the words that have been relentlessly playing in my head. I can't escape from his echoing voice. I keep trying to make his face disappear, but every time I close my eyes, I see him.

The words seem to hold more meaning than I ever imagined, but now they're worthless. Something made him stop fighting. Or even if he did, at this point it's pretty moot.

March 9th, 2013

I sit up on my lumpy bed in the Ritter Inn's lovely room—not really.

I let out a sigh as I hold my head in my hands. Sleeping has been practically useless. When it's not his voice, it's the Scotts' words following me around. Scenes of Cal and me in the past haunt my thoughts every second, or even worse, my first meeting with "Chris."

It's been two days since I found out the so-called "truth," whether or not I believe it. It is implausible, but makes so much sense, connecting so many dots that have been scattered about in my brain for years—all of Cal's sudden disappearances, his void connection with family, with everyone except the Crestfields—but to believe that he isn't real, that he's a forged personality . . . I'll never believe that. I can't.

I try to forget the look on the Scotts' faces; they carried a quiet honesty and a sincerity—even Mr. Scott. His bitterness was too genuine to be an act. Mrs. Scott's tears were too real, her eyes so full of sorrow when she spoke. If this is all a scheme, they should both win an Oscar.

I look over at the side table where my phone is vibrating once again. It's Hillary this time. She, Angela, and Raven have all called numerous times, but I haven't been up to the task of talking to them. I can't face not being able to answer questions that I don't have answers for myself. This entire thing seems like I'm in a nightmare, just waiting to be woken up, as if everything is playing backwards in my head.

I grab the remote beside me and turn on the television in the hope that it will take my mind off of my complex thoughts. I think of Caylen; this is the longest I've been away from her. I miss her so much. I know Raven is taking great care of her. She would die before she let anything happen to her, but I still miss her.

I feel guilty for my lack of communication back home, but I'm just not ready to talk to anyone right now.

I can't begin to think of what this means if it's all true. Whenever I do, I feel as if I'll throw up or pass out. I don't know anything about this Chris person, and he knows absolutely nothing about me. He's in love with another woman, or he's engaged to another woman. I can only imagine how his parents will explain me to him.

I think back to Mr. Scott's words about the possibility that Chris won't be able to handle the truth, the chance that it'll make things worse. But what does that mean? Would Cal come back?

I've seen movies about split personalities, story arcs in the soap operas Raven watched when I was younger, but facing it in reality is something completely different.

A knock at the door interrupts my thoughts. It's probably room service, which means Ms. Ritter is making sure I haven't trashed her room. I lazily get up from my bed and open the door.

"I don't need . . ." I start to say, but freeze when I see the person looking back at me.

"Hi," he says softly, his eyes as wide as mine.

My heart crawls up into my throat. Here—he's here, standing in front of me. I try to move my eyes from his, but they're locked there. I search for the intensity in his eyes that I haven't seen in years, but there's only uncertainty.

My hands are starting to shake, my body taking on directions of its own. I can feel my emotions start to swell from the bottom of my stomach, ready to overflow if I don't gain some sort of control over them.

I can't blow up here; I can't boil over. I have to use this time, if not for me, for Caylen. I have to see if this is him, if he's playing me, if everything is a lie, or even worse—if it's the truth.

Right now he has the upper hand, the element of surprise. I have to use this. I have to think . . . I jump out of my thoughts at the knocking of the door once again. I realize I subconsciously closed the door in his face.

I can do this. I can do this. I reassure myself.

"I'm sorry for coming like this. I-I just thought . . . I can come back later when you're ready," I hear the timid voice say before his footsteps lead away from the door.

"No!" I quickly open the door and step out halfway to see him.

He turns around and slowly approaches me. With each step he takes, I feel my chest tighten, making it harder for me to breathe. My eyes avoid his now, inadvertently landing on his chest since that's where I am height-wise with him.

"My parents said you were coming tomorrow, but . . . I thought we . . . I wanted to talk to you alone if it's okay." He stumbles over his words.

I glance up and see that his eyes stare over my head; we both seem to be using the same tactics. I try to respond, but nothing comes out, so I step back and gesture for him to come in. I take a deep breath as he passes me, stealing a quick glance at him before I shut the door.

I reassure myself again that I can do this. I walk over to the sofa, trying to decide if I'd rather sit or stand, but my eyes still gravitate to him.

I can't believe it's been almost two years since I've seen him, not including that disaster the other day. As much as I don't want to look at him, I can't help it at the same time.

I fold my arms across my chest and wait for him to say something; after all, he's the one who came here. Our eyes meet, and the look in his scares me. They seem so familiar, yet foreign. He looks at me as if I'm a stranger.

Whenever Cal looked at me, even when I was upset with him, or he was upset, there was always something that held me, something so intense that I hated it when I was angry and became enraptured with it when I wasn't. But now, as I look in Chris's eyes, I see confusion. Something solemn and apologetic, and it terrifies me because Cal has never been any of those things. He never took anything back, and he rarely apologized.

The room seems to be filled with things that need to be said, questions that beg to be asked, at least on my part, but I don't know what to say, where to begin. Where do you start with someone who you've known for what seems like forever who, in fact, you don't know at all?

I convinced myself that if I had him alone, I could instantly know if this was all a lie. I tried to convince myself that it was a lie. And now, just from the look in his eyes that always gave away so little and so much about him, I do know. I don't see Cal. I hold on to my wrist and start to squeeze, a nervous habit I've developed.

"I don't really know what to say to you, or where to start," he begins in a quiet tone, his eyes looking into mine for the first time, as if he's seeing me for the first time, almost. It only lasts a second before he looks away. He opens his mouth to say something else, but then stops, as if he's at a loss for words completely.

I try to think of something to say, to cut through the dead silence in the room. There are so many things I want to say, but not to him. Not to the person standing in front of me.

Tears start to cloud my vision, and I fight with everything in me to keep them from falling. I turn away from him and wipe my eyes quickly. I see that his eyes are glued to his feet. I realize I have to talk to him for who he is, someone I know nothing about, and that's one of the hardest realizations I've come to.

"Um," I try to say, but my throat starts to burn. I look up at the ceiling, trying to be stronger than I feel right now.

"I don't know what to say to you either, to be honest," I say, angry at the new tears that are falling down my cheeks. I quickly wipe them away and notice how uncomfortable he looks.

"Your parents told you everything?" I ask unsurely, commanding my voice to steady.

He sighs, still avoiding eye contact. "They told me they've been lying to me all of this time. That when I didn't remember things, another person was living my life for me, that they felt they should keep it from me," he says with obvious bitterness.

"Everyone I know and trust has been lying to me. My parents, my so-called doctor," he says, his mouth formed into a frown.

"Welcome to the club," I mumble, rubbing my temples. I've had a continuous headache since I got here.

There's another period of silence. I notice he's wearing scuffed work boots; his jacket is clean, but it's apparent that it's been worn more than casually. His hair is different too, shorter almost. He looks like a model for Old Navy, so much more innocent than Cal. No dark colors, no mystery; it's almost like what you see is what you get.

"I should have known something was wrong," he says quietly, his words snapping me from my thoughts once more.

"I would wake up and days, sometimes months had gone by. I should have known it was bigger than what they were telling me. They made it seem like I was okay, like they had me under control. I thought my treatments were working. I didn't know how bad it'd gotten," he says, but it's as if he's talking to himself instead of me.

"The people I trusted most lied to me," he says in frustration.

"You can't blame yourself. It's human nature to want to believe things are always good. When I talked to your parents, they thought they were doing what was best for you. Your interest was the only one they were looking out for."

He looks at me, a little surprised. I'm surprised myself; I don't know why I just said that. I barely know the Scotts, and we didn't exactly get off on the right foot, but it seems they truly love him, so much that they'd screw anyone else over for him. Though they did horrible things, they did it all for him.

"I didn't expect for you defend them. Especially after . . . they lied to you too," he says uncertainly.

"I'm not defending them," I say quickly. "What they did was wrong; it hurt a lot people. But I don't think they did it to be malicious or cruel. They thought they were protecting you. As a parent, you'd do anything to protect your child from what you believe could hurt them. If I was in their situation, and I believed that I could keep you safe by lying to you, I would have," I admit.

He doesn't say anything for a moment, and then he turns his attention to his pocket and pulls something out. He starts to walk closer to me, and I swallow every nerve in my body. I feel my breathing speed up.

I know he must think that I'm crazy, but his expression doesn't show it. His earlier facial expression softens, and I find myself taking a step away from him. He notices my discomfort and stops walking toward me, instead reaching out his hand.

"My mom said . . ." He drifts off, and I notice it's the picture I gave Mrs. Scott of Caylen. I feel a small smile spread across my face. His eyes are still locked on the picture, his expression a cross between puzzlement and worry.

"Caylen," I say softly, touching her face on the picture. When I look up, I notice his eyes are on me, and we both look away.

"You named her after him . . . after Cal?" he asks.

I nod mechanically. His eyes stay locked on the picture as he makes his way over to the sofa and sits down.

"How old is she?" he asks, releasing a breath that he seems to have been holding in for a while.

"She just had her first birthday three days ago," I tell him, sitting on the edge of the sofa, feeling more at ease with Caylen as the topic. I see his eyebrow rise, and he turns fully toward me.

"You've been raising her alone." He looks at me sympathetically, which I feel angry about for some reason.

"No. My aunt and friends have been there since the beginning to help me with her. She doesn't lack anything," I explain.

"But a father," he says quietly. He said it, not me. "Is . . . is she okay?"

"She's fine." I smile, missing her the more I think about her.

"I-I mean is . . . is she healthy?"

"As a one-year-old can be."

"Are you sure?"

I frown as my gaze goes toward him. "Of course I'm sure," I tell him, a bit annoyed. I'm her mother; I think I would know if she wasn't.

"She doesn't do anything strange?"

"Like what?"

"In general?"

"Caylen isn't strange," I tell him sharply.

"No, I didn't mean that. I just wanted to make sure she was okay," he says, trying to clean up his words.

I stand up. "She's been okay an entire year of her life without you making sure she was okay. I've made sure she's okay!" I say, more bitter than I intend to be, but I've raised her alone since birth, and he thinks I wouldn't know if my daughter was okay.

"I didn't mean anything by it. I-I don't know what I meant," he says, seemingly genuine. He offers the picture to me. I feel guilty for some reason, and it dawns on me he's referring to his mental condition, even though it may be over-reaching. I guess that's something I'll need to worry about sooner or later if this is hereditary, but that'll have to go to the back of my queue of things to go crazy over.

"I'm sorry. I overreacted," I say apologetically, "I'm-I'm just not used to this, all of this . . . It's all—" I say, unable to excuse my erratic behavior.

"No, it was my fault. I was out of line. I shouldn't have asked such a stupid question," he cuts me off.

Silence fills the air again, and we both sigh.

"She's fine. She's a perfectly normal, healthy one-year-old." He turns his attention back to the picture with a slight smile at first, and then it spreads widely. It's almost as if half the worry from his expression is gone. It's the first time he's smiled since . . . well, in a long time. Actually, it's the first one I've seen from him . . . from Chris, but it's still one that I've missed. He sits down on the sofa again, and I cautiously sit beside him, looking at Caylen's picture in his hand.

"She has your eyes. They turn like yours do," I say cautiously, almost as if the comment is too personal to be allowed. He looks uncomfortable.

Maybe I shouldn't have said that. I knew I shouldn't have . . .

"I-I mean I . . ." I stumble further, embarrassing us both until he looks up from the picture and smiles at me.

Butterflies start to go crazy in my stomach. I start to silently pray that my cheeks aren't as red as I think they are. He turns his attention away from me, pretending not to notice, and then his smile disappears into an almost worried stare.

"How are we supposed to deal with this?" he asks quietly, like he is uncertain of what more to say. "I-I don't know how to deal with this . . ." he says, wringing his hands as he lets out a sigh of frustration before standing again.

"You don't know anything about me. I don't know anything about you. And this Cal guy . . ." He covers his face, exasperated. "I mean . . . I have a daughter I don't even remember . . ." He drifts off, laughing angrily.

"Years of *my* life," he continues. "All of these things happened, and I don't remember any of it. No one bothered to tell me. What am I supposed to do with this?" He anxiously begins pacing the room. "I'm trying. I really am. I thought if I could make the first step in talking to you that I could do it, but . . ."

I can see the confusion in his face, the worry, the uncertainty. He's just as lost as I am, maybe even more. I don't know what to say to change that, or if I *can* say anything to change it. I'm not used to seeing him so frantic and on edge. This isn't the *him* I'm used to at all.

"I know this is hard for you. I can't begin to imagine what you're going through right now," I say honestly, trying to comfort him in some form.

"I don't know *anything* about you." His tone is apologetic, but his eyes and expression are compassionate. *Still* his words hurt; they feel like a knife penetrating my heart. That familiar face is looking back at me, but his eyes show no sign of recognition, nor do his words. "But when you look at me, it's like you know everything about me," he says. His eyes are on me, staring into mine as if he's trying to see inside me, as though if he stared hard enough, he'd have the answers to all his questions.

"I have enough trouble with one life," he says with a sardonic laugh. "How am I supposed to deal with one I don't know anything about? One that . . . that isn't really mine?" he says to himself.

I open my mouth to respond to him and then realize that he thinks this is easier for me. He doesn't realize what I've been through . . . what I'm going through. I pause, trying to carefully choose my words so as not to agitate or overwhelm him.

"When your parents told me about you," I begin warily. "It was the hardest thing I've ever experienced; the most difficult thing I've ever had to listen to. I was hurt and confused; I didn't even believe them . . . I didn't want to believe them," I say, clenching my wrist as I continue. "I'm *still* hurt. I am *still* confused. I don't know what to do. I don't know what to say to . . . to *you*," I hear my voice crack and he turns around to face me.

"I can't compromise with someone I don't know either." I take a few breaths to try and steady my heartbeat, but it's futile as my pulse continues to race. I can feel his eyes on me and I continue to stare at the floor.

"When you look at me . . . it's as if I'm a burden . . . a problem, and you have no idea how much that hurts," I swallow the lump in my throat, hot tears in my eyes as I finally look up at him. He looks as if he's going to say something, then doesn't. His eyes take my place and become glued to the floor.

"I don't blame you for it," I quickly add. "I can't . . . but you have to understand that you have Cal's . . ." I laugh as the tears are unavoidable, but I try to maintain a steady voice as I continue.

"You . . . you have his smile, his voice, his eyes . . ." I feel myself smile through my tears when I think back to when Cal would smile at me, without being condescending, manipulative, or arrogant—those rare moments when he'd truly smile.

"When I look at you . . . I can't help but see him. And it hurts knowing that you weren't the one who stole my heart when you first smiled at me, who took me bungee jumping on our first date, that you weren't the one who told me I'm the only woman you have ever loved. But you're . . . you're not him, and you're in love with someone else." I feel embarrassed as the tears stream down my cheeks, but he needs to see them, to know that I'm a person.

"So, I'm sort of having a hard time with this." I chuckle, finally wiping away some of the fallen tears. "Even knowing all of it, I don't how I'm supposed to get past it," I explain. "How I'm supposed to deal with this . . . if I even can, but I'm willing to try because of that little girl in that picture. I'd do anything for her, including giving up the only person I've ever been in love with . . ."

He looks at me, dumbfounded. I feel myself starting to break down and I take a deep breath, wiping away all of my tears once more, commanding my eyes to stop it. I walk over to him, forcing myself to see someone new, to not see Cal, but to see . . . Chris.

"I-I'm sorry. Please don't cry." His voice is shaky, his expression one I've never seen before. I see him looking around nervously. He searches his pocket and he pulls out a napkin, the rough kind that usually comes from a fast food restaurant. I take it and wipe my eyes.

"I know you didn't ask for this," I say. "I know this isn't your fault. And I know that you want to believe none of this is your problem, but it is, and it's mine too . . . but it's not Caylen's.

"I'm willing to accept that you're not Cal, that you aren't my husband; I can learn to do that. But I can't relieve you of being Caylen's father. You're part of her," I say, sternly enough to get the point across, yet tender enough to not frighten him. "And that's all I'm really sure about. That's all that I can think of to say to you."

The silence returns.

I walk over to the sofa and sit down, resting my head in my hands. A few minutes later I feel him sit beside me. I look over at him; he's in deep thought with his hands clasped together. I've never seen him . . . Cal . . . like this before. Cal never let me know when anything was wrong except that one occasion; when he was upset about anything, he always tried to hide it. He was very good at doing that.

"My parents say that he's . . . they describe him like . . ." He trails off as if he's trying to find the right words, afraid of offending me.

"Oh, I know," I answer. "Your father didn't hesitate to tell me what he thought of Cal," I say with a sigh.

"Is he—was he . . . ?"

"The person your parents describe isn't who Cal was to me," I tell him, busy looking at my hands.

"Don't get me wrong. He could be arrogant, mean, and snide . . . a lot," I say honestly. "But that isn't all there was to him," I add in defense. "He's so much more than that. He could be kind . . . caring . . . protective." I smile as I reminisce on the earlier part of our relationship, how infatuated I was with him, like I was in high school with a crush on a teacher. He had me wrapped around his finger, for God's sake. I laugh at the ridiculousness of it.

"He's extremely intelligent, confident, and persuasive; he could talk anyone into doing what he wanted. He's handsome, incredibly sexy . . ." I say with a laugh before I realize what I just said . . . oh God, I did not just say that out loud!

I glance over and see that his cheeks are bright red. He's blushing! I realize that in my entire life I've never seen him blush. I'm staring; staring isn't good, not good at all . . . *Say something!*

Thankfully, his phone rings and breaks this embarrassing silence. He takes it out and looks at it.

"Excuse me," he says. I nod, and he walks a few feet away and answers it. "Hello? Yeah, I know, something came up." I can tell by his tone of voice it's *her*. "I'm on my way right now . . . I'll see you then . . . I love you too."

I can't help but feel a twinge of jealousy. Well, more than a twinge—a lot more. More like someone just kicked me in the stomach and is standing on my chest. The man I love, well, this man who resembles the man I love, in the exact same voice, is professing his love to another woman. Knowing it's her he holds in his arms, her lips he kisses . . . oh God, I have to stop thinking like this.

"About the other day . . . I-I'm not usually like that." I rub the back of my neck.

"No, it's forgotten," he says sincerely.

"Does she know about all of this?" I ask as he hangs up, but my focus is on the ceiling fan.

"About some things," he says, letting out a deep sigh. I nod. I don't know what kind of answer that is, but I decide not to push any further.

"I-I have to—" he begins to explain. I smile weakly, letting him know it isn't needed.

I walk with him to the door.

"My mom says you're from Chicago. How long are you going to stay here?" he asks hesitantly.

"Well, I'm from Saginaw, but I live in Chicago," I correct him as we walk the small distance to the door. I scratch my head and realize I only have enough money with me to pay for another day at the Inn ,and I left my credit cards.

"I have to get back to Caylen, most likely tomorrow morning," I say when we reach the door.

"Oh." He frowns slightly, as if he thought I would be staying longer.

"I have some things to take care of back home. It'll take me a couple days, but I can come back, and . . . let you see her. We can start to work something out," I say, almost incoherently due this unwanted situation we are in.

"That would be good. I'd like that since we have a lot to work out," he says. I'm not sure if he's joking or not.

"Um, let me give you my cell phone number," he says.

I turn to get my phone and hand it to him; after a few seconds he puts it in. He hands me his, and I do the same.

"You have my home number too," he says after I'm done, and we exchange phones awkwardly, almost as if we're trying to avoid touching one another.

He opens the door and steps outside. It's an awkward moment, and we both laugh at our obvious discomfort.

"I just realized we never got a chance to really . . . uh . . ." I look at him, confused, as he extends his hand.

"I'm Chris," he says with a soft smile. I let out a small laugh, realizing we never really did get a chance to properly introduce ourselves.

"I'm Lauren," I say, taking his hand.

IT'S FUNNY HOW one day I can change the whole course of your life. Not even a day really, just a few seconds. The moment you find out you're having a child or the day you receive a bad medical report. Those life-altering moments when you know your life will never again be how it was before those few seconds happened.

March 10th, 2013

I've walked through the door to the penthouse over a thousand times, each time secretly hoping he'd be there, sitting on the couch, his eyes giving away so much and so little. And then time would freeze and in that moment it wouldn't matter where he'd been, or who he'd been with—just that he was home, and that he loved me and couldn't stay away. I hoped that, of course, there would be a reasonable explanation, circumstances that were beyond his control that kept him from me, from us, our family.

Each scenario I imagined played out differently and vaguely. Deep down, I never cared what the explanation was, just that he was home, and that my family would be complete again. That longing feeling of missing him so much that I felt a part of me was missing, gone. That part of me would be returned in pieces, but not quite broken.

I think back to the days in the house alone, when I returned after finding out I was pregnant. Even then I was trying to run away from the memory of him, hating him with every fiber of my being. Yet each day my stomach grew larger as a part of him grew inside of me. Love and hate crashing together in a never-ending battle that I fought within myself. I wanted to erase his existence from my mind, but each and every day I walked through the door, returning home from some mundane task, I still secretly hoped he'd be there.

I know how ridiculous an idea it was to try and keep my hope a secret—even from myself. The thought of wanting a man back who walked out on his pregnant wife was too pathetic for my own subconscious to comprehend. Well, he didn't know about the pregnancy, but still . . . I held on to some quixotic *hope*. It was unwarranted, almost incomprehensible. But I did; I still had hope for Cal and me. Now there is no hope. It's the first time that I know for a fact he won't be there. That the man I've loved and loathed all of these years is a mere figment of the imagination of a man named Chris . . . or not—my mind is too exhausted to cope with the logistics of this entire situation.

On my drive back from Madison, I imagined this all going differently. After all the convincing I did to myself that this is an opportunity for me to start anew and to leave the past where it was, making myself see this as a freeing experience, I pictured myself walking through the door, taking a deep breath, and a weight being lifted.

All of the days which went before, when I was left not knowing if he was alive or not, if he was hurt, who was he with, if he thought about me, if he knew about Caylen . . . The burden of all that was gone—liberated from me.

But now, as I *actually* walk through this door, the feeling is overwhelming, almost as overwhelming as the day he left. I thought I had convinced myself on the long drive back home that I could exorcise him from my life, from my mind, and my thoughts. I convinced myself that I could deal with this and that the reality I have now has given me the closure I needed to move on. But walking through this door now, in real time, I feel like I've been punched in the chest, the wind gone from my body, and I can't breathe.

The true reality of this situation hits me likes a ton of bricks, and I can't help but make my way to the floor to prevent from falling. I'm trying to stop myself from crying, but the more I try, the more I can't breathe. I reach back to try to push the door closed behind me and rest my head on it. I promised myself I would cry my last tear over him back in Madison and that I would walk through this door stronger, not weaker, and would be ready to close this chapter of my life, ready to begin afresh.

Now I realize I was an idiot thinking I could just will myself to be prepared for this; I'm not. I'm so tired of feeling like this. I don't know what I did to deserve this. To fall in love and wrap my life around a man who doesn't even exist, and now sharing a child with someone who doesn't even know who I am. How do I explain this to anyone? I'm barely coming to terms with this myself. And now I'm supposed to pretend this all didn't happen, while staring at the face of the man I've felt bound to?

"Lauren, Lauren, honey, what's wrong?"

I see through my cloud of tears, a fuzzy vision of Raven and Angela. I try to get a hold of myself, but their touch seems to make my emotions pour out even more. Raven kneels down and wraps her arms around me, rubbing my back. I know I have to pull myself together; her seeing me like this is going to cause her to think the worst. What could be worse than this though?

"Lauren, what happened? Did you find him? Lauren, talk to me," she says, her tone calm but growing more frantic.

I try to catch my breath, feeling that I might as well get it over with, when I see Hillary hurry to my other side near Angela. I make another attempt. This is not how I wanted things to go. Nothing is going how I wanted it to.

"Where's Caylen?" I say, bewildered, knowing that one of the only things that can calm me down is her in my arms.

"Caylen's fine, honey, she's sleeping," Raven assures me.

"Lauren, it's eleven at night. You haven't answered your phone in two days. We've been so worried about you! What's wrong? What happened? Did you find him?" Angela asks frantically.

"I-I want to see her," I whimper.

"Lauren, no, not like this. You'll upset her terribly," Raven scolds me.

I realize waking up to her mom crying hysterically isn't the best idea for my daughter at all and I relent.

"H-he's not real," I stutter pathetically, trying to calm down.

But I think all of this hugging and coddling they are doing is making it worse.

"What? Who's not real, honey? Cal? He was really Chris?" Hillary tries to infer. She's partly right, at least. How do I even begin to explain this to them?

"That fucking son of a bitch bastard! I knew it, I knew it all along!" she continues. Her voice grows from uncertain to angry in a matter of nanoseconds.

"No-no, it's not what you think. It's worse," I say in between sniffles.

"Come on, honey, let's get you up and cooled down with a glass of water so you can tell us all about it," Raven says authoritatively.

They help me get off the floor. We head towards the kitchen, where Hillary and I sit down. Angela paces the floor nervously. Raven grabs a pitcher of lemonade out of the fridge and pours a glass for me, herself, and Hillary. I quickly take a few sips and try to think of how I can explain it. They both look at me, full of anxious curiosity.

"I don't really know where to start. It's . . . it's all so . . . so surreal is the only way I can explain it," I say, staring into the cold glass of lemonade.

"Take your time, L," Hillary says reassuringly. Raven nods in agreement.

For the next hour I give them a play-by-play of the events that transpired over the past two days. I tell them everything from discovering 'Chris' on the porch with another woman, who is actually his fiancé, and that he had no clue who I am, to his parents revealing his mental illness to me, then to me and Chris coming to an agreement for him to be in Caylen's life, and finally me basically giving him a pardon on the obligation Cal had to me besides Caylen. Not once during the entire story do any of them interrupt. They've all been silent since I finished and the silence is frightening.

"Please say something," I urge nervously, trying to cut the thick tension in the room.

I'm sitting in between three of the most opinionated women I've ever met, and I think for once they are all speechless.

"I, I don't know what to say," Raven says. She looks unsure. Then I look at Hillary, who looks angry. I was sure she'd have a mouthful to say.

"Hillary?" I ask, almost afraid to hear her opinion, but today can't get any worse.

"I don't know what to say either. I-I mean, what can I say to something like this? I mean, basically . . ."

She stops and clasps her hands together as if she's actually pondering the right words to say. I've never known Hillary to edit her words before speaking them, and I'm touched by the fact she's trying to be thoughtful, but at this moment, whatever she has for me, I'd rather her dump it on me now so that after today I can try to leave this feeling behind.

"Hillary, whatever you have to say, just say it," I urge her. Out the corner of my eye I see Angela shoot her warning glare.

"The last time I did that, you ended up fainting." She chuckles dryly.

"It wasn't what you said; it's what you didn't say," I assure her.

Words hurt, but she didn't have to use any. She wasn't spouting knowledge I had been hiding from; she had just pulled out a newspaper with my husband's picture in it under a different name.

"Well, I think this is a load of bullshit," she says brashly, and for the first time in days I laugh.

It starts out as a small giggle and grows; Raven looks at me strangely and then begins to laugh too. Hillary folds her arms and then joins in. Angela looks at us as if we've all lost our minds, but I can't explain what a wonderful feeling it is to laugh—truly laugh and not cry.

"I mean, I don't have a degree in Psychology or anything, so I could just be misinformed but . . . Multiple Personality Disorder? Give me a break! Do you know how many guys will be using this excuse if you let this slide, L? It'll catch on like wildfire. *"Honey, it wasn't me fucking that other chick, it was my alter ego."'*

She explains this in between her laughter, and then it subsides, and the seriousness of the situation creeps back into the room.

"What do you think of this, Raven? You're the old—most mature of us all?" she jokes lightly. Raven lets out what seems to be a much-needed sigh and nods her head.

"Well, I know this may be telling my age, but I remember seeing an episode on Oprah about this psychologist who interviewed this woman who said she had fifteen . . . umm . . . I forgot what she called them . . . not personalities. It was another word. Oh gosh, it's slipped my mind."

I watch her brow furrow as she seems in deep thought.

"Alters?" Hillary offers.

"Yes, that's it!" Raven says excitedly, like she's won a prize on a game show. I turn surprised eyes to Hillary.

"I watch a lot of soap operas." She shrugs. "Well, Ang, you're the one who's spending all of your daddy's money on that degree of yours. You took a couple of psych courses, right? Let's see how much they were worth," Hillary jokes.

"Well, I admit I know a little. In a course I took, this was one of the disorders that we went over, and from what my [rofessor said, it's a diagnosis that's still highly debatable in the mental health community. There are doctors who swear that it's real and others who think it's something that's "therapist induced." A misdiagnosis of what could be several other disorders including schizophrenia, bipolar disorder . . ."

"Okay, so is it real or not?" Hillary interrupts.

"Like I said, there isn't a general consensus yet. There was one study, however, that recorded neurological changes when the alleged 'alters' or 'changes' were said to take place. However, it could have been due to a number of factors . . ."

"Well, regardless of whether this 'condition' exists or not, the question is, does he have it? Let's face it, the chances of him having this are, what?" Hillary exclaims.

"Hillary, I don't know. I'm not his psychiatrist. But some of the behaviours Cal exhibited, from what Lauren has shared with me . . . I wouldn't completely rule it out as a possibility,"

"Give me a break," Hillary mumbles under her breath.

"Hey, you asked for my opinion and this is how you respond?" Angela retorts sharply.

I rub my fingers in soothing circles on my temples. This conversation is starting to be overwhelming.

"Ladies!"

Raven interrupts the two of them and they immediately become silent, having obviously sensed my stress level rising.

"I don't think any of us here are qualified to agree or disagree with Angela's comment on the validity of this illness," she says, eyeing Hillary, who looks away from her gaze.

Her attention focuses back on Angela.

"And I think Angela would agree, without knowing the specifics of Cal's or . . . Chris's condition, she can't be certain whether he does in fact have this condition."

Angela nods in agreement.

"The most important thing right now is to support Lauren in what she believes and in how she decides to move forward from this point."

I glance up and notice that all of their gazes are on me. Raven reaches for my hand and I hold it. She squeezes it, giving me a bit of encouragement. The gesture lets me know whatever my answer is, she's behind me, which means so much at this point.

"I didn't want to believe them. I didn't want to believe any of this, but when it was him and me alone, it wasn't him. It wasn't Cal."

"Well, honey, if that is your decision, I stand behind you one hundred percent, and I will be there to support you on it." Raven smiles and squeezes my hand reassuringly.

"We all will, Lauren," says Angela, hugging me from behind. We all look at Hillary and she takes a deep breath, and for a moment it looks like she's contemplating.

"You and Caylen mean the world to me, and I'm sure this is hard enough for you without me bitching about the situation. If you can deal with all of this, I'm not going to be the one to make this harder on you," Hillary says.

She comes over and wraps her arms around me. I let out a huge sigh of relief. Just knowing that I have the support of the people around me makes things not seem as bad. Certainly not as bad as when I walked through the door an hour ago, but I'm so afraid. I've held on to the past for so long. Not knowing what happened to Cal was like having a crutch to lean on, and now it's been taken away.

"How do I pretend the last few years of my life didn't happen?" I say frantically.

Angela gently grabs my face and lifts it up so that I'm looking directly at her.

"You don't. You don't pretend that the past didn't happen, but you don't dwell on it. You accept the past, but you don't live there anymore," she says in an affectionate tone, but her words are stern.

"You've chosen to look forward, and to let go, and you can do it. You've been through so much, and you've bent a few times but never broken. We won't let you now!" Angela says and squeezes me a little tighter.

"Okay?" she asks, the authority disappearing from her face and the warm smile I know returning.

"Okay." I nod, calming down.

She's right. As much as I've talked about moving on and forward, I haven't. It's the reason I'm still here. Everywhere I look, I see a memory of Cal, enrapturing, comforting, and appeasing me. And now I can't rest in memories, in false hope. I have to let go. I have to let him go and believe that the future can take the place of my past.

I T'S BEEN TWO weeks since the catastrophe of a lifetime happened to me, since I found out about, met, and, well, almost fought with Cal—Chris—and the woman he loves. The woman who, unfortunately, in some bizarre, unimaginable way, will be my daughter's *stepmom*. I try not to think about that, or how I'm supposed to accept it. I said I would accept it, and my mind says I must, but my heart and mind have never been able to agree on anything. But since I've agreed to head back to Madison

March 23rd, 2013

tomorrow, so Caylen can meet Chris and his parents, I've found myself thinking about it more and more. Today, I worked up the confidence to try to start moving forward. Still, it's funny how when you try to move on, some habits from the past creep in and wrap around you.

I haven't had any alcohol since before I found out I was pregnant with Caylen. Actually, the last time I drank was the night I most likely conceived her. That night, I packed my things with the wine's help, determined to leave Cal. Tonight, I need it to aid me in packing up his things, trying to be content with the fact that he's gone.

I look at the last box I packed, the remainder of all things "Cal" that I could find. It's the first step of many that I'm taking to try to "cleanse" myself of him, even though the thought of it makes my heart sink, even though my own tears choke me as I gather everything together. I keep trying to remind myself I have to do this, that this is for Caylen, but how do I shake the feeling that I'm in mourning? I know it's only been two weeks since all of this happened, but when do I feel "fixed"? When will I be able to get over all that has happened? When do I start to feel a little less numb than I did the day before? Because now, the same hole within me just seems to be getting deeper, and what Angela described as a way of taking my life back, in actuality, is like burying myself deeper and deeper. I squeeze my hands together and take deep breaths. I can't stand this.

After spending hours going through his things and packing them, *cleansing* myself, I've been searching unsuccessfully, looking at old pictures of us, trying to find some sign. Was there some secret hidden behind his eyes that I failed to unlock? I replay every conversation we had, trying to think. Was there something I missed? Did he ever try to tell me? Was there anything I ignored which would have prevented me from being here? In the end, I realize I'm surrounded by the past, by lies, by a ghost of a person who never really existed.

That thought sends chills through my body, and if I believed it, I wouldn't be in mourning for a person who's still alive. At least his body is here. I try not to think where Cal really is. What happens to an alter when it's not here? Has he completely dissipated, or can he see from behind Chris's eyes? At first sight, when I threw myself onto Chris and called his name, was Cal somewhere in there? Could he hear me call him? Could he see me?

I know I have to stop thinking like this. It's not going to do me any good. I can't hold on to the belief that Cal exists on any level. I have to move on for Caylen, our little girl—to whom I heard him talking that night. At that time, Chris didn't know who Caylen was, so it had to be Cal. Was he able to escape from whatever mental desert he was lost in, for that purpose only?

Ugh! I told Chris I could deal with this, but they were just words. I kick over a box I packed and throw my wine glass at the wall, watching the small amount run down the grey wall, leaving a vivid stain. I have to get a hold of myself. I'm so glad Angela took Caylen for the night while I do this. I guess she knew it wasn't going to be as easy as she led me to believe.

You're being ridiculous, Lauren, I scold myself. I go to close the box and remember there's only one thing left that hasn't been packed away. I walk over to my drawer, and underneath all of my blouses is a button-up of his, studded with tiny black buttons and smelling faintly of cologne— Cal's. When he first left, I couldn't bear to get rid of his things. I always hoped he'd be back to reclaim them. After a few months, I avoided them, never once opening his closet.

But this one thing, this one shirt, I couldn't bear to put in the box. I didn't hide from or avoid it, though I hid it from everyone else. It's the one I wore for sleeping, on the nights when I missed him so much that even the fabric that last touched his skin gave me comfort. His scent, faintly clinging to it, calmed me, while a part of him rested inside me.

Going through an entire pregnancy alone, without him, was one of the hardest things I've ever had to do. I put on a brave face for those around me, especially Raven, Angela, and Hillary. They were there with me every day, making sure I was never alone. I was still lonely when they were with me, because they weren't him.

He wasn't there to rub my belly, to banter about whether it'd be a boy or a girl. To just hold me. I missed all of that. Going to childbirth classes with Angela, while all the husbands and boyfriends of the other pregnant women were with them, made me want to hide in a corner.

So many times, I imagined him bursting into the room the moment Caylen made her appearance. I guess a thing like that only happens in the movies, because that day never came. But on those nights when I was home alone, I'd put on his shirt and pretend it was his arms around me. For a while, it held his scent, and when it faded away, I'm embarrassed to say I sprayed his cologne on it. Little moments like these, I'm sure if I told anyone, they'd think were insanity or an odd form of self-torture. But those rituals somehow kept me sane all those nights alone.

I sit down on the floor with the shirt in my hand, and hold it to my chest as tears escape from my eyes. If I'm saying goodbye, trying to escape him tomorrow, I can still make a fool out of myself tonight. I pull my shirt over my head, stand up, slip out of my jogging shorts, and put on his shirt, and for a moment I pretend this is all a bad dream.

But this room feels suffocating. I glance through the glass in the doors that lead to the terrace. The sky is dark and raindrops start to paint it, and the clouds echo my pain. All those times I wished the weather matched my mood; this is not one of them. I step over the broken glass from earlier, make my way downstairs to the kitchen, and pour myself another glass of wine. After finishing it, I crawl onto the couch. I close my eyes and pretend I'm visiting an alternate reality where my husband is not my husband. Here, he doesn't wear jeans that cost in the upper hundreds but ones that come from Old Navy. Here, he lives in a house on a farm, instead of on one of the top floors of a high-rise in the city. Here, he slings manure instead of stealing away on jets around the world, and it's not so devastating that he's in love with a woman named Jenna, and not Lauren.

But I know I'm not in an alternate reality, because in an alternate reality, the weight of his absence wouldn't feel like a tomb on my chest, and any distraction wouldn't only be for seconds. And in an alternate reality, as I'm lying on this couch, closing my eyes, I wouldn't give anything for him to be next to me, to feel him kiss the back of my neck, his fingers to trace his name on my lower back. I wouldn't still be so in love with a man who's a ghost, myth, fairy tale, and tragedy all wrapped in one, and I wouldn't trade half my soul just to hear him say, *You're all I ever wanted.* I pull my throw over myself, hug my knees, and will myself to sleep, to start over with another day.

The thunder crashing outside my window awakens me from my slumber. My head is still spinning. The banging on the door rouses me, and my body feels as if it weighs a thousand pounds. There are boxes all over the living room floor I don't remember bringing down. The door swings open and the adrenaline coursing through my body is replaced not by relief but by utter confusion. What is he doing here?

"Chris?" I say hesitantly, making my way to the doorway. "You scared the hell out of me!" I say, one hand covering my pounding heart as I make my way toward him

But as I get closer, I see his chest is heaving up and down. He's sucking in as much air as he can, his clothing and hair wet from the storm and clinging to his body. My mind says to ask him if he's okay, what he's doing here, but when I look at his eyes, which are set directly on me, he shakes his head, and a grin appears on his face, and I know.

"Close, but not quite right," he says, seemingly winded but with a familiar grin on his face. When we're face to face, I'm able to separate my tongue from the roof of my mouth.

"Cal?" It's barely a whisper, since my throat has closed up. I wonder if he heard me. But as I look at him, even though he hasn't answered yet, as his breathing slows down, the grin slowly becomes a seductive smile, and I know.

"So it's that easy, huh?" His voice stops me cold. The moonlight from the window highlights his grey eyes. I try to move but I can't. "So you're giving up on me—on us. Just like that?"

He walks toward me and I try to reach out to him, but my limbs are frozen. He bends down, looking at the box I packed earlier.

"You're going to pack me away and pretend I never existed?" he roars and kicks the box over. The sound is so loud it echoes through the entire house.

"What about us, Lauren? What about our family?" he growls. He's so angry that I see the veins in his forehead throbbing. I keep trying to talk or to move, but I can't manage either.

"Do you really think the Scotts are going to accept you into their life? They want to pretend I never existed! Do you think they want a constant reminder of me walking around, spoiling their delusional little world? I'm the bastard child . . . their prodigal son!" He laughs angrily, circling around my frozen body.

"Caylen needs a real father who's here," I whisper, somehow breaking my catatonic state.

"I'm her father!" he shouts angrily in my face. He grabs my arm roughly and ushers me to the couch and pins me down on it. His weight feels like a house on top of me, and I can't breathe.

"Was it Chris that made love to you here? Was it his name you called out?" he whispers vehemently in my ear. He then rips my shirt in two.

His lips touch mine firmly and I turn my face. I'm so angry at him. I keep trying to speak, but my I'm mute. He grabs my face and turns it back towards him.

"There's a lot you want to say to me, huh, Lauren?" He laughs in my face.

"YES!" I scream.

I WAKE UP from a dream so real, I can still feel Cal's hands on me. I'm on the floor in a cold sweat. I don't remember falling asleep, but I must have drifted off after I put Caylen down for her nap. I try to catch my breath and slow my heart down at the same time. It's the third dream I've had this week about Cal.

Each one was slightly different, but I notice a few things stay consistent. He's always dressed entirely in black, his eyes are gray, and I can barely speak. He's also furious with me for not fighting for us. Whatever that means? I fought for us for over five years, two of which he was completely absent from. I don't know what more he wants me to do other than knock Chris on the head until he comes out?

If Cal were dead, I'd swear he was haunting me in my dreams. But it's not really Cal, of course. I've held on so tightly up until now that there's a part of me having trouble letting go. I can only describe it like an addict detoxing. I guess it's the right time for this to happen. I don't want Chris to think the mother of his child is a complete lunatic.

Yet, wouldn't it be ironic for him to think that, considering the circumstances? At least I'd like to find my bearings, especially since I'm back in Madison, staying at the lovely Ritter Inn. More importantly, I've agreed to take Caylen to see Chris and the Scotts later on today, and I've been having so much anxiety about it.

What if Chris freaks out and can't deal with all of this? What if Caylen doesn't like him? What if she likes him too much? Aside from all of the obvious weirdness of the situation, how am I going to adjust to sharing my daughter with a person I don't know? I've been a single parent so long I don't know how co-parenting really works. I grew up with Raven raising me pretty much on her own. I wonder how people do this—make long-distance parenting work? I guess I'm jumping too far ahead of myself. In three hours we'll all find out.

The last time I met him at this house, I had a complete nervous breakdown. He offered to come to Chicago, but I thought that would be weird for both of us. I'm trying to be optimistic about getting away from there. It's become increasingly difficult staying after everything that has happened. I really think I'm going to sell the penthouse and start over.

I pick up Caylen's gray sweater and pink leggings with her khaki Ugg boots. It took me twenty outfits before I decided what she should wear.

It's a surreal feeling getting her dressed to meet Chris. Especially after all the days when I wondered what it would be like for Cal to hold her in his arms. To see how he'd be with a tiny version of himself. *Well, that's not going to happen now*, I remind myself. Even if she wasn't going anywhere special, I always dress her like my own little doll.

These days I spend more time planning what she wears than I do for myself. It's actually been a while since I've worn more than a t-shirt and jeans. I haven't had anyone to dress up for in a long time. But today I've tried to plan the appropriate thing. I don't want to look like I didn't put any thought into what I'm wearing, but I also don't want to look like I spent too much. I mean . . . there's no reason for me to worry, anyway. It's not like I haven't already made a first impression with mascara dripping down my face and my hair tangled about my head.

I decide on being Caylen's twin with a long gray sweater and leggings. But instead of bubble-gum pink I decide on black, of course. I'm hoping to redeem myself from the image of the hysterical, yelling crazy woman they met before. Not that they didn't deserve it after everything that's happened. I shake away the thoughts of the last meeting at the Scotts' and the last time Chris was here in this same room. I think about how he seemed just as nervous as I was, almost more so. Still, other than the nervous energy, there was something about him that was a little calming. Do I dare say . . . comfortable?

I glance at the clock. I have less than an hour before Caylen's usual wake-up time. I grab my things and head to the bathroom for a quick shower, hoping to relax at the beginning of what's sure to be a nerve-racking day.

"OKAY, LAUREN, YOU can do this," I say to myself. Then I look in the rear-view mirror and see Caylen smiling up at me.

"You must think mommy's crazy, huh?"

I smile at her and a few of my nerves dissipate. She's so innocent. I'm glad she's young so none of the awkward weirdness of all this is affecting her. I start to wonder if I should call or just go up to the Scotts' door. That didn't turn out so great the last time. At least I know I won't go into emotional overload today. I can't. Not while she's here. I drum my hands on the steering wheel to calm my nerves. I mean, the worst is behind me. The only thing that would make this worse than last time would be if Chris came to the door in drag. I giggle to myself at that image.

I tried to kill time by having breakfast with Caylen at a little diner named Goldman's on the way here. I haven't had a good, hot bowl of grits since I moved from Saginaw. Caylen enjoyed *playing* in her applesauce and hash browns more than she enjoyed actually eating them. I look at my watch and notice its 9:15 A.M. I told him I'd be here at 9:30 A.M. Is it rude to show up early? I glance back at the house and see someone holding the curtains open at the front window.

Oh no, they see me!

Well, someone does. If I sit out here now, I'll look like a stalker or weirdo. Okay, it's now or never.

I get out of the car and take a deep breath. I pull Caylen out of her car seat and close the door. I guess this is it. I never really prayed before, but I quietly ask God to give me strength to deal with this and not make a complete fool out of myself.

The door to the house opens and I watch as the six-foot figure walks through it. I feel myself getting nervous and I take another deep breath. I squeeze Caylen's little hand as we walk towards the towering front porch. Her tiny steps are making this the longest walk ever. I look up at him and I'm caught by his eyes—they're bright green with glimmers of grey now. As he walks closer, his smile widens. I glance down at Caylen, whose little steps start to quicken.

"Hi," I say, my voice light and unfamiliar.

"Hey," he replies, his voice warm but shaky. His smile widens even more as his big hands squeeze the little stuffed animal he's holding. I can feel my heart starting to speed up. I let go of Caylen's hand once we're on the sidewalk. She quickly makes her way over to him.

She reaches up for the penguin he's holding and he chuckles, staring at her in what I can only describe as amazement.

"Umm, my friend's daughter loves the penguins in the *Madagascar* movie. I thought she'd like it," he explains nervously.

"She watches that movie all the time," I reply, and notice the wonderment on his face. I watch him as he squats down to her eye level.

"I thought you might like this," he says, holding out the little penguin.

"Pepe!" she says excitedly, taking the penguin from his hands and putting it in her mouth. He looks up at me in wonder.

"She looks so much like my baby pictures," he says aloud, but I think he didn't mean it to be heard. Watching him take in the sight of her gives me a feeling I've never had before. The emotions evident on his face as he watches her play with the little stuffed penguin are indescribable.

"I'm Chris, Caylen," he says, his voice slightly cracking.

His eyes glisten, and I think I see tears in them. I walk closer towards them and squat down as well. I apprehensively touch his shoulder gently. Caylen takes one of her hands and touches his face and giggles.

In this moment I know for sure the man beside me is not the one I knew. I take a deep breath and prepare myself to say something I didn't plan on saying. I didn't know how or when I would say it to her. If there would ever be the right time to say it. But now I know without a doubt.

"Caylen, this is your daddy."

I promised myself I wouldn't do this. But it's impossible not to. I never thought this moment would turn out this way after all the anger, worry, and fear. The anxiety and stress in the pit of my stomach are replaced with something I haven't felt in so long.

Peace.

I lift my hand to wipe away my own tears, which are starting to fall, and he stops me, holding my hand gently in his.

"Thank you, Lauren." His voice and eyes are full of sorrow, sincerity, and concern.

And for the first time in my life, I'm able to read the face looking at me. There's nothing hiding the emotions resting there, nothing trying to camouflage them.

"Hey, gorgeous," he says to her, and in the briefest second he turns towards me, his smile is familiar and he winks at me. My breath hitches. And as fast as the moment happened, before I can verify it even did happen—it's gone.

"Lauren?" he asks, a look of concern on his face. He's staring at me and . . . it's still Chris, but I know for a second it wasn't. *He* was here, Cal. I move closer to him. I hesitantly bring my hand to his face, wondering if he'll even let me touch him. He does.

I ignore the familiar emotions that pass through me.

Before this moment I felt like I was giving up the only person I've ever been in love with. Doing it for the only person in the world I love more than him, his daughter. I have to . . . right?

"I-is everything okay, Lauren?" He lets out a light laugh, his cheeks turning red. I only nod, looking down at the ground. Everything will be okay.

I'll make sure it stays that way.

I have to . . .

. . . even if I break.

Thank you for reading! If you enjoyed *If I Break* and would like to be kept up to date on when the sequel will release along with any other new releases, promotions, and giveaways from Portia Moore Books, sign up for her newsletter.

about the author

I'M OBSESSED WITH blowing kisses. I guess that makes me a romantic. I love books and cute boys and reading about cute boys in books. I'm infatuated with the glamour girls of the past: Audrey, Dorthy, Marilyn, Elizabeth.

I'm a self confessed girly girl, book nerd, food enthusiast, and comic book fan. Odd combination huh, you have no idea . . .

Like Portia Moore on Facebook
www.facebook.com/portiamoorebooks

Follow on IG
www.instagram.com/portiamoorewrites

or visit
www.portiamoore.com

books by
portia moore

THE *IF I BREAK* SERIES

If I Break

Before I Break

Almost Broken

Beautifully Broken

STAND ALONE

What Happens After

For a sneak peek into the next book in the If I Break Series, Before I Break a novella from Chris' POV continue reading for the first two chapters.

before I break

chapter 1

March 7th, 2013

SILENCE, DEAD SILENCE. There's nothing I hate more in the world. It's the sound that fills the room when you know the people you're talking to are searching for something to say. Not just something, the *right* thing to say. They know if they speak too quickly or the wrong words are spoken, everything will shift. The wrong response could tilt the world—your world—off its axis. I get why my parents are so careful with their words. Words changed our lives, and not for the better. It all started when I told them, "I don't remember where I was last week." The last time was when they told me, "Your mother is sick."

In each instance, dead silence followed. Time stopped, and everyone tried to think of what was the right thing to say next. Now I've made an announcement that will change our lives forever, for what I hope is the better. That same silence follows, and they stare at me blankly. They're shocked. I expected that, but what comes next is what's worrying me. My dad cracks a smile, but my mom is still stoic. Her expression is unreadable, and that's not a good sign.

"Wow. Engaged?" my dad's the first to break the silence in the room. His eyes are wide, the excitement in his voice apparent.

"What do you think Mom?" I ask, rubbing the back of my head. I thought she'd be happy. She and Jenna get along great.

"I—I don't really know what to say, Chris." She won't even look at me as she lets out a long sigh. She gets up from the dining room table and disappears in the kitchen.

What type of congratulations is that? No smile, no tears of joy, not a single question? In the back of my mind, I knew there was a chance it could be like this, which is why I didn't bring Jenna. I just told her I'm getting married. That I've chosen a woman to spend the rest of my life with, who is going to be the daughter she always wanted, and she walks out as if I just told her to grab me a sandwich. My dad looks behind him and sighs before his smile returns.

"Did you get a good deal on the ring?" he asks, trying to convey enough excitement for the both of them. My dad has always been a deal maker. I would have taken him with me to buy it if I thought he'd be this happy

"I think so." I chuckle.

"I took Lisa with me to pick it out." I smile. I'm sort of proud about it. It's one of the first big decisions I've made in my life without their input or influence. Lisa's been my best friend since kindergarten, and she knows jewelry like nobody's business. She knows her stuff but wouldn't force a decision on me. Even though she and Jenna aren't the best of friends, Jenna loved the ring Lisa picked out. My dad makes his way over to me and pulls me into a bear hug.

"Well congratulations, son." He gives me another pat on the shoulder. It's like I'm in bizarro world. My dad's excited and accepting, but my mom looks as if I told her I've dropped out of college.

"Thanks, Dad," I reply, still a little in shock. My mom is in the kitchen banging pots around.

"She'll come around." He notices my meandering glance towards the kitchen.

"I don't get it. She likes Jenna, right?" I scratch my head. Now I'm confused. I mean, I thought she liked her, but this reaction is causing me to think she's a good actress.

"Of course, son. It's not that she doesn't like Jenna. I don't think it has anything to do with her, really." He motions his head to living room. I follow him there. We sit down across from each other on separate sofas.

"So what is it? To be honest, I expected you to be the one upset," I admit with a dry chuckle. My mom runs away from the problem. If it was him he'd confront it right then and there head on. They really balance each other out.

"I'm happy for you, son. You deserve this. You deserve to be in control of the important decisions in your life," he says a wide smile on his face. He almost seems more excited than I am.

"She doesn't think I'm ready, does she?" That has to be it.

"I haven't had a black out in two years. I've been doing really well," I say defensively, but the truth is I have to tell myself every morning that I'm ready.

"I know! This is exactly the thing you need to put the past behind you. To move into the future," he says encouragingly. *"Your future,"* he adds with a smile. I don't know who else's future it would be, but I'll take it as long as one parent's on my side.

"Jenna and her parents are still coming over for dinner tonight. I've got to talk to Mom. Jenna is going to be really hurt if she thinks mom is against this." I let out a deep breath and stand up.

"I'm going to grab some champagne for tonight." My dad grabs his jacket off the coat stand.

"I'm proud of you, son." And at that, he slips out the door. I shake my head in disbelief and head to the kitchen. *My dad, is actually happy about this?* Never would have thought it. Once I'm in the kitchen, I see my mom pulling a bowl of potatoes from the sink and setting them on the counter.

"Need some help?" I ask, turning on the faucet and washing my hands. She smiles at me.

"It's been a while since you helped me in the kitchen," she says with a laugh and handing me a knife. "I remember when you were a little boy. After you'd finish working on the old engine your dad let you tinker with, you'd come in here, dirt and oil all over you, and ask to help cook," she jokes, starting to peel a new batch of potatoes. I laugh at the memory. I love both my parents. There's nothing I wouldn't do for either of them.

When I found out she had cancer, it was like the wind was knocked out of me. A bad joke.

Before that, my black outs had been worse than ever. Most of the time, they'd last weeks instead of days, sometimes months. I was losing my mind; the sessions weren't helping. The medication only made me depressed. Then with all of that, my mom gets diagnosed with stage-three cancer. I thought that was the worst thing that could happen to us, but somehow it was a blessing in disguise. After that my black outs and headaches were practically nonexistent. I met Jenna who helped me stay sane during a time I thought I would lose my mom, and less than eight months later, my mom was cancer free.

"Mom," I say quietly.

"Honey, I am happy for you. I am," she says, her voice perky, but the expression on her face seems forced. I touch her shoulders and turn her towards me. She lets out a small breath and holds both my arms.

"Tell me the truth?" She's been so strong through everything. There were days when I asked how she was doing, and I knew they were hell for her, but she kept up her smile and never complained. She never let us know how much pain she was in. Her eyes meet mine briefly before they find the floor.

"Please," I ask again, giving her my best puppy dog eyes, and she hugs me.

"I want you to be happy, Christopher. I want nothing more in this world than for you to be happy," she says and her voice breaks. I feel tears wet my shirt, and she walks a few steps away from me.

"Mom, you're scaring me now." I chuckle, but my heart is speeding up . . . I thought she'd cry because she was happy, not this. My stomach drops when I realize what could be causing this. I put my arm around her and lead her to the kitchen table and sit beside her. She takes a Kleenex and dabs her eyes.

"You're not. You're not sick again are you, Mom?" I ask, afraid to hear the answer.

"Oh no, honey! I'm so sorry to make you even think that." She shakes her head vehemently. I let out a big sigh of relief as she squeezes my hand.

"I just . . . things have been going so well, and I know you care about a lot about Jenna," she says, a small smile appearing, but her eyes avoid mine.

"Are you ready? *Really* ready?" she asks, her eyes finding mine again and looking so hard into them I think she's trying to see inside of me.

"I asked myself this over a thousand times already, Mom," I reveal with a laugh. "Everything you're thinking about, I've probably thought it five times over. The thing is, I don't think there is ever going to be a time where I know that I'm cured from this—if I'll ever be," I say honestly. Her lips tighten, and she nods her head.

"If not now . . . when? I'm tired of being afraid to live my life because of what may happen," I tell her.

"I never know when these black outs will happen. But for now things have been good. In a few months it will be almost two years since I had the last one. It was hell, but I've finally finished school. I have an amazing woman who knows about my condition and doesn't think I'm a weirdo or some sad puppy that needs to be taken care of. And you're doing better." I finally see a genuine smile start to appear on her face even though her eyes are still watery.

"I want to get married, maybe get you some grandkids." I give her a playful nudge. I thought that'd make her laugh, only it doesn't. Instead she looks anguished, maybe even a little guilty, but that can't be right. She won't even look at me as she gets up from the table and starts to pace the floor.

"Mom, what is it?" I stand up and walk towards her. Something's wrong. She finally stops and looks at me.

"There's something we haven—"she stops mid-sentence as my dad comes through the door with a bottle of champagne in hand. His smile is wide as he eyes the chilled bottle. When his gaze finds us his expression turns grim.

"What's going on?" I look at my mom and then at him.

"You haven't what, Mom?" I ask her again, glancing at my dad.

"What haven't we done?" he asks, his tone is low. My mom glares at him, and that awkward silence has returned, the tension so thick I could choke on it.

"What?" I ask more firmly, causing their stare-down to end, and they both turn to look at me. My mom's eyes dart away from me but my dad's eyes stare straight into mine.

"Dexter Sr. is here in Madison," he says abruptly. The grandfather from hell. Whenever he comes here it's usually bad news for the town. He's either shutting something down or opening something that will destroy someone's business. Most of the people here tend to forget our family's association with the Crestfields, but their presence always serves as a reminder. My mom never liked him but for her to be this upset . . .

"Is that it, Mom? Is that what's been bothering you?" I ask, a little relieved. My gut says it's something else, especially when I notice her lips tighten.

"Gwen, today everyone else's problems aren't our concern. This day is about Chris. We're celebrating the step he's made to marry the woman he loves. Let's not ruin this day for our son," my dad says firmly. There's something off about this.

"Mom, what is this really about?" I don't believe Dexter's visit is causing this type of tension. She looks from me to my Dad, then clears her throat.

"I heard through the grapevine that your grandfather is eying the property Kreuk Place is on," she says with a sigh. I immediately frown. Kreuk Place is the community center my mom and I have been working at for the past year. It not only helps people in our town but neighboring towns too. It has a free clinic, gym, and daycare center. Only a monster would even think of displacing it. It's a landmark. I want to say, he can't do that! But, the Crestfields can do almost anything.

"No. That's bull!"

"It's just a rumor, but we all know how those start," my dad says, a frown on his face.

"I heard from Ms. Jaber's daughter, that Dexter Jr's in town. She was just hired as one of the groundskeepers. He's leaving this evening, supposedly," she mumbles. The community center helped my mom and me through some of the toughest times in our lives. It's a cornerstone of the community.

I look at my watch. I have a couple of hours before Jenna and her parents get here for dinner.

"I'm going to talk to him before he leaves," I say, grabbing my keys off the counter. "I'll be back in enough time to change before Jenna and her parents get here." I say over my shoulder and rush out of the front door. I climb into my truck and head towards the one person who can stop this before it gets going.

Dexter Jr.

CRESTFIELD. THE NAME alone evokes envy, fear or anger depending on who you're talking to in Madison. They own almost half the town and have the biggest everything in the entire county. It wouldn't be a problem if they were permanent residents, but they're not. It's mere extravagance—all for show, adding to their theatrics when they come in town to raise hell.

I've heard the phrase, "It's nothing personal. Business is business." But destroying families and ruining lives isn't business as usual.' Messing with people's livelihoods makes it personal.

Once I arrive at the Crestfield estate, I have to wait at the gate to be cleared by security. When I'm in, I feel repulsed by the decadence of it all. The house and grounds are huge. The house alone is four times bigger than the community center. I'll never understand how people can be so selfish and greedy.

I get out of my car and head towards the house my when phone starts to ring. I smile, seeing it's Jenna. I slide my finger across the faceplate to answer the call.

"Hey future hubby." She giggles.

"Future wife." I chuckle, playing along.

"So . . . how'd your parents take the news?' she asks, a hint of nervousness in her voice.

"Great. They're really excited," I say. It's half true.

"Really? Even your dad?" she asks in disbelief.

"He took it even better than my mom did," I tell her, making my way up to the large French doors. I roll my eyes at the discreet camera above the door before ringing the bell.

"*Better* than your mom? What was wrong with your mom?" she asks, her pitch elevating slightly. I immediately regret my choice of words. Jenna picks up on almost everything. She's like a bloodhound when someone's hiding something. She's good at reading people.

"My mom thinks it's great," I say, hoping to throw her off.

"You said better than your mom did. Meaning, your mom must have not taken it well," she rattles off.

"I thought your mom *loved* me? She's against this?" She's gone from five to ten on her panic-o-meter.

"No it wasn't like that. She was just surprised that's all." I sigh. I had to say "better." That one little word triggered all this. The large doors have opened, and the Crestfields' maid smiles warmly at me as she gestures for me to come in. I smile back to acknowledge her and walk in.

"My parents and I are coming over for dinner tonight and your mom is totally against us getting married. This is terrible!" she says, her panic rising with every syllable.

"Jenna. My mom loves you. She loves your parents, dinner is going to be fantastic I promise, but I've got to go. I'll call you back in a few. Love you," I say as I hang up the phone, despite her protests.

"Mr. Christopher Scott?" the maid asks, a little hesitant. I've known her for years, but she always asks as if she's unsure of who I am.

"How are you, Ms. Alma?" I smile as she leads me up the large winding stair case.

"Wonderful. Would you like something to drink?" she asks right before we reach the door to Dex's office.

"No, I'm fine," I reply.

"Mr. Scott. Christopher," she announces as we enter Dexter's office, even though he can see me.

"I always feel like I should bow or something," I say sardonically. I notice Ms. Alma cover her laugh by clearing her throat.

"A little courtesy would work just as well," he responds dryly, barely glancing up from his computer screen.

"Will you be needing anything else, Mr. Crestfield?" she asks.

"That will be all. Thank you," he says.

"Good to see you, Mr. Scott," she says to me before leaving the room.

"You too," I say, walking over to Dex's desk.

"So what brings you here today, nephew? Long time, no hear from," he says. I hear the amusement in his voice as he leans back in his large leather chair. I don't understand why he always has remind of me of our relation, but I guess if it didn't matter I wouldn't be here.

"Kreuk place. Just leave it alone. You guys own half the United States. Do you really need it?" I say, exasperated.

He chuckles. "Why don't you have a seat, Christopher," he says, gesturing towards one of the chairs in front of his desk.

"I'm okay standing," I tell him. I'm not going to sit and shoot the breeze with him. I just want him to leave Kreuk place alone.

He frowns. "I'm sure Gwen has taught you better manners than that. When a host offers you a seat, you take it. Especially when you're asking a favor of said host. You smile and grant the request," he says smugly. I take a deep breath and sit down.

"So, how have you been?" he asks as if we're best friends. We're cordial, distant relatives at best. It didn't always used to be this way. Ten years ago after my grandmother died, Dex was sent to boarding school and the traits that were reminiscent of the better half of his parents seemed to be left behind.

"Fantastic," I say shortly.

"You haven't been seeing Dr. Lyce," he says with an accusatory tone. I fold my arms.

"My condition is neurological not psychological. I don't understand the point of me going."

"She's a Neuro-psychiatrist. It's important that you see her in conjunction with—"

"Kreuk place, Dex. That's why I'm here," I interrupt him. He's getting off the subject, and I don't plan on being here all day.

"We'll talk about this first," he says calmly, but there's an edge in his voice that I'm sure causes his employees to cower. Good thing I don't work for him.

"She's one of the best in her field. You're being remiss to disregard her expertise," he says, a hint of anger in his voice. I take a deep breath and bury the urge to flip him off. I grit my teeth. This guy capable of bringing out the absolute worst in people.

"Your dad is being *remiss* by destroying a historical land mark—a place that helps a lot people. What's he going to do? Build a parking lot?!" I shoot back. He leans back in his seat amused.

"Look. It's important to lots people here, our family included. Before he starts anything can you get him to just leave it alone," I say with a deep breath.

"You know once something's underway with my father, it hasn't just started, it's already done," he says nonchalantly. I fold my hands in frustration.

"But . . . that's not his interest at the moment," he adds lightly.

Great then, I can leave. "Well, I guess that's it then," I say rising from my seat.

"Congratulations are in order aren't they? I hope we'll be getting an invitation to the big event," he says before I'm even a step away from my seat.

"What?"

"You're engaged to . . . Jenna Mallory," he says dryly.

I try to hide my surprise. I just proposed to her yesterday. I'd ask how he knows but there's so many ways. He probably holds the lease on the jewelry store I bought the ring from.

"Are you ready for that step?" he asks. Lucky for me, this is the one person that I can care less what he thinks about anything.

"Well since you know everything, you tell me," I say sarcastically. He smirks and stands up from behind his desk.

"Marriage and family are the greatest gifts humanity was given," he says, walking around his desk. I fold my arms across my chest, wondering where this is leading. Dexter has always irked me since he left. He's only three years older than me but he always feels the need to talk like some Ivy League college professor.

"Sometimes things happen, and they don't always turn out how you hope or plan for." There's a lingering hint of regret in his voice. "Today, for instance, I'd give anything to attend my goddaughter's first birthday party." He picks up a picture frame off his desk and reflects on it. I wonder what kind of desperate person would choose him as a godparent. The money hungry kind, no doubt. I know he's not religious. But for teaching a kid values like honesty, integrity, and hard work, he's not the ideal candidate.

He glances up at me from the picture. "She's beautiful. Take a look." He holds out the picture. I don't care much for the guy, but refusing to look at a picture of his goddaughter would be a prick-ish move.

I take the picture and my eyes lock on it almost involuntarily. It's a woman and a little girl. The woman in picture is beautiful with long dark hair and wide almond shaped eyes. The little girl in the picture doesn't look much like her, she looks like . . .

The picture drops from my hand as a shooting pain shoots through my head. "Ahh!" I grasp my head and hold it.

No. Not now. Not in Dexter's office.

"Christopher, are you okay?" Dex asks, walking towards me. I stumble backwards, finding the chair I was in earlier. I hear my heart beating in my ears. I haven't had a headache like this since I can't even remember, but it's never hit so fast and hard.

I groan, gripping my head. I hear Dex's voice, but it's starting to sound far away as my vision starts to blur. "Call my parents!" I try to say, but I'm not sure if I've even said it at all as everything turns black.

chapter 2

I'M COLD BUT my face is warm . . . almost hot. My eye lids feel like bricks. I manage to open them as they adjust to the sunlight. My back hurts. I stretch my body. It's stiff, and cramped up. I lift myself up and see that I'm laid out in the back seat of my truck.

How did I get here? My eyes scan the truck for my cell phone and wallet. I have to have my keys, otherwise how would I have gotten in my truck? This is bad. Out of all of the times for this to happen! Why now?

I see an envelope taped on the rear view mirror, and there's a word on it. I can't really see what. My contacts have dried out and feel stuck to my eyelids. I reach and grab it; it's heavy. The envelope is tightly secured, and it takes some effort to free it. Once I do, I can read the word "Open" in red ink. So I do, and in it I find my wallet, phone and keys. My phone is dead. I'm afraid to know what time it is or day even.

I get out of the truck, and thank God, I'm parked behind my parents' house. The sun is bright; I'm praying its mid-afternoon. That'd mean I've only been out a few hours. If it's morning, I'm screwed.

I reach the back door to our house and fiddle for my door key. How did I get here? *Think, think!* But it's no use. This has happened a thousand times before.

I walk into the kitchen. It's empty, no smell of food and my stomach drops. That means my mom isn't cooking dinner. Which also means it can't be the same day, and I've missed dinner with Jenna and her parents. She's going to kill me!

My eyes find the clock above the table in the kitchen. It's 9:30 and definitely not pm. I've really screwed up.

"Mom! Dad!" I call out. I rush to the living room. Most likely they went out looking for me when I missed dinner. This is bad, *really* bad. All my talk about being better, and my two-year, blackout-free stretch has gone down the drain.

"Chris." I hear a light, groggy voice call out from behind me. I turn around and see Lisa sitting up on the couch. I didn't even notice her. I let out a sigh of relief that it's her. Out of all the people, I'm glad Lisa's the first to see me. She'll let me know what's happened while I was out and not freak out or be pissed at me.

"Sorry you don't have a better welcome wagon. Your parents had me driving around all night looking for you. They went out looking for you again early this morning, and had me stay here in case you got back," she explains.

"How bad did I screw up?" I sigh and take a seat beside her.

"On a scale of one to ten, with your parents like a five. They're more worried about you than anything. With Jenna like a 12."

I throw my head back into the sofa.

"Ugh. How long?" I groan. *Of all days for this to happen . . .*

"Your mom said you'd been gone since three o' clock yesterday. You still don't remember anything?" she asks, starting to fold up the blanket she was under. She's surprisingly calm. Well, not surprisingly. Lisa's always pretty calm and laid back even in the most hectic situations, but when she's pissed, she can go from zero to ten pretty fast.

"The last thing I really remember was telling my parents that I had proposed to Jenna. Everything after that is a blur," I admit.

"Look. Go get in the shower and clean up. Call Jenna and apologize like your life depends on it," she sighs.

"But the bottom line is, if you guys are going to be together she's going to have to get used to this. It's not like she's going into this blind. She knows about your condition," she says simply. I wish it was that simple.

"Easier said than done. Her parents were here from Seattle, and her fiancé doesn't show up. That's a promising beginning of an engagement. Her dad already can't stand me."

She turns towards me. "She loves you. She'll get over it. It's not like you skipped out on her to go get drunk with strippers or something," she says, patting me on the shoulder.

"Were you?" She grins.

"No!" My eyes bulge. I bet that's what Jenna thinks.

"You're no fun Chris. Go get in the shower. You look like hell. I'll call your parents and 'the fiancé' and tell them you're safe and sound," she says and pushes me toward the stairs.

"Give me your phone, I'll charge it up for you, go and fix yourself up. You'll have a much better chance if you flash those 'forgive-me' green eyes at her without eye crust and accompanying morning breath," she jokes.

THE SHOWER CLEANED me up, but my brain is still fuzzy. I lost 18 hours. Not bad, considering some of my other blackouts lasted weeks at a time but the timing sucks. If I could remember one thing. Some clue as to how I ended up asleep in my truck in the back of my house. Why wouldn't I just go to bed? And then that weird envelope on my mirror almost as if I knew I wouldn't find it if it wasn't there. That means I had to have some form of consciousness or someone was with me. But where'd they go? If someone wanted to rob me, they wouldn't leave me with my wallet and car. I hear voices down stairs. They're both women. My stomach drops. I know one has to be Jenna. She's going to be pissed.

"Look give him a break. Don't you think he feels bad enough?" I hear Lisa's voice before I'm down the stairs.

"Don't tell me how to act or how to feel. You're not the one who sat here for hours waiting on her fiancé with her parents, looking like an complete idiot," Jenna's voice screeches.

"I'm sorry, but you do know that he has a neurological condition, right? You act like he did this deliberately!" Lisa fires back. Jenna starts to say something, but they both quiet when they see me.

"Hey." I let out a breath as I walk towards Jenna. She is wearing big round black sunglasses and her arms are folded across her chest.

"So you're alive," she states sharply. Lisa huffs.

"I got to get out of here." she starts to walk off but turns and curtseys. "Queen Jenna, it would be nice if maybe instead of freakin' out on the guy, you give him a fucking hug," she says before storming out of the dining room.

"Have a fantastic day, Lisa!" Jenna shouts sarcastically before turning her attention to me. She takes off her glasses and what I see breaks my heart. Her eyes are puffy. I can tell she's been crying.

"So you think I'm being a bitch too? That I don't have a right to be upset? That I'm just this selfish angry pre-bridezilla?"

"Jenna, I'm sorry." I try to pull her into a hug but she pushes me away. She sits down and covers her face.

"So what happened, Chris?" she asks, and I really wish I could give her an answer.

"I—I don't know. The last thing I remember is telling my parents we were engaged," I admit, sitting in the chair across from her.

"You know you talked to me right?" she asks sharply. I shake my head. I don't remember talking to her after telling my parents.

"Yeah you told me your mom wasn't thrilled about us getting married and then rushed me off the phone," she says in a huff. I know I wouldn't have told her that. At least, I wouldn't have used those words.

"Did I tell you where I was?" I ask confused.

"No. You rushed me off the phone and said you'd call me back in a few minutes. Next thing I know, my parents are at my house, and I still haven't heard from you. Then we're at your door, and your parents have no clue where you are. That was *so* much fun," she says in an exaggerated tone as the doorbell rings.

"I thought I was doing better, Jenna. I never would have dragged you into this if I knew this was starting again." I stand up and hold my head in frustration. No woman in her right mind would want to deal with this. I don't want to deal with this." I hear her sigh.

"You're not dragging me into anything, Chris. I'm sorry. I know this is hard for you too. It's just, ugh, the timing couldn't be worse, could it?" She laughs, and her slender arms wrap around my stomach. I wrap my arms around her back and take in her scent. It's berries mixed with a hint of cigarette smoke. I pull back from her.

"Come on, Jenna. I thought you were done with that?" I say, disappointed. She's been cigarette-free for the past three months after my guilt tripping and nagging. I blame my mom being diagnosed with cancer for that.

"I pretty much earned one of these after yesterday, and it wasn't that many," she says, defending herself. I can't argue with that. The doorbell rings again and again, and then there's frantic knocking.

"Who the hell is that?" Jenna asks.

"I don't know." My parents have keys, and Lisa would come through the back of the house.

"Let me get the door," I say. I feel like a load of bricks has been lifted off my chest. She's mad, but she's still with me.

I open the door, and see a woman retreating down the stairs.

"Can I help you?" I ask. She sort of stumbles over her own feet and grabs the railing. I instinctively step forward. Maybe she's disoriented. She says something but she's facing the opposite way. Her voice is light, and I can barely hear her. She turns around, and her eyes lock onto mine.

They're bright, hazel, and almond-shaped. Her stare is ethereal, almost haunting, and won't let go of me. They make me feel like I've seen her before, or known her forever but that's impossible. She's not someone I'd forget. Too beautiful to be forgotten.

Maybe I saw her in a movie, or she was in a show I used to watch when I was a kid. She's grown up, and that's why I can't place her. That has to be it. Maybe she's an actress whose car stopped in our little town and she needs her tire changed or something. But none of that explains why she's crying. And now she's touching my face, and I'm frozen, stuck in place. I can't move. I'm telling my feet to step backwards but they won't budge.

"It's you," she says, throwing her arms around me. The wind blows her long dark hair in my face. I steal another glance at her and even though she's crying her face is lit up with recognition. She knows me, or think she does. I'm getting more freaked out by the minute. She's holding me so tight I can feel her heart beat. It's almost stampeding through her chest. Hell, maybe it's mine. This random, albeit beautiful woman is crying and hugging me while my fiancé is less than a few feet away, and I can't move. The worst part is that my brain isn't connecting with my body because my arms are moving to hug her—well, they're trying to, but that sure as hell isn't happening!

I'm all for helping a woman in distress, but if Jenna finds me out here hugging this girl, especially after yesterday, I'm screwed. But it's taking so much to stop them. I'm literally shaking, or maybe her shaking is causing me to shake. Before I can open my mouth to ask who she is, I hear footsteps behind me.

"I've missed you so much," Hazel Eyes says, squeezing me tighter.

"Chris, who is this?" Jenna's voice sends a chill up my spine, and the girl lets me go. She looks up at me, confusion replacing the previous euphoria on her face.

"Chris?"

She steps away from me, her attention turning to Jenna.

"Chris? His name isn't Chris!" Her voice is sharp and a little terrifying. Her gaze is directed back at me, the vulnerable exterior she previously had now changing. There's fire behind her eyes. Jenna walks closer to us, surprisingly calmer than I thought she would be.

"I—I don't know!" I answer quickly. I'm trying to move again but my freakin' body isn't working. I can't move away from this girl.

"Who am I? Who are you?" she asks, her voice raising an octave and a second later, with the look she gives me, I swear she's about to throw a right hook my way. I'm starting to think this woman, with eyes like an angel, no taller than maybe 5'3, could be out of her mind crazy, and my damn feet won't let me get away from her.

"What!" she shouts angrily, but the disbelief in her voice and despair in her eyes makes my heart break. I don't know who she thinks I am, but the moment the hurt replaces the once-frightening fire in her eyes, I'd be whoever she wants me to be .

What is wrong with me?

"I think you have me confused with someone else," I tell her hesitantly. I turn to Jenna. The calmness I was surprised with earlier is suddenly replaced with the anger I expected.

"She just started crying when she saw me," I try to explain to Jenna's, whose face is flushed, lips pressed together.

"What the hell are you talking about?!" the girl says, her tone loud but her voice weak, almost pleading. My chest is tightening like someone's standing on it. I try to control my breathing. The last thing I need is

Jenna thinking this is something it isn't.

"She doesn't seem to have you confused!" Jenna says angrily, eyeing the woman.

"Cal, what the hell are you trying to pull?" the girl yells. I glance back at her. At least the fire is back. My feet are finally able to move.

"My name is Chris," I tell her, moving towards Jenna, who seems a little less angry since this girl seems to be looking for a guy name Cal. This all just has to be one big misunderstanding.

"Look, who are you?" Jenna asks. She seems more annoyed than angry now.

"I'm his wife, that's who I am. Who the hell are you?!" the little brunette spits, and with those words I'm in hell, literally hell. I'm afraid to even look at Jenna, but she's laughing. She's lost it. I'm standing in between two psychotic women.

"Ooh, I see. This is a joke. Good one, Chris. You almost had me for a minute, but you know I see right through your pranks." She pats me on the chest. Then I realize that this *has* to be a joke, a prank that Lisa is pulling. I let out a little sigh of relief, but the other woman on the porch is livid. Her nostrils are flaring, eyes wide and if this were a horror movie, this would be the part when her head starts spinning or she sets the house on fire.

"Does it look like I'm joking?" she asks frantically, tears welling in her eyes. This woman is way too good to be in Lisa's budget.

"Cal tell her!" she demands, and I'm afraid this prank is getting way out of control.

"My name isn't Cal," I'm about to have an anxiety attack right here. I've been lucky enough to never have one of those, but I'm pretty sure this is what it feels like.

"Chris, who is she?!" Jenna yells. No one thinks this a prank anymore.

"Jenna, I've never seen this woman before in my life!" I shout.

"You ass hole!" The brunette is now pushing me. If she wasn't so small, I'd be pushed into the door.

"You don't know who I am now?"

I don't know what to do. I'm trying to avoid touching her, but Jenna's looking at me like she's about to push me next if I don't do something.

"Well who gave me this?" Thankfully she's stopped. But then she starts to pull something out of her jacket and hurls it at me. Whatever it is, Jenna snatches it up and inspects it. *Oh no, please don't be what it looks like.*

"Chris, this is a wedding ring!" she shouts, thrusting it my face. Jenna should know that this isn't from me. The thing looks like it costs more than I make in a year.

"I've never seen that before in my life! I've never seen *her* in my life!"

"Chris, don't lie to me! "Jenna's shouting, and she's starting to cry. I've never seen her cry before.

"She doesn't even know my name! She's crazy!" I shout just to get her to hear me. This is crazy. How could she think I could be *married* to anyone one else? I just proposed to her, that's illegal. Jenna's still staring at the ring. I grab her hand.

"Jenna, I swear to you. I have no idea what she's talking about," I try to tell her more calmly, and now the other woman is laughing hysterically.

"Who the hell is she to you? This is why you left? *Is this who you left me for?!*" Hazel Eye's grabbing me now.

"He's my fiancé!" Jenna yells at her.

"How the hell can he marry you when he's still married to me?!" she shrieks. Now, I'm pissed. This isn't a game or a joke. This crap she's selling can destroy my life.

"I don't even know you! Who are you? How do you know me?" I ask her, not hiding my anger.

"All of this time—*all of this time!*—you've been lying to me and now . . . Now! You act as if you don't even know who I am!" She's crying hysterically, and I instantly regret yelling at her. I feel a dull headache coming on, but that's not happening now. I won't black out now! She's leaving the porch. Slowly, but leaving. I want to tell her not to drive in her current state. But the best thing for me, is for her to be as far away as possible so I can to try to salvage this mess.

"I want a divorce! I never want to see you again! Don't you ever come near me or Caylen again! I'll send your shit through Dexter. I want it all out of my house!" she shouts. Oh no. *How the hell would she know*

Dexter?

"How does she know Dexter? How the hell does she know Dexter, Chris?" Now Jenna is shouting at me.

"I don't know, Jenna! This has to be a joke!" And now I'm the one who's laughing. There's nothing else I can do but laugh. My life is about to crumble around me, and I don't know what the fuck is going on.

"Joke! I'm a joke?! You think ruining my life was a fucking joke?" the woman screams, now rushing towards me. She throws all her weight against me, her movements frantic and all over the place. She swings her fists at my face, and I have to grab her to stop her because if I don't, she'll do some serious damage.

"Get your hands of him!" Jenna screams and attempts to tug her away from me, but I don't need the help. This girl is pissed, but she weighs almost nothing.

I grab the girl by her waist to lift her up and carry her to the other side of the porch. When I lose my grip on her hands, she jabs one directly into Jenna's face hard, and Jenna tumbles to the ground. I let the brunette down to try to go help Jenna, but now she's up and rushing toward the brunette. I grab her to stop what's about to be a fight. Jenna tries to reach over me and manages to capture a hand full of Hazel Eyes's hair. I'm able to somehow able pry her fingers loose but I also get elbowed several times in the process. After trying to juggle both women, I pick Jenna up and carry her to the other side of the porch. I hear the door open from my house and have never been more grateful to see my dad appear, even though the brunette has calmed down.

"What's going on?" My dad asks, looking bewildered.

"This psycho just attacked us!" Jenna yells, finally settling down in my arms when she sees my dad.

"This has nothing to do with you! This is between me and my husband!" The brunette says sharply, catching her breath.

"What?!" My dad asks her angrily.

"Tell her, Dad. She doesn't believe me!" I plead. Will someone try to wake me up from this nightmare? The brunette is slowly moving off our porch but she seems unstable. She's about to pass out, and I run over and catch her right before she collapses. I pick her up as my dad looks at me disapprovingly, and Jenna's eyes shoot daggers at me. What was I just supposed to do? Let her collapse to the ground?

My mom steps onto the porch, joining in on the freak show.

"What's going on?" she asks, panicked.

"I'd sure as hell like to know!" Jenna laughs bitterly. My mom walks over to me and looks at the girl in my arms. Her breath catches.

"Lauren?" She looks down at the woman passed out in my arms, her eyes wide with recognition like she's just seen a ghost. Her lip quivers, and her hand shoots up quickly to cover her mouth.

"You know her?" Jenna and I both ask in unison. My mom looks between Jenna and I me.

My dad lets out a gruff sigh and covers his face. "Shit! Shit! Shit!" His groans escalate with each expletive, and I know something is wrong.

"Honey, go lay her down in the living room and take Jenna home. When you get back we have something we really need to tell you," she says, tears in her eyes.

"I'm not going anywhere! Who the hell is this woman, and why do you know her?" Jenna screeches.

"Jenna calm down," tell her. I know she's mad and confused. So am I, but I refuse to stand back and let her scream in my mom's face.

"I will not! Who is this? She shows up saying she's married to you with a ring that costs a hell of a lot more than the one you gave me! You claim you don't know her, but she knows Dexter. Your mother obviously knows her, and you think I'm going to be sent home like an errant child. I want to know who this woman is right now or I swear to God I will never speak to you again, Christopher!" Jenna says as tears stream down her cheeks.

"Jenna, please!" My dad roars, and we're all taken aback, especially Jenna. The authority in his voice, for once, reminds me of a Crestfield.

"Please let Chris take you home. It's not what you think. I promise you both will have answers by the end of the day, just let us take care of this for now." His voice calmer, but no less authoritative. Jenna looks at me, and I shake my head. I don't know what's going on, but I know Jenna and I staying here will only make things worse. Besides, I really don't want to be here when this girl wakes up.

My dad comes over and reaches for the woman lying in my arms. I want to hand her over, but my body is hesitant and I'm confused as to why I'm protective of someone I've never even met, especially with my dad, the man I trust him with my life. My mom looks me in the eye and reassuringly squeezes my shoulder.

"It's okay. She's safe with us," she says, looking me directly in the eyes.

"Oh, FUCK me," Jenna shouts, and I realize how this looks. I don't understand anything that's going on. I hand the girl over to my dad but by the time I do, Jenna has shot down the porch and is headed towards her car.

"Jenna," I shout, running after her. She whips around and holds her hand out.

"No. You stay! That is obviously where your concern lies right now!" she says, hysterically opening her car door.

"Jenna, no! It's not like that!" I plead as she slams the door in my face. I try to open it but she's locked it. She lets her window down.

"Stay the hell away from me, Chris. Go attend to your *wife!*" she yells before pulling out of the driveway. I kick the dirt and punch the air. My life has turned into a living hell. I glance up, and my dad is back in the house. My mom stands on the porch looking at me with tears in her eyes.

"How do you know her, Mom?" I'm shouting now. I know it's not her fault but she knows something. I'm so mad, there are tears in my eyes now.

"Christopher," she pleads.

"Tell me!" I shout again.

"Chris." My dad has reappeared in the doorway and comes down to meet me. "Go after your fiancé. We'll explain later," he says. His voice is calm as he hands me my phone and keys, ignoring my perplexed expression. He takes my mother's hand and leads her into the house.

I'm in the twilight zone. *How is he so calm right now?* I don't take time to question him. I hop in my car, ready to go after Jenna but slam my hands on the steering wheel. She's not going to hear anything I have to say unless I have an explanation for all this.

I pull out my phone to call her. I see all the missed calls from yesterday. Jenna, my parents, and Lisa. There are voicemails from each of their numbers plus one unknown. I hit the prompt to play the one from the unknown number. At first all I hear is a lot of static and wind. Then it starts.

"You really are more fucking dense than I thought. All of these years and you still think you're just having black outs?! I don't have much time so I'll get to the point. You can't get married because you already are, dumbass. Talk to Dexter. Make this right or I'll have to do it for you. Stay away from any Altars." The voice chuckles. *"No pun intended. If you don't, there will be hell to pay. You can bet on that. Oh and by the way, since no one gave two shits to inform you, I'm Cal."*

I replay the message again and again. My hands won't stop shaking. The scary part is, this is the second time today I've heard the name Cal. But, what *terrifies* me is the voice in the message is *mine*.

Before I Break (If I Break 1.5) is available now for purchase on all platforms. Thank you for reading! Almost Broken book 2 and Beautifully Broken book 3 are also available for purchase.

Printed in Great Britain
by Amazon